Louise Candlish studied English at University College London and worked as an editor and copywriter before writing fiction. She is the author of five previous novels – including *I'll Be There For You*, *The Double Life of Anna Day*, *Since I Don't Have You* and *The Second Husband*, which are all also published by Sphere. She lives in London with her partner and daughter.

Visit her website at *www.louisecandlish.co.uk*.

Before We Say Goodbye

Louise Candlish

SPHERE

First published in Great Britain as a paperback original in 2009 by Sphere
Reprinted 2009 (twice)

Copyright © Louise Candlish 2009

The moral right of the author has been asserted.

A CIP catalogue record for this book
is available from the British Library.

Typeset in Sabon by M Rules
Printed and bound in Great Britain by
Clays Ltd, St Ives plc

Papers used by Sphere are natural, renewable and recyclable
products sourced from well-managed forests and certified
in accordance with the rules of the Forest Stewardship Council.

Mixed Sources
Product group from well-managed
forests and other controlled sources
www.fsc.org Cert no. SGS-COC-004081
© 1996 Forest Stewardship Council

Sphere
An imprint of
Little, Brown Book Group
100 Victoria Embankment
London EC4Y 0DY

An Hachette UK Company
www.hachette.co.uk

www.littlebrown.co.uk

For Kitty

Acknowledgements

Thank you to Claire Paterson, Lucie Whitehouse, Tim Glister and Kirsty Gordon at Janklow & Nesbit (UK) – your enthusiasm and tirelessness makes it all so easy for me! At Little, Brown, Jo Dickinson, Rebecca Saunders and Caroline Hogg have all helped reshape and improve the manuscript immeasurably. Thank you to Jo and Caroline especially for all your extra patience and care. A big thank you also to Emma Stonex and Nathalie Morse. My thanks to Jenny Richards for the perfect cover! Thank you to Kirsteen Astor, Tamsin Kitson and Hannah Torjussen; also to the fantastic sales and marketing team at Little, Brown and to the countless others there who have supported and promoted this book in different ways.

The quotes about swans come from the Royal Society for the Protection of Birds (www.rspb.org) and the Cornell Lab of Ornithology (www.allaboutbirds.org), both of which have excellent online guides. I recommend Abbotsbury Swannery in Dorset to those who have not yet discovered it (www.abbotsbury-tourism.co.uk). The information about leaving children at home alone is based on guidelines issued by the NSPCC (www.nspcc.org.uk).

Finally, thank you, as ever, to family and friends for your love and support during the writing of this book – tradition demands a special a special name check for Mats 'n' Jo.

PART ONE

'The mute swan is reported to mate for life. However, changing of mates does occur infrequently."
The Cornell Lab of Ornithology

Chapter 1

I knew the moment Lindy opened the door that there'd been a change. Her eyes were several tones paler, the usual warm optimism drained right out of them.

'What is it?' I demanded. 'Oh God, she hasn't . . .?'

'No, not that.' Her hand was on my elbow, reassuring and ushering in one. 'But something's not right, Olivia. She seems to be feeling a lot more pain than usual. I've just called for the nurse.'

I barely glanced beyond the herringbone parquet of the hallway before turning left into the ground-floor room where my mother had been cared for these last months. I hardly thought now of the atmosphere that had reigned in the house when Alec was alive, when you'd come through the door and be tugged at once in this direction or that, drawn by a gale of laughter or some sudden whoosh of calamity. Now, in this home-cum-hospital, all voices, all gestures were designed to deter such excitability. Sometimes it felt as if the mood was controlled by a switch.

'How was the drive?' Lindy asked me. These days, she paid almost as much attention to my welfare as she did Maggie's.

'Fine, it's always better coming west—' I started, but was quickly distracted by signs of motion from the patient's bed. 'She's awake?'

'Olivia . . . here . . .'

3

Now I saw the change in her – or, rather, heard it – for Mum's voice was not so much a whisper as a shatter, as if the original had been dropped on the floor and broken into a hundred pieces. As a small child I'd felt protected by that voice, by its depth and swell and all-powerful presence; as an older one I'd listened only for its insincerities.

Lindy withdrew, pulling the door shut behind her, and I slipped into the bedside armchair. 'How are you feeling, Mum? You're not in too much pain?'

Her right arm, the one not attached to the IV drip, was tucked under the bedclothes but I quickly found the shape of her hand through the linen and gave it the gentlest of squeezes.

'I'm . . . alright . . .' She didn't see well now and as she spoke her eyes strained through heavy lids, the skin puffed and discoloured. Despite the deterioration, I seemed to have caught her in one of her urgent, lucid moments, which meant there would be no small talk required of me this evening, none of the commentary of routine events at home that always seemed to offer more comfort to me than it did her.

'I wanted to say . . . there are things I feel uncomfortable about . . .'

'OK.' In spite of the circumstances, I couldn't help smiling at that. 'Uncomfortable' was Mum's word for guilty. She also favoured 'misguided', which had the added benefit of passing the buck to someone else (or, better still, to some other, higher power).

'You and him . . . I shouldn't . . .'

But each word was rasped so painfully that I couldn't bear to let her continue.

'Who? You mean Dean?' At the thought of my brother my chest tightened and I wished that he was here beside me. For this was surely it, the scene we'd never really believed would come: the big apology. Maggie Lane was finally ready to tell her children she was sorry.

4

But the voice that spoke next was mine, 'It's all right, Mum, you don't need to say it,' and we both looked a little surprised at that. It was the kind of platitude that belonged in a movie, and God knew I hadn't rehearsed it. After all, wasn't this the plea for forgiveness I'd craved my whole adult life?

The truth was, she *didn't* need to say it. Yes, she'd been a difficult parent; yes, she'd let us down, especially Dean, who'd begun as her favourite and had further to fall, but what did her crimes amount to, really? If I broke it down – and I didn't mean in a court of law, but in my heart – then there was actually just one thing I knew I couldn't forgive her for, one true betrayal.

And it was a betrayal that I couldn't even be certain had happened in the first place.

Her hand moved under mine – it had all the strength of a trapped butterfly – and her mouth struggled open once more. 'No, it's important I tell you both . . .'

Again my voice easily smothered her broken efforts. 'Mum, don't worry, honestly, it doesn't matter. And I'm sure Dean feels the same.' That was an outright lie and I could see his incredulous face in my mind's eye, his hissed protest in my ear: *Why are you letting her off the hook? After all this time! Why, Olivia?*

But I wasn't letting her off the hook, not exactly, for there was still that one unanswered question. Suddenly it burned hot in my throat. If I didn't expel it I would be suffocated by it. 'There's something I need to know,' I said, in a low, urgent voice. 'It's about something that happened a long time ago.'

There was a pause in her breathing and a faint widening of those waterlogged eyes – she had no control of her tear ducts now. Under my hand the butterfly lay quite still. In the silence I became conscious of the sound of water splashing from the taps in the kitchen next door; Lindy filling the kettle. She'd soon be back to offer me coffee.

I leaned closer to Mum's face. 'Did you keep us apart? That's all I want to know.'

5

She didn't reply, but I read the guilt in her eyes.

'Just say it, please. Yes or no?'

The tension between us could almost be smelled, until she at last made an attempt at movement – unmistakably a shake of the head. No. But she was not answering my question, I realised, she was simply feigning confusion.

'I know you remember!' I cried, the sound abrupt and violent in the calm of the room. 'Did it happen like you said it did? Why can't you just tell me, one way or the other? Don't you think I deserve that?'

My cry had attracted Lindy and I turned to find her standing just inside the doorway, doing all she could to mask her alarm. Everything about her manner and appearance was gentle, from the slope of her nose to the curl in her auburn hair; I'd come long ago to rely on her as the pacifying antidote to Maggie, just as I'd previously relied on Alec and, in the beginning, Dad. But for once her presence did nothing to soothe me.

'We were just talking,' I said, breathlessly. 'She was answering my question, weren't you, Mum?'

But she had turned her face away, straining on the pillow to escape me, her throat making a noise like the whimper of an injured animal.

'Maybe she's a bit tired for conversation,' Lindy said, kindly choosing not to point out that a seventy-year-old patient in the middle of a pain management crisis might not be best suited to drama of this sort. And if I weren't so worked up still, I'd have been mortified to have created such a scene at anyone's bed-side.

'Why don't you just sit with her for a while, while she sleeps? She'd like that.'

Indeed, when I turned back, Mum did seem to be slipping into sleep. I couldn't allow myself to suspect that *that* was feigned, as well. Now, with no chance to apologise, I felt like the worst kind of bully. And it wasn't as if I didn't know the rule – don't say

6

something you might regret in case you don't get the chance to take it back – one I had followed assiduously until now.

'I ought to go,' I said, rising. 'You said you've got the nurse coming, I don't want to be in the way.'

Lindy was dismayed. 'Not yet, surely? You've only just got here. Stay and have a cup of tea, at least?'

'Thank you, but I won't.'

She watched me leave without further protest. And though she couldn't possibly have known what had caused this unscheduled bedside flare-up, her eyes let it be known that I had her sympathies.

Often as I drove home alone from my mother's I would see her face in the windscreen in front of me, crushed and cold, like a reproach, though a reproach for what I was never quite sure. For having left her house so soon (I was in the habit of keeping visits short where I could so as not to disrupt my family's schedule too much)? Or for not having forgiven her her faults, when this was so obviously the proper thing to do, the right time to do it? Well, tonight I'd at least got halfway there. *You don't need to say it.* Before I'd gone and ruined it with all that sourness.

But this evening it was a different Maggie Lane who appeared in front of me as I drove: it was the full-powered original, the ringmaster with the bright, all-seeing eyes. There were voices, too, beginning with my own, decades younger and painfully shrill: 'I need to know, did you make it up? Did he really do it?' And then my father's, puzzled and anxious: 'What's she saying? What does she mean?' Last came Maggie's reply, full of false tenderness: 'I think she must be hallucinating or something, poor love. We'd better talk to the doctor in the morning.'

I blinked the face away, my thoughts returning to the scene that had just passed. There were no two ways about it: I was in the wrong. A dying woman had been trying to make amends and I'd interrupted her, allowing old feelings of rivalry to rise at exactly the point where she couldn't be expected to fight her corner. Fight? She could scarcely speak! Well, I'd be the one to make amends tomorrow. I'd come back and I'd listen to whatever it was she wanted to tell me, however long it took. I'd let her be the judge of what needed to be said. As for my own question, the one that *still* had the power to keep my life in a suspended sentence, well, she hadn't answered it the first time and I had to accept that she wasn't going to answer it now.

On the passenger seat beside me, my phone was ringing. I pulled over at the next service station and checked the display: MISSED CALL: LINDY. Still with the engine running, I dialled.

'Olivia, I'm so sorry, but is there any chance you could come back tonight? She's woken up and is asking for you.'

'I'm almost in London,' I said, sighing.

'It's just that she's quite distressed.'

Lindy never did this; she *had* to consider it exceptional. The problem was that my body was heavy as lead and I wasn't sure I could find the strength to finish the journey in either direction. Home was closer. 'I need to see the boys,' I said, at last. 'Why don't I come back in the morning? And Lindy, I'm really sorry if I upset her earlier. I didn't mean to, I just . . .'

'Of course you didn't,' she said, hushing my distress. 'There's no knowing how she's going to react at any given time, we all know that.'

'Thank you.'

'Tomorrow then,' Lindy said. 'Can I tell her you'll be here in the morning?'

'Yes. I'll set off as soon as the boys have left for school.'

I told myself afterwards that there was no way I could have known that was the night Maggie would succumb to her last – and fatal – haemorrhage. It happened in her sleep, an eventuality Lindy described as 'merciful'.

I told myself there was nothing to feel guilty about, that that was not what she would have wanted.

The problem was, with Mum, you never knew.

Chapter 2

The story begins when I am eleven – or at least that is when it changes. That is when Mum leaves us for the first time.

She goes out one Saturday night with a group of girlfriends, 'raging' – her own word and one I find a little frightening, as though the women will spend the evening bellowing at each other in anger. Whatever it is they do spend the evening doing, all have returned to their families by the end of it, all except Mum. She has *not* come back. On Sunday morning, Dad tells us there must be some innocent explanation: a missed lift home, an eleventh-hour saviour and a sofa for the night. He sets about making the Sunday roast as if expecting her back in time to help with the gravy. But by late afternoon the beef is uneaten and there is still no sign of her. Now he tells us he is calling the police.

The officer who comes to the house is bemused: there has been no row, no 'incident'. Nor are there any local murderers on the loose to justify the setting of sniffer dogs on Mum's trail, or the launch of a police helicopter like the one Dean and I have seen before from our bedroom windows. We are fascinated by the way the searchlight sweeps the neighbourhood's streets and playing fields like a giant's torch. As we watch we hold our breath, remembering the day's crimes, rigid with the fear that we might be the ones its beam hunts.

The two of us listen at the banisters as the officer asks our father questions; he sounds mechanical, as if he's reading from a list.

'Dad hasn't offered him a cup of tea,' I whisper. It's the kind of nicety Mum normally takes care of and I feel a prickle of shame on his behalf.

'Cops prob'ly only drink whisky,' Dean whispers back. 'I bet he's got his own hip flask.'

A sober voice carries towards us: 'Would you say this is out of character for your wife, Mr Lane? Is she normally a steady kind of person?'

As Dad hesitates, Dean and I exchange glances. 'Not exactly,' comes the answer, finally, and we have to strain to catch the words that follow. 'She can be a bit . . . excitable, I suppose you could say, but she's never done anything like this before. That's why I phoned.' His voice cracks on the last word and although I sense Dean turning again to me, this time I just can't bring myself to look back at him.

'OK, well, let's hold our horses for the time being. It hasn't been forty-eight hours yet.'

By Monday morning – thirty-six hours – Mum has still not returned, which means that Dad has to iron our uniforms (they still look creased) and drive us to school (we are late). I'm young enough to get so absorbed in the day that I can forget a background crisis like a missing parent, remembering it again only when it's Dad and not Mum who picks me up at home time, but Dean, sitting in the passenger seat in front of me, looks as if he has not spent his school hours so easily.

'Is Mum back?' he asks straight away.

Dad keeps his eyes on the road. 'Yes, she is.'

It's obvious even from here in the backseat that Dean wasn't expecting him to say that, because when he speaks again his voice matches the opposite answer, all pained and brooding, as if he wasn't able to switch in time. 'Where was she then?'

'She was taken ill,' Dad says. 'She couldn't get to a phone to let us know.'

'What? She's been in hospital?'

'No, not hospital.'

'Where then?'

A pause, then, 'Just drop it, Dean. The important thing is she's back.'

This doesn't sound right, but I forget that the moment we reach the house, flying straight to the kitchen like homing pigeons. There is Mum, shuffling pans on the cooker, calling out an everyday greeting and generally behaving as though nothing has happened. Dean hugs her, which is unusual now he's thirteen, and I do the same. Her answers to our questions are as short as Dad's, but gradually we discover that she became ill after her night out and spent the rest of the weekend at a friend's house (though not one of the friends she was out with; Dad can't pretend he didn't phone each one of them in turn on Sunday morning and draw blank after blank). Dean calls their version of events 'the party line'. He points out that neither the friend nor the illness is ever actually identified.

I am much too young to imagine that another man might have been involved.

It happens a second time. This time Dad knows not to bother the police and by now Dean thinks he has an inkling what the mystery illness might be.

'D'you think maybe Mum's an alkie? Like Irene Robbins's dad? She could be out on a bender.'

I have no idea what a bender is, but I hope with all my heart that Mum is not like Irene Robbins's dad. Once I was in Irene's kitchen having tea when he came swaying through the door, chuckling like a demented clown. He smelled so revolting I put my fork down so I could hold my nose. I would never forget how Irene had looked at her mother, panic pouring from her eyes, as if to say, *Make him disappear, please!* Then I remember how last

11

time Mum returned magically to the cooker, neither chuckling nor smelling, and I relax again. 'She'll come back,' I say, confidently.

And she does. Again she returns to us after only a day or two, but this time Dean doesn't hug her. I do, and afterwards he takes me to one side and asks if I thought her breath smelled of rum.

'No,' I say, considering. 'More like mint.'

He nods. 'Tic tacs. A classic cover up. It was definitely a bender.'

There are other times after that, frequent enough for me to lose count but infrequent enough for each to bring real fear into the house. It's like someone has walked from room to room spraying the stuff from a bottle; just as it fades, you get a fresh hit. A pattern develops, a running order: first the announcement that she is going out with friends; then Dad's offer to collect her himself at a pre-arranged time and place; next her refusal; last, her disappearance. Soon Dean and I need only a half-glance to read one another's lips: *Here we go again.*

And then, when I am fourteen, she *really* goes away. She goes away for a whole year almost to the day and my fifteenth birthday is the first family occasion she misses. This time Dad is in the loop, or at least he's been formally dismissed from it. He explains to us that she has met someone new, a man from Croydon named Nigel, and that he and she are now separated and we will stay with him. It is, he says, a bit like what is happening or has already happened with many of our friends' parents.

'Does that mean you're getting a divorce?' I ask, hating myself for beginning to cry. As far as I'm concerned it doesn't happen *that* often. None of my closest friends comes from a broken home. Even Irene's mother hangs on in there with the giggling alkie.

'I don't know yet.' Dad touches me awkwardly on the shoulder. We've always been close, Dad and me, and Dean and Mum too, that's just the way our family has naturally broken into pairs. I wonder how it will work in a three. He says Mum has promised to be in touch 'just as soon as she's settled. She may not have a phone yet.'

'Settled where?' Dean asks. 'Why won't she have a phone?'

'I don't know yet,' Dad repeats.

'Why didn't *she* tell us?' I demand. 'Why didn't she even say goodbye?'

But he has no answer to that, either. It seems to me that he is protecting her, though of course what he is really doing is protecting us.

Mum writes several times over the next few months. She never gives us an address to reply to and Dad says this is because she is moving around so much. We inspect the postmarks for clues: Croydon, Harrow, Manchester and then, after one particularly long silence, Los Angeles. This causes a stir, despite ourselves.

'Maybe she's got a part in a soap opera?' Dean says. 'She'd be good in *Dallas*.'

'She's a shorthand secretary, not an actress,' says Dad. But he doesn't look especially convinced.

Chapter 3

The speaker's voice was steady and proud, easily audible at the outer reaches of the congregation. 'What I will remember most about Maggie is the life she brought to every occasion.'

Dean, by my side, muttered, 'Yeah, when she actually bothered to turn up.'

'Shh!' I told him. 'People will hear you!'

'I hope they—'

'Just listen, Dean. Dad's doing a great job.'

'Hmm.'

If you were looking at it on paper, you'd think our father a strange choice to deliver a eulogy at Mum's funeral – they'd been divorced for over twenty years, after all. In the final analysis of family and friends it was agreed that she had never cared enough about his feelings, either in the marriage or out, but had simply been fortunate that he had cared so much about hers.

But Dad was nothing if not a good sport. In fact, he had come forward to offer his services today rather than waiting to be cajoled into taking part. Apparently, he had no difficulty in gathering enough evidence of his first wife's good character to fill a five-minute speech. He stood before the congregation looking exactly what he was: the sombre and respectful survivor of a potentially fatal force of nature. A force of nature now contained in a wooden box just feet from him, beautifully crowned with lilies and gerbera. The coffin shone in the glow of the candelabrum like sun on glass; did they polish the wood especially to catch the light like that, I wondered? To create some kind of effect of holy radiance?

'Maggie always brought people out of their shells,' he told us. 'She had a kind of spark that set situations alight.'

My brother's mouth moved closer to my ear. 'And left third degree burns . . .'

'Dean!'

Lindy and I had agreed that he would be the loose cannon today and, sure enough, when he'd arrived at the church he was practically giving off the smell of gunpowder. As we took our seats I'd noticed him look up and eye that grand brass candelabrum, as if plotting to leap up in the middle of a hymn and swing from it like Tarzan.

To my relief I saw that his wife Beth had become aware of his subversive commentary and was quick to issue whatever silent sign it was she used to keep him in order. He shut up at once. On my other side, unaware, Russell squeezed my hand. He was following the eulogy with particular attention, as if genuinely making a stab at seeing Maggie through new eyes, re-casting her after all this time as the guileless life and soul Dad portrayed. He was a good husband, Russell, not the kind to have stepped back and left my difficult family relationships entirely to me. Over the years he'd come to understand as well as I did that any hope I felt would more often than not be chased by disappointment, and that the only way to diminish the disappointment was to qualify the hope. Which had left him with what? A wife who never quite trusted in good news.

I blinked back to the present as the words 'good news' in my thoughts chimed exactly with those spoken by my father. He was sharing a Maggie anecdote, one of the less controversial ones, obviously. 'So I said to her, "OK, give me the bad news first."

And she said, "The bad news is the bedroom ceiling's fallen in." "What's the good news?" I asked her, and she said, "The good news is you can see enough of the sky through the hole to know that *that* hasn't fallen in, at least!"'

There was an appreciative titter, most audibly from my eldest son Jamie, whose sense of humour was unpredictable. I leaned forward a little to bring into view the line of Chapman males on my left – Russell, Jamie, Noah – men, really, for both boys had shot up this year, their mid-brown hair losing its pubescent flop and taking on the coarser springiness of their father's. Each had the same appraising dark eyes under low slanted brows, the same slight pull of a pout about soft, unreadable mouths. From a distance, or perhaps from close by too, you wouldn't have put my children with me. I was separated from them not only by my colouring (fair hair, blue eyes) but also by the emotional clues. I was sensitive and easy to injure, whereas they could be teased non-stop for a week without taking the slightest offence (Russell once said they could contest the award for World's Thickest Skin without any need whatsoever to open it up to outsiders). Sometimes it felt as if they were a team to which, through nothing but blind luck, I had found myself attached. Sometimes it felt as if they loved me like a star athlete loves his first coach, the one he knows he's outgrown but keeps in touch with for sentimental reasons. There was a kind of unspoken tragedy about it.

But I was being melodramatic again. First that outburst at Mum's bedside, now this maudlin reverie. Recently, it was as if my imagination had split its skin and seeped into other areas of my brain. And no wonder, I told myself, look at the situation now: the church, the grief, the dazzling coffin, the sheer perverseness of hearing Dad talking like this – *as if he meant it*. (And he did!) It was enough to send anyone mad.

Behind us feet shuffled as he finished up his address: 'And so, to misquote *The Pilgrim's Progress*, "All the trumpets sound for her on the other side."'

17

There was no way Dean was going to let *that* pass. 'Yeah,' he said under his breath, 'warning everybody.'

At Maggie's house the ground-floor hospital room had been cleared out and closed up. It was to be redecorated before the estate agents' valuation as a small second sitting room, a place to sit and muse. All doors and windows throughout the rest of the house had been thrown open to the late June weekend, bringing just enough sunlight to lift the gloom that naturally settled over any space where someone had recently died. The combination of fresh air and flowers took care of any lingering medicinal odours.

Lindy had suggested I bring some family photographs to pass among the guests and get conversations going, and so I had set large framed ones on bookshelves and sideboards, as well as leaving loose piles of prints on the tables where food and drink had been laid out. Seeing them again had been a surprisingly pleasurable experience for me, and so it was proving for other people too: little ripples of guests radiated from each picture, issuing 'ooh's and 'aah's and cries for someone to check the backs for dates and locations. There was baby Maggie in antique monochrome, done up in the various bonnets and sashes of the age; here, teen Maggie in a wasp-waisted cocktail dress, posed on a chaise longue like some sort of Buckingham Palace deb – even though the picture had surely been taken in her home town of Wolverhampton; next, Maggie reintroduced to the world in colour and as a mother (it was as if the two developments were scientifically linked), with Dean preserved as a narrow-eyed toddler and me an uncomprehending babe in arms.

The one that was proving the favourite was a portrait from my own wedding album – again, Lindy's idea – the one of Russell and me with our parents. Mum had eschewed the usual mother-of-the-bride chic for something bolder, outlandish even, depending on how you rated aquamarine fluted swirls, but that wasn't what I liked about the picture, or why I had chosen it. It was the way she had her arm around me, right around my waist so you could see her pale fingertips at the other side, as if guiding me and claiming me all at once. That was what I liked about it. They'd done well that day, Mum and Dad; if you hadn't known they were both married to people standing out of shot, you'd have thought they were still quite happily together.

But one person was less than delighted with today's exhibition and as he approached, his head bowed slightly as if preparing to butt someone (me!), I felt an instant pang of disloyalty. 'Dean! Which one have you got there? Let's have a look.'

In the photograph he, I and two other infants circled a birthday cake like baby sharks – *my* birthday cake, judging by how close my hair hung to the flame. I wondered what my wish had been. For a kitten or a pony, perhaps; it would have been years before I'd begun wishing, above all else, for a normal mother.

'Rewriting history already?' he asked in a dangerous tone. If ever a man's appearance matched his character it was my brother's. His eyes and nose were sharp, his hair a black and silver carpet of pine needles. Everything about him was prickly, as if he'd been designed to repel aphids.

'What?' I laughed, hoping to brazen this out. 'You can't say this birthday party didn't happen. Was it my fifth? I can't make out the—'

'You know what I'm saying,' he interrupted. 'All these pictures. I mean, I can understand that Dad had to do it in the church, he could hardly have started slagging her off. But you, here – this perfect Disney version you and Lindy have cooked up. Maggie Lane as Snow White: yeah, right!'

I stared at him in dismay. 'Oh, don't be ridiculous, Dean, this is a funeral, not a murder trial. It's not appropriate to draw attention to the dead person's faults, is it? Half the people here haven't seen Mum for years. They want to remember her at her best, not listen to us dredging up old family grievances.'

'Well, I'm glad *someone* had the opportunity to see her at her best!' But he paused in brief concession. 'Just so long as we haven't forgotten what she was really like. All that unforgivable . . . *crap* she put us through.'

Unforgivable: it was a word he used routinely to describe our mother's behaviour towards us, but one that I had slipped from my vocabulary during the last few months, resulting in that spontaneous capitulation at her bedside. *You don't need to say it, Mum.* How I wished now that I had let her say it, if only to discover what it was that she remembered of it all. The difficulty for Dean and me was that her crimes had been mostly in her absences, not her actions, which made them harder to classify, let alone grade. One of the more damning of our adult years had been her missing of Dean's wedding, a drama still debated now and clearly on his mind in the church when he'd made that quip about her not bothering to turn up. Perhaps passing around a picture of my own happy day wasn't such a good idea, after all.

'Anyway, forget that. You're right, it's just for show. It had to be done.' He tossed the photograph to the nearest flat surface besides the floor (he still had *some* sense of decorum) and said what he really wanted to talk to me about was Mum's will. He planned to put in a call to her solicitor the next morning, maybe even this afternoon if he got home in time. 'Not that we can count on anything. I wouldn't put it past her to have cut us out just to spite us.' He cast about for inspiration, spied a watercolour of some coral reef on the wall to his left, and added, 'Leave the whole lot to Save the Octopuses or something equally ludicrous.' He directed a meaningful look over my shoulder – turning, I followed his line of vision to where Lindy stood offering a platter of sandwiches to a group of Mum's neighbours – and added, 'Or to *her*, more like. I know they were close, but when it comes down to it she was just a paid employee, wasn't she? It's not like she's flesh and blood.'

'Lindy deserves a reward,' I said, with as much fire as I could muster. 'You know she does. She's looked after Mum for years, long before she got ill.' Having come to Maggie originally through a cleaning agency, Lindy had spent almost ten years of devoted service as housekeeper, secretary, companion, and, finally, nurse. She was as good as flesh and blood, as far as I was concerned. '*And* she's handled all of this for us,' I pointed out.

In fact, the funeral itself, followed by food and drinks for fifty people, was only a part of the task undertaken by Lindy since our mother's death a week ago. The day after we'd got the news I'd looked up some legal websites and made a list of all the authorities that needed to be contacted after someone had died. It was three pages long – completely overwhelming. But when I'd phoned Lindy about it she'd assured me she already had it under control, that I shouldn't worry about a thing.

I sighed. If Dean couldn't see what I could – that Lindy had fulfilled our family duties far better than we had – then he was more of a lost cause than I'd thought. When I spoke again I hoped it was with finality. 'We don't need Mum's money, Dean. And, anyway, we don't even know for sure that she had any.'

He scoffed at this. 'Of course she did. She owned this place outright for starters. Plus Alec left her a fair bit, and I don't see how she could have spent it all since. She hardly left the house since finding out she was ill herself.'

It was true that Mum had reacted to her diagnosis in an unexpected way, withdrawing into herself and embracing each new symptom with an obedient grace. There had been none of the denial and anger and rush to seize what remained of life that I'd read about in the books Lindy had lent me.

I frowned at Dean. 'Even so, neither of us is badly off as we are.'

He flashed me a parting look of disbelief before turning away. 'Speak for yourself, sis.'

Recently, during the final stages of Mum's illness, I'd felt like I was losing energy, losing life, at the same rate she was. Every day

21

a drop emptier. I put it down to a strange mirroring effect, like fathers-to-be who feel mysteriously nauseous in the mornings or develop backache if they don't get a seat on the train. Of course just as likely a culprit was the hours of driving I'd been doing, back and forth between her house near Cheltenham and ours in South London, three or four times a week in recent months. I suppose rest was what I was searching for when, the reception in full swing across the hallway, I was found by Lindy sitting in the window seat in Mum's old room. Without the hospital bed and nursing equipment, the space looked curiously smaller.

'You need a holiday after this,' she said, joining me. 'It's been a long slog.'

I smiled gratefully at her. 'Oh, but I haven't done anything, you've done it all. You've been amazing, Lindy. I don't know how we can thank you.'

'You don't need to thank me, Maggie was my friend. She asked me to take care of things and I did. But seriously, Olivia, have you planned a break?'

I shook my head. 'Not until August. The boys' school holidays.'

'Maybe you could try to fit something in before then? Just a weekend? A change of scene really helps.'

'Yes.'

There was a picture on the wall adjacent to the spot where the bed had been, a still life of a bowl of yellow roses on a polished tabletop. How many times had I looked at that picture, my eyes drawn to it as if to a flickering screen, and thought how incredible it was that the shine of wood could be recreated with buttery paint? Directly opposite the visitor's armchair, it had been the natural place to look as the painkillers pulled Mum under and gave her – and us – respite from her wakeful self. But I'd never seen it from this angle; from here it looked all wrong.

I turned back to Lindy. 'I suppose I thought that when it was over I would feel, you know, relief or something, like you're supposed to. But I don't. I just feel exactly the same.' The same inability to relax, the same grinding pressure, the same sense of sinking, always sinking.

'Give it time,' Lindy said. 'A delayed reaction is normal. It's only been a few days.'

That's not what I meant, I thought. *I can't remember when I didn't feel this way.*

She looked delicately at me. 'Have you thought about seeing your GP? They have people you can talk to, help you work out what it is you're feeling.'

'Yes,' I said, my voice just bright enough to stop the suggestion in its tracks. 'You're right. That's what I should do.'

Noticing through the window the approach of a late arrival, she rose. 'I should go back through. Can I bring you something in here? A drink or some food?'

'No.' I pulled myself to my feet, forced a smile. 'No, I'm not the patient. Let's go back together.'

But as we walked back into the main room there was a strange, weightless moment when I didn't recognise any of the people in it – including the boys, who were standing near the refreshments with Dean and Beth's daughters, and my husband, and even the woman in the photographs. Then Russell stepped forward to take me from Lindy. It was a seamless, practised manoeuvre, almost as if he were taking a physical baton from her.

'I wondered where you'd got to. You look tired, let's get you another drink pronto. What's the strongest thing on offer? Whisky.'

He had started to lead me to the drinks table when I burst out, unexpectedly fiercely, 'I did love her, you know!'

Russell stopped moving, his features caught in an expression of alarm. 'Of course you did. No one's ever doubted that.'

'She wasn't all bad, whatever people think. And she loved us just as much as any other parent loves their kids. She just didn't understand that she had to . . .' I broke off in frustration, unable

23

to define what it was that a mother needed to sacrifice of herself in order to be upgraded from the merely loving to the properly good. I felt blood flood my cheeks. 'Sorry, Russ, I didn't mean to cause a scene.'

'It's OK, I know.' Without another word he stationed me by the drinks and closed my fingers around a glass of whisky. It was tears he dreaded, I knew, and in a funny way wished for. He had it on good authority (Beth's – she was training to be a counsellor) that until you cried you weren't properly grieving. There was an established process and few deviated from its path. Were he to consult Lindy, he'd probably agree that this was all part of a delayed reaction, nothing a change of scene couldn't solve. 'Hang on in there,' he said, gently chinking my glass with his. 'Not long now.'

And he was right. This wasn't a wedding; already people were starting to say their goodbyes and leave.

Chapter 4

On the surface nothing much changes without a mother. You still have all your fingers and toes. True, Dad has had to shorten his working hours a bit, rope in a few friends and neighbours to help make sure Dean and I are where we need to be at about the time we're expected to be there, but otherwise, on the surface, it's the same. There is still a meal on the table in the evening, homework still gets done, chores are still fought over. Dad even, accidentally, introduces a reduced-family motto: 'We're fine on our own.' He doesn't notice how often he says it until, as sorry for him as we are for ourselves, we start repeating after him, 'We're fine on our own.'

But it is not fine. It is awful. Not only for the permanent gnawing sensation in my stomach that doesn't let up even when I sleep, but also for the way other people are behaving towards us. As the months wear on I don't know which is worse: the ones who pity or the ones who mock. My school teachers, friends' mothers, half the adults on the street, they can't look at us now without that same mixture of sorrow and indignation. They say they want to know if there's anything they can do but what they really want to know is how she could have done it. How? *How* could she have left these kids?

As for the bullies, they've never had it so easy. Being abandoned by your mother is as bright a beacon as weighing thirty stone or coming to school in foul-smelling rags. There's one girl I'm especially wary of: blonde, bony Samantha Culler. If Samantha were in the wild she would never go hungry; those quick hazel eyes are always the first to spot a change of pace, a dip in confidence. We're not in the same registration class, but we're in the same year, which means our paths cross beyond the standard danger zones of break and lunch hour. For one, we've both been selected for the fifth-year netball team and we both want to be captain. The teacher picks me (I get picked much more this term – maybe it's to balance out the being picked *on*) and when she announces it to the squad everyone crowds around me to say congratulations.

'You'll get the yellow sports tie now,' my best friend Melanie tells me. 'All the captains do. They'll do a special presentation in assembly.'

But Samantha just jeers, 'Who wants a crappy tie? I'd rather have a mum who doesn't hate me so much she's *emigrated*.'

The games teacher overhears her and gives her a detention on the spot. I'm almost as pained by this as Samantha herself. Don't teachers realise it just makes it worse? Now this cow has the perfect opportunity to tell the meanest kids in the school that Olivia Lane has been rejected by her own mother – which she most assuredly does. More comments, more looks, more *pity*.

Dean is getting similar reactions in the sixth form, but he is smarter than I am and has turned the whole thing into a comedy routine. He and his friends openly refer to Mum as The Deserter. 'It would be better if The Deserter had just died,' he tells me. 'OK, everyone'd feel sorry for us for a while, but at least they'd go away eventually and forget about it.'

'That's a horrible thing to say!' I protest.

'It's a horrible thing to do. Who else's mum just ups and leaves? Only ours. The Deserter. If this was a war she'd be shot for cowardice.' He considers. 'They'd have to find her first though.'

It is true that we've heard of a few fathers disappearing (and then reappearing on birthdays with oversized presents), but we've never heard of a mother doing it. When mothers leave, they're supposed to take their children with them. They're not supposed to *miss* the birthdays.

'You realise she's not coming back this time?' Dean says, dropping the act and looking at me properly. That's when I know he hurts as much as I do: I recognise what's behind his eyes from the reflection in my bedroom mirror. Despair, basically.

'I think she will,' I say, softly. And I do. I still think this is all some terrible misunderstanding. Sometimes, on nights I can't sleep, I imagine her lying murdered in a ditch, undiscovered and unmissed, and I feel guilty for ever having thought she had gone because she didn't love us.

I have other theories, too, and decide to test one on Dean. 'Maybe she's got amnesia? You know, no memory whatsoever of her family back home. And she's not in any of the official systems in America, so they can't work out who she is. People are asking her all these questions, but she's gone completely blank. Her mind is just . . . *empty*.'

He just grimaces, the hard guy again. 'Yeah, she's empty all right. She's morally bankrupt.' *Morally bankrupt*, that's a description he uses a lot for The Deserter. It's hard to remember that a few years ago they were still so close I called him Mummy's Boy.

Dad gets wind of the badmouthing and summons us for a chat. 'It doesn't do any good to blame her,' he says. 'I know it's hard to understand, I don't expect you to, but Mum sees you as practically grown up. You're fifteen now, Olivia, and Dean's in the sixth form. When we were your age we'd already got full-time jobs.'

'Yeah, but you were still living at home with your parents,' I point out. '*Both* of them.'

He sighs. 'Come on, love. For the time being, we don't have any choice. And we're fine on our own.'

27

It doesn't matter what good things he makes happen, what treats and presents our grandparents arrange for us, nothing removes the underlying knowledge that we may be fine but we are not good enough. Every night when I go to bed, I whisper a secret prayer to God. It's ten years since Dean and his friends told me He doesn't really exist but now I have a strong need to overrule the older kids and resurrect Him. I pray that when I wake up in the morning Mum will be back. Best of all would be if I woke up and Mum was back *and* I discovered this had all been a bad dream. The last few months just hadn't existed.

I wouldn't even mind having to do the school work twice.

When she finally comes back in July of the following year we hardly recognise her. What I've been praying for so devoutly is no longer actually there. She used to have shiny conker-brown hair curled neatly into her shoulders, but now it is cropped as short as a boy's and bleached white-blonde. She used to wear a lot of sensible jumpers, but now she wears bright cotton blazers with big exaggerated shoulders. She has a startlingly deep tan, too, and some flashy turquoise rocks around her neck that reflect blue in her (strangely whiter) front teeth. She also has a new husband, though not, as it turns out, Nigel, the man for whom she originally left Dad. This one is called Warren, an American who she has known for less than six months. And nor is he, technically, her husband, even though she calls him that, because she and my father are not yet divorced.

'I can't wait for you to meet him, you're going to *love* him!' she exclaims to Dean and me, trying to clutch us to her with an excitement we're clearly supposed to share. She acts like she's been away for a short holiday, not a year, or, the way she speaks about this Warren character, just down to the high street to collect a long-awaited pet. I picture him being delivered to our door in a hutch.

'Don't grab me like that,' Dean protests, and I have to agree I don't like it either. She didn't do it before, she didn't need to.

'Oh, come on,' she says to him, 'don't you love me any more?' And we stare at her, off balance, because that's what we want to ask *her*.

It's weird, being in the same room as her, finding her in front of my eyes wherever I go. I marvel that I'm not more overcome with emotion – not overcome at all. I would have expected to be crying and squealing and praising the Lord to have had those nightly prayers answered.

'It's too late,' says Dean, glumly, and he's right. She is too late. It's as if she has stayed away just a day beyond the point at which we might still have been won back. Or maybe it isn't the length of her absence that's been the problem but our ages during it. Maybe she's missed the formative year; maybe there was a single moment when we just grew up.

It doesn't matter, because she is still bubbling over with plans for us all. 'As soon as Warren gets in we'll start looking for a house, as close to here as possible so you guys can come over whenever you like. How does that sound? If Dad doesn't mind, of course.' Like *that* would concern her. 'And it's almost the school holidays, what perfect timing! Oh, I'm *so* happy to be back!"

That's when I first notice her new way of speaking. Mid-Atlantic, Dean says it's called. 'Gets in', for instance, so casual, like she's used to flying in and out of different time zones at the drop of a hat (as a family we have flown only once and she was the most nervous of all of us). As for the 'you guys', does she *really* think she can make us believe we are one happy, equal band of brothers?

Dean is the first to respond. 'I don't think so,' he says, and refuses to look her in the eye. 'We live *here*, remember?'

'Yeah,' I add, sullenly. 'We've already *got* a house. We don't need another one.'

Mum just smiles bravely and turns her big-eyed, thickly mascaraed gaze on Dad. She seems to be appealing to him for help in winning us over. Talk about nerve! But Dad just retreats wearily to the sidelines. He no longer needs to protect us. By now we know our own minds and they are full to the brim with resentment.

Of course we don't know yet that she still has her trump card to play.

Chapter 5

'So, are you feeling OK, Mum? Hold up all right today?' It was Russell who spoke, not Jamie or Noah, though he did so with a deliberation that was clearly meant to demonstrate to the two of them the concern they might be showing for their poor mother but glaringly were not. ('I never thought we'd have to teach them to *care*,' I'd said to Russell, years ago. 'Isn't that supposed to be innate?' And he'd shrugged, considering. 'Maybe not for boys.')

I thought, on this occasion, he was being a bit ambitious. After all, this was a first for the boys, who had been too young to be affected by Alec's death and had not known him particularly well, anyway. No, the funeral had done its job in drawing a line under the experience for them – if not for me – and I knew we should be pleased that it had.

Jamie briefly puckered his brow in my direction before returning to the computer printout he was reading. This had just been pressed on him by Noah, who sat opposite him at the kitchen table. Head to head, that was the typical arrangement for the boys, rarely, these days, side by side. The advantage Jamie had in intellect was easily balanced by Noah's confidence, his savvy. They were complementaries on the colour wheel.

Both had finished eating and had pushed their plates aside to devour the printed word. They always brought schoolwork to the dinner table, or something to read; opportunities for learning didn't stop with the requirement to refuel. It was just one of the million ways in which they differed from the national average.

'You've hardly said a word since yesterday,' Russell continued. He had also wolfed down dinner, eating far too quickly for his taste buds to have had anything but the most glancing contact with the various food elements. Sometimes I felt like testing them, asking what it was they had just been served. It might have been warmed-up papier mâché for all they cared. Not that I wasn't used to male feeding habits by now, of course – Jamie was fourteen and Noah approaching thirteen – but that didn't stop me from yearning sometimes for a fellow female who might savour her meals or, since we were on the subject, murmur a word or two of appreciation once in a while.

'I think you're in shock, you know,' Russell looked thoughtfully at me. 'You seem a bit numb.'

'It can't be shock if what's caused it didn't happen suddenly,' Jamie said, finally prompted to contribute. His antennae for technical inaccuracies were permanently abuzz. 'Grandma was ill for *ages*.'

Russell frowned at him. Normally very patient with Jamie's need for preciseness, this evening he wasn't in the mood for it, I could tell. 'I don't see why it can't still be a shock,' he said. 'The death of a parent is one of life's major traumas, however much warning you get. Hopefully you won't come to realise that for a very long time, eh, mate?'

At this Jamie and Noah exchanged a secret look. I liked to pretend that it was a recent thing, this certainty of theirs that they knew better than us, but we all understood that it was not.

'Any word on the will?' Russell asked me. That made me think of Dean and our sour little exchange at the funeral.

'I think wills are totally macabre,' Jamie remarked.

'What does macabre mean?' Noah asked.

His brother shrugged. 'It means fucked up.'

The phrase jolted me for reasons beyond the obvious. 'Boys!'

'It wasn't *me*!' Noah protested, but only half-heartedly, because he knew they could get away with anything at the moment. My perspective had shifted, had done ever since I'd increased the frequency of my pilgrimages to Mum's house, leaving the two of them – the three of them – out of focus. And Noah was not one to look a gift horse in the mouth.

'Macabre means gruesome,' Jamie corrected himself, matter-of-factly. 'It's from the French and refers to the dance of death.'

'That sounds about right,' Russell said, smoothly, though he knew as well as Jamie did that he could never have produced so dictionary-perfect a definition. He reached for their plates and stacked them on top of his own. 'Now hop it, boys, if you've finished. Mum and I need a minute on our own.'

I had never ceased to admire his natural command of our children, a knack I still lacked even after fourteen years of practise. There'd been times when I'd worried my lack of instinct might be genetic, that I might take after Maggie, but I'd learned to suppress the fear and concentrate instead on simple gratitude that at least one of us was able to get them to vaguely do what we wanted them to do.

As they retreated to the PC at the far end of the room, Russell got up and began transferring the dishes to the sink. This was new; I wasn't used to being treated as helpless, even if I felt it. I looked about the kitchen, unable to stop myself noting the jobs that needed to be done. It was a long, narrow space taking up most of the basement floor of our terraced house and with its stripped floorboards and battered wooden units had the feel of an old boat. Not exactly shipshape, though, for the mess was back, I saw, despite Russell's efforts. The low tide maintained over the last week had been replaced once more with the churned-up breakers of newspapers and magazines, circulars and bills, dumped bits of uniform, the school newsletters that never stopped coming. In a way, it was a relief.

My eye drifted to the calendar that hung from a nail by the corkboard. I looked at this at least twenty times a day, sometimes for a specific reason, other times in the way a dog might check its empty bowl – for comfort, out of habit. Lately, I'd spent so much time staring at it I might as well have scheduled slots for the activity in the same way I did the boys' dental appointments and after-school clubs.

The calendar was of a kind designed especially for busy families, with a column for each individual as well as one for the whole family to share (this, presumably, was where one noted the clan picnics that never took place, the family theatre trips that didn't get booked). Each person was supposed to fill in their own column but in reality I did it for all of us, cornering the other three in turn every Sunday evening and writing down their commitments for the week ahead. The manufacturer had anticipated this, it seemed, for the rules, type and array of witty little illustrations were all in pink.

Tomorrow's entries were fairly typical:

Russell: meeting in Swindon, home late.
Jamie: 8.30 school. After-school debating club, will have
    art project – collect from Newton building, 5.15.
    Remember PE kit for tomorrow.
Noah: 8.30 school. Tennis match at AHS, back for
    dinner. Important!! Also needs tennis kit Fri.

My own column was empty; I kept a separate, portable list of duties, too long to cram into the space provided. In any case, few items related to me, even though I was the one undertaking them. It was all about the boys in this house: their schedules, their needs – and those of their school, the famous, much-sought-after Herring's School.

It had taken a while to notice what was unusual about Jamie. He was our first child and there was no one to compare him

34

with, not openly. At mother and toddler gatherings it was under-stood by all who attended that the smallest boast, the faintest put down, would put one at risk of expulsion, a policy I endorsed to the full. Who wanted to get jealous about small children? They did that perfectly well on their own. Family offered a better opportunity for observation, for Dean and Beth had had their daughter Isobel only nine months after we'd had Jamie, but the problem was that Dean got so competitive about the two cousins. I quickly learned to play down any sparks of talent Jamie might show – if my brother hadn't already done so ('Well, he *is* that bit older, Olivia!').

Then his nursery school teachers began making remarks: 'He concentrates so well for a boy.'; 'He's very serious.'; 'He gets so frustrated. We think he wants to do things a lot more compli-cated than his hands will let him.'; 'He told us he was trying to make a high chair for his brother – out of toothpicks and Play-Doh, imagine that! Normally they just do a hedgehog!'

Soon, a crop of questions followed: 'Have you taught him to read at home?'; 'Does he spend a lot of time with older chil-dren?'; 'Have you noticed how extensive his vocabulary is?'

The school assessments spelled it out more formally. He was only just four but he might have been six or seven. He was advanced.

When the offers of places were made, the headmistress of our favourite school phoned to ask when we expected to hear from Herring's. She wanted us to know that there would be no prob-lem with our taking a few extra days beyond her own deadline to make our decision. I realised that she assumed we meant to accept *her* offer only if this Herring's turned us down. I was too embar-rassed to say I'd never heard of the place but as soon as I'd put the phone down I looked it up in the phonebook and drove the few traffic-clogged miles west to pick up a prospectus. The pic-tures showed small children with unusually determined faces and the introductory text spoke of a special provision for the gifted.

Gifted. Well, I'd seen the movies and read the newspaper features: gifted was a bad thing, it meant your child couldn't relate to ordinary people or, worse, that *they* couldn't relate to him. I'd seen child geniuses occasionally on TV, being gently mocked on chat shows or gaped at as they completed some devilish puzzle, and I'd thought, What was the use of a university degree at thirteen? Who wants to be different at that age? Logically, though, a school like Herring's might be the only place where Jamie *wouldn't* be different and so I rang to arrange to take him for a visit.

'I don't understand it,' I said to the headmaster, Mr Kendall, when the tour had been completed and he'd offered us a place on the spot. 'Neither Russell nor I are particularly talented at anything.'

He nodded. 'It's a common misconception that gifted children must come from gifted parents. But with two geniuses for parents the child would actually be *less* likely to be one himself. In that situation he would simply revert to the mean.'

'I see,' I said, already a little lost. I had a sense that the mean might have made for an easier life, especially when I considered Noah. Since his arrival eighteen months after Jamie, he'd consistently been pronounced 'normal'. How would he feel when he went to a different school, one for the *un*gifted?

But I needn't have worried. Though he didn't have Jamie's natural abilities, Noah had excellent coat-tails from which to hang or, as Kendall put it, the best one-to-one tutor you could ask for from the first day of his life (and he didn't mean me). In some ways he was in a better position than a gifted child who lacked direction. Besides, not everyone at Herring's was super-bright, some were just bright and, when the time came, Noah was accepted alongside his brother without argument.

Later, as we applied ourselves to a bottle of wine, Russell said, gently prompting, 'So, Maggie's will. When do you think we'll hear?'

I took a gulp. 'Any time now, I think. Dean was talking about it yesterday. Lindy's in charge, she's Mum's personal representative, that's what they call it. In fact, I'm sure she said she was meeting the solicitor today in Cheltenham. Or maybe it was tomorrow.'

He nodded. 'She'll let us know later in the week, then.' Though he spoke casually enough, when you'd been married to someone for this long the casualness merely alerted you to the more profound emotions below the surface. Despair in this case, or exhaustion. Like many men new to middle age, Russell was tired of his job, could hardly bring himself to call it a 'career' any longer. In his early forties and already counting down to retirement; his condition had become self-fulfilling. An outsider would think it wasteful, absurd, but when it came to careers, I was in no position to judge, not having one myself. I was the one who was wasteful.

'Dean seems to think we'll just split the proceeds of the house down the middle,' I said. 'Plus whatever else there is.' I felt no thrill at the prospect, in fact I felt detached from it, but I knew Russell would be reassured by the information.

Yes, a legacy would be a convenient rescue package, especially if it was enough to facilitate an escape route for him, perhaps even a return to old passions – so old I had trouble remembering what they were and wondered if he did, too. Woodwork was one, that was right. It had been Russell who'd been attracted to our hull of a kitchen. Once he'd dreamed of being a cabinet maker, coaxing boards of walnut and oak into gentle curves, smoothing the joins together to a quality of finish you never found in shop-bought stuff.

And Dean, as well; perhaps the money might do something towards easing *his* heartaches. I hoped so. How unrecognisable he now was from the boy I'd huddled together with at the banisters, desperately transmitting our support for our father while willing Mum to walk back through the door and end the torment.

He'd been about the same age then as Jamie and Noah were now and in many ways he'd been more appealing. There'd been more vulnerability to him, more humility.

But remembering now the way a grimace had contorted his features yesterday, making him look almost demonic as he brandished that photograph, I became aware once more of the terrific heaviness in me. It was as if I was twice my age and my bones could no longer bear their own weight. Rising to fetch an aspirin from the drawer, I thought of that phrase Jamie had used earlier: the dance of death. Yes, I had no doubt that was what we all squared up to now.

Chapter 6

Mum's letter came the next day. The first shock was in receiving it at all, in seeing her handwriting on the envelope – upright and rather hesitant, not at all what you would have imagined of someone so headstrong – and knowing that the blood in her fingers had still flowed when she'd held pen to paper; wondering if this might have been the *last* thing she'd written, whether these counted as her final words.

The second shock was that it should come now, with only the second rattle of the letterbox since we'd buried her. But that, at least, was easily resolved: surely she'd only put into words what I had not allowed her to say at our last meeting? This was her apology for those 'uncomfortable' times she had put us through. I imagined her pressing the envelope on Lindy with that frail free hand, finding final energy where it had been all but sucked dry.

The third shock was the contents, for it wasn't a letter at all, and nor was it even in Mum's handwriting – she'd only addressed the envelope – but in a stranger's scribble:

Richie Briscoe
2 Angel's Lane
Millington, Dorset

That was it: a half-sheet of lined paper with a name and address on in. No covering note, no explanation. So much for a last attempt at penitence! Unless . . . The nerve ends in my fingers flared slightly, causing the paper to flutter, and I closed my eyes. Unless she'd understood only too well that final anguished question of mine, the one that had burst from me after decades of being held in abeyance, the one she had turned her head from as if from the devil himself . . . Unless this was her answer?

Richie Briscoe. The first man I had loved and the *only* one there had been to love, hate or otherwise before Russell came along and offered the alternative that had brought me back to life. Was I to take this missive at face value and understand that the address I held in my hands was *his* address? Could it be true that he was living now in England and not in the United States? Or was this something quieter – just a place that held a clue or a connection to something I didn't yet know? Whatever it was it was clearly intended to be somewhere to start. To *re*start.

Reading the words a second time, I allowed my thumb to trace gently over the characters that formed the name: *Richie Briscoe*. I wasn't sure how much time passed before I heard someone whisper the words aloud, or how many seconds later it was before I realised the voice was mine.

Rooted to my seat in the living room, I allowed my gaze to sweep every wall and surface, every object, and to wonder. I'd done this before, not often enough to call it a ritual, more a kind of occasional treat – or torment, depending on my mood – but never had it felt so necessary as now. To look in turn at the family photographs, the pictures Russell and I had chosen for the walls, our vases and books and DVDs, and to wonder what would be in their place had it been Richie instead of Russell. Had he not left me, had it been *me* he had married and not – well, I knew only the name that Mum had supplied me with and it was just as likely false as true. What would the faces in the photographs show, then? And, when I looked in the mirror, what would *mine* show?

Sometimes I felt like a teenager again, only instead of dreaming of the future, *our* future, I dreamed of the past, the past I had never been allowed to live but which I believed in my heart was the one that I'd been meant to live.

But I knew the answer to that, I'd repeated it to myself often enough as I sat on the sofa and wondered: stop dreaming. I had made my great leap of faith to Richie Briscoe long ago and I'd landed not in quicksand exactly, for it hadn't sucked me completely under, but on volatile ground, on a fault line. The adventure had shaken me, it had taken something from me that had never been recovered: innocence, perhaps, or grace.

Whatever it was that Mum was asking me to do, I wasn't sure I could do it.

Unendurable though it was, I managed a full twenty-four hours before extracting the road atlas from the car and looking up Millington – just as I had known I would and, more to the point, as *she* had known I would. It was a village in West Dorset, not far from Weymouth. Maybe because of the mental image I still held of Richie himself, I had automatically pictured some sort of surfers' resort right on the beach, tanned teenagers with beads in their hair and lifeguards dressed in red, but a quick search on the internet told me Millington was not like that at all. It was a small country village a mile or so inland, tucked picturesquely between ridge and sea. The area was rich in archaeological interest and attractive to tourists for its nearby swannery and botanical gardens. Zooming in on the digital map, I was able to locate Angel's Lane easily, a street on the southern edge of the village nearest the coast.

I estimated that it would take about three and a half hours to reach Millington by road and probably less time still by train.

Hardly knowing why, I prised from the bookshelf a second

atlas, this one containing maps of the world, and my fingers found North America: the West Coast ... northern California ... Santa Cruz. I remembered how Richie and I had looked together on the antique-style globe in the living room at Dad's, the one that lit up from within and doubled as a lamp. He'd shown me his hometown, as well as the town further north where he'd been born and had lived for most of his childhood. We'd traced a route across the Pacific to Hawaii and on to Australia, to the Great Barrier Reef and Ayers Rock, the cities of Sydney and Perth, and we'd talked about making our fortunes and going travelling. 'Making our fortunes': like a line from a child's fairytale, as though the idea of travel was completely out of reach.

Perhaps we'd sensed, even then, that we would meet greater resistance from our parents than a pair of step-siblings-to-be might ordinarily expect to when proposing a trip together. Or maybe the obstruction was more practical than that: Richie was two years older than I was, our gap years would not coincide and it would be another five years before we were both free of college. On top of that our educations were taking place in different continents. Travelling together *was* out of reach.

At the sound of the phone ringing I put the atlas away, grateful for the interruption.

'Olivia, is that you?' It was Lindy. 'How are you bearing up?'

'I'm fine,' I said, adding, 'I think. And you, are you OK?'

'Oh, not too bad. It's a bit strange in the house now the funeral's out of the way, a bit ...' She stopped, and I imagined her catching herself, not wanting to presume that her grief might be a fraction as intense as mine. I longed to fill in the word for her, but I didn't know which one to choose – empty, flat, anti-climactic, *lonely*? – and in the end I left to her to break her own silence. 'Olivia, the reason I'm calling is I've just spoken to Dean and I'm afraid he got quite angry.'

I groaned. 'What's wrong now?'

'It's a bit awkward, actually. I mean, I do understand, but there's really nothing I can do about it. I met with Adrian Bellamy, your mother's solicitor, yesterday and it seems she's left very specific requirements regarding her will.'

'Really? You mean we know the details already?' Instantly, an image of Russell's face filled my mind, that shoot of hope in wintry eyes.

'No,' Lindy said, 'the opposite. It's going to take a little while.'

'Why? Is there a problem?'

'No, it's just that . . . well, for one thing, she wants a formal reading. Apparently they don't normally do that, not any more, they just send out copies to everyone concerned and take it from there, but Maggie didn't want that . . .'

This time she didn't need to finish the sentence. I knew the story. Mum would have insisted on the arrangement she knew from films and novels. Where was the drama in everyone opening their copies separately, jotting down little calculations on the back of a Sainsbury's receipt? Where were the collective gasps and the fists clenched in triumph? Knowing Mum, she had probably left a strict seating plan, a script to refer to, a personalised feud for every family member.

I sighed. 'OK, no problem. When is it? We're looking at next week now, I suppose? Let me just grab the calendar.' As I reached for a pen I willed her to agree, as though a delay until the following week might make some sort of difference to me. (Why this should be, I wasn't yet prepared to admit to myself.)

'That's the thing,' Lindy said. 'She doesn't want it to take place for another six weeks.'

'Six weeks?' I was taken aback. 'Can she stipulate something like that?'

'I'm not sure, but she *has*, and Mr Bellamy felt there was no reason not to respect her wishes. It's not like these things move particularly quickly at the best of times. Getting the house on the market will take a few weeks, anyway, and I have access to enough money to settle her final bills and that sort of thing.'

'Of course. All right, then, if you're sure it doesn't complicate things for you, that's fine with me.'

There was the sound of pages turning. 'We've provisionally agreed a time for the last week in August. Does that work for you? It will mean coming to Cheltenham.'

'OK.' I flipped the pages of the calendar until I found the right one. She was talking about the week before the start of a new school year, a whole summer holiday away. As well as a family trip to the Algarve, the boys had a variety of activities lined up for the break, leaving me the breathing space to resume my job hunt. At least that was how Russell put it: breathing space, resumption – such easy, positive words. I thought of it more as standing on the edge of a high cliff and waiting to be blown off.

I marked in the solicitor's appointment. 'Lindy, while I've got you on the phone, can I ask you something?'

'Of course, go ahead.'

'I just got something in the mail from Mum this morning.'

'Yes, I posted it for her. I'm glad it's arrived safely.' Her voice was matter of fact, unintrigued.

'Did you see what was inside?'

'No, when she gave me the envelope it was already sealed.'

'I just wondered if you knew who might have written it?' But even as I spoke I realised the obvious answer: Richie's father, Warren Briscoe. No one else in Mum's address book would have kept up to date with Richie. Mum must have written to him to ask for it. But when? And what had made her do it?

'I assumed it was from Maggie herself,' Lindy said, sounding puzzled.

'No, only the envelope is in her writing. When did she give it to you, Lindy? Was it that night? Just before she . . . went?' We were still experimenting with euphemisms for death, but I already knew that 'went' was definitely not going to work and nor was 'gone'. There'd been far too many wents and gones while Maggie was alive.

'No,' Lindy said, 'it was a while ago, actually, before she got too weak to hold a pen properly. You saw how she was in the last few months; she was having to dictate all her final bits of correspondence and even that was a real struggle for her.'

'Of course, I'd forgotten that.' How could I have been so stupid? During my last few visits Maggie had not been able even to prop herself up on the pillows. There was no way she would have had the strength to sit up and address an envelope. And that was before you considered the problem of her failing eyesight.

'I don't understand,' I said, frowning. 'She gave it to you months ago but she didn't want you to *send* it until now?'

'That's right. She was very specific about that. She wanted me to post it the day after the funeral, not a moment before.'

'Did she say why?'

'No, but she didn't need to.' Lindy paused, tactfully.

Because she wanted to be sure she wouldn't be around when I read it. I supposed I ought to be grateful that she hadn't saved it for this big meeting with Bellamy, had him announce it in front of Russell and Dean and the rest. Unless . . . unless *that* was part of the point.

'I don't suppose there were any other letters, were there?' For the first time I considered the possibility that Richie had received one too, a copy of *my* address, and the thought frightened and exhilarated me at once.

'No,' Lindy said. 'That was the only one. I'm sure of it.'

'OK. Thank you. Thank you for everything.' Remembering her original reason for phoning, I sighed. 'And just ignore Dean, you know what he's like.' *He takes after his mother*.

We hung up. I wondered if Lindy's thoughts were working along the same lines as mine but, on reflection, it seemed unlikely. Her natural discretion, if not her ignorance of the contents of the letter, would prevent her from seeing what was clear to me: there was a link between this mysterious delay in the release of Mum's will and the mission she had set me in her letter – a direct link.

For it was a mission, I was certain of it. She had known I would agonise and dither about it and so she had created a way to give me time, six whole weeks' worth.

She wanted me to go and find Richie. She wanted to give us a second chance.

Chapter 7

It is the summer of 1984 when Warren Briscoe arrives in the UK to be converted by my mother to the joys of suburban London living. Though he is from the city himself – San Francisco – he has the brute energy, stocky proportions and checked shirts of a rodeo cowboy. He is younger than she is, well-mannered and generous, impossible to dislike in spite of the circumstances. And, most importantly, he does not come alone. Along for the ride is his son Brian (after Jones or Wilson, the story varies) Richard Briscoe, known to everyone as Richie.

For me, Richie changes everything. Straight away I see that everything until now, every*one* until now, has been second best. He is eighteen, not quite a year older than Dean, and has just graduated high school in Santa Cruz, where he lives with his mother and will be returning in late August for the fall semester of his freshman year at college. Just hearing terms like 'fall semester' and 'freshman year' gets Dean and I all excited. Until now our exposure to American culture has been limited to soap operas and music videos; family holidays have hardly taken us further than Calais. To us, California, with its surf parties and Harley Davidsons and Pacific Coast Highway, is glamorous beyond words.

Unlike his father, Richie looks the part. If I'd been asked in art class to paint a Californian beach boy, he is what I would have painted. He is blue-eyed and blond, of course, his hair long over his ears and neck, and deeply tanned all over ('sun-kissed', I tell Melanie in an American accent, making us both collapse into girlish laughter). He wears his clothes loose over a lean, muscular body, but is equally comfortable with bare skin, often going about barefoot and sometimes bare-chested, too. I know long before touching him how he will feel: taut and hot and with a pulse you can find all over him.

'This is a seriously fucked-up situation,' he says to Dean and me that first day, just as soon as the three of us are left alone together. Richie, we quickly learn, thinks a lot of things are fucked up and this serves only as a source of amusement to him. His voice is exactly the slow drawl I would have hoped for, the sound of someone who's just been pulled out of a long snooze in the sun. 'My mom is going crazy back home.'

'Why?' Dean asks.

Richie sends him a conspiratorial look. 'Because she's a control freak and I'm a million miles away?' He says this as if it's a question for us to reply to, but then supplies the answer himself. 'She's lost *him* and now she thinks she's losing *me*.'

'How did they meet?' I stammer, finding his assertion breathtakingly insightful. 'I mean, Maggie and Warren?' It's the first time I use her name as he does and it feels disloyal somehow.

He tells us they met in Warren's office, a construction business in the Bay Area with a couple of big contracts and a workforce of forty or so. Warren has been instrumental in sorting out Mum's work permit 'and stuff'. Richie laughs out loud when we ask if you can see the Golden Gate Bridge from the office. 'Are you kidding? He's an hour from the city. I grew up in a great neighbourhood but it's a real pit where Dad lives now. Mom seriously screwed him in the divorce. Our house in Santa Cruz is a million times cooler.'

'*Really?*' Now it is we who are disbelieving and, in my case, seriously crestfallen. Mum's desertion was a whole lot more understandable when I pictured her in Hollywood or Las Vegas or perhaps travelling between the two in a bubble-gum pink convertible. But now all I can think is, Why did she prefer working in a low-grade job in a 'pit' on the other side of the world to being at home with us? 'Where she belongs', that's the phrase Dad uses in conversations with the grandparents, though not when he thinks we are in earshot.

In any case, whether she's here to show Warren and Richie off to us or us to them, Mum *has* come back. There is no denying that. Now it is Warren who leaves his real life in the hands of a partner, albeit a business one, a man called Brad who phones frequently to campaign for his return. Richie tells us Brad disapproves of Warren's proposal to invest his money in a property over here.

'Don't know why the Bradster's getting so mad about all this. Dad won't go through with it,' he says. I watch his lips as he talks; they look dry and sort of salty, as though he's joined us directly from the beach. 'There's no way this will last.'

'Why not?' I protest.

'Nothing lasts with our mother,' Dean agrees, over the top of me. Though he matches Richie in nonchalance, I can detect the raw hurt in his voice even if Richie can't.

Richie himself does not seem to be doing any hurting. This turn of events means nothing more to him than a free holiday, a mellow way to pass the summer, to use his own favourite adjective. He says he's always thought Europe would be mind blowing, especially England (he seems to think this includes Scotland), and now he's here it looks just as wild as he'd pictured it. It is incredible to us that he might consider anything about suburban South London mind blowing or wild, but apparently he does.

To us it is obvious that *he* is the mind-blowing one, he's the wild factor, and soon there is evidence to back this up. Being

49

male and closer in age to him than I am, Dean is his natural guide and on one of the first nights in town he takes him to the eighteenth birthday party of a mate from school. All the girls start 'acting weird' at the mere sight of him, my brother reports the next day, even before he puts on tapes with music they've never heard and makes everyone Kamikazes (some kind of vodka drink, I learn). After they've all, at his instruction, downed several of these in one, they form a human chain and jump into the pool, even though it's raining and the water isn't heated. Some of the girls take their tops off. For this last detail alone, my brother has dropped his cynical act and declared himself a convert.

Already Dean doesn't say 'Goodbye', he says 'Sayonara' like Richie or, if he's going the whole hog, 'Sayonara, sucker!' Richie got that from his friend Troy back home (Troy! No one in England is called Troy!). Dean thinks it's cool and soon we're all saying it.

My mother, of course, is just as enchanted by Richie as we are. 'Isn't it fun having a new brother?' she asks me in her breathless new accent.

'He's not my *brother*,' I argue. 'You and Warren aren't married.'

'We will be, though, just as soon as the divorce is final.' She rolls her eyes. 'Why does everything have to take so long in this country? In the States you could sort this out in a jiffy. Why is it that here people always want you to suffer for your mistakes?'

There's a lot I could say to that, like everything that's happened is her doing and maybe she *should* be suffering a little bit; or like, if she's saying her whole marriage to Dad has been a mistake then doesn't that imply that we are, too, Dean and I?

But instead I make the point that's suddenly more important to me than any of that. 'Even if you do marry Warren, Richie would only be a *step*-brother.' I feel my face flush and hope she won't notice.

She does, of course. 'What's got into you? Oh, Olivia, don't tell me you're developing a little crush on him?'

'I'm not developing anything on anyone!' But my hot cheeks say otherwise.

She groans, pulls a face of exaggerated motherly concern. 'Well, I hope not, sweetie, because he's a lot older than you.'

I know it won't help, but I can't resist arguing with her. 'What, two years? That's not a lot older.'

'Excuse me, it most certainly is when one of you is only fourteen! And it's a lot more than two years!'

'I'm fifteen,' I correct her, disgusted. 'Sixteen next month. We're two years and four months apart.'

Mum nods, too ashamed of her error to mock me for the preciseness of my calculation. 'But that doesn't change the fact that Richie is a grown man. No offence, but I don't think it would occur to him to think of you like that.'

'I don't want him to! Don't go on about it!' I wish I could take this horrible liquid heat from my face and scald her with it. The only way I can think to get out of this conversation is to blurt out a question I've longed to ask her since she's been back but not dared: 'Mum, why did you bring Warren to England? Why didn't you just stay in California where he already has a house?'

Her mouth gapes and I see the line inside the lower lip where her matt cherry lipstick stops and the moist blue-pink skin begins. 'Because *you*'re here, of course, Dolly. You and Dean. I missed you guys!'

'Oh.' I'm not sure whether I should enjoy the pleasure that floods my body at this declaration, not to mention her first use of my childhood nickname in years, or simply pretend it isn't happening.

Either way, I think she is as relieved as I am when Warren swaggers into the room and breaks our little moment.

Chapter 8

In the end, I went suddenly on impulse, or at least that was how it felt, though of course the urge must have been brewing from the moment I opened the letter. It was Saturday, mid morning, and the boys were out. Jamie had made his own way to Mind Stretchers, a Saturday maths group run by the school, while I had driven Noah to the swimming pool for his diving lesson. Parental attendance at either activity was so far out of the question as to be a punishable offence; even delivery duties were permitted only grudgingly. As for goodbye kisses, well, any public display of affection had been forbidden for years (I could probably find the exact day on an old calendar somewhere, the day an older boy had first sneered at the presence of a younger one's mother at the school bus pick-up). I wondered sometimes if all of this was the same with daughters.

No, it certainly didn't feel like the last time I would see my sons for a while. Though Noah and I had chatted quite happily on the way to the pool, it hadn't worried me that Jamie had been running too late for conversation. His only communication was to ask me if Dad and I had looked at the details for the residential course he wanted to sign up for during the summer holidays. Yes, I said, but I didn't think we could afford it. These courses were expensive. And he'd groaned, not sullenly, more in the way a scientist might if his lab experiment had not turned out as hoped: there had to be another way to get the result he needed.

Did that groan of his amuse me or irritate me, cause me guilt that I couldn't always meet his needs (or even understand them, if I was honest)? Either way, it was a pretty standard Saturday morning – at least that was how it felt as I parked the car and climbed the steps to the front door.

'Russell?' As I let myself back into the silent house I breathed a sudden confidence through my lungs, a feeling I hadn't experienced for so many years I didn't even recognise it at first: freedom. In that moment I knew that if I didn't do it now I never would. Now or not at all, that was my choice.

Now. Instantly adrenaline flooded my veins, making an easy glide of the two flights of stairs to my bedroom. Pausing only to stuff my overnight bag with a change of clothes and a handful of toiletries, I skipped back down to look for Russell.

He was in the back garden, still in his dressing gown, chopping away at the ivy-choked hedges. A large heap of trimmings lay at his feet and as he side-stepped them tendrils began tangling around his ankles as though still growing. He did this sometimes, woke up in a gardening mood and went straight out to get on with it, no thought even to brush his teeth.

I stood on the patio a while just watching. Noticing me at last, he wiped his brow with a dirt-caked gardening glove and asked, 'Any chance of a coffee?'

I eyed the full mug on the wall near his feet. He never finished a drink when he was gardening. 'Russ, how would you feel if I went off by myself for the weekend?'

'What?' He took another swipe with the shears and stepped back to judge his work, the unnoticed shackles of ivy causing him almost to overbalance. I reached forward to move a stone duck out of range. 'Er, I think that's a great idea, Liv, exactly what you need, some time with friends. Just let me know when and I'll make sure it's in my diary.'

'No,' I said, 'not with friends. And I mean *this* weekend. Now.'

At last he stopped his hacking and gave me his full attention. '*Now*? Why?' Still clutching the shears, he moved towards the steps. The lawn was raised from the patio by a few feet and I had to tip my head back slightly to meet his gaze. Its innocent bafflement reminded me of Noah when I interrupted his computer game to remind him to have his bath.

'I don't know how to explain it. I just feel a bit odd.' And though I was concealing something from him I was also telling the truth, because I *did* feel odd and I *didn't* know how to explain it.

'Odd in what way?' Russell asked.

'I . . . I just feel like I need some *air*!'

As my eyes pleaded with him to get it, to nod and let me go, he dodged the rose bush and came slowly down the steps to join me. Next thing, a gloved hand had landed on my shoulder and was giving it a clumsy squeeze. A flake of dried dirt dropped to the ground.

'Well, that's understandable. It's a huge thing, what's happened. Why don't you spend a bit of time with your father? You didn't get much of a chance to talk at the funeral, did you?'

I shook my head. 'No, Dad's fine. He's about to go on holiday, anyway, he won't be around much this summer.'

'Dean, then?'

'No!' My vehemence startled both of us. All at once the hedges, grown for privacy, felt confining and oppressive; it seemed vital that I be unfixed from this spot immediately, placed in the street, pointed *away*. And though Russell was as mild-mannered a man as any I'd met, it took every ounce of my energy to contain my fear that he might prevent my escape. 'Dean's driving me nuts,' I added, keeping my voice as normal as I could. 'He's the last person I want to see. No, I think I need to be on my own. It's not such a big deal. I'll be back tomorrow.'

I fled inside. Russell followed me across the kitchen to the basement door at the front, his gardening boots clumping heavily on the boards. He noted at once the overnight bag by the window.

'When did you pack this?'

'Just now.'

'Oh.' He was looking not so much ambushed – as we both knew he was entitled to – as eager to find a way to make a joint initiative out of this. That meant more questions, and I decided it was better to keep moving as they were being asked rather than stand still and allow myself to be talked around.

'Did something happen when you were out?' he began.

I twisted the key in the lock and pulled open the door. 'No, not at all.'

'The boys got off OK?'

'The boys are fine.'

'Don't you want to wait for them to get back and say goodbye?'

'You explain,' I said, brightly. 'Anyway, by the time they get home I'll virtually be back myself.' A thought struck. 'You do know where they are, don't you?'

'Sure.' Russell's gaze settled on the fridge and I realised he was looking for the pink calendar in its old spot between fridge and oven. I'd moved it months ago.

'Noah's at diving practice,' I said. 'Then he's at his friend Harry's for the day, the number's on the board. And Jamie's at the school all morning. He'll probably come straight home after that. They've both got their mobiles if you need to speak to them. And there's plenty of food in the fridge. You shouldn't need to go to the shops at all.'

'Thank you, executive housekeeper Olivia.' It was a familiar joke, but his heart wasn't in it and my own smile felt weak on my lips.

'Bye then.' I kissed him and made for the steps. As usual, they needed sweeping. Home all day and I'd never been able to keep on top of it all, never. The list in the pocket, in the handbag, on whatever surface I'd last wiped clean, it never came to an end. Only the bit of paper changed, the colour of the ink. Executive housekeeper I was not. There was just that once when I had, I *thought* I had, everything up to date – meals, beds, laundry, school uniforms, shopping, bill paying, travel arrangements, even birthday cards to the children of lapsed friends – and I'd had the almost supernatural sense of being able to reach out and touch the peace with my hands. Then the mail arrived, bringing with it a bill that had to be queried and a reminder for an optician's appointment that had to be made. By the end of the morning a damp patch had appeared on the ceiling in Noah's bedroom, the tumble dryer had developed an ominous rattling, and the whole painting of the Forth Bridge had begun again.

With one foot wedging the door open, Russell stood at the bottom of the steps, a curious figure in his towelling dressing gown and mud-smeared boots. 'Olivia, hang on a bit, where is it you're going, exactly?'

'I'm not sure,' I said over my shoulder. 'Maybe to the south coast. I feel like some sea air.'

'Are you taking the car?'

'No, I'm sick of driving.' And nor did I want to take the risk of having Mum's face projected onto my windscreen for the next three hours. 'I'll get the train.' I turned a final time and we stood looking at each other as we had in the back garden, only now our positions were reversed and I was up high and he down low. 'Thank you,' I said.

'What for?' When I didn't answer, he added, 'Well, phone when you get there, all right?'

I put up a hand in farewell, fingers lightly keying the air. 'All right.'

Later, when I looked back on that morning, I saw that the disconnection had begun at once, almost as I walked down Sterling

Avenue to the bus stop to catch the bus to the train station. Perhaps it had begun earlier, when I had chosen to keep my mother's letter to myself or, earlier still, at the time of her death – after all, Russell had said himself that he thought I was in shock. Perhaps, most likely of all, it had begun before any of that, long before. The letter was not the first important piece of information I had hidden from him, after all. Whatever the answer I was already aware of it as I bought my ticket and took a window seat on the Waterloo train to Weymouth.

I had imagined I would start crying, right then and there, and had chosen a quiet carriage for that very purpose. Alone, anonymous, this was surely the natural moment for me to succumb to the grief that was expected of me, that I expected of myself. But, to my surprise, the opposite was happening. As I looked out of the window, London falling away from me as vertiginously as if I had taken off in a plane, I felt unusually light-hearted, almost serene. There was no sun, but the city light had never been so clear and beautiful.

I was reminded of the first weekend Russell and I spent away from the boys, years ago, when Jamie was two and a half and Noah not quite a year. We'd left them with Russell's parents and taken the Eurostar to Paris for two nights. Two nights: negligible on paper compared with the nine hundred or so straight that I'd devoted to the boys (when I worked it out, the only night I'd spent away from Jamie had been the one on which Noah was born), but not negligible to me. It was like the unstrapping from my back of an enormous pack. It didn't matter that I would have to buckle it back on again soon enough; any relief from the weight, however brief, was to be cherished.

'I miss them already, don't you?' Russ had asked, before we'd even reached the tunnel. He'd looked genuinely bereft and I couldn't help smiling. 'Olivia, I'm serious! Do you think we should really be doing this?'

'Of course we should.' I didn't point out that he had spent

many nights away from the children on business trips and that it was illogical for him to be especially nervous about this one. I supposed it must have been the idea of *me* leaving them that worried him, or perhaps the idea of the two of us being together without them, on our own, no infants sandwiched in the bed between us. Our family had doubled in size, but somehow the concept of the two of us had more than halved.

'They'll be fine,' I added, more gently, touched by his woebe-gone face. 'Nothing can go wrong. They're in safe hands. Your mum knows what she's doing.'

'You're right,' he agreed, bravely. 'We need this.'

'Exactly.' And it had amazed me that he had needed to brace himself for something I considered a gift.

As the train pulled out of Winchester I bought a cup of coffee from the buffet car and returned to my seat. The carriage had filled up; I couldn't cry now even if I wanted to. I took the lid off the coffee but the liquid was much too hot to risk putting any-where near human skin, so I just placed it in front of me and watched it slosh gently back and forth. Finally, it began dripping over the sides and I replaced the lid and mopped up the spillage with a paper napkin.

That was when I first heard the whisper – or at least that was when I first allowed myself to *listen* to the whisper. The words that told me that what I was about to do might very well make a mockery of my entire adult life – and the loved ones who had filled it – overwriting all that had fallen into the chasm between then and now, between Richie and me. And how could it not? If, when I saw him again, I felt anything like I had the first time, it would. If my attraction to him was a hundredth as powerful as it had once been, it would.

One summer. That was all it had been in the end, no time at all. For him it was no more than a brief punctuation in his long surfer years and yet for me it had made a punctuation of the rest,

59

it had come to represent my whole adolescence – and beyond. Time passed, my life expanded, but that single summer had never shrunk to the size it ought to have. Maybe that was why I hadn't noticed the years slipping by recently. My heart processed them differently from the calendar on the wall.

I gulped at the scalding coffee in an effort to silence the whisper. I wasn't going to Richie to try to resurrect our first love – that was ridiculous! Maggie couldn't possibly have meant me to do that. No, I was going to Richie to lay a ghost to rest. A meeting with him after all this time would act as a memorial, just like the one we'd held for her last week, a chance for a proper goodbye to the past before I got on with the real life of the present. *That* was what I should be reclaiming, surely, my family life with Russell. I should be making up for all the time I'd spent in Cheltenham, for the feeling of falling away I had allowed to spill through the front door with me every time I came home.

Reaching in my pocket to finger once more the envelope that contained his address, I thought again of what Lindy had said about it: how Mum couldn't have written anything by hand in her last few weeks, maybe even months. She'd given the letter to Lindy to hold on to 'a while ago' and, if I was right about her source of information, she'd made a special effort to seek it in the first place. But if Richie had been on her mind – then, later, whenever it was – then why had she been so intent on *not* talking to me about him? There'd been any number of mother–daughter opportunities for her to tackle the subject, not least that last shameful confrontation. How could she possibly have imagined that a slip of paper given after she had died would be enough for me?

And then the whisper came again, too fast for me to close my ears to it. The only explanation for her refusal to speak was that she must have known for certain what I had only ever been allowed to suspect: that she had been responsible for destroying us. She, and no one else.

Her silence was her admission of guilt.

Chapter 9

Jamie used to say that the nature of the universe meant that 'out there, somewhere' there was another solar system exactly like ours, another earth, another Sterling Avenue, London, an identical suburban family sitting at just the same kitchen table as ours. They looked like us, too, the same hair and eye colour, shoe size, everything – they might even be *talking* about us as we were them. Then Noah, who was going through a competitive phase, said that *he* thought it would be even better there than it was here. It was planet earth without the bad bits.

I thought about that now as I travelled by taxi through jewel-green countryside from Weymouth to Millington, the soft sunny land rolling and folding just so, guiding me smoothly to my destination. It was as if there could be no other place for the car to end up; I was a smooth glass marble pitched with absolute precision towards my own perfect pot in the ground.

That feeling of sureness continued as we entered Millington itself and proceeded gently downhill past rows of stone cottages towards the old coaching inn, Victorian school building and medieval church that constituted the heart of the village. The driver had said he didn't know the place at all, but still he found Angel's Lane without once resorting to his map. It was so simple, in fact, that at the last minute I asked him to pull over by the village store on the high street rather than turning into the lane itself. Suddenly, this was happening too fast for me. I didn't know if I was ready to discover exactly what this remote address held. In fact, I was no longer sure that it held anything at all. Might this not turn out to be nothing more than a wild goose chase? Was I forgetting too easily how much confusion there'd been in Mum's mind during her decline? Might she not have joined someone else's address with a name that had surfaced randomly from the past, slipped it absentmindedly into an envelope meant for some other purpose?

Then I reminded myself that the name and address had been written by a third party – probably Richie's father – and could not possibly be the fabrication of a jumbled mind. The house number *did* exist, the address *was* Richie's (or at least it had something to do with him), my instincts *were* to be trusted.

The driver gave me his card and told me to phone when I needed taking back to Weymouth. He'd be free again after five.

'Oh, I'm not going back today,' I said, my sureness restored. 'I'm staying overnight.'

He nodded dubiously towards a trio of elderly ladies exiting a tearoom across the road. 'Don't look like there's much going on in the evenings round here.'

I just smiled, pocketed his card and closed the door behind me. Only after he had pulled off did I turn to look properly down Angel's Lane. It was a short, straight road, which meant I could see a part of every house from where I stood. Counting ahead I calculated number two to be the last on the right, beyond which the road continued in a rough track in the direction of the sea.

After several minutes of simply standing there in the heat, drawing energy from the sun like some sort of desert creature, I at last began walking towards the house. Even at a relaxed stroll the task took less than a minute and then there it was in front of me: number two, a fact confirmed by the neat brass numeral above the letterbox.

It was a small brick-built cottage, ivy feasting on its front and a spray of yellow roses around the front door, and there was no gate or fence of any kind, only a pale gravel drive that led directly to the back of the property, separating it from open countryside. A green-painted veranda, raised a few steps from the ground and presumably wrapping the full width of the rear, had been extended around the side to finish just below a small square window. If I saw that arrangement in the city I'd think at once of burglars, but here I just marvelled at the incredible position, at its uninterrupted views to both the south and the west, complete with glittering wedge of Atlantic. How peaceful it felt! To London senses the space and the silence were otherworldly, almost magical. And it didn't connect with the Richie Briscoe I knew on any level but one: the ocean.

And then, almost as a detail I might have overlooked, I saw him. A broad, barefoot figure in jeans and a sky-blue T-shirt, who had suddenly and noiselessly appeared on the side section of the veranda. He had a paintbrush in his right hand and held it ready as he stooped to inspect the lower section of the window frame. He was no more than four or five metres away from me.

I took a step back, flattening my palms against the brick of the house to steady myself. Could it possibly be this easy? After so many years, could it actually be that all that now divided us was this short stretch of gravel and the timber structure of a veranda? A dozen steps forward and I'd be able to reach between the balustrade and touch him! But I found that for now I could do nothing of the sort, I could only stand and stare as though watching him on a screen.

He began applying flat, deft strokes of pale pink to the wood, crouching low and bringing his face so close to the brush he'd be lucky not to paint his own nose in the process. *Was* it him? If so, then he was no longer the lean and bony boy of my memories, and he was certainly not as blond, but one thing had not changed – he was tanned, his face and forearms several tones darker than my own. An ancient memory burst suddenly to the surface: our fingers entwined, our legs hooked around one another's, the colour of his skin so exotic next to my milky, pink-flushed tones, like sugar and syrup melted to make toffee. (Truly, a teenager's metaphor – never had a suntan elicited so much admiration! I'd even resolved, back then, to ask his mother if he'd been born that colour; I'd been so convinced we would one day meet.)

I continued to watch as he wiped drips of colour on to a cloth and leaned back against the handrail to inspect his work. It was only then that, sensing spying eyes, he turned to look towards the street. There was a slow moment of complete stillness and then his hands resumed their wiping, reaching behind him to prop the brush in a tray sitting on a box or chest of some sort. Then his eyes were on me again, checking I was really there and not some apparition he'd glimpsed in the dazzle of the sun. Cool, easy Richie, this was his version of the startle reflex. A languid double take.

'Hello, Richie. I'm so glad you're in.' I crunched forwards towards him, coming to a halt at the bottom of the steps. Now that I'd spoken I felt utterly calm; unnaturally so. If I was unnerved by anything at all then it was by my *lack* of nerves.

'Hey, Olivia.' His blue-eyed gaze was steady and friendly. There was no bewilderment or incredulity, no spontaneous blaze; it was almost as if he'd been expecting me. It occurred to me that the strange calm I felt might have the power to infect others but, no, it was crazy to imagine he experienced what I did. The fact was he had always been unflappable ('He's so laid back he's horizontal,' Warren used to say of his son, the first time I'd heard the expression). No, Richie would be as casual as this with any unexpected visitor. The sense of there being anything more meaningful to the occasion belonged only to me.

I stood before him, smiling. 'You recognise me then?'

He grinned. 'Sure. You look pretty much the same.' That

covetable, much-mimicked Californian drawl was muted now; you might not detect it at all if you hadn't known him before.

'I doubt that,' I said, 'but thank you.'

He wiped his hands on the paint-spattered cloth and dropped it into the tray. Then he brought his left hand up to his face and squeezed the end of his nose, pressing the nostrils together in a reflective mannerism I hadn't thought about for over two decades but that now seemed the most familiar thing in the world. Still I stared, absorbing all the lines and textures of him. His hair was shorter, paler, a little thinner, his skin more wind-beaten than sun-kissed. Back then he'd been lithe and elastic, quick to slide away from – or towards – trouble; now he was solid and strong. Responsible. A different age, a different life, but he was pretty much the same, too.

'What are you doing in this part of the world?' He leaned his elbows on the rail and looked directly down into my face.

I hesitated, considered telling him about my mother's cryptic part in this, inviting him to debate her intentions then and there, but the prospect was awkward by anyone's standards. How could I explain why the sight of his name and address had caused almost immediate flight in me, when I knew he had likely not given me a thought from one year to the next?

I cleared my throat. 'I heard you were living down here and I thought I'd drop by.'

He nodded. 'You're on your own, are you? I didn't hear a car.'

'No, I came on the train. I would have phoned, but I didn't have a number. Maybe I should have written to you first . . .'

He dismissed this with a quick gesture. 'No, no, it's no problem. It's just lucky I was in, is all.' He gestured to the steps at the back. 'Come on up. Mind the paint, though, it's still wet.'

'So I see.' I tore my eyes from his face and took in the space beyond. A high rear window with the same gleaming new paint-work as the one at the side; a back door, ajar, its surface prepared for the new colour but not yet begun; a battered storage chest being used as a stand for materials. There was a row of trees in squat metallic pots and lots more ivy, roots of the stuff coiling to the ground and bringing briefly to mind Russell in his dressing gown and boots (had that really been as recently as this morning? Already our parting felt like a month ago). To the far left, the space was as sheltered as it was open to the right, with a line of closely set yews screening it from the neighbouring garden and making it impossible to tell if that had a deck like this one. I suspected not, it felt too American; I felt sure Richie had had it built. And it was exactly what I would have wanted to do, too. A foot or two of elevation meant a centimetre or two more of ocean view.

'Grab a seat,' Richie said, motioning.

There were two options: a wooden bench that had been shifted away from the wall, presumably to allow access to the window behind it, and on the right a basket chair hanging from a chain attached to a beam overhead. I didn't think that would hold my weight, let alone his, so I took the bench, placing my bag to the side to leave room for Richie, too. Instead he settled on the top step, lowering himself with a satisfied flop, like a dog just returned from a long walk. More lost-and-found body language – and to think I'd been so sure I'd logged every bit of it!

'It's been a while,' he said, eyebrows raised. 'I would have thought you'd forgotten about me a long time ago.'

I couldn't help chuckling at the idea. 'Actually, I've been thinking about the past a lot recently. Maggie died. My mother. Two weeks ago.'

'I'm sorry to hear that.'

'It's OK. We weren't . . . well, you probably remember, we didn't have the best relationship.'

He nodded. 'You and your brother, I remember you guys . . .' But the comment faded on his lips, presumably as he reminded himself that two weeks was a little too soon to start being honest about the dead.

'Gave her hell?' I finished. 'Yes, we did. It was complicated

between us. And you were probably there at the most complicated time.'

'Tell me about it.'

Yes, I thought, I will tell you, I'll tell you everything. But there
was no hurry.

'There were a lot of old friends at the service, people I hadn't
seen for years. I thought about your father. I wondered if he
might have been planning to come?' This was not quite true;
Warren had been sent word of Mum's death and of the date for
the service, as had everyone in her address book, but having not
heard from him we had had no reason to expect him on the day.

'No,' Richie said. 'He doesn't leave the States much these
days. And I guess they must have lost touch.'

'Like us,' I said, quietly. I glanced over his shoulder at the
lawn, admiring the way it tumbled towards a brook at the
bottom, as if just this second freshly unrolled. The brook presumably marked the boundary between Angel's Lane and the
farmland beyond, which connected in turn with the ridge of hills
that backed the shore. It was a simple, beautiful view made of
compass curves of green and blue, the lollipop trees and cotton
wool sheep of a child's collage. Planet earth without the bad bits.

'I love your sloping lawn,' I told Richie.

'Oh, yeah. All lawns slope in Millington.'

I grinned. 'That sounds very profound.'

He grinned back. 'I guess, if you want it to be.'

'Well . . .' I pretended to ponder. 'I think I do.' Again I marvelled at my uncharacteristic calm. All those hundreds of times
over the years that I'd imagined this moment of reunion, and
every single one had been something grand, elemental, like some
great whooshing together of two walls of water. But now that it
was happening there was only a lovely gentle floating feeling, as
though I'd been bobbing beside him all along, just waiting for
him to put out a hand. It may not have been the feeling I was
expecting, but somehow it was exactly right.

'So how long have you lived here?'

His gaze narrowed as if he were calculating the answer for the first time. 'Pretty much thirteen years now. In Britain, I mean, not in this house. I was over in Southampton before.'

I stared, amazed. The thought that he might have been here all these years, perhaps even commuting to London for work and spending eight hours a day there, for the full stretch of my own retreat from office life, it seemed inconceivable to me. It flipped everything and demanded reassessment, like travelling to the southern hemisphere and seeing an upside-down moon.

I composed myself, gestured to the can of paint. 'And you've just moved in?'

'No, no. It's been almost three years. But I'm a little behind with my renovations.'

Almost three years! How long had Mum been in possession of this fact? I tried to banish her from my mind. Having not mentioned her role in my arrival here, it already felt too late. 'You know, I couldn't believe it when I found out you were in Britain at all. I'd just assumed you were in California all this time.'

He shrugged. 'I was for a few years.'

'After college?'

'Yep. I worked for my father for a while, before I got into the whole Silicone Valley thing. Then I travelled a while.'

'You came back to England?'

'No, not that time. I went to Asia, Australia. Then back home. And eventually circumstances brought me here.'

Circumstances in the form of a woman, I thought, but I didn't want to know about her, not yet. She obviously wasn't home – not unless she was doing something in complete silence indoors – for there'd been no other signs of life since I'd arrived. I was sure we were on our own. I realised now that I had not envisaged this meeting any other way. Stumbling upon him as he sat on this very seat with his arm around his wife, surveying their magnificent view together, him kissing the top of her head as she rested her cheek on his chest, no, that would not have been the same.

'How is Warren?' I asked.

'He's good. Retired. Remarried. Getting fat.'

'My mother married again as well,' I said. 'A man called Alec. Not long after you went back, actually. I'd just started college, so it must have been eighty-seven, something like that.' It felt surreal to talk about that period so casually. *After you went back*: as if his departure had been just one of a crowded calendar of inconsequential comings and goings.

'A nice guy?' Richie asked.

'Alec? Yes, great. He was a big traveller, a bit larger than life, he was good for her. He died about five years ago and I don't think she ever really recovered. When she was diagnosed with cancer herself, it was as if she didn't really care, not in the way you would have expected. Without him with her there seemed less reason to fight, I suppose.'

Richie nodded; he seemed genuinely sorrowful, which touched me. 'And your dad?'

'He's still going strong. He lives with his second wife up in Cambridge.' My fingers felt for the wooden seat on either side of my knees as, once more, I gazed beyond the green to the sea. 'This is beautiful, Richie! You're so lucky to live somewhere like this. It's really peaceful. Not at all like London.'

He adjusted his right leg, wedging a bare foot against the gate post. 'I bought it after my mom sold her place in Santa Cruz. She got ill and went to live with my aunt in southern California.'

'Oh, I'm sorry. Is she better now?'

'She's just getting old,' Richie shrugged. 'And she was on her own for quite a while, which I guess doesn't help. She wasn't so lucky as Maggie in that respect.' Though his body language remained relaxed, there was a new guardedness to his voice. There was a limit to the information he was willing to give; he wasn't as sure of me as I'd thought. Well, that was understandable. Here I

69

was, an uninvited guest, an uninvited ghost. He wasn't prepared for me.

'Normally on a Saturday I'm running around after my two sons,' I said, eager to keep the conversation going. 'That's my job: housekeeper, cook, bag packer, chauffeur.' I laughed. 'Actually, less and less chauffeur, they get the bus or Tube everywhere, or they cycle. They claim they don't need adult supervision any more. That's how they think of me, a supervisor.'

Richie raised an eyebrow. 'How old are they?'

'Fourteen and twelve.' I paused. 'And the sad thing is they're right. They *don't* need me. They already seem to know more about life than I do.'

'That can't be true.'

'It is. They're cleverer than me, both of them. I can't even help them with their homework. I haven't been able to for years.' In the past observations like this had caused me grief, or at least guilt, but now I found myself speaking about it quite acceptingly, even with amusement. 'Washing and ironing, that's the bit I do that they really couldn't do themselves. I'm their charlady.'

Richie laughed. 'Charlady? That sounds so English.'

'Doesn't it?' Jamie would know the origins of the word, I thought. He never looked up a spelling in the dictionary without also checking the etymology. 'Not that I mean to give you the wrong idea,' I said, quickly, 'like I'm Cinderella or something, because Russell helps with the domestic stuff. He cooks a bit. He does the garden. He's great with the boys, better than I am, in fact. I'm lucky.'

'Russell's your husband?'

I nodded, finally falling silent. I could understand why people often responded with a joke to questions about their marriages, one of those 'for better or worse' or 'for my sins' quips. It removed the temptation to blurt out the truth. Which was that you no longer dared think about what it meant to be a husband or a wife because deep down you knew you'd failed at it somehow.

'I heard you got married,' Richie said. 'I guess Dad must have told me.'

'And how about you?' It was impossible to delay the question any longer. 'Did you . . .?'

'Yes,' he cut in, shortly, and his gaze moved from my face to the back door, as though he'd been distracted by a noise from inside. Had I been wrong then, *was* she here? Was I about to meet her? Beneath the coolness of my skin I felt the hot thread of my pulse. But it turned out he was only thinking about his host's duties. 'Hey, what am I doing? I should get you a cup of tea or something. A beer, maybe?'

'A beer would be nice.' I made to rise and follow him inside, but he gestured for me to stay where I was.

'It won't take a second. Enjoy the view.'

I did as I was told. My eye was drawn to the left, eastward towards Weymouth, where one of the shield of hills rose higher than the others. At its brow, as stark against the sky as black ink on paper, stood a ruin of some sort, an old chapel or watch tower, perhaps, and I could see an ant trail of walkers negotiating the sheep-dotted terraces to reach it. I would walk that path myself, I decided. The views from the top must be wonderful.

'Here we go.' Richie was back, handing me a bottle. It was wet with condensation and my nails automatically began picking at the label, sliding it away and touching the glass beneath, a nervous habit I hadn't done for years. He remained in the doorway, leaning away from me against the frame, his glance oblique, and I could sense the tension in his body. He needed more from me, I saw, more than this impression I was giving that I'd simply drifted in with the breeze.

'I'm sorry to just turn up like this,' I said. 'You must think I'm completely mad. It's just that after Mum died I had this urge to look you up. Like I said, I've been thinking a lot about the past, about some of the crazier things Maggie did when we were

71

young. It's weird how it comes back to you, things you thought you'd forgotten.'

There was as much chance of my having forgotten him as there was my need to breathe in and out, but I reminded myself that I was an adult now – a wife and a mother – and whatever torments of the imagination had taken place over the years there was as little *real* residual love for Richie in me as there was in him for me. That was why I was so relaxed. But the thought had hardly been completed before I knew it to be false. This supernatural calm of mine was a defence, it was what held me upright and stopped me from spilling myself to him – my true self.

In any case, my words seemed to have done the trick because he was looking at me with gentle sympathy. That was different from before: he took emotions seriously now; he didn't make a joke of them.

'You didn't want to bring your family with you?'

'No, they're in London. Weekends are busy, the boys have commitments, and there's all the school stuff to get sorted for Monday.' Stuff that I had not thought to brief Russell on, but that hardly seemed to matter right now. Hadn't I just been bemoaning how well the boys looked after themselves?

Richie put his beer to his lips and swallowed. 'You know what? I looked *you* up once.'

'Really?' I glanced up at him, startled. But he'd shifted his position and his face was in the full glare of the sun, making it impossible to read his expression. 'When was that?'

'Years ago, when I first came back. I tracked down your brother and he told me all your news.'

I frowned. 'Dean? He never mentioned it. How strange.'

Richie shrugged. 'It was just a phone call. We never got as far as getting together in person. I guess it must have been ninety-five, maybe early ninety-six, something like that.'

I wound my mind back to that period. I must have recently had Noah, which meant we had moved into the house on

Sterling Avenue and discovered the dry rot problem. And the mice infestation. We'd only been there a few weeks when Jamie pushed some wire wool into his right ear and had to go into hospital to have it surgically removed. The anaesthetic was a traumatic experience for him, he'd had bad dreams for weeks afterwards, his wails waking Noah, who was a light sleeper at the best of times. Breaking down in tears was not uncommon for me then. There would have been all sorts of reasons why Dean hadn't remembered to pass on Richie's enquiries, some of them possibly even involving human sympathy.

'So how is Dean these days?' Richie asked.

'He's fine. He works in computers. He's got two daughters, similar ages to my boys. They don't live far from us, it's easy to get together.' Though we don't do it as often as you'd think, I added, silently. We need each other, Dean and I, but we don't make each other feel good.

Richie tilted his beer bottle from side to side. He seemed to have relaxed again. 'Who was that girl he was going out with when I was there? Red hair, freckles. Cute.'

I said straight away, 'You mean Amy Jukes?'

'That's it. Wow, you've got a good memory.'

Only for that summer, I thought. I can't remember the names of colleagues or neighbours from a couple of years ago, and yet I can play that summer in my head like a recording, every single detail, all our meals together, our conversations, our precious hours alone.

'You mean you *don't* remember?' I said, only half-joking, and my heart was suddenly painful in my chest, as if the muscle had been stretched over a frame and beaten with a stick.

Richie just chuckled, amused by the question, and I waited, wondering if he might mention something else, something about us. But instead, to my dismay, he was checking his watch, draining his beer, preparing to bring the reunion to an end. 'Look, I have to shoot off in a minute, but if you're not in a hurry, why don't you stay and have dinner?'

There was nothing I wanted more. 'I'd love to, if you're sure.'

'Sure I'm sure.' He eyed my bag. 'Are you checked into a B&B or something?'

'Not yet.' It was my cue to get up and do exactly that, the obvious way to fill my time while he ran his errands. The coaching inn opposite the church would probably have rooms and was only a couple of minutes from here. I could have a shower, take a rest from the sun – that was if I weren't rooted to the spot.

I must have looked as helpless as I felt because Richie added, 'Or hang out here if you like. I just need to pick up Wren and I'll be right back.'

'All right, thank you.' For a second I was so busy feeling pleased about not having to move, about being able to sit here a little longer and watch the fields and the sea and think about us having dinner together, that I didn't get his meaning. Rewinding, I thought I might have missed the name of a foodstuff he wanted to pick for supper. Then, as he vanished indoors in search of his car keys, pushing the back door wider open, I finally used my eyes. Inside, just visible by the doormat, was a child's Wellington boot, green and shiny and printed with ladybirds. Across the deck the basket chair I'd worried might not hold my weight *wouldn't* hold my weight – because it was not designed for an adult. Richie, a man in his early forties, was painting his house *pink*.

He re-emerged, car keys dangling from his index finger, and stood in front of me. 'OK, I'll see you in a . . . hey, what?'

I smiled broadly up at him, not knowing why I was so delighted. 'Richie, you didn't tell me you have a child. A girl?'

'Yes.' *Now* the sun blazed from his eyes.

'What's her name?'

'Wren.'

'Wren, like the bird?'

And he glanced to the sky. 'Exactly like the bird.'

Chapter 10

Richie is a hedonist, everybody says so. Mum has seen it first-hand (or at least its morning-after effects): the crazy beach parties, the stadium rock gigs at which the kids at the front faint in the heat and have to be shunted to the sidelines along a track of lifted hands, the romances with college girls who either don't know he's still in high school or are unusually willing to overlook the fact. His father is worried about his recklessness and about the friend called Troy, two closely related reasons, we gather, why he's been sequestered over here for the summer.

I listen to the stories with excitement and jealousy, an unfamiliar blend that reminds me a little of dread.

'He's a popular boy, all right,' Mum sighs, looking all girlish. 'But then I suppose that kind always is.'

'What kind?' I ask.

'You know, the free spirit kind.' She uses her fingers to put inverted commas around the term, another imported mannerism Dean and I have noticed (we are keeping a list). 'Then again, you probably haven't met any free spirits before, have you, Dolly? Your father and brother are always so bloody sensible.'

I don't know whether I'm imagining the sneer in her voice or not, but either way I don't like it. 'What about you?' I say, bridling. 'Aren't *you* one?'

She cackles with laughter at that. 'Oh, darling, that's very flattering, but mothers are not allowed to be free spirits. Didn't I tell you? It's against the rules.'

I consider this remark quite seriously. Doesn't leaving your children and travelling halfway around the world to start a brand-new life count, then? Not even sending word of a new address? Not coming back for a *year*? From where I stand, it is *fathers* who are not allowed to be free spirits, fathers who must play by the rules. 'But when you went to Ameri—' I begin, but she cuts right across me, her passions roused.

'It's not about *where* you go, Dolly, or even for how long. You're not free *here*!' Clapping one fist to her heart and covering it with the other like a game of one-potato-two-potato, she cries: 'Which may be how it's supposed to be, and how it always will be, but it doesn't change the basic fact that women are *never* allowed to forget they're women. Never!'

She's so wild eyed, I wonder if she's forgotten it's just me she's protesting to and not someone else (God, perhaps, or one of my grandparents). Whatever it is, I automatically retreat. Mum never admits she's wrong. Besides, though I hate to side with her against my father and brother, she's right about them, they *are* too sensible.

Later, several years later, when I meet Russell, I see straight away that he is not a free spirit. But nor is he a tethered one and that is important. He is optimistic, but grounded. One of the first things he says to me is that he wants to have his children while he still has the strength to keep up with them. His own parents had him later in life and he has been forever reminded of the problems of this, the frustrating gulf between his energy levels and theirs. He wants a brace of boys who he can chuck into the swimming pool, one after the other, safe in their matching rubber rings, and then he'll jump in after them and chase them about so they all squeal with terror and delight. Afterwards, happy and exhausted, they will sit in a line wrapped in towels and eat hot dogs, or blow into cups of cocoa. He has a very specific idea of what family life involves.

When he asks me to marry him I have no hesitation in saying yes. I've forgotten about Richie by then, or at least I've told myself it's *time* I forgot about him, which is as far as I'm ever going to get. I've consigned him with some ceremony to the compartment in my past labelled 'First love', or 'Teenage dramas', or, maybe, 'Free spirits'.

The plan is for Mum and Warren to rent a place near to ours while they look for a house to buy. The rental property on Acacia Street is surprisingly run-down, considering how particular Warren is reported to be about kitchen and bathroom fittings, but it's big – big enough for Richie to be assigned the whole basement floor to himself. He has his own shower and toilet down there and a sofa and TV, plus the electric guitar shaped like a bolt of lightning that he carried with him on the plane (his 'heavy duty' musical gear is back home in Troy's care. There are plans for a band on his return). He has his own private exit to the garden but no door at the front, so he must enter the house through the main front door, like everyone else.

Mum suggests that I get into the habit of staying over. 'I don't mean you have to move out from your father's lock, stock and barrel,' she says, 'I just mean come and use your bedroom here occasionally. Maybe at the weekends? You could think of it as your holiday home.'

Following his initial resistance, Dean is already crashing there after nights out with Richie and I have to admit I want to do the same. Despite myself, it feels quite glamorous having two houses to choose from, two bedrooms of my own. In a matter of weeks life has transformed from the weak, dismembered creature it was into something strong and whole. Now it feels like we're a family from a soap opera in a *good* way. OK, we never know what will happen next, but we are old enough to handle that now.

Or maybe not. For one thing, I'm not nearly worldly enough to second-guess my mother's motives. Only gradually do I suspect that there is an element of sport to what is going on.

Dean spells it out: 'She wants to win us back. She wants to beat Dad.' He says Mum is the kind of person who always thinks the grass is greener on the other side of the bridge, like the Billy Goats Gruff. If that's the case, then he has cast himself in the role of the troll. He might be willing to sleep in his designated second bedroom and eat food from the new oversized fridge and superpowered microwave Warren has drafted in, but he has not forgiven her.

'I'll never forgive her,' he says. 'There's no excuse for what she did. She shouldn't have had kids if she didn't want to be with them.'

Personally, I'm not sure I mind the original abandonment nearly so much as the fact that now Mum has returned she seems to be passing herself off as someone she is not. The younger style of dressing, the yellow streaks in her spiked-up short hair: all that is unremarkable compared to the changes in her speech and attitude. Does she really think we don't notice? Or is the whole point that she wants to make sure we do? To show us how different from us she thinks she is?

There are the Americanisms, of course, of which she is studiously unselfconscious (she'd have us all believe they've been incorporated into her speech without her having even been aware of it), not to mention the hammed-up Englishness (I never heard her say 'golly' before she left, or 'goody gum drops'. Dean winces when he repeats some of the phrases.). There is also the way she calls the Briscoes 'my boys' and yet calls Dean 'his father's son – through and through'. The sensible dig again. And then, ever since that conversation she and I had about Richie, there is the new personal edge to any comment that comes *my* way, too:

'That dress is going to look terrific when you've filled out a bit more.'

'Fifteen! You know what, Dolly, the Californian girls your age are something else.'

And to Warren, right in front of Richie, 'Why is it that the less make-up they need, the more they insist on wearing? It's a crime!'

Oh, and she wants us to start calling her Maggie instead of Mum. That's the one suggestion that Dean actually welcomes. Now there's no verbal clue that she's his mother at all.

Me, I'm not so sure.

Chapter 11

R, got here safely.
Thank you for understanding.
Love to the boys. Ox

To my frustration, my phone bleated pathetically in my hand before displaying the alert, MESSAGE FAILED TO SEND! There was obviously no signal here. I slipped it into my jeans pocket, just in time to hear the approach of a vehicle in the lane at the front and the sound of car doors crunching shut. Then a small child's voice cried out: 'Have you *really* done it, Daddy?'

'I have,' came Richie's voice from the drive. 'I thought it would be nice to surprise you.'

'Am I going to be *really* surprised?'

'Well, let's see. Come on, have a look.'

Footsteps scampered lightly across the gravel, followed by Richie's heavier tread. In the few minutes I'd had to picture Wren I had already overlooked the information that she was being collected from a party and so had not prepared myself for the full princess costume, which included faux sable shrug, bejewelled tiara and a pair of plastic heeled slippers. Miraculously, infant ankles had survived the gravel untwisted – she must have had practice. In one of her hands she gripped a party bag and a pink balloon trailed behind on a long red ribbon. There was chocolate all over the front of the ball dress and more around the mouth that opened now into a delighted 'O'.

'Oh, Daddy! It's gorgeous!'

Even through the party regalia I could see that she was a very slight child. I might have taken her for as young as three had not her speech already told me she was of school age. Her hair was soft golden-blonde and her skin very pale but for an apple of high colour on each cheek. Other than the very resolute set of her eyes as she appraised the new paint colour, she did not look like her father at all.

Richie, coming up behind her, tried to redirect his daughter's attention. 'Wren, sweetie, this is the lady I told you about just now in the car. She's called Olivia.'

'Oh!' Her confidence deserted her and she turned to cling to the nearest of Richie's legs, hiding her face from me.

He prised her free. 'Come on, don't be shy. She's totally friendly.'

I stepped forward, smiling. 'Hello, Wren. Have you just been to a party?'

No response. Well, it *was* a stupid question. Richie continued to peel her from his leg, but no sooner had he succeeded than she had nestled back into place.

I squatted to the floor at the top of the steps. 'How old is your friend, the one whose party it was? Four? Five? There's no number on the balloon.'

'*Five.*' Now she emerged. The urge to correct was not confined to my own children, then. Her eyes were bright, the colour of clear honey. 'But Daisy's a younger five than me,' she added.

'I see. And when were you five?'

'April the sixty thousandth.' She giggled, showing the tiniest teeth; it was ages since I'd seen milk teeth close up.

'Wren, don't be silly,' Richie said. 'Answer the question properly.'

She sighed. 'April the sixteenth. That's in the spring, not summer. When lambs are born. Who are you?'

'My name's Olivia. I'm an old friend of your daddy's.'

'Why are you at our house?'

Richie laughed. 'You can see I've raised a real society hostess here! Come on, chickie, let's take our guest inside.'

'No, I want to see the pink windows some more!'

'But the colour will change as it dries. We won't know the real colour until tomorrow, after I've done the second coat.'

Wren frowned. '*My* paints don't change.'

'It will still be pink,' I said. 'I think it's a beautiful colour for windows. Is pink your favourite?'

'Yes, and purple and green.' She eyed me with interest, before admitting, 'And blue and yellow. And silver.'

Richie grinned, cupped the back of her head with his right palm and eased her forward. 'That's it, keep your options open. Now let's get you inside. It's almost time for your bath.'

But now she'd spotted the open door and stopped in her tracks, gasping. 'Oh no, the door is open! Has a yogre been?'

'No, Olivia's been minding it.'

'There've been no yogres,' I said. 'I've guarded it very closely.'

She nodded solemnly and finally led the way in. The door opened straight into the living room, a square, light-filled room with beams overhead and polished boards underfoot. Two small sofas faced one another by the fireplace, both covered with patterned throws and mismatching cushions, the most prominent of which featured an embroidered mother duck and her ducklings. Drawings, presumably by Wren, were tacked higgledy-piggledy to the walls, alongside framed seaside prints of various sizes. It was cluttered and cosy, instantly sheltering.

Wren plopped herself down on the nearest of the sofas and immediately emptied the contents of her party bag onto the coffee table. Expertly sifting the haul of toys and pencils, she

83

quickly found the only edible item, a chocolate lolly. 'Daddy, can I eat this now? You can have the birthday cake. Is it a deal?'

Richie unhooked the fur wrap from around her throat. 'You already gave me the cake, remember? I ate it in the car?'

'Oh yes. I was very kind to share, wasn't I?' Uncertain now of her bargaining position, she nibbled at the foil wrapper while keeping her eyes on her father for signs of censure.

I settled on the sofa opposite. To my delight, from here you could still see the sea, a faint slim ribbon just above the window sill. Now that Wren was here there was no chance of conversation between Richie and me, a dynamic I'd forgotten from the boys' infanthoods. It made me remember something I hadn't thought about for years, how Russell and I used to take the two of them to Saturday morning swimming lessons, a forty-minute window in which we could converse without interruption. Afterwards, without fail, we'd be chastised by one or both of them for not having watched their progress properly. 'Did you see what I did with my flippers?' Noah would demand. 'Did you see?'

'They were talking,' Jamie would tell him. 'They *never* watch.' And invariably his accusing eye would settle on me.

Richie brought me a mug of tea before taking Wren upstairs for her bath. Clearly she was of an age when every instruction existed to be challenged.

'Can I miss bath time? Can I stay up? *Please*. It *is* a special occasion.'

'The party's finished. It's just a normal Saturday now. Come on, you're a tired teddy.'

'I'm not a teddy, I'm a *human*. And it *is* a special occasion. *She*'s here. *Lily*.'

'Not Lily, *Olivia*.'

'That's what I said!'

And so on. But, in all of this, there was no mention of a mother expected home or staying away overnight or being anywhere at all. While the two of them were upstairs I studied the various family photographs on display around the room. Most were of Wren, either alone or with children of the same age. One showed her on Richie's shoulders when she was about two, gripping his chin so that his head was forced up towards her, mouth wide with laughter; in another she was flanked by a man I recognised as Warren, silver-haired and portly, and by an elegant, blonde-bobbed woman in her sixties. That must be the new wife, the woman who might have been Maggie. Then I found what I was looking for: a baby picture. Wren – for presumably it was she – was being cradled by a young woman with shoulder-length mid-brown hair and a soft-featured face. The exhausted set of her shoulders and the array of hospital equipment in the background suggested this was the day of birth itself, or near enough. The woman's eyes were cast towards the baby rather than to the camera but I knew that if they had been they'd be that same rare golden colour as her daughter's.

A nearby stack of mail caught my eye. The top one was addressed to Mr R Briscoe, innocuous but for the stamp above it that read 'Beechwood C of E Primary'. Wren's school, presumably. But why would the school office address only the child's father? The answer was it wouldn't, not if there were a mother's details on file as well. I looked again at the hospital photo and felt a chill on the backs of my hands. Something had happened to this woman. She was no longer in the picture.

Though still light outside, shadows were lengthening indoors, so I turned on all the lamps and pulled shut the blind to the street (not that I imagined there'd be too many passers-by out here at the edge of the village). I took my empty mug to the kitchen – a tiny space at the side of the house – and rinsed it in the sink, then came back into the living room and gathered Wren's party goodies back into the silver bag. I was just putting the discarded princess slippers next to the ladybird wellies at the door, when Richie reappeared, crumpled and smiling.

'Hey, thanks. You didn't have to clean up.'

'No problem. Is she in bed?'

'Technically, but a bit too wired to sleep. This always happens after a party – she's had way too much fun. We may not have seen the last of her, let's put it that way. She likes to re-enact musical statues with all her toys.'

I thought of Jamie and Noah, their intensive, overwhelmingly academic schedules, and could think of nothing comparable to contribute. 'You have such a lovely house,' I told him, instead.

'Thank you. It's small, but it has a nice vibe, doesn't it?'

Any place would have a nice vibe with these two in it, I thought. 'Did you choose all the pictures and things?'

'Wren helped. She's my interior designer.' He pawed at his right hip pocket, an old mannerism from his smoking days, perhaps. He'd given up now, of course. When, I wondered? What were his bad habits now? It was one of a million details I longed to know.

'Right,' Richie said, 'adult time. Beer or wine?'

'Whatever you're having.' I followed him into the kitchen. 'It's so nice of you to let me stay for dinner.'

'You're welcome.' He reached for two glasses in a cupboard overhead and began opening a bottle of red wine.

'You don't have to cook though, really.'

He looked sideways at me. 'I'd forgotten how you always used to say that.'

'Say what?'

'"Really", at the end of every sentence, like you think people might think you don't mean it otherwise. You know, "It looks great, really."'

'You make me sound very insincere!'

'Really?'

We smiled, looking easily at one another for a second or two.

'I'd forgotten how you notice things like that,' I said, though I hadn't. It was one of the things I'd cherished about him, the way he picked up on the little things, as though the quirks were what counted the most to him. It had taken me a while to understand that that was what he saw, quirks rather than faults, and it had been, at the time, doubly welcome for being the exact opposite of how Maggie saw them. 'Or I could help you with dinner,' I went on, frustrated by how hard it was to dismiss my mother from my mind for any longer than five minutes. 'I know what it's like with little ones. You get to the end of the day and you just want to collapse.'

'Yep, that pretty much covers it.' He handed me a glass of wine and set about transferring a dish of food from the freezer to the oven. It was cottage pie, I saw, obviously homemade.

'I see you've embraced English cooking.'

'Huh? Oh, yes, actually we've got Wren's childminder to thank for this. But I do cook. I make sure Wren knows her American classics.'

'Like grilled cheese sandwich with coleslaw.' The words, along with the memory, were quite spontaneous. Oil from the sweating cheese on a plate abandoned by his unmade bed, an empty Coke can, a packet of Camel cigarettes, a treasured Zippo. 'I'd never seen anyone *fry* a grilled sandwich before.'

He grinned. 'You really *do* have a good memory. I dread to think what else you're going to come up with this evening.'

That made two of us. All I knew was that it was not going to be anything that questioned the rightness of my being here. I felt absolutely certain that this was where I should be. I couldn't think when I had last felt this contented.

As Richie sliced tomatoes into a salad, I stood at the kitchen window that overlooked a small paved area I hadn't noticed from the deck. It evidently doubled as a storeroom for bikes, scooters, sandpits, the detached plastic limbs of a couple of dolls, and I imagined Wren making a den down there. Who were her friends? What other games did she like playing besides musical statues? *Where was her mother?*

'Are you OK inside,' Richie asked, finishing up, 'or would you like to sit out again?'

'Oh, outside would be lovely. You know, I was trying to remember the last time I spent a night by the sea. I think it must have been last August, almost a year ago.'

'That's way too long. I don't think I've ever spent longer than a week or two away from the ocean. And Wren, I think she's seen it every day of her life so far.'

'How wonderful.' I settled on the bench again, once more leaving space for him, but this time he dragged a chair from indoors for himself, tossing me a cushion from the sofa. The sorrowful sound of a sheep carried across the fields from the hills and the birdsong was clear and sure. I couldn't quite hear the sea, but I thought I could smell it.

'Richie,' I said. 'I hope you don't mind me asking, but where is Wren's mum? Are you divorced or something?'

'Or something.' He spoke softly, and to my surprise he went quite still, as though frozen by indecision. Then, just as I was warning myself to drop the subject, he gave an answer of sorts. 'Let's just say she's not around, but we're doing OK. Do you mind if we talk about it another time?'

'Of course, I'm sorry.' Though buoyed by the promise of another time, I was saddened by the inference that he'd suffered somehow, *they'd* suffered. There was also an unexpected echo to his words that took a moment or two to come to me: my father speaking, Dean and me repeating together after him: 'We're fine on our own. We're fine on our own.' She must have left them, then, just as Maggie did us. She didn't live here any more. I wondered if they knew *where* she lived, or if she had chosen to withhold that from them. That, for us, had always been the cruellest part. I remembered how I used to will Mum to hear us wherever she was, how I'd imagined her finding a shell in the bottom of her handbag, one I'd given her years ago when I was little, and putting it to her ear to listen for our voices. I'd never asked her if she did, I hadn't dared hear the answer.

'You're doing more than OK,' I said, lightly. 'Wren is great. A real little character.'

'She certainly is,' Richie said, then, after a pause, 'Tell me, how long have you and – what was his name again? Russell – how long have you been married?'

'Oh, a long time now.' But the idea of counting up the years was suddenly an exhausting prospect and it was my turn to want to hold back.

Richie pre-empted me. 'Or maybe you'd rather talk about that another time, as well?'

'Yes please. There's so much to catch up on, but it's quite nice to just forget it all for a bit, isn't it?'

In response he sent me a quick, curious look, and then we settled back in our seats, looking out in the direction of the sea, which had blurred by now into the dusk horizon.

A new memory dripped into my mind, a safer, more distant one. 'Hey, do you remember that family trip to Lymington? It's not too far from here, is it?'

Richie considered. 'An hour or so. Over the border, in Hampshire.'

'That's right.' It had not been the most memorable event of the first and last Briscoe–Lane holiday, not by a long chalk, but it had certainly had its drama. My mother had got lost, an incident in pre-mobile phone times that had led to the rest of us spending most of the afternoon searching for her. Warren had directed the manhunt, moving us through the cobbled streets in an evenly spread fan formation. It was one of the first times we'd seen him grow exasperated with her and Dean had muttered to me, 'Can you believe it's taken him *this* long to see what she's like?' We didn't say it out loud, but we both thought it: *She's gone, she's taken off again.* We were wrong, as it happened, she really was plain lost, but we'd glared at her anyway when she was finally discovered, treated her like the boy who called wolf. It occurred to me now that it must have been hard for her to have her children undermining her at every step, and drawing Richie into our hostilities, or at least doing our damnedest to.

Richie must have been remembering the same episode, because he said, 'Poor Maggie. She didn't mean to spoil the day.'

'Hmm.' I wasn't so sure about that. What had Dad said in his eulogy: *She was the spark that set situations alight*? But what about all the situations that hadn't called for any spark, the ones that would have been better left unlit?

'How did the funeral go?' Richie asked. 'Not too rough on you, I hope?'

'It was fine,' I said. 'The church was lovely. We went back to Mum's house afterwards and I think people had quite a good time. It was a celebration rather than a miserable occasion.' At least that's what Lindy and Russell had told me after the event; for me, the day had passed with blurred edges and I'd yet to bring any of its images back into focus. 'She knew she was dying and so she was able to plan a lot of it herself. She had this friend, Lindy – she was a bit of a saviour from my point of view, did all the stuff I probably should have.' I laughed. 'Mum liked to call her her amanuensis.'

'Amanu-what?'

'It means secretary. A kind of scribe. Towards the end, when she didn't have the strength to write letters herself, she'd dictate to Lindy.' That made me think of the envelope tucked inside my bag just a few feet away and the thought gave me an odd little twinge in the pit of my body, right at the bottom of the sternum. I didn't know if the feeling was guilt for not mentioning it to Richie or something more complicated, more grudging – a reluctance to give Maggie credit for what was proving so pleasurable a reunion.

'An interesting idea,' he said, 'though it's hard to imagine writing *anything* by hand these days. Even Wren sends emails.'

90

'Oh, Mum was very proud of not having used a computer. Anyway, you know what she was like. She didn't exactly suffer from an inferiority complex. She liked to make everything seem grander than it really was.'

He chuckled. 'I remember when she first showed up, Dad thought she was some kind of English lady, you know, like a duchess or something.'

'Really? That's funny. She was just an ordinary woman.' But that didn't sound at all right; Mum had been anything but ordinary. I tried again. 'She was just a wife and mother, I suppose.'

A current passed between us. It was as though the words I'd chosen were the most charged in the English language, and yet neither of us understood why that was the case for the other. I thought of the framed image of the woman in the maternity hospital, just metres away from us on the dresser inside the door, but for me, for now, she was quite hidden. I didn't even know her name.

'So will you keep in touch with this Lindy?' Richie asked, eventually.

'Yes, I'd like to.' But the idea of Lindy, of all of those connected with my real life, except, perhaps, Mum herself, was already fading into two dimensions. And they were losing their colour, too; they no longer had their own flesh tones. It was as if I'd left one realm and entered another, an enchanted one, like Jamie's parallel planet. I was Odette. I wouldn't have been surprised if I looked in the mirror and found I'd taken on another form entirely.

And I wasn't at all frightened by the idea. Being here, being with Richie, I felt only a strong, unequivocal sense of belonging, a feeling I had always remembered but had never dared believe was real.

I felt *returned*.

Chapter 12

That first night in Millington I never did get around to finding a hotel. Once we'd eaten, drunk some more wine, listened to the sounds of the village dying around us, and *still* I sat motionless on his veranda with just a cushion on my lap for warmth, Richie had no choice but to offer me a bed for the night.

'It's way too late to check in anywhere, and you'll never find your way. There are no street lights in Millington.'

'There aren't? Why not?'

'Something to do with how the roads were built. Some of them have been here before the Civil War. It's a very old village.'

'I shall have to explore tomorrow.' The lack of street lighting explained the night sky, which had begun to glitter gently an hour or two ago and now appeared to contain more silver than black, an effect I'd never seen outside of Noah's sci-fi films. Even Richie said it wasn't usually so star-filled.

Finally indoors, he began hunting for spare pillows and blankets. 'You take my room upstairs. I'll sleep down here on the sofa.'

'No, don't do that,' I said. 'What about Wren? What if she wants you in the night and gets a fright when she sees me?'

'She sleeps like a log, usually. Speaking non-stop for twelve hours without pausing for breath is pretty exhausting, you know.'

I smiled. 'Just in case, though. *I*'ll take the sofa.'

So in the end he kept his room and I snuggled under a patch-work quilt, sleeping a sweet, dreamy sleep more restful than any I'd had in months and waking to blissful silence. Opening a window I saw that last night's extraordinary star cloth had been replaced by translucent blue and the fresh morning air in my lungs seemed to lift me slightly from my feet.

Richie, his hair ruffled from sleep and face unshaven, made us coffee and asked me what I was going to do today.

'I want to take a walk, look around. See all your Civil War nooks and crannies. After that, I don't know.'

'You're not due back home then?'

I felt myself shake my head. 'I think I want to stay here another night. Not here in your house, I mean,' I added, realising how presumptuous that sounded, 'but I'll find somewhere in the village.'

'OK. It gets pretty booked up in the village during the tourist season, but I guess it's still a week or two till the school holidays.' He paused. 'When do your kids break up?'

I had to think about this, which was odd, because term dates were normally engraved onto my eyeballs, accessible whatever my state of mind. 'On the eighteenth, I think.'

Wren, who had not yet dressed but was already at work on a picture of a mermaid as she ate her toast, looked up, interested. 'Do you have darlings, 'livia?'

'That's what she calls children,' Richie said to me, his eyes soft and indulgent. 'Because we always told her, "You're our darling."'

'I'm Daddy's darling,' she agreed. 'And Grandma Jane's.'

'Both grandmas', Richie said. 'Don't forget the one in California.'

'I've only met her three times,' Wren said, precisely. 'But I've seen Grandma Jane *zillions* of times.'

That was an interesting exchange. So there was a mother's

branch of the family based somewhere close enough to be regularly involved.

'I have two darlings,' I said to Wren, kneeling next to her. She smelled of toothpaste. 'They're both boys.'

She pulled a face. 'I don't like boys – except my best friend Chas, of course.'

'Of course. You have to like your best friend, don't you? Well, my boys would seem like grown ups to you. The biggest is as tall as I am.'

'Does he have his own baby, then? Are *you* a grandma?'

Richie's mouth was in his coffee cup a fraction too long and I saw that he was hiding a snort of laughter. I giggled and Wren copied me. All at once I felt a spasm of pure pleasure in being here with the two of them, just standing in the space between them, sharing the morning with them. I didn't want to leave.

'Not yet,' I said to her. 'He's only fourteen.'

As she translated this into school years, using her fingers to count the grades, Richie added, 'Olivia's kids are in big school.'

'No. *I'm* in big school.'

'OK, even bigger school. You're in elementary school.'

'*Primary* school,' she corrected him. 'I'm in Reception. Which is *much* older than kindergarten.'

'Oh, gosh, yes.'

Hearing him use so English an idiom stirred a memory somewhere of Mum and Warren discussing faucets and muffins, always making such a big deal of their differences, as if they were the first transatlantic couple in history. And Dean and I making such a big deal of *them*.

Once Wren was dressed, Richie told her to put on her fleece and trainers because he was taking her to the beach for a run around. I found myself hoping he might invite me to join them, but instead he glanced at my overnight bag, still sitting unzipped by the sofa, and said, 'I'll show you the way to the B&Bs when we go. They're mostly off the other end of the high street, and there's a couple more on Rope Street. I recommend Valerie's, if you can get in. They've got a bar there and they do food all day.'

'Thank you, that sounds great. I'll try there first.'

We left just as soon as I'd gathered my few things together, Richie striding ahead and Wren trailing behind. Torn from her unfinished picture, she was in a contrary mood, twice insisting we return to the house for items she couldn't live without and then protesting that her shoes hurt and she wanted to go bare-foot. Once on our way, however, it was only a matter of minutes before we reached my turn. Richie gestured uphill. 'Valerie's is a right turn into Rope Street just past the butcher's. There's a sign, you can't miss it.'

We lingered on the kerb as I thanked him for the previous night's dinner and the last-minute bed. Wren was already off in the opposite direction, pale hair streaming in the breeze, spotty skirt swishing against bare legs. I noticed a sign a little way down for the swannery and had an instant picture of her dancing among the sleek white birds, a stray feather caught in her hair.

'Bye, then,' Richie said, half-distracted by his daughter's reced-ing figure and, it seemed to me, half-preoccupied somewhere else entirely. Already I missed his undivided attention of last night.

'Bye,' I said, brightly. 'Have fun at the beach.'

'Not sure how much fun today will be,' he said in a murmur, more to himself than to me, and before I could answer he was gone.

I didn't have his phone number and nor had we made any arrangement to meet again before I left, but it hardly mattered. If I checked into the place he suggested, I'd virtually be within whistling distance.

Millington was surprisingly bustling – surprising to me, since I'd yet to take a wider view of life here – but presumably normal for the time of year. It was, after all, a picture-postcard Dorset village by the sea, the weather the best you could hope for of a British summer. Families may not yet have arrived in force but other groups had: older couples in sturdy walking boots who brandished fold-out maps of the coastal paths, tourists with overseas accents stopping to exclaim over the produce left for sale outside people's houses – eggs and herbs and hand-picked posies – and at the notices explaining that payment should simply be posted through the letterbox. It seemed just as quaintly trusting to me, too.

Valerie's was on the eastern edge of the village, a lovely old stone house with wooden casement windows and a grand front lawn that led down to a millpond, beyond which was nothing but that beautiful cobalt-green hillside decorated with ponies and fat grey sheep. There were potted flowers near the entrance and a hand-painted sign for legendary cream teas. Ringing the bell, I had no difficulty in picturing Valerie herself – if she conformed to the Millington idyll she'd be a rosy-cheeked farmer's wife – but as it happened it was a teenager with winged black eye make-up and a pierced lip who hurried through to answer. I suppressed a smile; I'd enjoyed getting carried away with the fantasy.

'Morning!' She introduced herself as Val's daughter Martha and consulted the register with a practised eye. 'We've only got a single left, I'm afraid.'

'That's fine. I'm on my own.'

'Just the one night?'

'I'm not sure,' I said, truthfully. The way I was feeling I could have answered 'twenty' and I wouldn't have surprised myself – or felt the need to retract it. My mouth felt completely at the mercy of my mind's impulses. Maybe that had something to do with why, when Martha asked, I gave my maiden name, Lane, rather than my married one.

'The room's free for the rest of the week,' she told me.

'Oh, I'll be gone by then.'

'Well, just let us know the night before you decide to leave.'

'All right.'

The room was tiny, with a window to the front set deep and low in the stone wall. There was as much furniture as space would allow: a single brass bedstead, the mattress raised high off the ground and tucked tightly with a floral eiderdown; a small oak wardrobe, the door of which opened only partially before making contact with a velvet-covered armchair; and a matching footstool, on which rested a tray of tea things. There were painted plates mounted on the green fleur-de-lis walls and a pink and white striped rug hardly bigger than a bathmat. The tiled shower room, an equally tight squeeze, was clean and well lit – all I could ask for.

I unpacked my few bits and pieces and spent the morning resting, only half-aware of the sounds and smells of Sunday lunch rising from the terrace below. I felt safe here, cocooned by the patterns and textures of the room; I was no longer so eager to climb hills and explore churches. There was plenty of time for that, I decided. Later, I whiled away an hour or two in the sun having a cup of tea among the tourists. One group had just visited the nearby botanical gardens, a terrific success judging by the cries of delight as cameras were passed back and forth, before the arrival of a cream tea brought fresh excitement. It was a while before the exclamations died down and I quite missed the jolly group once it had departed.

Still I felt detached from myself, from my mind. Thoughts drifted in and out of my head, but I could not hold one steady. It was like chasing dreams: by the time I'd recalled it, it no longer made any sense. I wondered if Russell had remembered to make the boys something to eat. They were used to a proper lunch on Sunday and there was a chicken in the fridge from my last supermarket shop. I should phone them, I knew, to tell them I had arrived safely and that I was extending my stay, but there was no hurry. No one's life was at risk. I deserved my break from roasting chickens.

I thought of my friend Jill, who lived on the other side of the park from us and who'd phoned me a few times since Mum died. We'd said we might meet for a stroll in the park today. She'd urged me to surround myself as much as possible with nature, with living things. Well, she'd approve of this glorious bowl of green, surely – I'd never seen so much nature in my life. Checking my mobile phone, unusable at Angel's Lane, I saw that it did not get a signal here, either. Well, if anyone phoned the house for me, Russ would explain.

I checked the clock – four o'clock – and without even making the conscious decision, I got to my feet and set off once more for Richie's cottage.

He and Wren were out on the deck again, he painting the back door and she busy with a tray of felt-tips. Her picture was of a vase of flowers and I could make out the word 'Mummy' in wobbly purple letters in the bottom corner. She'd changed from her beach clothes into a full-skirted sundress tied behind the neck, an old-fashioned cotton print of scattered red cherries, and the style made me think of my own childhood, the notion of 'Sunday best' that was all but lost to my sons' generation. I noticed her pen lids scattered all about; Jamie and Noah had always been so precise with theirs, counting them up, keeping them separate from one another's, devising ways to preserve the last of the ink. Not once had there been a blue lid on an orange pen.

At the sound of my tread on the veranda step, they both looked up from their work.

'I wanted to invite you to Valerie's for afternoon tea,' I said, without preamble. 'Scones and jam and cream. It's supposed to be good.'

'I don't like jam,' Wren said, with suspicion.

'That's OK,' I smiled at her. There was something about Wren that drew the corners of your mouth towards your ears without you even thinking about it. 'You could just have the cream. Or

99

maybe they'll have honey or lemon curd. Do you like either of those?'

Her eyes widened. 'I haven't tried churd, but I like honey. Did you know I've seen a *real* bee hive? I wasn't scared at all.'

Richie, who had resumed painting during this exchange, now interrupted his work a second time to reach down and ruffle his daughter's hair. 'Wren, we have to do your handwriting homework once I've finished this. *And* the reading book we forgot on Friday.'

She scowled. 'That's boring!'

I caught the look of irritation on his face. 'Is everything all right?' I asked. 'I could help Wren with her homework if you're busy with that?'

'Everything's fine. We just have a million chores to do, that's all.' His voice was flat and when our eyes met I saw a wariness in his that had not been there that morning. Evidently the beach walk and the rest of the day's activities had stirred in him more of the natural questions one might consider asking a figure blasted from a past of almost a quarter of a century ago. 'Why is she here?' must be top of the list, followed closely by 'And why again so soon?' Once was a pleasant surprise, but twice . . . what was that? Harassment? I felt hurt by the idea, as hurt as if he'd opened his mouth and accused me of it directly.

'Aren't you taking in the sights this afternoon, anyway?' he asked, at last. 'Make the most of the great weather?'

'Yes, you're right, I should do that.' I took a step backwards. 'I'm sorry, I know how busy weekends are. Forgive me, I shouldn't be bothering you like this. I just . . .' I trailed off, not knowing how to explain, and he looked at me with greater uncertainty. 'I'll go.'

Wren frowned up at her father. 'Aw, Daddy, I want scones.'

'Another time, sweetie. You heard what I said about the homework.'

She pushed her pens away. 'It's not fair! I don't like today!'

Richie just sighed, dipped his brush into his can of pale pink and gently blotted the drips onto the rim. 'Well, I'm sorry, Wren, but that's just the way it is.'

As he spoke his voice sank with an unfamiliar sadness and I found myself holding my breath, unable to move. Then, murmuring my goodbyes, I hurried away, hating to think I'd caused a disagreement between the two of them. At first, as I walked back to Rope Street, my stride was restless and my mind fretful, but even before I'd reached Valerie's both had returned to an even keel. Those mysterious new powers of relaxation were back again, just in time to protect me from the fear that I had had my moment with Richie; that our reunion had already been and gone.

Chapter 13

Dad says Warren Briscoe is a perfectly nice guy, that he has nothing personal against him. He talks as if Mum were his daughter and has brought home a suitor to meet him: since she is smitten and there's nothing he can do to change her mind, he might just as well be civilised about it.

But Warren is not going to be Dad's son-in-law, he's going to be his wife's second husband. It seems odd to me that Dad can't see the difference.

Sometimes I wonder about Warren. I wonder if he has reinvented himself like Mum has, exaggerating his Americanness the way she has her Englishness. All that swaggering from room to room at the Acacia Street house, the exclamations over the smallness of food items – packets of cheese and cartons of orange juice seem to be a particular source of obsession – the grumbles about the rain ('Jeez, not again! Maybe we should go build ourselves an ark!'), even though it's an unusually fine summer for us. The whole cowboy act.

Like Mum, he has embraced his new partner's foreign vocabulary with gusto. The difference, Dean points out, is that he doesn't pretend he isn't doing it deliberately: he knows full well the words don't belong to him. Instead he puts on a comic British accent: 'Shall we all have a *cuppa*? Maybe a *tea* cake?' '*Filthy* weather, isn't it?'

But there's something stifled in his chortle that I would not have thought of a cowboy; I would have expected a proper shout of laughter, like the way Richie laughs. Warren's laugh is small and cautious, as if he knows that what is going on is not funny, not really.

'Would you say your Dad is the same?' I ask Richie, dropping into his basement one evening before dinner.

He looks up from the black pages of his music magazine (all the magazines Richie reads have black pages). 'The same as what?'

'The same as himself. Is he acting the same here as he does back home?'

Richie pulls a face. He has such beautiful bone structure that even pulling a face looks pretty on him. 'If you mean has he made a fool of himself before this, then yeah, he sure has. They all do it, my mom as well. She's worse, actually. You don't wanna know some of the sleazebags she's been dating.'

'Why do they do it?' I demand. 'It's really embarrassing.'

He snickers. 'That's why, I guess. It's the only way they can keep our attention.'

We are talking about different things, different people, but it doesn't matter. I like the way he finds everyone's behaviour so entertaining. For me this is a brand-new way of looking at your family. And he makes me feel confident, like I can ask him anything at all and he'll give me a straight answer. He won't dismiss me.

'Did my mum ever talk about us? About Dean and me?'

'What, you mean back home?' He closes the magazine and frisbees it to the floor. 'Sure, all the time.'

'Really? Didn't you . . .' I falter and he waits a while before prompting me.

'Didn't I what?'

I feel suddenly overcome with sadness and am terrified I might cry. 'Didn't your dad ever ask her why she left her own children for so long?'

He *must* realise this is shaky ground, he must know how much rests on his answer, but neither his eyes not his voice waver. 'Not when I was there, no. I guess they must talk about all that stuff when they're on their own. Hey, don't forget he's divorced as well. He's gone months without seeing me. Like my mom is right now. He probably thinks it's normal.'

'Do you think it's normal? I mean, *a whole year?*'

He shrugs, rubs at the end of his nose with his knuckles. 'Course not. I think it's fucking *weird*. Not unless there's some actual reason, you know, like there's a restraining order or whatever.'

No restraining order; only her own free will. 'And did you know she never sent us her address, so we couldn't write to her? Dad said she was moving about too much, but I think she just didn't want to hear our news.'

His eyes widen. 'I didn't know that, no. Wow.'

'Why do *you* think she did it all then?' I ask.

He rubs his nose again. 'She must have been having some kind of breakdown, yeah, like my mom.'

'Yours had a breakdown? When?'

'A few years ago, when she and Dad broke up. She was depressed, they gave her all these pills. But it was OK once we moved away and she started over. Sometimes that's the only thing that works. That's what *she* says, anyways. Maybe that's what your mom was doing, only . . .'

'Only without us,' I finish, flatly.

'Right.' There is a silence. This is the most confidential we've been with each other and I'm teetering on the edge of something deeper, something new. But I lose my nerve and pull back. I don't want to offend him; I don't want to embarrass myself. And I still have too many questions to ask about my own mother.

'So what did she say when she talked about us?'

His considers me for a long time with his so-blue eyes but I don't see the blue then, only the kindness. 'Just how much she

105

missed you, that kind of thing. Pretty cheesy. She said she wanted to call you but your dad wouldn't let her speak to you.'

'Really?' I'm indignant on Dad's behalf. 'Dad would never do that. She didn't ring us once.'

'She said Dean would be out. He was always partying.'

'Dean's her favourite,' I confirm, though I'm not so sure about the present tense. Neither of us are her favourites now. Rather, Warren and Richie are her favourites. She's her own favourite.

'Oh, and she had photos in her purse,' Richie tells me. 'Your brother looks exactly the same, I recognised him right away, but you . . .'

I wait, hardly daring breathe.

'You looked a lot younger in the photo. And the way she described you, I was expecting something totally different.'

I frown. 'How d'you mean, totally different?'

'I don't know. I guess you must have changed a lot in the last year.'

The way he studies my face, his gaze bold and knowing, makes me hopeful that he means 'changed' in a good way, a special way, but again, to my disappointment, I am the first to crack. I can manage only a second or two before looking away.

Chapter 14

R, not back tonight. Will
phone tomorrow. Ox
P.S. trouble with signal!

I didn't eat tea, I hadn't eaten anything since a slice of toast at breakfast, but my brain did not seem to register my stomach's neglect. It wasn't anything new: when I thought about it, I hadn't had much of an appetite for weeks now. Often I'd drop my fork at the same time as Russell and the boys did theirs, but their plates were scraped clean while mine was hardly a third cleared. Reminding myself at least to stay hydrated in the sun, I took a bottle of water with me into the garden and settled with my book in the shade of an apple tree.

Late afternoon slipped into evening and presently the hotel bar opened for business. It didn't take long for the tables to fill, high-spirited voices collecting in sudden rushes of volume before falling into murmurs again as the food arrived and everyone ate. Every so often Martha came out to clear tables and tuck in chairs, ready for the next group. It was she who had told me of the much-prized lone square foot of Rope Street where a mobile phone signal could be had – right at the top of the car park behind the crafts centre – and having visited the spot and successfully sent a text to Russell I now had no other responsibility to honour between now and bedtime. It was a long, long time since that had been the case.

I laid back my head on the grass and closed my eyes, thinking how completely different the air was here from in London; smoother, newer somehow. I felt it on the hairs on my arms and neck and if I turned my head suddenly it was like brushing my face against a length of silk. Or sinking into a giant pillow of the stuff . . .

'Olivia? *There* you are!'

I sat up, blinking to life. It was Richie, standing a little lower down the lawn and tilting his face up towards me at a querying, childlike angle. Focussing, I found that my vision was just as intensified as my sense of touch, the colours in front of me unusually rich and saturated. The line of his blue jeans against the green of the grass was almost fluorescent, the tan of his arms against the yellowing dusk sky as defined as in a cartoon. He looked, in this perfect light, as eye-catchingly beautiful as I remembered from years ago, the boy we'd all wanted for ourselves and who I had won, at least I thought I had, for a little while.

I brushed a leaf from my arm and smiled at him. 'Hello again.'

'Hello again.'

A sensation ran through me like déjà vu, but I knew it wasn't that because this was something that *had* happened before: the way he stood before me, awaiting my attention, the way we echoed each other's greetings because neither was sure of what was coming next, of what there was between us.

'Where's the little one?' I asked. 'Still drawing her pictures?'

He gestured in the rough direction of Angel's Lane. 'In bed. A neighbour's minding her for me.'

'Do you have time for a beer? I owe you one.'

'Sure. Thanks.'

When I returned from the bar I found he had claimed my spot

under the tree, so I cleared a second area of fallen apples and arranged myself at a polite distance from him. He responded by stretching out his legs between us in an obvious barrier. He seemed to be having trouble getting comfortable, a far cry from the spontaneous flop to the floor of old – and of yesterday. Clearly, he had something on his mind.

'Olivia, can I ask you a question?'

'Of course you can.' I sipped my drink and waited.

'Please don't get me wrong, but, well . . .' – another minor adjustment of the legs – '. . . what are you doing here, exactly?'

'What do you mean?' I didn't allow myself to glance at the envelope tucked into my paperback for a bookmark. For a moment I feared its proximity to me, to us.

Richie gestured to a group of hikers who'd just settled on the other side of the lawn in a chaotic heap of backpacks, maps and water bottles. 'You're obviously not like the rest of the tourists here. The ramblers and the history buffs.'

I looked at him, torn between blurting out the truth (and more besides) and guarding it with my life. 'The thing is I'm not really sure *what* I'm doing here. But now I *am* here, well, I like it. I don't know why, but I feel very safe here.'

'*Safe?*' He pounced on the word as something significant. 'So do you not feel safe at home, then?'

I didn't know what to say to that. 'No, yes. Of course I do.'

He tipped back his beer and drank, his eyes still fixed on me. 'Look, I know this is none of my business, but have you left your husband or something? Has there been some sort of incident with him?'

'No, not at all.' I couldn't imagine how he had come to this conclusion. 'Russell and I are fine.'

'You're fine,' he repeated. 'OK, my mistake, I'm sorry.' Though he smiled, I noticed that only one side of his mouth curved upwards, making it less apologetic than doubtful. 'But I guess that's kind of why I'm a bit confused by this sudden visit.

You and your husband are fine, your kids are still in school, so how do you come to be on holiday on your own?'

He didn't know any other mothers who did that, that was what he was saying, any other wives – and nor did I.

I sighed. 'It's not a holiday. It's hard to explain *what* it is really.'

'It's to do with Maggie passing away, is it?'

I took a deep breath. 'Yes, I think it must be. All of this year, I've been rushing backwards and forwards to her place, trying to see her as much as I could and still do everything I needed to at home. It's been exhausting, like working and working for something huge, but when you get to it it's actually just a huge empty nothingness!'

How horrible and selfish that sounded, as if her illness and death had had no meaning in the world except for their impact on me. I was glad Lindy wasn't here to hear it. Gentle, selfless Lindy.

Richie just stared, not betraying any reaction. I guessed his silence was to give me a second chance to explain.

I tried again. 'I suppose what I mean is that since her death I've been wanting to take stock a bit.' I liked that much better: *take stock*. It sounded like something anyone might do, it had purpose. 'I needed some time on my own, you know, a breather. To be somewhere that feels like a kind of retreat from the chaos.' I didn't add that in the last few years I'd come to make an elaborate daydream of this idea of a retreat, of being whisked away from my life and installed somewhere else – and not in a spa or by a pool, but something closer to a hospital or a religious sanctuary, a place of peace and order. A place where someone looked after *me*. More selfishness! But at least I hadn't confessed this portion of it aloud.

'Taking stock, OK.' Richie scratched at the curve of his upper lip. 'I guess I was wondering why Millington in the first place? You didn't come down here especially to look me up?'

I hesitated, resisting another glance towards the bookmark at my side. If I'd come to any conclusions during my day alone it was that I should not mention my mother's part in this. An envelope, empty but for a single address, *his* address – it would sound absurd, and I would look absurd for having acted on it. The word macabre sprang to mind, Jamie's voice, deliberately camp: *It's totally macabre, Mum*. Well, maybe it was. Maybe that was why its presence made me so wary.

I looked brightly at Richie. 'I came to this village to look you up, yes, that's true. Hearing about you being here gave me an idea for where I could go.'

'Hearing about it?' Again he regarded me unblinkingly over the top of his drink.

'Yes,' I said, 'someone must have mentioned it at the funeral.'

To my relief he accepted this without question.

'But I think I was going to go somewhere anyway. I had to get away before I lost my mind once and for all.' I laughed, showing I meant this purely as a figure of speech, but, for the first time in this conversation, Richie was nodding in recognition, as though this was exactly what he'd expected me to say.

'So what about your family, then?'

'Oh, they're quite capable of looking after themselves for a few days. I'm not the first woman to need a break from her family.'

'I'm sure you're not,' he agreed. 'You've spoken to them, then? They know you're down here?'

'I've sent a text. I *think* it got through, but it's obviously a bit hit and miss around here.'

'You could use a landline. Val must have one here? Or you're welcome to come back and borrow mine?'

I shrugged. The truth was that this problem with the phone signal suited me just fine. I didn't *want* a long conversation with Russell, or with anyone in London; if I did, I need only have stayed there to have it. But I sensed such an answer would only

111

fuel whatever suspicions Richie had developed about the state of my marriage. 'I'll talk to Russell tomorrow,' I said. 'Honestly, it's no big deal.' It was a subconscious imitation of Richie (or my Richie of old): his attitude, his phrase, his shrug. No wonder he could do nothing but concede the point.

He swallowed another mouthful of beer. It was obvious he had not yet finished what he had come here to say; perhaps he had not yet begun it. And a part of me was thrilled that he evidently cared enough to say it at all.

'What? You're worried about something? There's honestly no need.'

'The thing is, Olivia . . .' His fingers began to pluck at the grass, scattering the blades over his trouser legs – he had definitely not fidgeted like this yesterday. 'I might be completely out of line here, but you seem like you're not really coping that well. Your mom's death has obviously hit you hard. You seem totally traumatised, like you've just walked away from a plane wreck or something.'

'Oh.' My eyes widened in surprise.

'Don't get me wrong, I realise you're probably different from how I remember you from however many years ago – hey, I know I am. It's just . . . well, I guess I just know the signs.' His voice dipped then and he had to consciously retrieve it before he could make himself heard again. 'I was a complete zombie after Lisa died. I mean, you function OK, you do what you have to, but you know you're not reacting right. Some things feel way too intense and other things don't feel like anything at all. It's like you can't even remember what your normal self *is* anymore. Not that I can say what yours is, of course, like I say, it's been a long time, but whatever it is, d'you think maybe you're not it right now?'

I stared at him, riveted. Despite his tangled delivery, he was describing how I felt better than I could myself, except perhaps for the most mysterious bit of all: that feeling of lightness in my blood, that unshakeable sense of rightness I'd had from the moment I began walking down Sterling Avenue yesterday morning; that sensation I'd had in the taxi of bring propelled forward by some force far greater than any car's engine could give me. There had been no plane crash, no, but there was still wreckage to free myself from and my body seemed to know instinctively that home was not the place for me to do it.

None of which I said aloud, but, finally breaking the silence, asked only, 'Who's Lisa?'

He didn't flicker. 'Wren's mother.'

'When did she die?'

'Four years ago.'

'So . . .' Having finally been presented with the information, my mind was slow to work it out. 'Wren must have been tiny? Just a baby?'

He nodded. 'She wasn't much more than one; almost fifteen months. It's hard for her to remember, which in some ways is a good thing.' He inhaled sharply before continuing. 'Today was the anniversary. We'd just got back from the cemetery when you came over earlier. It's a bit of a way away, a long drive, and Wren was tired. I was trying to get the day back to normal before school tomorrow.'

'Oh, God.' I thought of Wren in her special grown-up dress – her favourite, probably – her picture of the flowers, the little, wobbly 'Mummy' in the corner. 'I don't like today,' she'd said. And into their private grief I had blundered, offering scones and cream! Not only that, but I had sat here just now complaining to him about *my* terrible sense of nothingness! My eyes brimmed with tears. 'I'm so sorry, Richie, I should never have bothered you – today *or* yesterday. I had no idea this was such an important weekend.' I gaped at him, hardly bearing to picture the little girl I'd met so much tinier and newly motherless. 'I had no idea,' I repeated.

He shrugged. 'How could you?'

'But if I'd known you were down here, when it happened . . . It's only a few hours away, I would have got in touch, tried to help.'

He dismissed this with a quick smile. 'I had family and friends to help. We've been OK.'

We're doing OK. *We're fine on our own.*

'How did it happen?' I couldn't stop myself from asking, knowing it was intrusive, but to my surprise he replied quite readily; he was almost matter-of-fact about it.

'She drowned in a swimming pool. She'd had quite bad asthma as a child, but there'd been nothing for years, no reason to take special precautions. Then she went swimming when there was no one else around. She had an attack and couldn't get help in time. It was a freak accident, nobody's fault.'

I wondered how long it had taken him to perfect this tone, to make the horrific sound so everyday. 'Where were you and Wren?'

'Wren was at home with her grandma. We'd gone away without her, just for a couple of days. I was in our hotel room sleeping. I was probably no more than fifty metres from the pool, close enough to have got there in time if I'd known.'

'Oh, Richie.' Though he was still perfectly composed, looking candidly at me, I could sense the pull between his hands and his face, that ancient instinct to bury grief.

'Hey,' he said, at last. 'We've both had our tragedies. I'm not the only one.'

I shook my head. 'I knew about Mum, though. We had months to prepare, and she was cared for at home right until the end. They told me her quality of life couldn't have been better, that it was exactly what most sufferers wish for for the end of their lives. But your situation, out of nowhere, and with Wren so young, I can't even imagine it—'

'*Don't* imagine it,' he said, quickly. 'I really don't recommend it. Pretend we never had this conversation.' Despite the words

114

and the blankness of his tone, his eyes were bright and spirited, and in that second I knew that he'd never pretended, he'd never shied away from anything in his life. He was as bold and honest as he'd been when I first knew him, only now he was applying those qualities to surviving loss, to protecting his little girl. I can never be like this, I thought: I can leave my home and cross the country and surrender to whatever it is that has stopped me from going back when I said I would, but I can never find strength like his. That was what had attracted me to him over twenty years ago, his courage, the bit that was missing in me.

Richie was motioning to the gardens around us, the pond and hills and horizon line of sea. 'That was the reason we came here, Wren and me, for a fresh start, a much simpler . . .' he sought for the word, '. . . framework. All that stuff. I looked around the area, drove around day after day, looking for the safest, quietest place I could find. And it had to be pretty, like something from one of her story books. You know, flowers everywhere, ponies in the fields, the full works.'

I nodded.

'And you know what? It's worked. She's happy. *We*'re happy. Every day something good happens. Millington is . . . it's a good place. That's what made me wonder when you said you felt safe here. It *is* safe – no matter what might have happened to you in other places.' His voice had become more emphatic and a tremor had started in his face, just above the right brow. As the silence between us grew, I wanted to break it by kissing him, just once, gently, in comfort or, failing that, to just reach towards him and touch his face. In all my thousands of imaginings over the years, I'd never predicted this for him: a widower with a young daughter, hidden away in the English countryside, doing OK.

'I think I'm going to stay here a few more days,' I said, at last. 'Do you want me to keep out of your way? I would understand if you did. No hard feelings. I know it must seem weird, my being here.'

The half-smile was back. 'You wouldn't be able to avoid me if you tried. This is a very small place, as you may have noticed.' He pressed his knuckles to the grass and pushed himself up. 'Thanks for the beer. I'd better get back. I'll see you?'

There was a suggestion of a question to his farewell, I was sure of it, but he was already out of earshot by the time I came to reply. 'See you, Richie,' I echoed into the silky night air.

PART TWO

'Swans are very attentive parents, so [the sight of] a young lone cygnet may mean that something is amiss.'
Royal Society for the Protection of Birds

Chapter 15

O, how are you getting
on? Any idea when you
might be back? Rx

Russell stood motionless by the kitchen window feeling only
unease at the evidence of another clear, sunny morning. It was
Thursday, the fifth day without Olivia and the fourth (of four)
that he would be late for work. Why was that, exactly? The
obvious excuse was Jamie and Noah – their discarded cereal
bowls sat on the dining table behind him, complete with the milk
spills of much younger children – but he could hardly blame
them for his own failure to adapt. The truth was they had
reacted to their mother's unplanned leave with surprising self-
sufficiency, getting their own breakfasts and leaving together for
the school bus at quarter to eight. They seemed to be seeing to
their own uniform supplies, as well, which was just as well as
Russell was having enough trouble getting himself dressed in the
mornings.

Shirts were his biggest problem. Having expected Olivia back
on Sunday and since then having addressed the issue of her
absence purely on a one-day-at-a-time basis, he had been ironing
his shirts singly. He had not, however, *washed* any and now that

there were none left to iron the inevitable impasse had been reached. (He knew this for sure because he had been the one to devise the family's laundry system: washed clothes on the rail above the washing machine, pressed ones on the rail above the ironing board. There were shirts on neither.) Just now, he had resorted to plucking yesterday's from the laundry basket, before biting the bullet and stuffing a bundle of others into the machine. As he wrenched open a new box of powder, spraying himself in the process, the frontage of the overpriced dry cleaner's next to the station had come temptingly to mind.

Childishly, he blamed the weather. It was this hot spell that was encouraging her to stay away, to prolong this sudden need for time alone. Not that he begrudged her it for a moment, of course – her mother had just died, for God's sake, she was in mourning! He'd have to be a complete brute to object. And he'd feel the same himself, no doubt, if she were here and he were there. Not that he'd quite got a grip on where *there* was.

'Where *are* you?' he'd asked, when she'd phoned him on Monday morning at the office. He'd tried hard to keep the haplessness from his voice – and not only for the benefit of any eavesdropping colleagues.

'I'm in Dorset,' she said, 'by the sea. It's doing me good, Russ, I already feel better.'

'Good, good. That's great news. So you're—'

She spoke over him. 'I think I'm going to stay for a few more days if you're all right on your own?'

'Of course, yes.' He remembered that weird, ghostly look she'd had about her when she'd left on Saturday and the way she'd thanked him, as if being granted leave by the most traditional, roost-ruling of husbands. This wasn't the nineteenth century, she didn't need his permission to leave her own house! 'Take as long as you need,' he added, bravely. 'We can cope.'

'You got my text message yesterday?'

'Yep.' He didn't mention that thanks to gremlins in the phone system it had not been delivered to him until close to midnight. He'd known not to worry, of course, even when his own calls went unanswered, but still he *had* been relieved when the message had finally come.

Texts had followed in the morning for the boys, pinging into their inboxes at the breakfast table within seconds of one another and glanced at only casually. So unconcerned were they by their mother's absence that Jamie probably wouldn't have thought to mention the message at all had not Noah passed over his phone at the first request:

Hi boys, have a good
week at school, I miss
you, love Mum xx

Two kisses for two boys, that was sweet. But it had seemed to Russell that the wording of it – *have a good week* – implied that she didn't think she'd be seeing them again until nearer the weekend, *next* weekend. Which was quite different from the 'not back tonight' content of his own message.

Still, he'd only had a few hours to wait before she'd got in touch.

'I did try you earlier,' she said, dutifully, 'but it's hard to get through from here.'

Before he could enquire once more where 'here' was, she was asking after the boys. 'Did they get off to school all right?'

Russell focused. 'Yep, they seemed to have everything they needed. And I should be able to slope off a bit early to get dinner together . . .' He'd wanted to add that they were missing her already, but she must have lost reception then because when her voice came back it was only to repeat, as though he suffered with a hearing impairment, that she'd PHONE AGAIN LATER when she had A BETTER SIGNAL! On reflection, it was probably just as well he hadn't said it; he didn't want to make her feel guilty

121

for taking this break, however impromptu, however inconveniently timed.

As the day wore on – and Tuesday and Wednesday, too – and no second call came, he knew not to let himself slip into fear or doubt for the simple reason that she had left him no instructions for the week's domestic arrangements. There were no extra litres of milk, no portions-for-three of lasagne in the freezer, no Post-its about trainers or swimming shorts designed to be spotted at crucial moments of male forgetfulness. (Once, when she'd gone to stay for two nights with an old girlfriend, there had been a three-page guide to decoding the boys' labyrinthine commitments – though he seemed to remember he had left them to their own devices then, as well). No, Olivia was an organised woman. This extension to her weekend was spontaneous and necessary. She'd be back any minute.

The kitchen clock said 8.45 am – so why was he still not moving? He had a shirt on his back for God's sake, even if it did smell of sweaty boxer shorts; the mug of Nescafé in his hand was drained to the last drop. And then, above his head, he heard a key turn in the front door. At last, here she was! Talk about the longest four days in history! He was ready to rush upstairs and gush endearments he hadn't made for years. So what if he got into work late again, he'd blame the Victoria Line, everybody else did.

His legs on the stair were as light as air. 'Olivia, you're – oh!'

'Hey-llo.' The tones that bounced back down the hallway were the gruff, slightly masculine ones of their cleaner Aniela. She looked up at him from where she was stooped by the stairs, exchanging her outdoor shoes for a pair of loafers. She had hung her jacket over the end of the radiator rather than using the hooks by the door, a detail that struck Russell as tragic, though he wasn't sure why (an image of servants sleeping in doorways flashed in his brain and vanished again). That was right, Aniela came on Thursdays – well, at least the place would be a bit more presentable for Olivia's return. And with Aniela on the case at least he'd get a clean shirt for tomorrow.

'Where is Olivia?' she queried at once. Though she had pretty features, her skin was subterranean pale and her eyelashes clotted with startling black mascara. She didn't look terribly healthy.

Russell swallowed. 'She's not here, she's taking a short holiday. But she'll be back for next time. I'm just on my way out but, Aniela, when the load in the washing machine finishes, could you iron one of my shirts? Any one will do.'

She looked blankly at him, obviously not following what he was saying. He considered miming it all out, but before he could begin she was leading him downstairs herself, not to the laundry room but to the corkboard and a torn half-sheet of notepaper containing a poorly spelled list of cleaning items.

'Aren't they in the usual place?'

She swept past him to the sink, opened the cupboard doors beneath and resurfaced at once with an expression of exaggerated query. The items on the list had obviously not yet been replenished. Russell grinned, embarrassed.

'Next week,' he said, too loudly. 'And can we pay you then, as well? I don't think I've got any cash on me.' He mimed this by putting his hand in his trouser pocket and showing her an empty palm, which made him feel like an extra from *Oliver!*.

'OK,' she said, turning away from him to get on. He got the feeling his hopelessness was nothing less than she would have expected of him.

Twenty minutes later, as he clung to the overhead strap on the Tube, Russell listened to a conversation between two women about dinner plans with their boyfriends and felt the belt of his chest muscles tighten a notch. No, he mustn't allow himself to feel neglected after so laughably short a time. Olivia needed time to herself, it was perfectly reasonable (if unprecedented), and she would be back in the next day or two, by Friday at the latest. They'd go for pizza with the boys and catch up on everything, and soon they'd all be on holiday together, and before they knew it August would have passed and they'd have Maggie's windfall. He hadn't liked to press his wife on the nitty-gritty of it, but he'd got the impression from Dean that they were talking at least half a million pounds between the two of them, possibly more, depending on the valuation of the house in Gloucestershire. She'd been an odd fish, Maggie, and not the greatest mother in the world, but when it came to property she and her second husband Alec had displayed pretty good judgment. Two hundred and fifty thousand pounds, minimum! That would pay off their mortgage, give them some breathing space.

Russell turned his face away from the huge guy squeezing past him to exit the carriage. He couldn't have been in a more awkward position if he'd tried and newsprint from the man's paper smeared across the sleeve of his already grubby white shirt. Breathing space . . . yes, he could understand just why Olivia needed some. He could do with a bit of it himself.

Russell had the kind of job that failed point-blank to inspire interest or enthusiasm in any third party. His was the career that no one could quite put their finger on and he was often asked at social events, even ones with close family, 'So what exactly is your job title?' This, he knew, was a creative way of saying, 'What is it you do again, I've completely forgotten?'

Well, if they were interested, his job title was Business Development Manager (Bolt-on Services) for a medium-sized software firm. Dull though it was, certain other individuals in the team had managed to flourish well enough – his friend Duncan, for instance, with whom he had entered the company as a junior exec all those centuries ago. Duncan was positively flamboyant in his success, gaining a promotion at most annual reviews and by now established as Russell's senior director, not to mention the possessor of significant stock options. For this reason, and despite their friendship, Duncan had come to cut a depressing figure for Russell. No sooner had he arrived at his desk in the morning than his old friend would be passing by in a better cut suit and a sharper haircut. Even his dentistry was demonstrably superior: as Russell's teeth yellowed over the years, drifting somewhat inwards, Duncan's seemed only to have pearlised and straightened with time. And it wasn't one-upmanship on Dunk's part, not in the slightest, for things had gone far beyond that stage. Now the difference between them was so settled as to be unremarkable. It was just the way it was. Duncan had made it, Russell had not, and the most galling part of it was that Duncan needed it less because his wife was a City solicitor and bringing in a healthy whack of her own.

'All set for our eleven o'clock?' Duncan asked him. 'The Falconer team have just got into Paddington. They're in a taxi on their way over.'

'Sure. Yeah. Great.'

It would take a good twenty minutes for the client to get here, so Russell took the opportunity to sign into his online bank account and scan the latest statement of his and Olivia's expenditure: no activity on her part since a withdrawal of cash at Waterloo Station last Saturday. Two hundred pounds, that wasn't going to last long. These days two hundred pounds left your hands so quickly the notes were still warm from the dispenser. Which meant she must be running up a hotel bill – that was a worry, though one he knew he would need to suppress. She was bereaved, in desperate need of a break; what was a bit of room service and a sea view when you'd been sitting at the bedside of your dying mother for the last six months? Not to mention clocking up more miles on the motorway than a professional trucker, and Olivia *hated* driving.

The balance was as close to zero as it usually was at this time of the month. As a rule, there was only one month in the year when the account showed a healthy surplus and that was April, bonus time, but that was always earmarked for whatever new bit of hardware the boys needed, or for the family's first new sofa in a decade. That, and a ten-day summer holiday, and the excess would be consumed without a trace.

He browsed the last few months' debits, the most startling being the large cheque written at Easter for the boys' summer term school fees. Now that was *definitely* an arrangement that had outlived the original plan. When Olivia had marshalled him and a three-year-old Jamie around the various school open days ten years ago her proposal had been simple and sensible: the local infant schools were a disaster, so what about three years at fee-paying pre-prep to get a head start and then directly into the state system at age seven? Meanwhile she would look actively into the possibility of their moving house into the catchment area of a decent junior school. There was no question that this would involve any more than a year or two of both boys at an independent school at the same time. School fees for one child was misfortune, but two was carelessness, that was the joke she'd made at the time. He remembered her exact words; they'd been in total agreement.

Then came the whole business of Jamie's giftedness and the arrival in their lives of the famous Herring's School. Sometimes, secretly, Russell liked to call it the Red Herring School: was he the only one who suspected an Emperor's New Clothes situation here? Not that he wasn't proud of his son, it was just that, well, if Jamie's brain was in the top two percentile of his age group, as the IQ tests proved, then wouldn't he fare well at any school? Not so, said Olivia and her experts. By putting him among lesser brains they ran the risk of his concealing his abilities in a bid to fit in; he might struggle socially and become introverted, all the while dying of intellectual frustration. They couldn't let that happen, could they? And so off Jamie went to be educated by the only people in the land up to the job. Then, a blink of an eye later, Noah was being fitted for the uniform, too, chomping at the bit to join his brother in his after-school clubs and his holiday courses and all the other genius essentials that cost Russell extra.

126

'I was thinking we might qualify for a scholarship,' Olivia said, but in the vague way that meant it wasn't going to make the top of her famous 'To do' list. To be fair she *had* passed him the information about applying, but it quickly became clear to him that there was no way on earth their family would qualify. They had to be having 'palpable' difficulties with paying, which as far as he could work out meant going about in rags and eating meals from other people's bins.

Today, almost half of their disposable income went on school fees. They had conversations about downsizing to a smaller house about as often as most families discussed Friday night takeaway options. Always Olivia would theoretically convert the stamp duty required to move into another year's school fees. Always this was what they went on to do. She murmured occasionally about grandparents helping out, but since both sets had other grandchildren, none of whom attended schools like Herring's, this was never actually proposed (he could only imagine Dean's reaction to such favouritism).

As for working herself, it was a well-known fact that very few jobs suited the hours available to the mothers of young children and those that did were as hotly contested as internships in the Oval Office. Together they had worked out that a full-time secretarial job, once before- and after-school care and/or an au pair or child minder were factored in, would earn the family about as much as a paper round. There had been one good spell not so long ago when Olivia had covered the maternity leave of an acquaintance in the office of a local primary school, her hours dovetailing perfectly with those of the boys, but the woman had come back at the earliest opportunity (which figured, since she would have known as well as the rest of them what gold dust she held in her hands) and Olivia was back to square one.

No, it was down to Russell and Russell alone to keep the carousel turning. And never more so than now.

'Ready?' Duncan asked, back already. His face was tanned, he must have been sunning himself in the evenings in the landscaped garden of his house in north London, a neighbourhood described by the papers as chi-chi and said to be thronged with celebrities. His next-door neighbour was an actor in a hit BBC spy drama and the two sometimes had impromptu barbecues together and cracked open the cigars. It was only a theory, but Duncan thought they got on as well as they did because he had no intention of behaving any differently with a famous face than he would with any Tom, Dick or Harry.

Or Russell. Closing the on-screen window that framed his paltry financial picture, Russell manoeuvred himself backwards as though confined to a wheelchair. For a moment he wasn't sure if his legs would lift him but they came through for him at the last moment, just as they always did.

'Yep,' he answered Duncan's question, 'onwards and upwards.' But he spoke with a sarcasm that was heavy even for him.

Chapter 16

Those first few days in Millington, I explored. I explored to the point of exhaustion. I would set off after breakfast with nothing but a bottle of water and a borrowed map and I'd strike out into the hills, climbing until my chest burned and I had to stagger into the nearest scrap of shade to rest. Other times, I'd meander down to the beach through lanes so narrow and overgrown I could hardly see above the high screens of nettles and wild grasses to get my bearings. It was still sunny, but sultrier than at the weekend and mostly breezeless. Falling into conversation with Valerie and other staff at the guesthouse, I was told that this was typical of the microclimate here, that the hills protected the village from the winds and rains of the Atlantic. Spared all but nature's best, the inhabitants felt lucky to live in the little sheltering cup of their village.

I began to feel lucky too. That phrase of Richie's came back to me often on my walks: *Millington is a good place.* What I thought he meant was that it was restorative, it had helped to heal him. Did that mean it would heal me, too? Was that the reason I had not returned to London on Sunday evening when I knew I had been expected? Nor Monday, nor Tuesday, nor Wednesday? Had I known from the moment the taxi set me down here that I was not going to leave? Perhaps Richie had sensed it when he'd talked about the hotels getting full in high season. He'd had a presentiment of what I hadn't yet understood myself.

I didn't see him those first weekdays. Not a glimpse in the distance, not a wave from the road (he drove a battered old estate; I'd seen it parked in Angel's Lane, but not once on the move). I presumed he had decided my sudden reappearance was too unsettling for him, that my new bereavement stirred up too much old grief of his own. I guessed he would simply lie low until such a time that my crisis had passed and I'd come to my senses and gone home to my family.

Until such a time.

And then, on Thursday afternoon, I ran into Wren. Delight flared inside me the instant I saw her. She was on the high street, on the raised pavement outside the grocer's, skipping about with another child as though on stage. It was four in the afternoon and both children were dressed in navy shorts and lavender T-shirts printed with the slogan '*Beechwood C of E. Learning for life!*' – they had finished school for the day, obviously. I watched as they began to argue about a game, each as insistent as the other – 'I won!'; 'No, *I* won!'; '*I* did!' – and then one indignant voice broke off to exclaim: 'Oh, look, that's my daddy's friend over there!'

'Hello, sweetie,' I said, approaching. 'How are you?'

'Fine.' She beamed at me, eyes shy. Under her sunhat her hair had been braided at either ear, but was unravelling fast. There were freckles on her nose.

'Who's your friend?'

'Chas.'

'Hello, Chas.' He was a sweet thing, plump and almost as short as Wren, with surprised wide-set blue eyes and a tiny pink mouth. 'That's a nice name. Are you really Charles?'

'No,' Wren answered for him, 'he's really *Chas*.'

'I see.'

She gave a sudden chuckle. 'Did you know he's *still* not five?'

'My birthday's in August,' Chas confirmed, woefully.

'He's the youngest boy in Reception Matthews,' Wren crowed as though this were a matter of public ridicule.

'But not as young as Maddy,' Chas protested. '*She*'s the youngest.'

'*And* the smallest,' Wren agreed.

'Are you with your dad?' I asked, squinting beyond her into the nearest shop, a grocers, bakery and tea room combined.

'No, Chas's mummy. She's buying potatoes.'

As I hovered, a woman emerged from the shop, concentrating at first on the task of wedging bulging paper bags into the large hessian shopper over her shoulder before settling her gaze on our little group. She was in her early thirties, I judged, her close-hanging dark hair and chunky clothes a little heavy for the weather and her face was flushed with the heat. When she spoke her voice was a little breathless.

'Hello. What's going on here?'

'Hello,' I said, stepping forwards. 'I'm Olivia. I was just being introduced to your son.'

'I'm Sarah. They haven't been bothering you, have they?'

'Not at all. I know Wren already, I'm an old friend of Richie's. I'm spending a few days in the village. It's a treat to bump into her.'

Wren's eyes flickered with pride just as Sarah's registered curiosity. 'You're staying at the house, are you?'

'No, no, in a B&B, Valerie's.'

'I was going to say, I didn't see you this morning when I picked Wren up. Hey, stop that, you two!' She broke off to pull back the children, who had begun to poke at the punnets of blackberries on display outside the shop.

'They're friends, then?' I asked.

'Yes. Well, they argue quite a bit. They're like an old married couple sometimes, I suppose because they spend so much time together.'

131

'They do?'

She gave me a more openly inquisitive look. 'Yes. I mind Wren while Richie's working. A couple of hours after school and in the holidays, as well.'

'Oh, I didn't realise.' I didn't like to add that I didn't even know what Richie's work was. What had we talked about on Saturday night? We'd spent hours together. Had I asked any questions, listened to any answers? I had an image of myself just staring at him across the deck in the fading light, not quite believing that after all this time he was back in front of my eyes, back within touching distance. 'He's got something big on, has he?'

'Yes, a renovation down in Bridport, a huge six-bedroomed place. It just came up the other night. Another chap cancelled at the last minute. Good money, as well.'

'My daddy's a *painter*,' Wren said to Chas.

'My daddy's a *manager*,' Chas returned. 'In *London*.'

This seemed to trump Wren's claim and she stood for a moment looking subdued, before brightening again. 'Well, my daddy's *taller*.'

'Nick commutes every day,' Sarah told me, the flatter note in her voice dictating my response.

'That must be hard. It's quite a journey.'

'Yeah, it makes it a long day, that's for sure. And the season ticket costs an arm and a leg.'

I didn't know what to say then. It felt unnatural to trade stories of my own husband's commuter hell and, in any case, I had always imagined Russell travelling to and from work quite contentedly, reading his paper in a corner seat of the Tube, time to himself; everything under control.

'I was just going to get something to read,' I said, at last. 'Is there a bookshop in the village?'

Sarah shook her head. 'No, but they've got a few paperbacks at the newsagent's. You could try there.'

'Thank you.'

'Well, I'm sure I'll be seeing you again,' she said, politely. 'We're off to see the baby swans now, aren't we, kids? Once we've dropped our shopping at the house. What are they called again?'

'Cygnets!' the children chorused.

'Have you been down to the swannery yet, Olivia?' she asked.

'No, no, I haven't, but I've seen where it is from the hilltop.'

'You should go down there. It's the right time of year.'

'You could come too,' Wren said, which started Chas off on a verse of 'Going to the Zoo'.

'Thank you,' I said, remembering Richie's reaction to my offer of tea on Sunday. 'I won't today, but maybe another time.'

'When?' she demanded, over Chas's singing, and she looked at me with that gaze of Richie's, the gaze that seemed to demand the truth of whoever it fell on.

'She doesn't know exactly when,' Sarah answered for me, rolling amused eyes.

'The next time you ask,' I said, firmly. 'If it's all right with your daddy and Sarah.'

Wren looked as if she suspected she might have been tricked, but Sarah ushered her away before she could object. 'Come on, gang, we need to get going.'

As they made their way towards a nearby parked car, I could hear the song start up again, *Going to the zoo, zoo, zoo, How about you, you, you,* until the door closed, abruptly sealing their little voices inside the car.

In the newsagent's I chose a thriller about a serial killer, the sort of story I had never been able to read in the past without getting horrible nightmares and asking Russell to double-check the bolts. I read it from cover to cover and slept like a lamb.

The following afternoon, to my surprise, Richie brought Wren to Valerie's.

'We thought we'd take you up on your offer of tea,' he said. 'It'll save me cooking.' His manner was warm and easy; it was as if that anguished conversation under the apple tree had never taken place and we had rewound to the unflustered companionship of the first night. Evidently he'd been working: there were traces of white paint all over his hands and forearms and there was a sore-looking red mark on one of his thumbs.

'How was school?' I asked Wren. She wore no sunhat and I had to resist the temptation to release her soft sandy hair from its pigtails.

'Fine. Daddy picked me up,' she said. 'Did you know it was Mrs Matthews's birthday? We sang "Happy Birthday" and I got the bit of the cake with the most icing.'

'So many birthdays in this village,' I exclaimed. 'Do you all get more than one or something?'

'No, of course not.'

'I think you do,' I joked.

'No,' she said, firmly, 'we don't.'

I straightened my face. Unlike my boys at this age, she didn't like teasing. For her, questions were clearly meant for factual answers, not for poking fun. 'I hear you work as a painter and decorator,' I said to Richie. 'I thought your job on the windows was a bit too professional for a bit of weekend DIY.'

He grinned. 'I've been doing it a few years now. You get good quite quickly. The main thing is I'm paid for the work, not the hours, which gives me a bit of extra time with Wren. I try to pick her up from school a couple of times a week.'

'Is there much work about?'

'Not so much in Millington. But there're plenty of Londoners doing up holiday homes further along the coast.' He looked at me as if to identify me with this group.

'Lucky them,' I said. 'I wish I had a place to come to. It's beautiful down here.' I imagined myself in a cottage right on the water, just reeds of tall grass separating my home from the

134

sand dunes. A striped deckchair on a small wooden veranda like Richie's – I could almost feel the weight of my body against the stretched canvas – wind chimes overhead, sand rubbing smooth the soles of my feet. I'd lived in the city all my life, this had never been my dream, but here it was, in my head, fully formed. It was as if someone else had taken possession of my mind.

Tea arrived. It involved so many bits of china there was hardly room for it all on the table. Wren loaded her plate with sandwiches and cakes, counting the various items and telling us how many of each we were entitled to. Again my own appetite failed; I could hardly distinguish one flavour from the next, even though the reactions of Richie and Wren told me that it was all as mouth-watering as the signs promised.

After Wren had declared she was full and got down from the table to explore the garden, Richie and I returned to the subject of work.

'You haven't told me what *you* do?' he asked. 'For a job, up in London?'

That, at least, was a question I could answer easily enough. I'd been asked it a thousand times and my response rarely varied. 'I haven't worked for a while, actually, and not much at all since the boys came along. I suppose by the time they were both in school I'd forgotten what it was I could do. Since then, well, I don't know what's happened to the time . . .'

I trailed off, sure that this succession of clichés would not wash with him, but he accepted them quite happily. He was treating me as fragile, then; he hadn't forgotten the plane-crash conversation at all.

'What *did* you do? No, hang on, you wanted to be a fashion designer, didn't you?'

I smiled. 'I think I probably just said that to impress you.'

'No, that's not true, I remember you had all those sketchbooks, and your hands were always smeared with charcoal.'

135

I was touched by his remembering such a detail. 'I didn't even apply to art college in the end. My A-level grades weren't great and I did some other courses instead, a business studies thing, then a secretarial programme. I couldn't make my mind up.' *I couldn't get my head together,* I corrected myself, silently, *thinking about you, thinking about everything I'd lost.* 'Actually, it was quite promising in the beginning. I got a job in the marketing office of a cable TV channel. I really enjoyed it there. But then I was made redundant and started temping.'

'Wasn't that the same kind of work as Maggie?'

'Similar. She was more of a career secretary. Before she left for the States she'd worked for the same guy for years. He really relied on her. She always said she was the wind beneath his wings.' It came back to me then, something else my mother had said, later, but I couldn't remember if it was before she'd left for America or after she'd returned. 'I'm sick of being the wind, I want to be the wings!' And Dean had said it was giving *him* wind hearing her go on about it. (That dated it, then, it must have been after.)

'And then you had the kids,' Richie prompted.

I nodded. 'And when I did work again, just temporary stuff, I'd sort of lost my nerve.' This was putting it mildly; I still recalled clearly the panic attacks I'd suffered in my last position in a local primary school office. Every time the phone rang I would be crippled with anxiety, certain that the caller would be about to complain about me, about a mistake I'd made, some error that had had disastrous effects for his or her child. And though I'd somehow pulled it off, concealing my terror day after day – the deputy head had even praised me for my work – I'd been grateful beyond belief when the contract had come to an end.

'I think Mum was disappointed I didn't end up doing something more ambitious,' I told Richie, remembering the to-and-fro of accusations concerning my decision to stay at home with the boys. 'You should go back to work,' she'd said, not just once but every time, 'the kids will be fine.' I disagreed. Wasn't I proof that without their mother kids were *not* fine? They lost their confidence, their faith in their own ambitions. But I knew that the cause of my own career failure was more complicated than that. It had not been Mum's absence that had contributed to it – or at least to the miserable college years that preceded it – but her presence.

'Well, I guess you just have to make your choice and stick to it,' Richie said, still keen to appease me.

I nodded. 'She kept asking me why I wanted to follow in my grandmother's footsteps, like I was personally pushing the women's movement back fifty years. I could never convince her it was a kind of progress just to have the choice in the first place. She just laughed at that.'

'Sounds as if Maggie's been a big influence on you,' he said, delicately.

'Bigger than I would have liked,' I said. We looked at each other. Could I *ever* tell him the full story, I wondered? Wasn't this easiness between us dependent on my concealing it?

'It's hard finding something with the right hours,' I said, finally. 'There didn't seem any point hiring someone to look after the kids when I could hardly earn enough to pay them.' But again, I knew it was a poor excuse. These last years at least, Jamie and Noah had been old enough to let themselves into the house and look after themselves for the hour or so between the end of their day and that of normal office hours. I could have taken any job I wanted – if there was anyone out there still willing to offer me one.

Richie tore at the edges of the last teacake before discarding it on his plate. 'Hey, I know all about that,' he said. 'I used to work for an insurance firm in Southampton but after Lisa died, well, it didn't fit around Wren, I didn't even attempt it. I probably don't make half as much money now, but it's worth it.'

'And you have Sarah to help you out?'

'Yep. If money's tight, I pay her in decorating or some other job, so it all works out one way or another.'

I liked the idea of that: a simple exchange of trades. In London, I couldn't remember a time when (lack of) money wasn't top of the Sterling Avenue agenda, when whatever services we needed that week were priced just out of reach.

'She seems nice,' I said. 'We met in the street yesterday.'

'So she told me.' He raised his eyebrows. 'You have to remember there's not much going on here, so you're a nice bit of gossip. I told her you were an old flame but I'm afraid she'd already got the idea that you must be a new one.'

I could feel my face getting warmer at this first direct reference to our personal history, and my pulse quickened. But now that the longed-for window stood open in front of me I found I had not the nerve to step through it – not yet.

'What's an old flame?' Wren was at her father's elbow, panting. She laid the heads of several flowers on the table in front of him, like a cat bringing its owner a dead bird.

'It means an old friend. I told you, didn't I? That Olivia and I knew each other back when we were teenagers?'

'*I* want to be a teenager.' She sighed as if this were beyond all hope and then eased herself up onto her father's lap. 'What was your number-one best age, Daddy?'

He knitted his fingers together across her tummy and lowered his chin to rest on her shoulder. 'Well, the age I was when you were born, kitten.' He paused. 'But I did like being a teenager, as well, I have to admit. I lived in California then. Do you know what we did after school, then? Not cream teas, that's for sure.'

'Surfing!' she supplied. 'Playing on the beach!'

'That's right. Every day after school we went to the beach.'

'But he was in London one summer,' I added. 'There was no surfing there. Only Big Ben and buses, red double-decker buses.'

As Wren frowned, Richie smiled at me in exactly the way he

used to, lips curling wickedly, teeth white against his tan. 'Yes, I was. We had a good time back then, didn't we?'

I smiled back. I was glad Wren was here to close conversations before they could be opened. 'Yes,' I said. 'Sometimes I think it was my number one best age as well.'

Chapter 17

Moving in with Mum and Warren for the summer is not my first selfish decision – I'm a month away from turning sixteen, after all – but it's the first to involve a boy. I tell myself I would have accepted Mum's invitation even if Richie weren't here for the summer, that the guilt I feel at having chosen her over my father is no different from how it would be if she'd moved out and married someone local, if there'd been no year-long separation involved in the process. Or if *Dad* had been the one to cause the break-up and to ask us to choose between them. Guilt is unavoidable in these situations.

In these situations: I hear that phrase a lot now, because no one really spells out what is happening in our family, no one defines it.

The saving grace is a change in Dad's own private life. He's seeing a woman, someone from his office called Rowena. She is younger than him, divorced, and has no children of her own. No baggage, Richie says. Dean thinks Rowena is just a pawn and that Dad, madman that he is, is still hoping Mum will change her mind about Warren and come back. How else do we explain his friendliness towards the Briscoes?

Mum, of course, declares herself relieved by the news. 'Well, that might help with the you-know-what,' she says to Warren, winking (winking? She *never* used to wink).

Dean has overheard her. 'You mean the divorce settlement? No need to be coy, Mother. We all know you're out for what you can get.'

Mum just laughs it off. That's how she deals with the dark new Dean; she just pretends his criticisms are hilarious jokes, as if in her absence he's grown the gift of stand-up comedy. Besides, she has other things to worry about right now: mainly, she's about to start a new secretarial job. Transferring American funds is proving more complicated than Warren had hoped and they have what they call 'a cash flow situation'. Another 'situation'.

For me, though, the job is good news. Now I know she'll be out during office hours I don't have to brace myself constantly for those backhanded compliments she sends my way, the little comments that, by now, everyone has noticed. The latest have been to do with my ambitions to become a fashion designer. During the summer break I've been spending time on my sketching, putting together ideas for clothes and thinking I might try for art college later.

'You'll have to design yourself a thick skin for that, Dolly,' she says, in front of everybody. 'You're much too sensitive. The fashion business is a *very* cruel world – one minute you're flavour of the month, the next you're dropped like a ton of bricks.'

'She said that totally without irony, did you notice?' Dean asks me, afterwards. 'She's got no idea. Like she was never The Deserter herself!'

If I can, I avoid Mum. It's just easier. I visit Richie in his basement or Dean in his room at the top, or I drink Cokes with them in the kitchen when she isn't there. Richie uses the place in a way I would never consider, let alone dare: helping himself to alcohol, taking risks about smoking joints. No sooner have the oldsters, as he calls them, closed the door behind them than he is lighting up one of his Camel cigarettes (he has a stash of duty-free cartons of which he says his father knows nothing) and pumping out his Californian rock. Every day his hair grows longer, wilder, blonder.

'Did you know Richie's done it?' Dean asks me, one time, when we're on our own, up in his room at the window, watching the fox cubs in the garden next door.

'Done what?'

'You *know*.'

'Oh.' I can feel myself blush but for once Dean doesn't pounce, just cranes to get a better view of two cubs in the flowerbeds. Maybe he's a little embarrassed by this conversation himself.

'Who with?' I ask.

'Oh, loads of girls. He's already in double digits.'

'You mean *here*?' How I wish I didn't sound so shocked, and so jealous – could Dean hear that, too?

He raises his eyebrows. 'No, moron, back home. Give him a chance, he's only been here a couple of weeks.'

I'm flushing deeper now, I need to deflect this somehow before my reaction becomes remarkable enough to be reported back to Richie himself. I move from the window seat and flop to the floor at Dean's feet. 'Have *you*, you know . . .?'

He shakes his head. 'Nah, but I reckon I'm on my way.'

He's been seeing quite a bit of Amy Jukes, a girl in the upper sixth, who is about to go off to university. She came over last week to party (Richie is the first person I've met to use 'party' as a verb and it's catching; maybe I'm not so different from Mum and her affectations, after all).

'Hey, a double date,' she said when she saw Richie and me on the bar stools in the kitchen, and I allowed myself a moment to bask in the idea. If only! I got the impression Amy was more concerned with impressing Richie than Dean, though there was no mistaking who she snogged on the stairs for the later part of the evening. That was my brother all right. I'd made Richie laugh about it the next day with my pretend gagging motions.

143

What with Mum and Warren, Dad and his new baggage-free companion, Dean and Amy, it seems like there's an inevitability to Richie and me, a kind of camouflage to the growing attraction. I fantasise about him kissing me all the time, but it goes without saying that I don't have the nerve to act on it (how can I when, according to the fantasy, it is *he* who must kiss *me*?). And since he can hardly be said to lack confidence himself, it's reasonable to assume that he doesn't have the same urges towards me. Those quick wicked smiles, the looks that seem to see straight through my clothes to the skin beneath, they are just part of who he is, how he is with all girls. I tell myself that this is OK, the last thing I want is to jeopardise our friendship (that's a line I got from TV), but I am getting to know myself well enough by now to suspect that it's the fantasy itself that I most fear losing. The fantasy is what I wake up to every morning and it is proving as impossible to shift as the previous one: that today will be the day that Mum comes back. Well, *that* came true, didn't it?

Then, one dinnertime in late July, Warren makes an announcement: we're all going on holiday together, a week at the 'seaside', maybe even a 'fortnight'. ('*Very* good,' Mum praises him for his use of native idiom, clapping her hands in front of his face like she's training a seal; I almost expect her to toss him a fish.)

I'll be celebrating my birthday while we're away. I'll be sixteen. And I know before we set off that this is going to be when my life will change.

Chapter 18

I could still remember very clearly the moment when I knew I was redundant in our family. Perhaps redundant was too strong a word – because that certainly wasn't the case in my roles around the house – more *demoted*. In a way, it shouldn't have come as the shock that it did, because I'd been used to Jamie preferring his father to me right from the get go. From the moment he could move his own body he would propel himself away from me and strain for Russell. It was out of the question that he would agree to go to sleep before Russell had come home from work. He was like a trained animal responding to the trigger sounds of his master's arrival: the faint percussion of house keys being chased around a trouser pocket, the brush of footsteps on the doormat, the drop of briefcase to stone. Instantly he would fret to get to the front door before it opened, tipping himself out of my arms and straight into his father's even before Russell had managed to get himself fully into the hallway.

'Hello, little limpet, how are you this evening?' he'd coo, his reward a radiant beam of happiness. Jamie would hardly look my way again for the rest of the night.

Noah was different. He did need me, at least at first, at least until he was sufficiently mobile to follow his brother about the place. And even then, he would still come to me for comfort when he'd hurt himself or felt unwell. I treasured our closeness, could at last share a little of what Dean's wife Beth enjoyed with Isobel ('I can't even go to the loo without her sitting on my lap!'). And I'd feel a twist deep inside me, like a flesh memory, at the idea that this was all simply a matter of gender. Of fate.

The shift occurred when Noah was about three. There was an episode in the garden, a Saturday in summer, when we'd filled the paddling pool and set all the toys out on our little square of lawn. The boys had been occupied for a while, and then Jamie had had enough and come for a drink at the table, where I was setting out cutlery and plates for lunch. Noah stayed on the grass, moving from the water to the mini cricket stumps. He picked up the bat and smacked it against the wall. He liked the cracking sound it made and repeated the action, laughing to himself. Then he misjudged and the bat came down on his foot. The yelling that followed must have been audible from orbit, his face dominated by that open mouth, anguish pouring from him as if through a wind tunnel. I opened my arms to shovel him up, but he pushed roughly past me to climb into his brother's lap. I rushed to check the foot but he kicked it into my face, startling me so with his strength that I cried out in anger. 'Noah! Stop it!'

Russell emerged from indoors, composed and unknowing. 'What's going on here?' He, too, bent to inspect the damaged foot and this time Noah permitted the handling. 'Hey, no broken bones, I think.'

I fetched the first aid box from inside and brought out a bandage. 'Jamie do it, Jamie do it!' Noah insisted, so Russell held the foot still while Jamie wound the fabric, Russell intervening now and then with gentle adjustments. Noah stopped wailing and Russell wiped away the last of his tears with his thumbs. Jamie secured the safety pin and Russell passed Noah a drink.

I just stood a distance away, watching. Three male heads all the same, bowed together in common purpose. It was a picture that needed no completing.

*

Hi guys, am staying a
little longer. Hope OK.
I love you, Mum xxx

It stood to reason that if you could get a signal to send a text message from the magical spot in the crafts centre car park, then you could also get a signal to make a phone call, but nonetheless it was another text I chose to send to Russell, Jamie and Noah as my first week in Millington drew to a close.

I did not feel worried about what was happening at home. For one thing, Russell had assured me he was coping well without me; for another, time had lost its normal insistence and I, without my lists and calendars and the heartbeat of the kitchen clock, my usual means of measuring it. It felt far too early to be missing the boys, and I could say quite without self pity that such feelings, when they did come, would reach me before they did them. If they missed my presence at all then it would be in relation to some errant item of sports kit, a school form that needed returning, a mug of tea Russell failed to deliver to their bedroom desks as they consumed their homework.

Here, decision-making was simple. In the morning Valerie or Martha would ask me, 'Will you be staying with us again tonight?' and I'd nod, yes, I thought I would be, if the room was still free. It was, and that was the decision made for another day.

There was another factor, as well, something equally unrecognisable to the Olivia of old. A mechanism was taking place inside my head that my thought processes could neither identify nor override: the moment I thought about Russell and the boys with even a hint of anxiety, the impulse was replaced with a warm, true certainty that they were well, better than well, better than ever. They simply continued with life exactly as they would if I were there – which only proved that I was not needed to facilitate it in the first place.

I remembered Beth describing to me once how it felt to take a

147

new kind of anti-depressant medication she had discussed in her training. 'It just removes the worrying, the negative thinking, the edges of everything.' I couldn't remember whether or not she'd approved of such an effect, but I thought I had an idea now of how it might feel. She'd told me I had a habit of catastrophising – seeing disaster ahead where there was none – but here I saw only what there really was in front of me. Green grass. A sunny sky. Richie and Wren.

I began to see them every day. Sometimes they dropped by in the morning before school when I was having breakfast and Martha and the other girls would direct them automatically to my table, as if everyone knew they belonged with me. I liked how that felt. Over the course of my stay, several sets of guests had already been and gone and I was getting used to the new ones eyeing me differently, acknowledging me as someone with a native connection, a longer-term position. I liked how that felt, too.

Perhaps that was why I reacted the way I did when I saw an advertisement in the newsagent's window for a summer lodger. It had been placed by a local couple whose daughter was off travelling for the summer before starting college in the autumn and the weekly rent they wanted was the same as a single night at Valerie's. I told myself that even if I stayed in Millington just another couple of days it would be a saving.

The house was at the top of the village, north of Rope Street near the road towards Weymouth, but still an easy stroll from the high street and Angel's Lane. On the way, I passed a front lawn full of children's bikes and cars and climbing frames and realised it might very well be Sarah's. This was where Wren played with Chas after school while waiting for Richie to come home from work. As if that weren't confirmation enough of how small this place was, I recognised the landlady, Tessa, as soon as she opened the door: she worked in one of the gift shops near the church.

'I saw your card about the spare room?' I began.

'Oh! Come on in!' She had the soft-eyed, forgiving face of contented late middle age, her hair tinted a majestic metallic gold and her Daddy-long-legs eyelashes reaching almost to her eyebrows when she smiled. This she did now, ushering me into the kitchen and insisting on giving me tea, regardless of whether I took the room or not.

We sat at the kitchen table, a polished pine oval with flowers at its centre that I knew at once had been cut fresh from the garden. This could be seen in all its splendour through closed French doors, a stone path leading past a pair of lovely willows to a rear section set with table and chairs. I imagined sinking into the shade there, as hidden from the world as it was possible to be.

'I've seen you about the place, haven't I?' Tessa asked, stirring sugar into her tea with a comforting sense of ceremony.

'Yes, I've been staying at Valerie's until now, but I decided I wanted something more homely.'

In fact, I hadn't 'decided' anything of the sort, but had simply seen the advertisement, packed my bag, checked out of Valerie's and turned up on Tessa's doorstep with little thought to the consequences. Were the room to turn out already to have been taken, I had no idea what my next move would be. Return to Valerie's? Return to London? It felt as if it were nothing to do with me, but left for the gods to choose.

Finally, I thought to ask: 'The room *is* still available, isn't it?'

'Yes, yes it is. It's been a relief in a way that no one's wanted it.' She didn't explain this remark and I didn't ask her to. Instead I took the shortbread biscuit she offered – of a kind I hadn't seen since my childhood, a favourite of Dad's – and I bit into it, exploring the sensation of the gritty sugar on my tongue rather than enjoying its sweetness.

'How long are you looking to stay?' she asked.

'I'm not exactly sure. Would it be possible to take it one week at a time?'

She nodded. 'All right, but if someone comes along who wants

149

the whole of August then I hope you'll understand that I'll have to reconsider?'

'Of course, no problem. You can throw me out whenever you need to.'

'Right then.' She looked at me curiously. Perhaps it had been an odd thing to say; well-spoken, educated-sounding women like me usually outlined their own expectations rather than waiting to be evicted at someone else's whim. They probably checked the room itself, too, rather than sitting ready to claim it no matter what its size and condition. 'Why don't we go and see if you like the room first?'

She took me upstairs, pausing to point out the family bathroom on the first floor that I would share with her, as well as her husband Peter at weekends (he stayed weeknights in London, she said). Then she indicated the short steep final flight to the top and followed me up. After the single at Valerie's it was a vast space to have to myself, the entirety of a converted loft, and the arrangement of narrow pieces of furniture around its edges only increased the sense of spaciousness. There was a single bed, a wardrobe (crammed full of a young woman's winter clothes, but that hardly mattered when I had so little of my own to hang up), a dressing table, a beanbag, a bookcase – and in the middle a collection of small patterned rugs in a higgledy-piggledy patchwork. Instinctively, I looked about for clues of its permanent occupant. On the wall by the wardrobe hung a framed montage of photographs, all featuring a teenager with long fair hair and Tessa's spidery eyelashes, and most involving the same group of friends grinning up at the camera in an inseparable cluster. They looked young and joyful, all of life ahead of them.

'My daughter Amanda,' Tessa supplied, her voice a little wistful.

'Your notice said she's off travelling?'

'Yes, she left a couple of weeks ago.' There was a pause. Now I guessed the reason for her earlier comment; while she was proud of her daughter's independence, she was struggling with the reality of an empty nest. Renting Amanda's room felt like the beginning of the end. 'Do you have children, Olivia?'

I nodded. 'Yes, two. Two boys.'

'How old are they?'

I felt myself hesitate. It would be so much easier to bend the truth, just as I had with staff at Valerie's when they'd casually asked about family. Keeping my eyes on the photograph to avoid meeting her gaze, I replied, 'A little older than Amanda. They've left home now.'

'Goodness, you don't look old enough,' she exclaimed.

I pretended to be flattered. 'Well, thank you, that's kind of you.'

'I shall have to pick your brains about coping with all of this.' She gestured to the empty room. 'It's harder than I thought. All I can think of is the disasters that might happen. I keep reading things in the paper, you know, all these terrible tragedies . . .'

At this, I quite forgot my own frenzies of the past, my visions of fatal falls or abductions whenever the boys went off on field trips; instead, the peculiar new mechanism in my brain got to work and I imagined Amanda and her friends in sarongs and sandals, arms linked as they headed to the beach.

'I'm sure she's fine,' I said. 'Don't think about it.'

When it became clear that I had no further wisdom to offer, we returned to the business of the room and agreed I would take it until either of us had reason to give the other notice. I handed over the last of my remaining cash.

'Where's the rest of your luggage?' she asked, noting my small holdall on the landing outside. 'Is it still at Val's?'

'No, this is it.'

I knew what she was thinking. I had so little I couldn't possibly intend staying for more than a night or two. 'I don't need much,' I said, 'especially in this weather.'

Clearly the type to give the benefit of the doubt, she nodded. 'Then I'll leave you to settle in. There's a key for you downstairs and when you're ready I can show you how everything works in the kitchen and living room.'

'Lovely. Thank you.'

After her footsteps had faded, I sat on the bed and cast an eye around my new quarters.

'Don't think about it,' I repeated to myself.

Tessa's house was on the most elevated street in the village, my room at the top of the house its highest point, and so it should-n't have come as the surprise that it did when my mobile phone, silent throughout its tenancy at Valerie's, began buzzing urgently in my bag. I checked for a dialling tone: for the first time it was strong and clear.

It continued to vibrate in my hand, delivering text message after text message until I began to lose count. I picked up the voicemail first: there were several messages from my brother and one or two from my friend Jill, his seeking me urgently, obvi-ously still fretting about Mum's will, she enquiring about our missed walk, content to assume I'd been unexpectedly busy and would return her call when I got the chance. Neither mentioned my sudden departure; they clearly knew – or thought – nothing much of it. Two further messages from Lindy resolved them-selves, the first asking me to call to clear up a discrepancy to do with Mum's house deeds and the second reporting that she'd got the information from Dean and didn't need me to phone back after all.

The rest of the messages were from Russell. Though his voice sounded perfectly reasonable, I was taken aback by the number of calls, as well by the way he ended each message quoting the exact time and date, as if passing on vital co-ordinates to a trav-eller lost at sea.

I took a deep breath, swept my eye once more around the pro-tective angles of my new home. Then I dialled the number of my old one.

Chapter 19

O, are you getting my
messages? When are
you back? Rx P.S. Call
your brother!

Russell was working from home today. Duncan had not been over-joyed by the request (nor, strictly speaking, had he granted it), since Russell would be missing a big HR announcement as well as caus-ing his day's appointments to be rescheduled, but Noah was off school with a temperature – nothing so serious as to keep him from his PlayStation, it transpired – and Russell had had no choice.

Jamie had announced the news at breakfast. 'His tempera-ture's 39.5, I've checked on the thermometer. That means it's technically a fever. And he was coughing all night. I heard him.'

Russell struggled to hide his exasperation. 'Why didn't you come and get me?'

'You were asleep. I heard you snoring. And then you were in the shower.'

'Yes, but if he's ill . . .' Sometimes with Jamie it felt like you were dealing with a traffic warden: it was all by the book and lacking the milk of human kindness. 'Do I need to take him to the doctor to get a note or phone the school or anything?'

153

'You need to ring the office, that's all. You don't need a note for just one day.'

'Fine. Are you OK getting in on your own?'

'Uh, yeah, Dad,' Jamie mocked, 'I've only been doing it every day for . . .' he broke off, brow creased, apparently prepared to calculate the precise number of school days in the last however many years. One boy in his class at Herring's could do this sort of thing instantly, he was a human adding machine.

'Course you have,' Russell said, moving away. 'I'm being stupid. You get off, Noah'll be right as rain after a day in bed. I'll make him a hot drink.'

No sooner had Jamie left than Aniela was on the premises – Thursday again, *already*? – clattering about, cracking the Hoover against the skirting boards upstairs. There was a loud 'Oh!' as she discovered Noah in his bedroom, followed by the unceremonious shove of his door closing. Then she popped her head down the basement stairs and called, 'There is problem, OK?'

You can say that again, Russell thought. I'm at home when I should be at work. 'What is it?' he asked.

Aniela angled a language dictionary under his nose and pointed to the word 'butterfly'.

'There's a butterfly in the house? I don't understand. Just open a window and let it out.'

'No, not on window, on ground.'

He had no choice but to follow her up to Jamie's bedroom, where she had discovered a bald patch on the carpet under the bed.

'Oh, *moths*, yes. We know.' Olivia had some dastardly potion to get rid of them (or not, as the case may be), but Russell couldn't remember what it was called or where it was kept. Now he came to think of it, nor had he shopped for those cleaning products Aniela had requested, though she'd at least not mentioned them this time. Presumably she had gathered for herself that things had fallen seriously apart around here in the last week.

'Leave it with me,' he said, and left her frowning over the consumed wool as he stumbled back downstairs. Moths! They were the least of his worries. On his way, he called out, 'All right, Noah?', getting only a grunt in reply. But that was OK, grunts were just about all he could cope with today. He reminded himself that Noah would need some refreshments at some point during the morning. What did ill children eat? What did *Olivia* give ill children to eat?

Back at the computer he rattled the mouse and felt a surge of forbidden self pity. It was impossible to concentrate, not with the calendar right there on the wall in front of him, 'END OF TERM' written in Olivia's no-nonsense capitals across Friday, twenty-four hours from now, for God's sake! Written diagonally across the whole of the following week was 'SCHOOL HOLI-DAYS' and, as if that wasn't clear enough, 'BOYS OFF!'. The days were ominously light on entries, the activities booked enough to fill only a fraction of the hours. Would it be all right to leave them on their own when he was in the office? Because there was no way he could take a second day off so soon after this one, let alone the whole of next week. He couldn't allow himself to imagine how many more weeks might come after that – somewhere in his mind he remembered someone saying the holidays lasted eight weeks, but could that really be true?

He returned to the original question: was it acceptable to leave the kids alone while he went to work? Was it legal? Jamie was fourteen: that *had* to be OK. And Russell was sure he himself had been left alone by his parents at twelve, Noah's age. But things were different now. The social services swooped if you so much as nipped out for a pint of milk without arranging for a state-registered nanny to guard the premises from paedophiles. He imagined himself in the local paper: *Single Father Leaves Child Geniuses Home Alone! Brainboxes Taken into Care!*

Abandoning work, he brought up Google and found a child welfare site:

The law does not set a minimum age at which
children can be left alone. However, it is an offence to
leave a child alone when doing so puts him or her at risk.

Great, he thought. Yet another thing in life that you only knew you'd done wrong after you'd done it.

There are many important things to consider when
deciding if you can safely leave a child alone, including:
* *the age of the child*
* *the child's level of maturity and understanding*

Well, that sounded OK. No child, or adult for that matter, could be as mature as Jamie. He could probably quote these guidelines himself.

* *the place where the child will be left*
* *how long the child will be left alone, and how often*
* *whether or not there are any other children alone with the*
  child

Again, all straightforward enough. The two of them would be together at home, or out on their bikes perhaps. They were of the age where they came and went as they pleased; what difference would it make if there was someone at home in their absence, sitting about, just in case? Just in case: that was rather the point, wasn't it? He would be out of the house from 8am to 7pm, at least, which was eleven hours. What would they eat? Far from being gifted in the kitchen, they'd never to his knowledge prepared anything but toast and even then Olivia complained about finding sticky trails of Marmite everywhere. And as for Jamie looking after Noah, he was mature, yes, preternaturally so, but it wasn't as if he was first-aid trained. Would he be so keen to play doctor if he had his head in one of those impenetrable tomes of his?

Russell thought about his sister-in-law Beth, just a twenty-minute walk away. Her psychotherapy training was not a full-time commitment and she prided herself on 'being there' for her daughters. Perhaps she'd be free next week and could be there for her nephews too? He'd hoped to avoid involving his in-laws in the issue of Olivia's unplanned leave, but there had to be a limit to how long he could remain secretly abandoned. (Where were the guidelines for that, eh? *How do you decide if you can safely leave a husband alone?*)

Behind him, on the kitchen table, the landline began to ring and he turned with balletic precision to pick it up. Seeing Olivia's name on the caller ID – *finally* – he hit the connect key and had his lips to the mouthpiece in an instant.

'Olivia! Thank God! I was beginning to get worried!'

Her voice replied quietly in his ear, 'Russell, I'm sorry. It's been impossible to get a signal.'

'No worries. What's the story? Are you on the train?'

'No, no, I'm not. Why?'

His mouth was suddenly dry. *Why?* 'Er, I was kind of hoping you might be coming back to London soon. The boys are about to break up for the school holidays. They keep asking when you're coming back.' In fact, Noah had asked only twice (and had presumably relayed the answers to Jamie, which explained why he had *not* asked).

'Oh. What have you told them?' Her voice was oddly toneless.

'I just told them you need some time to yourself after Grandma's death. Which is completely understandable, of course. But it's been almost two weeks and I think you need to get back.'

'Two weeks? *Seriously?*' She sounded so sincerely amazed that Russell was momentarily silenced. He didn't know whether to be infuriated or alarmed by her reaction; after all, it was hardly as if she'd been abducted by aliens, she surely knew how long she'd been away?

'Well, OK, twelve days, but still . . . .What's going on? Are you all right? Has something happened?'

'No, of course not. I'm fine.'

'Then why haven't you phoned? I know about the signal, you said that, but there must have been a landline you could use somewhere?'

'Yes,' she murmured, 'you're right. But to be honest, it's been nice not jumping up for the phone every two minutes. I'd forgotten what peace feels like.'

That made Russell wonder why she'd called him here and not at his office or on his mobile; she couldn't possibly have known he'd be working from home. She must have wanted to leave him a message without having to get into a conversation about it. To check in and out as quickly as possible. He began to feel a creeping sensation on his skin and it took him the length of an awkward pause to recognise it as the insect legs of fear.

'You sound a bit weird, Olivia. Are you sure you haven't hurt yourself or something?'

'No, no, of course not. The thing is, I need to be by myself at the moment, Russ, to take it one day at a time. Please understand. I need you to understand.'

Russell swallowed. One day at a time? How many one days at a time? She made it sound like she was recovering from some kind of drug dependency. 'I *do* understand,' he lied, 'but isn't twelve days enough?'

'I don't think it is, no. I need longer. Please understand,' she repeated.

There was a silence. Russell sucked in a mouthful of air. 'But what do you mean, longer? *How* much longer? Look, I know you've had a tough time these last few months, everything that's happened with Maggie, it hasn't been easy, and now she's playing silly buggers over the will—'

'I don't care about the will,' Olivia interjected, with more fire in her voice.

'Forget the will then, but you have to realise that you told us you were going away for one night! If you'd said in the first place it was going to be longer, we could have made arrangements. We're in chaos here.'

'I thought you said you were coping?' For the first time she actually sounded concerned and Russell was tempted to exaggerate for simple expediency – if she thought the boys were suffering then surely she'd get herself straight onto the next train? But, no, that would be wrong. He didn't want to do the wrong thing.

'I am, we are. Maybe "chaos" isn't the right word. But it's not ideal, Olivia. Apart from the boys, your brother's on the phone every five minutes. Can't you at least call him back?'

'I'd prefer not to talk to Dean at the moment.'

Russell sighed in exasperation. 'OK, well, why don't *I* just let him know you're incommunicado at the moment?'

He was being sarcastic, but she answered him quite seriously. 'Thank you, that would be great. And anyone else who phones for me, as well.'

Anyone else? What about *us*?

'I really am sorry,' she added. 'I honestly didn't realise how much time I was going to need. I still don't.'

Russell's glance fell on the computer screen, the web page he'd been consulting, and the problem of the school holidays reared its head once more. 'The thing is, I'm not sure you have the luxury of taking *too* much longer. We need you here.'

'I know.' At last Russell sensed capitulation, was already anticipating the guilt he would feel for his having applied pressure like this, but Olivia's next words surprised him greatly. 'But don't you see? For once I have to think about what *I* need, not other people.'

He was completely speechless.

'But you're right,' she said, sounding surer, 'I haven't been thinking. I'll call the boys next. Now I've got a signal, I'll phone them and explain what's going on. They must be getting worried.'

'They're not worried,' Russell said slowly, still digesting those last remarks. 'As you say, there's nothing to be worried *about*.' He thought of Noah upstairs, imagined calling him down to speak to his mother, and her repeating the kind of proclamations he would never have heard from her in his life – *What* I *need, not other people*. No, he needed to keep a lid on this . . . this whatever it was. 'They're at school,' he added, smoothly. 'They'll have their phones switched off. Maybe it's best if I just pass on your love? Let them know when you're coming back and leave it at that.'

'OK, if you think so.'

'So can I do that?' he urged, unable to give up. 'Can I tell them *when* you're coming?' When she failed to give an answer, frustration flared once more. 'I see. Well, it's not very fair, is it?' He sounded like a kid himself now. This was the strangest conversation he had ever had with his wife, with *anyone*; he wasn't sure he was completely convinced it was Olivia on the phone at all. Already he wished he'd censored himself better. They'd parted that last Saturday morning perfectly reasonably – he seemed to remember a kiss on the front steps – but now it felt as if he were on the back foot, making up for conflict. Was he making something out of nothing? What was twelve days, two weeks, even *three* weeks, in the grand scheme of a marriage? There were wives who went off for months with friends (weren't there?). Yes, Duncan's wife, for instance: she had cycled the Great Wall of China for charity, she'd been away for weeks for that. But Russell knew from the fuss Duncan had made about it that there'd been websites and blogs and pre-planned daily calls from the office – communications between China and the UK had been better during those weeks than at any time during the past hundred years! This was definitely not the same.

'Listen, I'll phone again soon,' Olivia said. 'Please don't worry about me.'

'Soon. OK.' And even before disconnecting he was already surrendering to the realisation that for now, for the foreseeable future, he was on his own.

Upstairs the Hoover had roared back to life and he waited for the noise to end, as though he couldn't think straight with it grinding above his head. On the desk his mobile phone beeped, alerting him to a call he had missed while speaking to Olivia. It was Dean, reminding him that the four of them were due to meet for dinner that evening. Russell recalled agreeing to put it in his diary some time last week, not imagining for a moment that Olivia would not have returned by then. 'Don't call me back,' the message finished, with Dean's customary curtness, 'I'm in meetings for most of the day. We'll just see you there at eight.'

Anyone would think he was chancellor of the bloody excheq-uer the way he went on! Russell dialled the Lanes' home number but immediately Beth's voice encouraged him to leave his mes-sage after the tone. He huffed in frustrated defeat before hanging up. There was no way he could summarise this situation in the required few upbeat seconds. He was going to have to meet them tonight after all.

He sat back down at the computer. After a while, he tore a sheet of paper from his notepad and wrote out a message, care-ful to keep the letters separate and clear. When Aniela next came into view, he held it out for her: *Can you cook?*

'Yes,' she said, reading it. 'I cook.'

Russell took the pad again and wrote out a new line: *Can you come every day next week? Keep an eye on the boys and make them lunch? Same money?*

Her eyes narrowed as she deciphered its meaning, then widened again as she studied his face. Clearly he looked as des-perate as he felt because she came quickly to her conclusion. 'OK, I cancel. At what time?'

Russell didn't allow himself to think about the other families

161

whose houses would go uncleaned over the course of the following week. This was survival of the most wretched. 'Nine o'clock on Monday morning?' he said, hopefully.

'OK.'

'OK, that's fantastic, thank you.' He wrote it on the pad and held it up: 'THANK YOU!'

'OK.'

Russell had to force himself to stop repeating 'OK' after her. He thought she might keep the chain going until they both went mad.

The thing about Dean and Beth Lane was that they were always so very pleased with themselves – not so much as individuals, to be fair, but as a pair. They admired each other, they respected each other and, worst of all, they agreed with each other. 'We speak as one,' Dean said once, grinning, but he was the only person present who imagined he was joking. Russell had never seen them bicker, not even after they'd had children, a stage at which most other couples had broken down, each burdened with the knowledge that they would never recover what once they'd had. Or maybe he was just feeling a bit down on happy couples this evening.

Either way, there was no denying it: Dean and Beth got his competitive juices flowing (and he was not generally, as Duncan had pointed out to him more than once, *nearly* competitive enough). Just the sight of them approaching, so strong and team-like, almost three legged in the matching rhythms of their stride, like something from a wartime propaganda poster, it automatically got him searching his mind for news of any latest triumphs passed on to him by Olivia (to do with the boys, of course, for neither he nor she contributed any glory to the family tally these days). This was not something he would have dreamed of doing with anyone else.

Today, though, attracted by Beth's waving from the corner

table in the pub and seeing the seating configuration that meant he must face the two of them as though an interview panel, he felt no prospect of one-upmanship, only instant defeat. For a family so satisfied with its own completeness, the Lanes were oddly attuned to others' vulnerabilities (he wouldn't go so far as to say that one fed the other). They'd feel sorry for him for his temporary wifelessness and, worse, they'd feel sorry for the boys.

'All right, Russ?' Dean said.

'No Olivia?' Beth said a beat later. She was a petite woman, with bluntly cut dark hair, kittenish features and a pretty smile. Olivia and he had once debated whether the sweet exterior might house a sour soul, but no definitive conclusion had been reached. The truth was they had made her more interesting than she actually was.

'Er, no,' he said. 'Just me.'

'She's with the boys,' Beth said. It wasn't a question, though the next was: 'You couldn't get a babysitter?' She knew it was odd, though. Dean was Olivia's brother, not his, and if anyone should stay at home for a cancelled babysitter it was Russell.

'No, I left them on their own, actually.'

There was a pause as Beth sipped her wine and considered. 'We haven't left the girls by themselves yet. But I suppose Jamie *is* older.'

'Exactly. He's more than capable and Noah's in bed with a cold, anyway. If there's a fire, they'll have more idea what to do about it than I would.'

She looked doubtful. 'The main thing is they know to get straight out? No hanging around looking for favourite possessions or putting coats on?' One of her habits was to seize on joking asides and address them with terrific earnestness. The implication, when it involved the safety of your children (and if you were in the mood to take offence), was that she took your parenting responsibilities more seriously than you did. 'You've got smoke alarms, right?'

Russell had not, at least not any that were operative, but his sister-in-law's expression was sufficiently cautionary for him to nod the lie. 'Yep, they're all sorted, don't worry.'

'Where *is* Olivia, then?' Dean demanded. 'I've left her a *hundred* messages about this collusion between Lindy and Adrian Bellamy . . .'

'Adrian Bellamy?'

'Maggie's solicitor.' He shot Russell an impatient look. Clearly this Bellamy was a household name *chez* Lane (and would undoubtedly have been *chez* Chapman had Madame not vanished and made every name but hers impossible to care about). 'Anyway, she *still* hasn't got back to me. I mean, we should have everything on the table by now, don't you think? But there's no point campaigning to bring the date forward if I'm the only one who wants it.'

'Oh, she wants it,' Russell said, quickly. 'Don't worry about that. I spoke to her earlier and told her you've been trying to get hold of her.' Saved by the arrival of the waitress, he ordered a pint, even though Dean and Beth were sharing a bottle of wine and already had a glass ready for him (plus one for Olivia). He felt petulant, reading their thoughtfulness as a bid to control him. Looking away, he saw a couple of blokes light up cigarettes on the street outside, breaking apart to laugh at something they'd spotted on the other side of the road. How he yearned to sweep all his responsibilities to the floor and dash out to join them.

'What do you mean, you *spoke* to her?' Beth asked, sliding a sideways look at her husband. 'Is she away somewhere, then?'

'Yes. She's spending a bit of time on her own.'

'Where?' Dean asked at the same time as Beth said, 'How long for?' and they acknowledged the clash with an exchange of small smiles. It seemed to Russell that Beth had posed the more crucial question, which was probably why it was Dean's he chose to answer first.

'She's down on the south coast. Dorset.'

'*Dorset?*' Dean spoke as though he'd said Jupiter. 'She doesn't know anyone down there, does she?'

'Like I said, she's having some time to herself.' Russell's drink arrived and he took a series of thirsty swallows. 'She's taken Maggie's death far worse than I expected.'

'I said that!' Dean turned triumphantly to his wife. 'Didn't I? She was so weird at the funeral.'

'Well, I suppose you could say it's weird *not* to be weird at your mother's funeral,' Russell said, defensively. He worried he might have gone too far, but saw at once he needn't have. Dean was, and always had been, unequivocal in his attitude to Maggie: she was a bad mother, that was his verdict, and even death could not redeem her. Sometimes it seemed to Russell that, without her brother, Olivia might have stood a much better chance at burying the hatchet.

'So when did she take off?' Beth asked.

Russell braced himself. 'The weekend after the funeral. She just meant to be away a night or two, but she feels she needs longer, you know, to recuperate. Recharge. It's been a hell of a year.'

'You mean . . .' Beth's eyebrows drew together in disbelief as she did the maths. 'Ten . . . no, *twelve* days ago? That's a long time to be away from the kids, isn't it? She's never spent that long away from them before!'

'I know. But it's not like they're toddlers any more. It's no big deal.'

'Well, when's she coming back?'

'I don't know, Beth, if I did, I'd tell you!'

There was a silence.

'Fuck,' Dean exhaled. 'You don't mean she's *left* you?'

Russell sighed. He knew this would happen. He knew they would make the very drama out of this that he was trying so hard to suppress in himself. Thank God the boys weren't here to listen to this scaremongering.

'She'd never leave the children,' Beth said at once to Dean.

'She hasn't left *anyone*,' Russell said, firmly. 'She texts me every day and we had a long talk this morning. She will be back *imminently*.' It was humiliating even to have to spell this out.

'The Dorset coast,' Beth said, getting the message. 'It's supposed to be nice. Why don't you go and join her? Take the boys for the weekend?'

I would do that, yes, but I haven't got the faintest idea where she is! 'The point is she wants to be on her own,' he snapped, 'so us joining her would just defeat the object.' At the sight of Beth's hurt face, he checked himself. They were a pain in the backside, Dean and Beth, but they were family and if it were to come to it – God forbid – then they would want to help him, he was sure of it. 'Sorry,' he said. 'You've caught me at a bad time. I'm a bit up to my eyes domestically, you know?'

He was saved from further apology by the return of the waitress. Notepad poised, she spoke in an absurdly carefree voice: 'Have you decided what you're eating over here?'

'*Are* we eating?' Dean asked Beth.

'I ate with the boys,' Russell said, vaguely. There was no way he was spending fifteen quid on bangers and mash, not when he was about to get hit with a two-week hotel bill.

Beth scanned the board. 'I had something earlier with the girls but I'll have a starter. Pâté, maybe.'

This had been discussed, he knew. There was no way they wouldn't have agreed the logistics of feeding in advance and since they ate here every other week they knew the menu by heart. They were buying time, which meant his news of Olivia's absence must genuinely have unsettled them – when had he last managed that? But there was no pleasure in the achievement, only the awareness of a nodule of fear in his throat, which stayed there no matter how much lager he washed over it.

He caught the waitress's eye and motioned to his glass – 'Can I get another one of these, please?' – and prepared to broach the subject that was the most pressing, the one Dean and Beth might actually be able to help him with. 'The thing is, Jamie and Noah break up from school tomorrow and I have no idea what I'm going to do if Olivia isn't back for Monday. I can't take time off work, especially since I've already booked two weeks off in August for the Portugal holiday.' Would she be back for that? *Surely* she'd be back for that?

'What about getting your mother down to help?' Beth suggested.

'She's away herself.' Russell prayed that this might all be resolved before his own parents got wind of it. Olivia was not the only one with a less-than-perfect mother; his was a panicker of the first order, the kind who created a Bay of Pigs out of a blown light bulb.

'Dad's away, as well,' Dean noted. 'He took the girls last summer holidays when we were stuck.'

Russell couldn't recall what kind of 'stuck' this had been, but he had a feeling that there was a dig in there somewhere – had he and Olivia not helped out appropriately?

'I'd step in myself,' Beth said, on cue, 'but I'm on a course all next week. The girls don't break up until the Friday after yours . . .'

At this, Dean stirred once more. If he so much as *looked* as if he was going to mention the shorter Herring's terms Russell decided he would tip his drink over his head. Ever since Jamie had begun at the school, Dean had waged his own campaign for a proper ordinary childhood, complete with warts-and-all local schools, like the one he sent his daughters to. He even went so far as to refer to Jamie and Noah (affectionately, of course) as 'freaks'. Damn this ridiculous competitiveness between them, Russell thought. He felt like crying out, 'Look, you win, you're a happier family. Just cut me a bit of slack, will you?'

'. . . and then we're straight off to Spain,' Beth finished.

'How long are you away for?'

'Two weeks. I guess it's just that time of year, Russ. *Everyone*'s away.'

Her words seemed to sit in the air between them.

'You'll need to get someone in,' Dean told him. 'Pay a house-keeper or something.'

'Yes. I'm on the case.' Russell thought of Aniela and her but-terflies. He wondered what sort of meals she would produce next week – that was if she didn't change her mind and cancel on him. Well, if she did he would just have to find a way to cope. Olivia was not the only stay-at-home mum in the area. He could ask the boys' friends' mothers for advice. They'd surely heard there'd been a death in the family; perhaps someone might offer to help out.

The next moment a huge platter of beef and dumplings was being placed in front of Dean, causing him to smack his lips, while a daintier portion of pâté arrived for Beth. That was quick, they agreed, but better than waiting half the night for something you could have made yourself in five minutes.

Russell applied himself to his second pint. 'I'll sort something out. It'll only be for another few days, anyway.'

'Of course it will,' Beth agreed, her soothing tone reinforced by the rhythm of her knife as it spread pink pâté on the griddled bread. 'Olivia's a wonderful mother. She won't want to be with-out her boys for much longer. Besides, she knows the school holidays are the whole point of her not working.'

Russell wasn't sure if Beth meant anything more by this last remark than she would appear to be saying. She, like many others, struggled with Olivia's decision not to work full-time (or even part-time – Lord knew, he struggled with *that* himself). But raising the toast to her lips Beth added that if Russell was *really* stuck he should phone her and she would see what she could juggle to help him out.

'Thanks, Beth,' he said, gratefully.

Returning to the house and finding the boys virtually unaware of his absence, much less smoked out by catastrophic fires, he decided that it had been the right thing to do, to meet Dean and Beth and get their take on the situation. OK, they hadn't come up with any magic solutions, but at least it was out there now. It had been beginning to feel like his secret. He was sure Beth would agree that sharing was the first step. The first step of what, he wasn't entirely clear.

Chapter 20

R, yes, still alive!
Will phone soon.
love to J & N, Ox

Richie's job in Bridport was taking up more of his time than he'd expected. Not an hour went by, he said, without some new complication being revealed that put further strain on his relationship with the builders. It didn't help that the client had arrived to live on site for the week, which meant an extra whip to crack. Often he would not get back to Millington until late, hardly in time for Wren's bedtime, and Sarah would give Wren tea with Chas, then bath her and have her waiting in her pyjamas for Richie to collect her.

Sometimes I took her from one house to the other myself. She'd ask for a piggyback ride, even though it was only a short walk, and she felt light, featherweight, the backs of her thighs slight in my hands. Taking advantage of the raised position, she'd talk directly into my ear, asking me about London, where she'd been taken once for a visit to the Natural History Museum. This she called the Actual History Museum, which made me smile.

Other times I'd arrive at Angel's Lane after she'd gone to

bed, so as not to encroach on their time together, often bringing with me groceries for dinner. This was not an arrangement we planned in advance, I simply turned up in the hope that it was all right and when I did Richie gave the impression that it was.

The magical weather held and we would sit on the deck with a glass of wine, just as we had that first night.

'What's it like here in winter?' I asked. It was hard to imagine drab greys and browns in place of the crystalline greens and blues of July.

'Kind of special, actually,' Richie said. 'We don't get much snow or frost, but we get mists on the hills. Wren likes that, she thinks it hides us from the outside world. Makes us a secret kingdom, like in a Disney movie.'

Maybe it does, I thought. 'She has a lovely imagination,' I told him.

'I guess it's hard for me to know with it being just her. I assume they're all like this.' His eyes seemed to turn liquid when he spoke about his daughter.

I smiled. 'She's different. She's got a special something.'

In a way, Wren had become our common interest, our talking point. There'd been an unspoken agreement between us since that conversation on the first Sunday, the one I'd come to think of as the plane-crash conversation, that we would not discuss the increasing length of my stay – even in light of my move from Valerie's to Tessa's. And if the future was out of bounds then we talked little of the past either, just safe reminiscences about Maggie and Warren and Dean, never anything of our own early, intimate relationship, what it had meant and how it had ended. The longer we left the subject, the less likely it seemed it would ever be broached.

'Are you all set for the holidays?' I asked. Wren was about to break up from school and so there were arrangements to be made with Sarah, as well as a holiday for her with her grandmother,

Lisa's mother Jane. This was an annual treat, Richie said. Lisa's brother and his family lived in France and every summer Jane took Wren there for two weeks or so to spend time with her three cousins. While she was away Richie would take on extra work and stockpile funds for leaner times. He and Wren might sometimes go away together in the winter, but not always; when you lived somewhere like Millington you didn't need to escape, you already had what everyone else was driving for hours to find.

'Just about. It's the usual countdown craziness.' He hesitated. 'What about you?'

I shrugged. According to the unspoken rules, he could not ask me directly if I had decided to return home for my own family holiday to Portugal. I had booked the trip myself, months ago, spent hours searching online, looking at hotel rooms far beyond our pocket, imagining a life without budgets. I could hardly connect myself to that person now. She was my reflection in a distorted mirror, her face pulled long, her voice dispirited. She was *never* happy. But I couldn't tell Richie that.

Nor did I tell him about an odd episode that had occurred the morning after my phone conversation with Russell, my first as Tessa's lodger. As I'd joined my new landlady in the kitchen for a cup of coffee she'd patted my hand and asked, 'Is everything all right, Olivia? Please feel you can get it off your chest if you need to.'

'I'm fine,' I said, taken aback by such fellow feeling at the breakfast table.

'It's just that in the night you sounded a bit upset.'

'I don't think so,' I said. 'I slept really well.'

Her gaze lingered awkwardly on my face. 'Of course. Sorry, it's none of my business. Probably just a bit of hay fever, eh? You drink your coffee.'

Hay fever? I dismissed it as a misunderstanding, but on my way out, passing the hallway mirror, I saw what she meant: my

173

eyes were quite red, the skin around them swollen, exactly as if I'd been crying hard. I frowned into the glass at myself; I had no recollection whatsoever of tears.

My next phone conversation with Russell was longer than the last, and trickier. He didn't seem himself; he sounded as if he'd prepared a script.

'Maybe I could drive down and pick you up? It's the weekend tomorrow.' He added, with great cheer, 'And where are you, anyway? You still haven't told me.'

I opened my mouth – 'I'm in a room, in a village . . .' – but the words got smothered in my throat. I tried again. 'It's near Weymouth.'

'Where near Weymouth? What's the village called?'

But again I couldn't say it. 'I'm sorry . . .'

'Olivia, just tell me where you are. I can't come and get you if I don't know where I'm going!'

'I don't want you to come and get me,' I said, but either he didn't hear this or he chose to ignore it, continuing with his rehearsed lines.

'I could come just as soon as I've taken the boys to their camp, so we could have some time on our own, maybe? It's out in Hampshire, this place they're going, pretty much on the way to Dorset.'

My brain took a moment to sort this new information. 'The boys are going to camp?'

'Yep, Camp Able, it's called. The camp for the exceptionally able – and their younger brothers, of course.' He laughed. 'Jamie said they asked you about it a while ago.'

'Oh. I don't remember.'

'Well, I've signed them up for ten days – at vast expense, I might add. It was the only thing I could think of. I can't leave them on their own all day long without proper meals and every-thing, and I can't just suddenly stop working, can I?'

His tone had lurched abruptly from breezy to plaintive. Not his intention, I sensed, but it threw me, nonetheless. 'Of course not,' I said, hastily. 'Well done. It sounds like the perfect solution. I'm sure they'll love it.'

There was a pause; another unsignalled change of gear. 'You need to be back,' he said, curtly. 'Seriously. I know you feel happier there at the moment, but you need to be back by the time the boys come home from camp.'

I didn't know how to respond to this sudden order. 'You've told them that?'

'No, but I'm telling you. Whatever it is that's going on you can have ten more days. After that, I can't fob them off anymore and nor can you.'

His words shocked me. 'I don't want to "fob them off"!' I protested. 'You know that! I thought you said you understood?'

'I do, I do. But you have to start seeing things from my point of view, Olivia. We've *never* been apart this long. I'm imagining all kinds of things that might have happened to you.'

An image crossed my mind of Tessa with her photos of Amanda; try as I might, I simply could not identify either with her disaster scenarios, or Russell's.

'But I've told you there's nothing to worry about,' I said, calmly. 'I'm all right.'

'But how can you be all right?' he demanded. 'If you were all right you wouldn't still *be* there, would you? You have a family, we need you—' The rest of the sentence was swallowed before I could catch it, and when he spoke again his voice was fractured with tenderness. 'We really want you to come back.'

'I know,' I whispered. But it was as though his sudden show of vulnerability had the reverse effect to what it should have: it was the final trigger to my sense of disembodiment. 'I'm sorry, Russell, I really am, but I can't promise I'll be back by then. I have to do this in my own time.'

'Do *what*, though? That's what I don't really get.'

There was another silence. It felt darker than the other ones and made me hold my breath low in my lungs.

'Just tell me: are you alone?' he asked, finally.

'What?' I felt my heartbeat accelerate. Had Lindy said something about the letter? Had Maggie sent something else in my absence that Russell had opened, some new riddle for me in case I had ignored the first? Russell might recognise Richie's name from ancient confessions, remember our history; it would be impossible for him to understand.

'You know what I mean,' he said. 'Wherever it is you are, are you with someone else?'

'No, of course I'm not,' I said, firmly. 'I'm on my own.'

He sighed, as wretchedly as if I'd given the opposite answer. 'I think we need to talk properly. Not on the phone. Please, just let me come and see you.'

'Not yet, Russell. *Please*.'

And it was with this trading of marital pleas that the conversation came to an end.

'Actually,' Richie said, 'it looks like I've got a bit of an issue with the first week of the school holidays.'

'Oh? What?'

We were in his kitchen, preparing kebabs for the barbecue while Wren lay snuggled on her beanbag watching a cartoon.

'Sarah's just told me they're going on holiday, a last-minute thing. Nick surprised her, apparently. A week in Lanzarote, kids' club for Chas, the full works. It's all booked.'

'Sounds great,' I said. 'I'm glad Nick's done that. When I picked Wren up yesterday I got the feeling Sarah was a bit cross with him. She says he's hardly ever home.'

Though I kept my eyes on the vegetables I was skewering, I felt the quick glance that came my way and I knew without looking up what it signified: couldn't I see the irony in a remark like the one I'd just made? *Hardly ever home*. Richie had been so good at not bullying me into confronting my reasons for not going home, but this time I could sense his reluctance in ignoring the opening.

'Anyway, I guess I'm going to have to take a week off,' he said, finally, 'which is going to cause big trouble at work. It's either that or take Wren with me.'

'You don't have to do that,' I said. 'I could look after her for you.'

'I wouldn't ask you to do that.'

I broke open a bag of mushrooms, leaned across to rinse them under the tap. 'You're not asking, I'm offering. I'd love to, Richie, really. It would give me the chance to do the rest of the things people keep telling me to, like go to see the swans. We could start a scrapbook together, she could take it to France with her . . .'

'I don't know if that's such a good idea, do you?' His hands were still.

'Why not?' Finally turning to look, I saw that his lips were pressed into a single worried line. I put the colander down. 'Look, I know you think I'm in the throes of some sort of post-traumatic stress.'

'Don't *you* think that?' he asked.

'I don't know,' I said, truthfully, 'maybe I am. All I can say is that I feel all right day to day. I really do. Whatever is happening to me, you can trust me with Wren. I can look after her, Richie. In a funny kind of way it might even be good for me.'

'How?'

'Because she makes me feel normal. She makes me feel the feelings I'm supposed to feel.'

Richie stared, lips still tense. 'Don't you think you'd feel them with your own children?'

'No,' I said, simply. 'The boys are much older, they don't need me in the same way. Another week won't make a difference to them and, anyway, Russell's sent them off to a summer camp. I can tell you hand on heart that they will never have been happier. They love those camps and we can't always afford to let them go. They'll see it as a treat.' This sounded as much like good sense as anything I'd said in the last few weeks and I could see that Richie was wavering.

'Maybe,' he said. 'I don't know.'

'Well, I do. Nothing would go wrong if I took care of Wren. I don't mind if you believe me or not, but there it is.' And it was really all that I could say. When it came to Richie and Wren, I *knew* that nothing could go wrong. From the moment I'd first set foot in this house I'd known that the right solution had presented itself, and that more would present themselves when they were ready. However confusing my conversations with Russell, however blocked my emotions about him and the boys, I still believed that.

We continued with our tasks in silence. When the kebabs were finished I began transferring them to a tray to take outside to the grill.

'Think about it,' I said over my shoulder. 'I'd be very happy to help.'

Chapter 21

I don't think Richie intended to accept my offer. It made perfect sense that he should not trust with his child a woman who was so singularly failing to care for her own. Then his client began talking of calling in other contractors to help, which meant taking the money from Richie's fee to pay them. He couldn't afford to let that happen, especially as he had no work lined up for afterwards.

'About Wren: if you really think you'd like to,' he said, a day or two later.

. I nodded. 'Of course, if she's happy with the idea.'

'She is. I asked her last night.'

'Good. Then just let me know what time you need me to start.'

I was given a list of emergency phone numbers – including one for Grandma Jane, who lived near Southampton.

'So close?' I asked, surprised.

'Yes, that's how I came to be on the south coast in the first place. Lisa was living at home when I first came over. Jane's normally over here every weekend, but she's been in Scotland for the last month looking after her brother. She doesn't get back until just before the trip to France.'

He didn't need to point out the obvious benefit of this, that he (or perhaps I) had been spared the sort of interrogations mother-in-laws were prone to making in such situations. A strange woman with unspecified family of her own turning up for dinner every night and stepping in when the childminder was away . . . she'd have every right to question it. And it only added to my conviction that my time here was charmed: to have Richie and Wren to myself these last weeks, when at any other time it might not have been possible. It felt intended.

Richie handed me a set of keys to the cottage. 'OK, one condition.'

'What?'

'If at any time over the next week you decide it's time for you to go back, then just phone me and I'll come straight away.'

'Fine.'

'You should go as soon as you do,' he reiterated. 'I can sort something out for Wren with another parent. Don't put it off because of any obligation to me.'

'I won't.'

He nodded. 'One more thing.'

'You mean there are two conditions?' I teased, but for once his attitude was one of proper rebuke and my smile faded.

'When Sarah's back, when I'm a bit less frantic, I'll drive you back.'

I stared, suddenly fearful. 'What d'you mean?'

'I'll drive you back to London. I think if you saw your house, where you live, if you saw your kids, you'd snap back.'

'Snap back?'

'Yeah, you know, recover. Like when people have amnesia in the movies. I think you need some kind of trigger.'

I imagined the boys then, coming out of the house together, transferring their bodyweight to their heels in that way they did, as if to make a slide of the steps, bantering back and forth, trading insults. And I imagined myself watching from the kerb, feeling nothing but that same automatic certainty that they were fine on their own. 'This isn't a movie,' I said. 'I don't have amnesia.'

180

'But do you agree? You'll let me take you back?'

'Yes, all right.'

That satisfied him. He was utterly confident I was going to reach this spell-breaking moment. He thought it was just a matter of time. And I did too, I must have done, mustn't I? Otherwise how was it that I could allow this distance to grow between me and the two boys I'd brought into the world? Three weeks, longer even, and still I had no intention of returning to them. *My own children.* How could I sit in some other family's house, at some other family's table, being briefed on the needs of someone else's child?

I'd have to be some sort of monster.

I had use of Sarah's car while she was away and on the very first day I took Wren to the swannery, or, rather, she took me.

She made straight for the rearing pens to inspect the cygnets, each of which she insisted she had previously identified and named, though they all looked exactly the same to me. She liked best the sight of a sleeping parent and baby: the baby with its neck curled into its own back, its beak buried snugly in its feathers. She called them daddy and baby, even though the adult was clearly female. She told me with impressive technical detail how the mating and egg-laying worked. 'They don't say family,' she said, gravely, 'they say clutch.'

'That's nicer,' I agreed. 'A clutch is like a cuddle.'

'That's what I thought.'

It was interesting that she reminded me so little of the boys at her age. Yes, she chattered constantly, as Jamie had, but whereas he had argued, face puckered and intent as he delved ever deeper into new knowledge, she was more conversational, her turns of phrase a mixture of Richie's and Sarah's, her eyes constantly scanning the space around her for a new curiosity to remark upon.

'Did you know the daddy's allowed to sit on the eggs sometimes? But only to keep them warm while the mummy has a drink of water. Only the mummy can *in-cu-bate*.'

181

'That's a big word.'

'Because it's a *very* important word. Did you know they *in-cu-bate* for thirty-five years?'

'Thirty-five days,' I corrected, gently. 'Look at this, Wren, it says here they won't be able to fly until they're four-and-a-half months old.'

She nodded, knowingly. 'That's because they need to wait for all their feathers to grow first. They're not ready to leave their daddies.'

The signs said that some of the cygnets were slow to imprint, to recognise their parents. I wondered if the same were ever true of humans.

After a happy hour's wandering, we took a break for a drink at one of the picnic tables. Sunlight trickled through the tall trees and threaded gold through Wren's long hair. Gradually, I was getting to know every last bit of her, from the newest freckle on the curve of her left nostril to the stubborn piece of sleep in the corner of her right eye. I thought she was the most beautiful girl I had ever seen.

'Look at you,' I said, 'with your gorgeous freckles. You're like a little speckled egg. You've got a speckle of freckles.'

She giggled, pleased with the rhyme, and sucked at her juice. Overhead, a sudden breeze caused quivers in the foliage and the sun fully broke through, spotlighting her face and making golden stars of those long-lashed yellow eyes; it was as if they'd been touched with a wand.

I sighed. 'You're lucky to be so pretty, sweetheart. You have no idea.' I'd seen a documentary on TV once about child development – I'd watched them constantly when Jamie was first diagnosed (diagnosed! As if he had some sort of illness!) – in which the presenter had asked the expert what people could do to make their children more popular at school. And the answer was make them pretty. Take time over their appearance and presentation because, like it or not, the prettiest children were the most popular. How sad, I'd thought, thank God I have boys and not girls. Maybe it had worked out for the best, after all.

''livia, did you know my mummy *really* loved birds?' Wren said, quite suddenly. 'That's why I'm called Wren.'

This was the first time she'd mentioned Lisa to me. 'I thought that might be the reason,' I said. 'It's a beautiful name.'

'Daddy says it's perfect for me because I'm so little and also I *really* like singing.'

'Well, he's right.' I paused. 'Do you remember your mummy much?'

'No, I was too young when she was here.' This was said matter-of-factly, just like Richie, and followed up with another noisy suck of apple juice. 'But it doesn't matter because *she* remembers *me*. Did you know she sends down love from heaven every hour?'

'Every hour? Wow.'

'Yes. I know how to tell the time. I'm the only one in Reception Matthews who can. Every time the big hand is on twelve, my mummy sends love down to me.'

Her eyes were wide with pure trust. It was all I could do not to grip her to me and not let go. 'I think she's probably sending it more than once an hour,' I said. 'All the time, I bet.'

'You mean even when she's sleeping?'

'I should think so. But extra when the big hand is on the twelve.'

She was thoughtful for a moment. 'Do you send love down to your darlings?'

Her question caught me off guard. 'Er, yes, I do.'

'Do they know to look at the clock?'

I smiled. 'I'm not sure they do, actually. But they're a lot older than you so it probably feels a bit different to them.'

You could almost read the workings of her mind in the patterns of her irises. 'Why don't you live at home with them?'

I breathed in. 'Well, I do usually. I know it seems strange, but they're busy doing exciting things of their own this summer and I'm here having a rest.'

'Looking after me,' she corrected. 'That's not resting.'

'Well, it is in a way. Because it's not what I'm normally doing, so it *feels* like a rest.'

'But it is what you're normally doing *now*,' she said.

There was hardly time to consider this when she thrust out her hand and proposed we compare clenched fists. 'Did you know your heart is the same size as your fist? That's how you tell.' Her eyes clouded. 'But how do you tell how big a bird's heart is? *They* don't know how to do a fist.'

'You ask such clever questions,' I said.

'That's what Daddy says.'

'I'm afraid I don't know the answer to that one.' *Or any of them, not really.*

'*Daddy* will know,' she said confidently.

Try as I might, I couldn't remember the boys invoking me like this. 'Mummy will know' – it had no familiar ring to it. 'Daddy knows more than Mummy,' they would say if there were ever a difference of opinion. Jamie had parroted Russell, and Noah Jamie *and* Russell, but before long it was a moot point for they were both quoting their class teachers at Herring's above any other authority.

Before we left, we checked the information board that announced the various interlopers spotted recently on site: the geese and black swans and occasional pink flamingo. I read the text aloud while Wren nodded sternly. 'Geese are naughty. *Very* naughty. But I don't think the swans would mind if a flamingo came to play. *I* wouldn't mind.'

Walking to the car park she slipped her hand into mine. Her grasp was trusting and confident, her little fingers smooth against my palm, the back of her hand soft, softer than anything I'd touched before.

Chapter 22

The first time Richie and I kiss we are on the beach, after all. After all, because this has always been the backdrop in my fantasy, the sun-drenched Californian beach of the movies, how I imagine Richie's home town of Santa Cruz to be, with sand and ocean swept up in a giant swirl of gold and blue. Our sand is not golden, however, but clay grey, and the ocean looks like stewed tea rather than liquid sapphire. It's a cold day, as well, the sky all angry and swollen, and it's probably true to say that all but those busy falling in love might wonder what on earth they are doing here.

In the old coastguard's cottage that Warren has rented for the five of us cabin fever has set in, causing Mum and him to bicker, the first strife I've seen between them. Dean, meanwhile, has disappeared into the nearest town to call Amy from a phone box; he's not expected back any time soon.

Richie and I go for a walk in the rain. I have the hood of my cagoule up to cover my hair and most of my face, but he just lets the rain flatten his hair to his skull and batter his skin until the tan is backlit with pink. He looks like a movie star, like someone's created the rain just for this scene. We kick soggy sand, throw stones into the water, and then when we're finally beaten by the wet, hostile wind we look for somewhere to shelter. At last we find an old concrete bunker from the war.

'They used to call these pillboxes,' I tell him. 'Because of the shape.'

He leans away from me to take a better look. 'No way! It's so tiny!'

'You see that hole? They'd look out through that for the Germans coming.' I am used to him being the one with the information, with the experience, so it feels good to be in possession of an unknown fact.

'Great for blowing smoke out, as well,' he observes, reaching for his cigarettes, and he taps one on the side of the pack in a ritual that has become familiar and wonderful to me.

After several attempts, he finally lights it and we settle just inside the doorway with our backs against the rough concrete. (I would never have done this alone in case of mice.) We're side by side, virtually shoulder to shoulder, like we're confined together in a lift, so close I can see the individual hairs on the lean calves that stretch from his cut-offs.

'D'you think igloos are this small?' I ask him.

He considers. 'I think igloos are probably any size you like. They probably have, like, *stadium* igloos.'

'Yeah, for ice rockers.'

He laughs and I feel my face glow with pleasure. I love making him laugh; I've noticed it's how he rates people: whether or not they click with his humour.

I ache with feelings for him, feelings I can only assume are love (I recognise them from descriptions in novels and from the faces of actresses on TV: a kind of joy jagged with terror). Day to day functions like eating and drinking have become mechanical to me, and that's how it will be until the moment I know for sure that he doesn't feel the same. That's how it is for me: I'm expecting a no. I could never allow myself to expect a yes.

It can't just be the cold that's making us sit so close together, there must be some other pull. Whatever it is there can never be a better time for me to make my move. We are completely alone, there's not another living soul for at least a mile, there's no risk of being disturbed. If (when) it goes wrong (as it will), whatever I've said or done can be denied later, definitely by me, preferably by both of us. But tethered by fear as I am, I do nothing but sit back and wait.

We talk about Dean and Amy, agree that they will lose touch when Amy goes to college in the autumn. He's been lucky, though, Richie says, to attract the interest of a hot older girl. Back home there'd be a lot of kudos in that.

That last comment doesn't inspire me with confidence since I'm two years younger than he is, but I've hardly had time to begin to wallow in it when Richie is asking, 'So, is there anyone *you're* into?'

'Not really.' I shrug. 'Well, not in school, anyway.' I hear the second part of my answer as if it's been said by someone else, a mischievous girlfriend or even an enemy, and I almost gasp at the treachery of her, landing me in it like this.

I open my mouth to suck back the words or, failing that, laugh it off, but it's too late: to my right Richie has turned his face towards me, giving me that stomach-melting half-smile of his. 'What does *that* mean?' he says, voice low and dry, breath warm on my cheek.

My hands are on the ground at my sides, and he reaches for the one between us and begins rubbing away the dust with the pads of his thumbs. Then, as I look to see if this is really happening, he moves his face closer to mine and says, 'You're very cool, you know. Cooler than your friends. Kids like Melanie.'

'I don't think so.'

'Well, *I* think so. *Dolly*.' He's picked up on my mother's girl-hood nickname, the nickname I've come to realise she's been using to make a child of me again, to stop anyone – Richie – seeing me as a woman.

'Don't call me that! It's embarrassing, like I'm five years old or something.'

'I think it's kind of obvious you're older than that.' His glance moves briefly downwards to my chest beneath the cagoule and the flush in my face surfaces at exactly the moment his mouth makes contact with mine. There's a delay before the nerve endings in my lips send the details of the sensation to my brain and then they explode and settle like moondust: it's salty and sweet at the same time; it's hotter than I'd imagined but it makes me shiver, too; it starts with my lips but it radiates towards every last molecule of my body.

He presses closer, blanketing me with his heat. It's a one-way process: he can warm me, but I cannot cool him.

'I like it inside the hatbox,' he murmurs into my neck. The damp causes a drag between his skin and mine. 'I *really* like it . . .'

I giggle. 'Pillbox.'

'OK, pillbox. Whatever.'

Then he says, 'Can I come to your room tonight? When the others are asleep?'

I don't hesitate. 'Of course.'

We sleep together for the first time on the night of my sixteenth birthday. Earlier, Mum has prepared a special dinner and seems pleased by my obvious happiness, even if she isn't quite as clear as she thinks she is about its source.

'Look how popular you are!' she cries, as a large heap of presents and cards is revealed, some, from my friends, transported from home by Dean. Everyone surrounds me as I work through the pile, nudging his or her own to the top. It reminds me of younger years, when everyone in the family would climb onto the bed of the birthday boy or girl, parent or child, and presents would be opened while he or she was still tucked under the duvet. If it weren't for the fact that Dad is missing, this would be a perfect celebration. But that's how it's going to be now: my parents are permanently apart. I have to be grown up about it, especially now I'm grown up myself.

Sixteen. As Richie has guessed, this is the first time I have had sex with anyone. It's hard not to tense, like I'm about to be inoculated, to use my hips to defend rather than invite, but in the end the pain is mostly lost in the breathlessness of his weight on me, the distraction of his lips, which hardly leave mine during the whole event, as if he guesses that I can only get through this if I share the breath from his lungs. Our bodies are joined at almost every possible point and I'm drunk with the closeness of it, with how safe his body feels, how sheltering.

Silently, stretching up from the bed, he eases open the window and lights a cigarette. I watch the rise and fall of his smooth brown chest as he recovers his breath.

I speak first. 'I don't think we should tell anyone about this.' For the first time I take the cigarette when it's passed to me.

'Oh, I think they already know I smoke,' he jokes.

'You know what I mean. Let's keep it between us.'

He raises an eyebrow, grins broadly at me. Already I feel more adult, wiser to his teasing, as if the club I've just joined is not the one for the sexually active or even the cigarette smokers but the one for people who've learned how to banter.

'Seriously, Richie,' I drawl, smiling back at him.

'Sure. Goes without saying.' His eyes narrow as he peers into the night; I wonder what he's trying to make out. 'I guess it could look a bit incestuous. But it's not, obviously.'

'No, but I still don't think they'd approve.'

'Do you?' he asks, staring directly into my eyes. 'Do *you* approve?' And I realise he really isn't worried about them at all, only about me. Here and now we are free of them all. I want to remember this feeling forever.

Maybe because of the cigarette, my voice sounds hoarse. 'Of course I do.'

'Enough to do it again?'

After that he comes to my room every night, except for the Thursday before we leave, when he and Dean go to a club in the local town and don't return until the early hours. The next afternoon I learn that they thumbed a lift at dawn with a lorry driver, got dropped a mile away and had to cross fields bogged with rainwater. Warren says there's cowpat on their shoes and Mum has chucked the offending footwear on to the path outside. Not only that, but one of them has been sick on the bathroom floor and they argue over which of them it was. When all this is related to me, they each gesture secretly behind the other's back in a bid to convince me of their own innocence and I feel suddenly at the centre of everyone's attention, at the centre of everything.

Maybe that's it, that's the shift that Mum notices: the focus is no longer on her and Warren or even on Richie, but on me, little Dolly Lane. For the whole of the final weekend she is walking about with her head angled to one side in that way she does when there's something niggling her, biting her lower lip in concentration, like she's trying to place a forgotten face or a half-familiar voice. It doesn't help that we're still trapped indoors, the rain causing floods in the drains outside and making brooks of the pathways. The conditions that have brought Richie and me together have also conspired against us and Mum has nothing to do but watch and listen.

Chapter 23

> Olivia, what's going on
> re Portugal? What am I
> supposed to tell the
> boys? Russell

As he waited in the cafe by his office for his sister-in-law to arrive, Russell examined the sent messages on his phone one by one, as if by looking at his own communications to his wife he might be able to reshape his feelings, to spot some clue as to her lack of response. He sensed it was not a healthy activity. *What am I supposed to tell the boys?* Looking at the words, he could recall exactly how he'd felt as he pressed the 'send' key: self-righteous and, worse, *hopeful*. He'd even waited a full five minutes with the phone in his hand, genuinely expecting her call to come. He should have known it wouldn't. This thing with Olivia – whatever it was, whatever it was turning into – was not going to be resolved in a single phone call. She could not be manipulated with emotional blackmail.

Nor could she, evidently, be manipulated with the reminder of their annual family holiday.

With a single command he deleted his collected pleas for mercy. Everything had changed, anyway, hadn't it? And not for the simple matter of time (two weeks was a break, but four was what? A *clean* break?), but ever since he'd done what he'd strictly forbidden himself to do: snoop. The previous evening he'd burrowed himself in Olivia's papers, working his way through the various places she kept her documents and correspondence – the kitchen drawers, the bottom bookshelf in the living room, the overstuffed filing cabinet with the lower drawer that wouldn't close. He'd scanned everything from bank statements to birthday cards (even a stack of teenage love letters) in his bid to find something that might constitute a clue.

And after two hours of looking, he had found it. It was in front of him now: a letter from his wife's GP, dating from over a year ago.

> *Dear Mrs Chapman,*
>   *Thank you for coming to see me recently. Following our consultation and your subsequent meeting with our practice counsellor Helen Meadows, I have concluded that you are probably suffering from moderate depression. Please phone our reception at your earliest convenience to book a further session with Ms Meadows. After she has made a full assessment, I will be better placed to advise you on a hospital referral.*
>   *Yours sincerely,*
>   *Dr Henley*
>   *Head of Mental Health, East Lane Surgery*

Russell had not the first idea whether his wife had followed up this request, whether she'd booked one session or fifty with Ms Meadows, whether she had ever set foot in the hospital (and presumably what they were talking about here was its psychiatric unit?).

That was when he'd phoned Beth, his almost-qualified counsellor sister-in-law. 'Beth, it's Russell. Could we get together some time soon? Tomorrow, if you possibly can? I think I may have a bit of a problem . . . with Olivia. I could really do with your advice.'

He ordered cappuccinos for both of them, though coffee was the last thing he needed; he didn't think he'd ever been so aware of his adrenal glands.

'Thanks for coming into town like this,' he said. 'I know it's out of your way.'

'That's OK.' Beth looked and sounded completely fresh. Her hair was in a kind of ballerina's bun, her glowing face bare of make-up; her voice was balanced and sane. She was nothing like the over-made-up office girls who filled the tables around them, crashing the acoustics with their screeching conversations. Was it just him or was working life turning into a permanent hen night? Sometimes he feared for the men of Jamie's and Noah's generation.

'I can't believe she's still not back,' Beth said, frowning. 'I was just asking Dean when I got your message: aren't you guys going on holiday next week?'

Russell nodded. 'Yes. To be honest, I'm starting to get a bit worried. That's why I wanted to talk to you alone.'

'We wondered about that.'

They'd have speculating about his phone message to within an inch of their lives, he realised. Since meeting in the pub almost two weeks ago, he'd been reluctant to keep them up to date. Pride had prevented him – until now..

'Whatever you need,' Beth prompted, politely.

He breathed deeply. He had decided not to mention the GP's letter, which was, after all, a confidential document. 'I found a book about depression that Olivia was reading before she left. I think she might be having some sort of, you know, emotional problem.'

'Emotional problem?'

'Yes. A few days away to think about Maggie is one thing, a week or two even, but this long is . . . something else, isn't it?'

He'd hoped for an immediate contradiction but Beth looked only relieved that he had said it first. 'I agree, it's worrying. And to not come back for the holiday. Normally she lives for these breaks, doesn't she?'

Russell didn't know quite how to respond to that. It sounded as if she thought Olivia had nothing else to live for. Was it as bad as all that? He couldn't bring himself to ask.

Seeing him flounder, Beth took charge. 'OK, let me get completely up to date. You've found a book about mental health. Did you mention to Olivia that you've found it?'

'No.'

'But you've spoken to her recently?'

'Yes, a few times.' Russell quoted the parts of the conversation that had made most sense to him. 'She's still taking time out. She can't say when she'll be ready to come back because she doesn't know herself. She feels better already.' This last was from her first call, weeks ago now – *I feel better already, Russ* – but he had begun to cling to it as to a lifebelt. He didn't add that the last experiences of speaking to her had been increasingly unsettling, even before his discovery of the letter. Something was wrong with Olivia, something he hadn't experienced before. There'd been an absentness about her, which, combined with the professions of personal emancipation, had made her sound sort of *brainwashed*.

'If she *is* having some sort of problem, then should I be looking for her a bit more seriously? Get the police involved, or whatever? I've been trying to keep it low-key for the boys' sake, but I'm starting to think I should be a bit more proactive.'

'No, I wouldn't contact the police,' Beth said, thoughtfully. 'Not if you're speaking to her regularly. She's obviously not at risk in any way. Would it not be easiest just to drive down there and talk to her face to face?'

Russell looked away, embarrassed. 'Well, it *would* but the thing is, I'm not sure where she is.'

'*What*? I thought you said she was—'

'—in Dorset, yes. But she's never actually told me where. All I know is it's by the sea, somewhere near Weymouth, and it's hard to get a signal on the phone. It could be a hundred different places.'

'I see.' Beth paused to sip her coffee, doing a decent job of hiding her shock. 'Has she been in touch with the boys?'

'They've had a text most days, not saying much, just that she misses them, that kind of thing, but I asked her not to phone them for now. Not while she's so unpredictable.'

'But they may be able to find out where she is?'

'I don't want to use them for that,' Russell said, firmly. 'I don't want them to know *I* don't know. Thank God for mobile phones, otherwise they'd be wanting an address to write to her!' He tried to smile. 'Not often you hear that kind of sentiment from a parent, eh?'

Beth's smile began gamely enough, but faded quickly. 'Have they tried phoning her?'

Russell shook his head. 'She never picks up her phone. The signal problem, I suppose. She always has to call you back. And I must admit I haven't encouraged it. I've told them she needs a rest and shouldn't be bombarded with calls from us. If they phoned her and she didn't phone back . . . well, I don't want them to be disappointed. She's never let them down before, they'd be devastated. This way I can keep them completely protected.'

She's never let them down before . . . there it was, he was finally acknowledging it publicly: he thought that what Olivia was doing was causing the boys damage. OK, damage was too strong a word, but harm. If it went on much longer, yes, harm.

He saw that Beth seemed to be struggling with herself – with the desire to admit something to him, he guessed. 'What is it? Don't hold anything back, Beth. This is getting serious.'

She nodded. 'I haven't told you this before, Russ, but I did mention medication to Olivia once.'

'Medication?' He wasn't expecting that. 'What kind of medication?'

'You know, anti-depressants – I thought it might be a help, just in the short-term, of course. I'm not saying she was at her lowest ebb, just that with everything going on she must have been a lot lower than any of us realised.'

'When was this?' he asked.

'Last summer. A little over a year ago, maybe.'

'So you've suspected she was depressed for a *year*?'

Beth gave another reluctant nod. 'But she said she didn't want to go there and I respected her choice.'

'Of course.' Feeling his pulse quicken, Russell made a spontaneous decision. It was time to break his wife's confidence for the first time that he could consciously remember. 'Did Dean ever tell you Olivia took something like that when she was younger?'

He could see that Beth was genuinely surprised. 'No.'

'It was before I met her. She told me she'd been prescribed some kind of tranquilliser when she was at college. There'd been all those problems with Maggie coming and going during her A-levels, messing everything up. She doesn't talk about it much, but it's obvious from what she *has* said that it got pretty serious. I remember when I met her, she said she'd taken time out from college because she couldn't cope, and there was a psychiatrist she'd been seeing. She hadn't had a boyfriend for years.' He groaned, overpowered suddenly by the idea of how little vigilance he'd displayed in this area over the course of their marriage – or at least latterly. You might even describe it as negligence. 'But she changed so much after we got together, she was really happy. She stopped seeing the doctor. I assumed it had been a one-off thing, to do with teenage hormones and not having a normal mother to support her.'

Beth shook her head. 'God, that woman did just enough to screw them up, didn't she? To keep them hanging on by the umbilical cord.'

Russell couldn't have put it better himself. There was a silence of shared regret as they both turned to their coffees. 'Shit,' he said, surfacing first. 'Is the same thing happening again? What the hell am I supposed to do next, Beth?'

Beth blinked brightly at him and he sensed her determination to turn this crisis around. 'Well, the first thing is to not jump to conclusions but to take her at her word. Accept that she's doing exactly what she says she is: clearing her mind, taking a break, a *temporary* one. Whatever she's feeling it's obviously fairly controlled, otherwise she wouldn't be phoning you to check in like this. Plenty of people just disappear without a trace. *That*'s when you really need to worry. This isn't an emergency like that. And it doesn't sound nearly as profound as what you've just described. Don't forget this has stemmed from bereavement, Russ. It's important we keep it in perspective, not least for Olivia's sake.'

At this pronouncement Russell felt his chest deflate with relief. He remembered the GP's wording in his letter: Olivia had 'moderate' depression. Moderate meant manageable, *salvageable*. 'Should I give her some sort of ultimatum then, d'you think? I mean, not in a heavy way, but if I keep on saying "Fine, no problem," maybe that's not what she needs to hear?'

It wasn't what he'd been saying, either, though he didn't tell Beth that. He was deeply ashamed of the way he'd spoken to Olivia that last time, not only for his attempt to force a deadline on her but also for that accusation he'd made that she was with another man. The notion had surprised him as much as it evidently had her. In all his speculations, as each new day added itself to the one before and deepened his doubt, he had not once believed her capable of the most common motivation for a spouse's departure: infidelity.

'No, I wouldn't get into any kind of deadline,' Beth said. 'I'm learning on my course that mental health doesn't really respond to that. A fragile mind will read a deadline as a new threat, something to fear, and that would only cause another flight reaction.'

Great, well done, Russ. 'You're right. And four weeks, a month, it isn't *that* long, is it? It's not like she's left the country.' Like Maggie did, when Olivia was Jamie's age. But neither of them said what he knew they were both thinking. Russell drained his coffee, licking the foam off his lips. 'I suppose I'm just going to have to try and find her from here.'

'How will you do that?'

He thought of the accommodation list he'd downloaded that morning from a Weymouth tourist site; if you counted all the guesthouses and B&Bs and holiday lets there were hundreds of them. He would take an alphabetical approach. It was probably too little too late – even if some receptionist did remember her from weeks ago, what was to say she had not by now moved on from the area? – but it was something.

'You could always use a private investigator?' Beth suggested. 'They'd ferret her out in no time.'

Russell thought irrationally of images from television: men in vans tracing phone calls and watching surveillance footage, uniformed teams swooping to capture. Large itemised bills.

'Just thinking aloud,' she added, seeing his face. 'It won't come to that, I'm sure. She'll probably be back in the next few days, in time for the holiday, and we'll all realise there was nothing to worry about.'

As they rose to leave, Russell asked, 'Will you fill Dean in for me?'

'Absolutely. And I'm sure he'll agree this is the right thing to do. Or *not* do.'

Russell nodded, remembered suddenly something Olivia had once said about him, years ago: 'It's great that Dean rates Beth's opinion so highly. Even if *we* don't always agree with her, how nice that she has that.' Had she been suggesting that such unconditional devotion was something she did not get herself? That *he* fell short. What had he said in reply? He couldn't remember; he couldn't remember saying anything at all. He'd neglected to notice. And now here he was discussing her fragile mind.

Beth kissed him on the cheek. 'Give my love to the boys. And if I don't see you before you go, try and have a great holiday.'

Without Olivia, that was what she meant.

He nodded. They hadn't even parted yet, but already he felt completely alone. 'I'll try,' he said.

Chapter 24

> J&N, I know it must
> seem like I've been away
> for ages. I'm sorry.
> I love you, Mum xx

Caring for Wren as her stand-in childminder was not the only commitment I was making here in Millington. There were friendships, too, early ones, casual ones, with Sarah and with Tessa. In a village swollen with summer visitors and depleted during the week of commuters, mine was a familiar face. I was becoming a local.

Several times I'd been Tessa's passenger when she drove into Weymouth or another nearby town for errands. There was no bank in Millington and I needed cash. Though she knew my 'real' home was in London, I had confided little else in her about my situation, only that my mother had recently died and I'd come here for a change of scene. I avoided mentioning my 'grown up' children again; when she asked what they did for work, I said something vague about their having not quite settled on their final career choices, before quickly returning the focus of the conversation to her own family. Amanda sent tantalisingly brief postcards every week or so and the decoding of them was an activity that could be extended to fill however many hours there were to hand. Tessa's husband Peter worried her too. He was older than she was and had only a few months left before retirement; what on earth was he going to do with himself all day at home? I let her chat on, burning off her anxieties and coming to the obvious conclusion that one would fill the void left by the other; I told myself that that was all that was required of me.

'Where does the boys' father live?' Tessa asked, on one early-evening trip that week. She delicately avoided the term ex-husband, though it was generally understood that I was divorced and I had done nothing to discourage the assumption.

'He's in London.'

'Are you still on good terms?'

'Yes.' I must have sounded doubtful, because she cast me a curious sideways glance.

'How long have you been apart?'

'Oh, it's fairly recent,' I said, vaguely. 'I expect it seems odd that I'm living like this, on my own?'

'Not at all,' she said, eyes back on the road. 'We get a lot of single ladies in Millington.' She meant spinsters and widows, not people like me, divorcees, runaways.

She risked another glance in my direction. 'Not that I'm saying I *know* you're still on your own. It's none of my business ... I mean, there's Richie ...' She left an inviting pause, which I realised I was going to have to fill.

'Oh, we're just old friends. We did have a thing when we were teenagers and our parents knew each other. We were about Amanda's age.' It was an easy deflection and I had only to follow it with a question about Amanda's romantic history to date and the subject was changed.

I supposed that Tessa had discussed me with Sarah and perhaps with Valerie, too; they were all friends. They had made other conjectures besides the divorce – to do with reasons *for* the divorce, I gathered. The fact that there'd been repeat showings of the mysteriously cried-out morning eyes only strengthened the impression that I was a victim of some sort.

But whatever they thought – Sarah and Tessa and the others whose lives overlapped with mine through nothing but serendipity – it seemed only right that false versions of me were being created in their imaginations. It was not so different from what was taking place in my own.

'She's a livewire, that one,' Tessa was saying, as I tuned back into her chatter. 'I don't know how you all keep up with her.' Ah, the safe subject of little Wren. Wren and I had been in Tessa's gift shop together the previous day and Tessa had taken pleasure in the telling of how her tiny, low-beamed work space had once been a home for four generations of the same family, great-grandmother living alongside newborn baby. Wren loved guessing how many children had squeezed into one bedroom, what they'd all eaten for tea, whether there might have been pets too. Yes, more even than Richie, she was my endorsement here, my validation.

'She's lovely,' I said. 'I don't think anyone has ever made me laugh as much.' And it was true; for all the evidence of my nervous breakdown, I'd been giggling non-stop during my days with her.

'You must be getting to know her well this summer. Had you met her before?'

'No. I hadn't seen Richie for years. I didn't even know he had a daughter. He's coping amazingly on his own.'

'Oh, he is,' Tessa said. 'I've not heard a bad word against him since he's been here. He's no trouble.'

And it sounded so normal, so natural, this idea of me as a woman with no responsibilities of my own, catching up with old friends, extending my stay to help out the valiant single father (never mind the man I'd abandoned in London to cope 'amazingly' on *his* own); I almost believed it myself.

*

It was Wren's falling asleep in the car that caused the first break-through – or at least that's what Richie would have called it had I chosen to report it to him at the time.

It was the Thursday of the week I was minding her, we'd spent the whole morning in the adventure playground of a neighbouring village, and she'd just fallen asleep in the car as we pulled up to the house. I turned off the engine and twisted around in my seat to revel in the stillness. How alike children were in sleep, I thought, stripped of all will and argument and energy. All that was left was eyelashes flat on flushed cheekbones and the gentle rise and fall of chest under cotton: pure child.

I remembered when the boys were young, younger than this, rarely had there been a night when both had slept straight through till morning. It was a time – a long time, so long that sometimes it felt like a sentence – of broken sleep for all of us. Gradually I'd learned what each needed to get him back under. With Noah it was cuddles, strokes of the head, long, reassuring sweeps from brow to nape of neck using the whole palm of my hand. Jamie wanted Russell, of course, but would, if half-asleep, settle for me. He liked me just to sit by the bed: it was presence he wanted, not touch. These days, at home in London, bedroom doors were closed, had been for years. It was a while since I'd thought to check on them as they slept. Now, looking at Wren, I felt a pull of yearning in my stomach – yearning for my little boys, not as they had grown to be but as they'd once been, years ago. It was the first pull since I'd been here, the first time my body had acknowledged who I was independently of my brain.

Suddenly I knew what I had to do. Leaving Wren to sleep, I let myself into the house and switched on Richie's laptop, kept on the desk by the door. Then I typed 'Camp Able' into the search engine and clicked the organisation's website. I was familiar with the company, all the Herring's parents were; it ran well-regarded residential courses in the school holidays, sometimes several at once in locations across the south east. Selecting their online calendar, it was clear that the course Russell had booked was the only one running this particular week and, just as he'd said, the centre was located on the Hampshire/Dorset border, not far inland from Bournemouth. Coldfield Manor, it was called, and I made a mental note of the address before returning to the car and pulling off.

The roads were busy, I wasn't familiar with the route, and the journey took over an hour. Luckily Wren slept throughout, which at least saved me from having to explain to her where I was taking her, why we were driving so far, what I thought I was going to do when we got there. I tested some options in my head. Persuade the boys to come back with me to Millington and hunker down together in Tessa's attic? Or behave as if it was a routine visit, have a cup of tea with them in the cafeteria and casually ignore the fact that they had not seen me for so many weeks? That I preferred to spend their summer holidays with a little girl I hadn't even known existed when I last saw them? Or throw myself at their mercy by confessing openly to this unnamed condition of mine, with its weirdly heightened and diminished sensations, its absence of proper, true feelings?

But none of this seemed within my capabilities. All I knew was that I wanted to see their faces again, to make them real, and that once I did I would know what to do next. Richie was right: they would be the triggers to my regaining my sanity. Nothing else would work.

The signs for Coldfield Manor appeared only at the last minute and so even after the lengthy drive its appearance in front of me seemed to come too soon. It was a down-at-heel Edwardian manor house, reached by a long curving driveway and surrounded by several newer outbuildings, as well as sports pitches, tennis courts and even some sort of BMX biking track. I parked by the main entrance, close enough to be able to read the notice by the door from my seat: 'July 25th–August 3rd: Camp Able'.

I felt more confident now, visualising the minutes ahead: I would walk down a long corridor of polished wood towards a broad, heavy door at its end, already ajar and needing only a nudge to open fully. The first thing I would see would be a run of high windows, open to let in the air, and then the arrangement of desks, in rows, like in an old-fashioned schoolroom. The children would all be in profile to me at first, but they'd turn together to see who the uninvited guest was, and I'd see Jamie and Noah near the front of the class, sitting side by side, their eyes full of . . .

All at once the picture broke into pieces and I felt my chest contract in terror. All at once it felt possible – unavoidable, even – that their faces would be as blank and unknowing as all of the others. Because I was different now, I was no longer the person they knew. It would be like Maggie coming home from America: they would no longer recognise me as their mother.

Shivering in spite of the afternoon heat, I left Wren sleeping in the breeze and climbed the stone steps to the entrance. The front door was wedged open to reveal freshly mopped tiles and a central staircase with passages leading off to either side. It was not at all as I'd pictured it so vividly a second ago: not only were all visible doors tightly shut but there was no sound of activities taking place behind them. The whole building felt empty.

Just inside the entrance was a large pin board on which the day's timetable had been displayed. The afternoon's sessions had already begun: two art classes were taking place in the grounds and three further groups had been taken off-site for a science project at a local river. The children had evidently been organised into teams named after artists – The Post-Impressionists, The Surrealists and so on – but the members of each team were not listed (the boys would be in different teams, anyway, presumably; which did I intend to pursue?). Set out on a low table were sheaves of printouts with headings like 'Court of Enquiry: who sank the *Lusitania*' and 'Old English in a Nutshell' and 'Why

206

Things Collapse'. There were also notes about a night hike and a stargazing session that evening.

Uncertain what to do next, I went to check on Wren, catching as I did the sound of a man's voice from the rear of the building. I followed it to a large sun terrace, on which a group of children stood painting, their easels arranged in a perfect crescent shape. In front of them lay a still life of objects that resembled an unlit bonfire. It took ten seconds to scan the backs of heads and deduce that neither Jamie nor Noah was among them. Edging into the open so that I could double-check the profiles, I saw that each face was identically intent with concentration and suddenly I wasn't sure I could tell them apart. I felt a fresh rush of anxiety, a feeling of being trapped, captive.

'Excuse me, can I help you there?' The teacher was by my side, a heavy-set man in his late twenties, dressed in casual clothes and an art overall. His sandy hair fell into his eyes as he peered at me.

'Oh, hi there. I was . . . I was just passing and I thought . . .'

None of the students turned at the sound of my voice, making me realise I was speaking too faintly to be heard, and, without touching me, the teacher marshalled me briskly away from them and back down the side of the building towards the car park. I could see he'd decided I wasn't quite all there, not a type he was comfortable with allowing near his charges. He, meanwhile, was exactly as I'd expect a Camp Able instructor to be, like the teachers at Herring's: quietly intense, unfailingly civil. It was so familiar I wondered for a quick confused moment if I might have met him before.

'Were you looking for anyone in particular?' he asked, self-consciously agreeable. 'The thing is, we've just started the afternoon activities and most of the students are out on field trips.'

Over his shoulder I could see Wren through the windscreen, stirring in her seats, and in a split second I made my decision.

'No, no, I just saw the sign and thought I'd have a look. I've heard of your courses. The children all seem very busy.'

'Oh, yes,' he nodded, 'they're very stimulated here. This is a fantastic camp, the best in the business.' He motioned to Wren. 'Were you interested in details for an older brother or sister?'

'No. I mean, maybe when she's a bit older.'

'Very forward thinking. Well, stay put a second and I'll get you a copy of our prospectus . . .'

I did as he asked, moving restlessly from foot to foot until he reappeared with the brochure. I noticed he waited until I'd pulled away and got halfway down the drive before he turned to go back to his class.

Soon into the drive back, Wren woke. 'Where are we? Where's Daddy?'

I spoke to her in the rear-view mirror: 'Hello, chicken, you had a lovely long sleep. You must have been worn out by the park. Listen, I just had to go somewhere a few miles from home, but we're on our way back now and we'll soon get something to eat. There's nothing to worry about.'

Within moments she was fully charged, describing her dream, exclaiming at the unexpected creatures who'd been her friends in it, making me smile despite myself at her descriptions of magical friendships with moles and unicorns. Then she broke her stream to say, "Livia, why are you crying?'

'I'm not crying.'

'Yes, you are.'

I felt it then: moisture cooling on my hot cheeks, drips beginning to gather at my jaw. It was the first time I had consciously felt tears since I'd left London.

'You must have an eye invection,' Wren said, wisely. She enjoyed playing the grown up. 'Did you know *I* had an invection? I caught it from Chas. I didn't go to school for two days *and* I missed sports days. They had ice lollies that day, as well. We had drops in a teeny little bottle.'

'Really?'

'Not the same bottle. We had our own. You're not allowed to share. Do you have drops? Drops will make you *much* better.'

'That would be good,' I agreed. 'I'd better get some. That will sort it out.'

And she settled back, comforts dispensed, and began her singing.

As we travelled, the traffic lighter in this direction and my speed faster, I thought of that stack of study notes by the board in the entrance hall: 'Why Things Collapse'.

Not a question, but an explanation.

I wished I had taken a copy.

'Someone phoned for you,' Tessa told me the same evening. 'Just after you left this morning.'

I looked up politely. 'Oh, you mean on my mobile? Don't worry, I always pick up my messages eventually.'

'No, on the landline, the number here. He said he'd got it from a list of B&Bs from the tourist board. We used to take guests sometimes before Peter started working up in London.'

'Oh. OK.'

'It was a man. He didn't give his name.'

I felt myself hesitate. 'What did he say exactly?'

'He just asked if there was anyone called Olivia Chapman staying here.'

I waited. I really had only one question, but there hardly seemed any point in asking when I already knew the answer. If she'd told him I was here, he would already have come.

Tessa watched me. 'I said no. After all, your name isn't Chapman, is it? It's Lane. I hope that was right.'

'Yes,' I said, resisting the need to close my eyes with relief.

'The thing is, I got the impression this wasn't the first place he'd tried, you know, like he was trying lots of different places on this list of his.' She paused. 'Looking for this Olivia Chapman person.'

My stomach twisted with indecision. I *couldn't* involve her in this. 'Thank you. I really appreciate you respecting my privacy like that, Tessa. I know this must all seem quite mysterious, but it's not possible for me to explain, otherwise I would, I really would.'

Her next question surprised me. 'You're not in trouble with the police, are you?'

'No, of course not.' But I thought instinctively of the art teacher's stance with me that afternoon at the camp; he'd been on guard, as if I posed some sort of threat.

She nodded, perhaps a little placated.

I did something strange after that, something that hadn't occurred to me until now. Up in my room I opened my handbag and went through its contents, all the bits and pieces from my London life, the papers that had gathered over the last months and I hadn't thought to remove before I left. A letter from the mortgage company advising of an increase in our interest rate – I'd scribbled a note to remind myself that the deal was about to expire and I needed to renegotiate; a tangle of shop receipts I'd kept in case items needed to be returned; slips I was supposed to fill in for the boys' school petitioning the local council for a change in the pedestrian crossing by the side gate; a reminder of my duties at the summer fete; acknowledgment of payment for the holiday. And the return half of my train ticket. I'd bought an open return, I saw; it was still valid for use.

I tore the whole lot into pieces and put them in the waste paper basket. My Sterling Avenue house keys I placed in a pot on the dressing table. In my bag now: phone, lip balm, paperback novel, key to Tessa's front door, purse. In the purse: bank card, credit card, driving licence, the two photos of the boys, forty pounds and some change.

This was all I had, all I needed.

Chapter 25

Mum strikes at once. When we get back to London from the coast, still two weeks before Richie is due to return to California and longer still until my own school term begins, she says to me, 'I think it might be better if you moved back in with your father for the rest of the summer.'

She might as well say, for the rest of the time that *Richie*'s here.

'Why?' I ask, feigning innocence.

'Well, because he's hardly seen you these holidays. He missed your birthday and I know how disappointed he was about that. He phoned me last night after you'd gone to bed and I said I'd talk to you this morning.'

All of this may be true, but it is not the reason she is asking me to leave. She's deadly serious, too, coming to my bedroom within minutes of detecting signs of waking life. She hasn't done that since I was in infant school and needed chivvying into my uniform. A flutter of fear moves across my stomach and solidifies – fear that I may not be able to see Richie as much as I want to these next two weeks, as much as I need to. Because need has set in already. I've been counting on spending every day with him until he leaves, and nights as well, if we can, down in his basement, safely out of range.

211

'Great,' I say, stonily, and fold my arms. 'You ask me to move in and now you want me out. Thanks, I feel really wanted.'

This provokes her, as I knew it would. 'I suggest we end this conversation now,' she says in a brisk, superior tone, 'before—'

'Before what?' I burst out, startling her. 'Before one of us points out it's weird to change where you live every five minutes? That most people stay in one house, you know, the one their *family* is in. And why would it bother you that Dad missed my birthday? *You* were quite happy to miss the last one, weren't you? *And* Dean's. Did you know your card arrived a week late? I'm surprised you even bothered to send us one!'

She gasps at this, a proper gasp, too, not her new wounded Edwardian duchess kind, and her face turns hot and furious. I feel both exhilarated and frightened now, exhilarated because I've broken the unspoken rule that we are not to make her feel guilty about leaving us, frightened because she'll now be so angry with me she won't want to see me wherever she is. That the next time she goes there'll no longer be any doubt about who is to blame.

There is the sound of footsteps on the landing outside, heading towards the bathroom, and at once Mum moves to the door and calls out a grateful 'Morning!'. She's expecting it to be Warren (not Richie, who stays in his basement quarters till late, and in any case she wouldn't have started this if she thought he was going to be about), but there's no response, which means it must be Dean. The bathroom door closes. Turning back to me, Mum's voice is mild. 'I don't want to argue with you. All I'm saying is that I think it's best if you sleep at the old house from now on, just to even things out a bit. We'll still see you regularly, you'll hardly notice the difference.'

So it's the night-time activities she objects to; she definitely knows.

Breathing hard, I gesture sulkily in the direction of the bathroom. 'What about Dean? Can't *he* even things out?'

212

'He's older and can choose for himself.'

Still I don't give up. 'I'm sixteen now, *I* can choose for myself as well.'

'It's different, Olivia, OK?' She looks at me, recovered now from her shock and intent on victory. 'Please just do as I say. It's for the best.'

'How do *you* know what's for the best?' I huff, but it's a last-ditch effort and we both know it. If I wanted to make her spell it out, I could, but the fact is I don't dare. She's won; she's still the stronger. After an argument like this I'll be leaving within the hour, just as soon as I've gathered together my things.

Downstairs, when Dean wanders into the kitchen, showered and bare-chested (the Richie look), and grabs himself a can from the fridge, Mum doesn't tell him as she normally would that Coke is no drink for breakfast time and she'll make him a cup of tea instead, but instead announces the news that I've decided to spend more time at Dad's place.

'Oh yeah? Cool.' Dean misses the point. He thinks Mum is hurt by my defection, and anything that hurts her automatically pleases him. He cracks open the drink, making her wince. 'Are you going there now? I might wander over with you and say hi to Dad and Rowena. Let's nip downstairs on the way and see if Rich wants to come as well. He gets on *really* well with Rowena.'

I'm not so devastated that I don't enjoy the sight of Mum bristling at that.

'OK,' I say. 'Good plan.' I love my brother.

The interference doesn't stop there. Soon it is obvious to me that they are in league, Mum, Warren and Dad, mysteriously passing information between the three of them like the Resistance, tasking Richie and me with last-minute – and always conflicting – chores and errands. I feel betrayed by Dad's part in it. To side with her, to become her informant after everything she's put us

213

through! I had assumed he would turn a blind eye to Richie and me, I had hoped that he might even act as he does towards Dean in his summer romance with Amy: with encouragement, pride, even.

'We kinda expected this,' Richie says, unperturbed, when I come to him booby-trapped and furious. 'We knew we'd have to humour the oldsters a bit.' He points out that during the day my parents are both at work, so our only concern is to dodge Warren, which is no great feat. And we can lie easily enough about what we're doing at weekends, play them at their own game by announcing separate plans at our separate breakfast tables and then meeting on the bus to go up to one of the parks for the day ('Sayonara, suckers!'). Clapham Common is our favourite; hanging out among the students and flat-sharers and down-and-outs. In the mornings I put on my bikini under my clothes, praying for the sun to hold, imagining Richie's hands all over my bare body.

Every day, from the moment I wake up (at Dad's) I am concerned with just one thing: counting down the hours to seeing him. My existence has shrunk to the moments when we're alone; everything else is just what happens before and what will happen after. Some days, to my great despair, it isn't possible to meet at all thanks to Warren's new checklist of cultural places his son must visit before he goes back (Mum's brainchild, of course). This includes day trips to Oxford and Cambridge and an overnight stay in Bath, concessions worth making, as far as Richie sees it, but to me nothing less than self-contained tragedies. On the days he is out of town I look at the hours ahead of me completely differently from the way I would have before, back in my pre-Richie life. Then, any day free of school-work was to be celebrated, to be made to last for ever. Now, though, without Richie, time is there only to be killed. It is too corny to admit to anyone else, but I only feel alive when I am with him.

'Am I your girlfriend?' I ask him, stretched out next to him on the grass, sunbathing on our own, free for once of the meddlers.

'You're my . . . let's think . . .' And he considers, kissing me expertly as he does so and prising the triangle of bikini top away from my right nipple. 'You're my babe.'

Chapter 26

Russell was feeling conspicuously solitary as he cooled off in a pool full of infants and their assorted inflatables. Clearly crocodiles were the thing this year, or alligators, it was hard to tell when they were plastic and, in some cases, pink. Also sharks, surprisingly fierce-looking as they prowled the water's edge – or maybe he was just feeling vulnerable. In any case, he had a cat's chance in hell of swimming a length in this pool. Half the headcount of London's primary schools was in there. Evading another bash to the head he clambered out and located his sun lounger. This, like everyone else's, came ready draped with a large green towel branded with the resort logo: a pair of fish, sardines, possibly. They weren't far from Portimao, which, according to Jamie, had the distinction of being the Sardine Capital of the World.

His eyes moved idly over the women in range, many of whom seemed to be occupied perpetually in the application of sun lotion. One, who'd halted at his feet to prise a small child out of wet clothes and spray it in a mist of the stuff, glanced up and caught his eye, gave him that look of assured fellow feeling. She was solidly built, her body contained within a bronze-coloured swimsuit in such a *structural* way that Russell feared it might fall to the ground in a large blob were the support to be unexpectedly removed. But it was a well-heeled crowd, generally, and most of the women were not so much overweight as properly curvy. If Olivia were here she'd be whispering to him, 'Am I as fat as her?', and she'd point out a particular person, not the one in the bronze rigging but someone slim and attractive, like the blonde at the shallow end who had a toddler on her shoulders and an older child clamouring in her face with a water pistol. When faced with such a question Russell had learned to his cost that he must not hesitate, not even for a fraction, but must reply straight away, 'No, much thinner,' and not over-egg it either by adding a 'definitely' or a 'no doubt about it'. It had to sound a hundred per cent natural. He could coach novice husbands in that tone of voice, make their future lives much the easier for it. The pang this thought caused startled him; a sharp, localised spasm plum in the centre of his body.

To be fair, it wasn't so bad here in Portugal or, as he'd come to think of it, the moon, for there were precious few references to the host nation beyond those intertwined sardines. It was, in some ways, how he imagined an old people's home to be – not that there were any old people about; the demographic scarcely varied from the two-parent, two-school-age-children basic model – but there was that same sense of being hidden from view that he remembered from visits to his grandmother in her care home before she died. Of course in this case you weren't quite clear who was being hidden from whom: those inside from those outside, or vice versa? In any case, *someone* had deemed it necessary to contain the hotel and apartment compound within a twelve-foot perimeter fence.

One welcome side effect of the arrangement was that Russell's feelings felt fenced off too. All except those occasional sensory memories that slipped through the cracks, not just the fat/thin poolside ritual, but others too: Olivia rubbing sunscreen into the boys' backs, gripping Noah's shoulders and saying, 'Look how tall you're getting!'; Olivia being more tactile than at home, touching him more as they passed items back and forth; Olivia lying beside him with her book, her legs in the sun, the rest of her in the shade, her eyes flicking over the top of the pages to check on the boys in the water, always checking on the boys, however tall they were getting, however little they noticed.

He tried to imagine what she'd say about this place. More often than not she was critical of her own holiday selections. 'It's not at all how I imagined it,' she'd say, or, the one he'd come to know as the most troublesome, 'It's just like home but hotter.' She was particularly disappointed to find people dressing alike – for some reason pool wear offended her, as if she'd expected instead some international costume parade. She'd certainly be quick to note this year's trend: a kind of Moroccan kaftan, all crusted with sequins and shells at the neckline. The mother three loungers down from Russell had dressed her two fair-haired daughters in the same sky-blue version she wore herself. With their confident, determined expressions the girls were their mother in waiting, literally cut from the same cloth. Would things have turned out differently if *they*'d had girls, he and Olivia? She'd longed for their second to be a daughter, though she never once expressed regret after Noah's arrival. She did, however, comment on the boys not needing her any more, on their reluctance to answer her questions about school or confide their troubles. Should he have paid more attention to that? The thing was, she had never actually sounded like she was complaining, but only making the same careworn murmurings of the next parent. Did Kaftan Mum make careworn murmurings? He was doubtful about that.

It was mid-morning and Jamie and Noah were at the hotel's golf academy. They'd signed up for a number of activities here, all at wincing expense. Russell had had to make an instant policy decision on arrival about expenditure: yes, he could agonise over a small beer costing six euros or an ice cream four, a bottle of mineral water eight (eight euros, it was criminal!) and so on, or he could assign some fictitious sum of money to the thing and tell the kids, OK, whatever you want, just sign it to the room. Poor motherless boys, how could he not? He'd release part of the lump sum from his pension, that was one theory that had struck during his first hours by the pool, as he watched families licking ice creams and slurping Cokes together and failed to stop himself from mentally totting up the total cost of their snacks. Another notion he'd had was to assemble every item in the house that had not been used in the last twelve months and sell the whole lot on eBay (Duncan had done this with his children's old baby equipment and raised almost eight hundred pounds). That was if there was anything left to assemble. He recalled that Olivia normally gave old stuff away to Aniela, who could usually be counted on to know of a mother in need of outgrown fleeces or a down-graded kettle.

Of course Olivia would not have considered the issue of spending money when she'd booked the holiday, using the entire budget for the flights and apartment alone, even though this was, in Russell's experience, only a half of the eventual cost. It wouldn't have occurred to her how awkward it might feel to not be able to afford the restaurants, or if it had then it would only have depressed her. 'We have to treat ourselves *sometimes*,' she would say, and with real self-pity, too, as if she really believed that for the rest of the year they were obliged to live like Amish.

But Olivia was not here this time. She had booked the holiday, but she had not turned up to take it.

The flight had been the worst bit. Travelling without her, without her reminders about train times and check-in rules and luggage restrictions, without that crocodile-skin zip-up wallet she insisted on using for documents even though it was slightly too big to fit in her handbag. The special treats she bought for the journey: little tubs of biscuits, tins of travel sweets, odd things she would never choose at other times. New perfume from the duty-free shop. It was as though she was trying to start over

220

every time they went on holiday, re-evaluating her tastes, freed at last to try something new. Until they got there and she found that it was just the same as home only hotter.

Russell had spoken to the boys the day before the trip and explained that their mother was still feeling low about Grandma's death and had decided that they would enjoy their holiday more if she did not come. This had been met with blank acceptance, and he had not felt the need to add, as he'd planned to if pushed, that she might still change her mind and turn up at the airport – there was still hope!

Waiting at the boarding gate, when it was finally obvious to him that she would not be joining them, Noah had piped up: 'Dad, is Mum mental or something, like Grandma?'

Out of the blue, just like that.

As neighbouring travellers looked up with interest, Russell paid for his hesitation when his son added, even more loudly, 'Like, has she been *sectioned*?'

Russell was completely floored. How on earth could Noah have come up with this when he'd been so careful to protect him? The fateful GP's letter was hidden in his desk drawer at work and all conversations with Dean and Beth had been conducted safely off site. Finally, he forced out a laugh. 'What are you talking about, mate? Mum's not mental, no, and nor was Grandma, thank you very much. What do you know about being sectioned, anyway?'

Noah shrugged. 'Well, why isn't she coming on holiday with us?'

Russell was aware of Jamie, his body quite still, on his other side. 'I told you yesterday, she's not coming because she needs a bit more time to herself. Grief is a strange thing. You don't get over it straight away. She needs a rest.'

'But holiday *is* a rest,' Noah said.

For you, maybe, Russell thought, but he would never say such a thing aloud. That was his one rule: he would never suggest to the boys that they had in any way caused their mother to leave. Not that he thought they *had*, of course, but he could certainly expect their imaginations to wander in that direction at some point soon and when they did he intended to be ready to refute and reassure.

'Sometimes being on your own is the only thing that feels like proper rest,' he said. 'That's why I've said we shouldn't phone her. We should think of her as having a really long sleep.'

That sounded totally wrong, like explaining a coma – or, indeed, death – to much younger children, and the boys looked duly unimpressed. Russell had never felt more grateful than when the announcement blared out that their row was among those now being boarded and the boys sprang up, their competitive spirit engaged, all conversation forgotten.

'Oops, sorry about that! Hello? Would you mind . . . ? Thank you.'

A ball had bounced to the side of Russell's lounger, spraying his book with water, and he rolled it back to the half-submerged mother who grinned her thanks and lingered for a moment looking at him. She was presumably making the same split-second assumption about him that he suspected of everyone, the assumption that he was only lolling about on his own because his wife was off somewhere on some sort of mum's treat, like a pedicure or a facial, or perhaps busy buying lunch materials at the resort's gourmet deli. It was inconceivable that he should be a Lone Parent.

Beyond the pool hut, on the shaded walkway that led from the golf academy, Russell caught sight of Jamie approaching, face downcast, and took the opportunity to slip from sight his poolside reading: *The Trauma of Grief*. He was not getting on well with the book, perhaps because he was now surer than ever that he needed to be reading up not on bereavement but on depression, a condition in his wife that, thanks to information from the

GP and Beth, he now knew had predated Maggie's death by some time. And the list of sources was growing: there was a third one now. How many times since getting here had Russell replayed that peculiar meeting with Joanna Lillywhite and hoped that he might have completely misinterpreted it? Or, better still, dreamed it?

Joanna was the woman whose maternity leave Olivia had covered a year or so ago in the office of a local primary school, and he'd bumped into her in the car park at Sainsbury's just the day before. Her baby was toddling now, pulling at his reins towards the stream of oncoming shoppers and protesting in high-pitched squeals when Joanna tried to pick him up.

'How's Olivia?' she asked over the cries.

Russell covered his hesitation with an indulgent grimace in the direction of the struggling child. There was no way Joanna could know what had been going on. 'Fine, thanks. We're gearing up for holidays, just spent a fortune on sun screen and mossie spray.'

There was an exchange about crêches and tummy upsets and the havoc to be played with naps by time differences, little of which had applied to Russell's family for years but he knew what the mothers of small children were like and he played his part obligingly. Then Joanna asked, 'So where's she working now?'

Russell gripped the handles of his trolley a little tighter. 'Nowhere at the moment. She could never find anything that suited as well as the school job.'

Joanna nodded. 'It's a shame she decided not to take the permanent position. I told her it was as good as it gets.' She laughed. 'Listen to myself! I suppose our idea of as good as it gets changes when kids come along, doesn't it? Ten years ago I would have thought that job was as *dull* as it gets!'

As she hooted merrily away, Russell could only stare in confusion. 'What d'you mean? How could she have stayed permanently after you'd gone back?'

Joanna looked puzzled. 'But I didn't go back. I decided to stay at home with Sam.' She repositioned the toddler from one hip to another.

'You did?' Russell frowned.

'Yes. I meant to go back but he was so unwell for ages . . .'

Now Russell listened with considerably less patience to details of a misdiagnosed lactose intolerance, all the while aware that his heart rate had just doubled. 'Oh. Well, I guess Olivia mustn't have realised. That's a pity.' As well as a bloody great under-statement, he thought. How much easier life would have been with that extra year's income, how much less time she'd have had to brood about Maggie and Dean and that whole family history of theirs that, when you really looked at it, was nowhere near as bad as they seemed to think it was.

But there was worse to come.

'But she *did* know,' Joanna said, the vertical tramlines between her eyebrows deepening. 'Of course she did. I was there when the deputy head talked to her about staying on. She defi-nitely had first refusal. But she was quite sure she didn't want to. They had nearly three hundred applications, you know, in the end. I thought that was incredible! Like I say, as good as it gets.'

Russell was starting to feel like a character in a film whose fatal flaw was his constant memory slips. He wanted to get out of there, away from this harbinger, so he could piece together in his own time what was apparently common knowledge to every-one else. 'Oh, OK, maybe I'm misremembering,' he told Joanna, backing his trolley away from her. 'It was a while ago.'

Maybe he had misremembered quite a lot, that's what he was thinking now. Maybe he had misremembered his whole mar-riage.

'Hi Dad.' Jamie's eyes were bruised and bloodshot from the hours spent in the water over the last few days. Noah had exactly the same look. The first day Russell had thought they'd been crying themselves to sleep. They'd seemed so untouched by their mother's absence so far, but after those remarks at the airport, well, it had made him think that maybe they were hurting more than he'd thought. Turned out it was just the chlorine.

'You're back early,' he said, cheerfully. 'How was golf?'

'Rubbish,' Jamie said. 'I was rubbish.'

He didn't seem unduly distressed by this, and had no particular passion for sports, so Russell let it pass. 'Where's Noah?'

Shrug. 'Still there. The instructor said he's a natural.'

'Is he? Oh. Well, think of all the things you're a natural at . . .'

'Yeah, I *know*, Dad, you don't have to say.'

'OK. You going to go in the water? I brought your kit down for you.'

Jamie surveyed the pool dubiously. One of his peculiarities was that he found small children intensely irritating. With the exception of his own brother, he had never been interested in children younger than he was. His focus had always been on those who knew more than he did; those who could already do what was next on his list to master. 'Nah. When's lunch?'

'Not till Noah finishes, I suppose.'

'I'm going to get an ice cream, then.'

This time the price on the bill was only a brief flicker in Russell's head, replaced instantly by an image of the three of them walking along together in their reduced, red-eyed little fraternity. They almost needed a little motivational motto to get through this holiday, like The Three Musketeers. *All for one . . .*

'Go for it,' he told Jamie, with a faint crack in his voice. 'Get yourself a double scoop.'

Chapter 27

After a period of feverish anticipation and a packing ritual that lasted over a week, Wren set off for her holiday in France. I didn't meet Jane when she arrived on the Friday to stay overnight in Angel's Lane before leaving with her granddaughter the following morning for the early Saturday flight from Southampton. Again no discussion was needed between Richie and me to establish that my presence there would not be a good idea, that he and I should avoid attaching questions that we didn't know how to answer.

'She's going to talk about you to Jane and the rest of the family,' he said, giving away nothing of how the idea made him feel.

'That's OK,' I said, lightly. 'I've been looking after her, it's only natural. She talks all the time about Sarah. There's nothing suspicious about that.' Which of course made it sound as if I thought there *was* something suspicious about me.

'I guess.' And he left it at that.

I said goodbye to Wren on the Thursday night. I had asked Richie if I could give her a small present to take away with her and she had chosen from Tessa's shop some egg-shaped soaps, each a different colour and scent, packaged in a real cardboard egg box. During our time together I had discovered her attachment to a babyhood toy – a tray of plastic eggs that squeaked when you pressed them into their shells. I wondered if her mother had given them to her, or if they'd played with them together. Another prized possession was an egg-shaped china dish from the swannery gift shop in which she kept special things like flower petals and sequins and the paste jewels that had come loose from her various bangles and tiaras. (The only eggs she didn't like, I was learning, were the ones Richie tried to get her to eat for breakfast.)

She was thrilled with the soaps. 'They'll be very small when I come back,' she said, 'but I won't let them wash away *for ever*. They know they live here with us.' There was something about the way she used 'us' that made me think she was including me in it, and that stirred real delight in me.

Before we parted, she asked me, 'Do you know the number one best thing about going away?'

'What?'

'Guess!' (Wren loved to get people to guess. One time, she asked me to guess which word she was thinking of and allowed no further clue beyond, 'It's in English, not French or Japanese.' Where to start with that?)

I pulled a studious face. 'Is it . . . sitting in the sun with a delicious ice cream?'

'No.'

'Is it . . . going to the seaside and—'

'No!' (Such games did not last as long as they might.)

'What then?'

She gave me an important look. 'It's how happy you are when you're together again.'

'That's a lovely thing to say, Wren. *And* it's true.'

'That's what Daddy says.'

'Well, he's right. Again.'

After she had gone, Richie drove to the Bridport site to get on with work. I knew he planned to work extra hours while she was away and didn't expect to see him at all that weekend, except perhaps on Sunday evening. It was a surprise, then, when he arrived at Tessa's house on Sunday morning.

'You are still here, then,' he remarked, when I answered the door.

'Yes.'

'It's just, when you said goodbye to Wren, I thought you might change your mind about your holiday. You could still get a flight, you know.'

I repeated the thought to myself. Russell and the boys were already in Portugal, far from reach. Had I ever been parted from all three of them by ocean before? I had a sudden glimpse of my mother's face, then, little more than a subliminal frame hidden in a film, but enough to make my breath quicken without my quite understanding why.

'No,' I said. 'I know how it looks, but I really think I would have done more harm than good if I'd gone with them. At least this way they'll be able to have some fun.'

'You think? I'm not so sure.' And he gave me a cool, direct look that was noticeably more challenging than usual. I was glad Tessa was not present to witness this exchange.

'What's in that?' I nodded to the pack on his back.

'It's a picnic.' His eyes didn't move from mine. 'Today is a day of rest, I've decided.'

'Day of rest?' I echoed. The bag was stuffed full; whatever he said, however he judged my actions, he must still have hoped I'd be here to join him and the thought caused a lurch inside me that had nothing to do with appetite. I wasn't sure if it was smothered anguish about my family far away or nerves for what might happen now we were on our own, properly free for one day. For the first time, neither of us had our children close.

'We're going to the beach,' he said. 'It's a crime you haven't been down to Abbots Bay yet.'

Just the sound of the words relaxed me. Abbots Bay was his

and Wren's favourite beach, a ten-minute drive away or a half-hour stroll along bridal paths. This was the route we chose now, just as soon as I had found my shoes and sunhat and hurried out the door after him. Without my bag, my purse, my phone, I felt like a child myself: absolutely free.

The tracks were so overgrown with grass and nettles we had to walk most of the way in single file, flies criss-crossing our faces and the heat rising with every step. My nostrils swelled with all the smells of field and soil and, behind them, the unmistakable tang of sea salt. When we finally reached the end it felt like emerging from a subterranean tunnel into open ground and I spun about, breathing deeply and letting my other senses get their bearings before I used my eyes. It was a magnificent view. The coast curved in both directions, drawing in on itself in a gentle horseshoe, and was dotted at intervals with fishermen, many of whom had pitched tents to shelter from the wind. The shore itself was a dramatically steep shelf of tiny pebbles – when you ran your fingers over them they felt perfectly smooth.

'No pillboxes,' I said to Richie. 'Do you remember?'

He nodded. 'I do. Actually there's plenty of stuff like that if you go a bit further along. Look in that direction, right in the distance, do you see?' I followed his gaze to a distant row of pale concrete cubes. 'They're from the war. They call them tank teeth.'

'You really are assimilated,' I teased. 'You'll be quoting Churchill next.'

He grinned. 'I *knew* I'd forget to pack the whisky and cigars . . .'

Despite the heat of the sun, the ocean looked forbidding: a cold grey skin stretching across the scorched stone. 'Do you ever swim here? It looks very chilly.'

He shook his head, his smile gone. 'Too rough most of the time. It's dangerous.'

I remembered Lisa then. 'I'm sorry, I didn't mean to remind you.'

He turned away. 'I know. Forget it.'

We walked for a while without speaking, before deciding on a spot for the rug, far from the fishermen, but not from the elements. The warm winds rushed past our ears to batter the hills behind us, out-voicing even the Atlantic, and the sun was high, roasting my skin where it was bare.

'This is like the fable of the Sun and the Wind,' I said, almost losing my hat. 'You don't know which is going to get your clothes off first.'

He looked at me then with a different kind of smile and I felt exactly as I had when I was sixteen, my insides turned molten, my senses tuned uniquely to his signal.

'Come on, let's eat something,' he said, at last.

We unpacked the food and uncorked the wine. As we ate, I found myself watching his hands, all calloused and grazed from his work. His face sagged with weariness; it was as though Wren's departure had increased his load, not lightened it.

'You look tired, Richie.'

'Yeah. I always seem to feel more tired when Wren *isn't* around. Some kind of weird law of parenting.'

I smiled. 'I know. It's like getting flu the first day of a holiday. The moment you relax, it attacks.' How many times had that happened to me over the years? Every trip I could remember. It occurred to me that I'd not once been physically sick since being in Millington, not even a sniffle.

'It's good to get some air, though,' Richie said. 'I'll be glad when this job is over. I'm not sure it's been worth the graft.'

'I wish I could help.' And it felt quite natural, when we had finished eating and settled back onto our elbows next to each other, that I should reach for his hand and begin squeezing it, gently rolling my thumbs over his knuckles to the fleshy ovals of his fingertips and back down to the ropes of his wrists. The rest of his body was completely motionless; I felt his eyes watching.

'That hurts,' he murmured, finally.

'I'm sorry.' When I'd finished, still holding his hand in mine,

231

I turned to look at him. His face was set with tension. 'What is it? Tell me.'

He groaned. 'Oh, Olivia. What do you think it is?'

'I don't know.' I brought my other hand over his now, pressing it between my two and feeling the roughness of his skin. Now that we were touching, it became instantly clear to me how scrupulous we'd both been until now in avoiding physical contact, even accidentally, in the passing of a wine glass or the holding open of a car door. Touch was what would alter this situation from being *my* madness and mine alone to being a shared one. Richie understood that too, I was sure of it, but what I couldn't yet tell was whether he was pleased or pained that I had made the leap for him.

'I just can't get over this feeling there's something you're not telling me,' he said, all his body's wariness in his voice. 'To do with Russell, why you left, what went on in London.'

'Nothing "went on". There was no one thing, I told you that.' And my voice sounded more persuasive than usual – not so passive and accepting as I'd become used to.

'He didn't hurt you, did he? He didn't threaten you, make it hard for you to go back in some way?'

My protest was immediate. 'Of course he didn't. Honestly, he would never do anything like that. He's a really good man, Richie, you'd like him.'

'Would I?'

'Yes.' But however I tried I couldn't construct an image that contained the two of them; it was as if they inhabited diametrically opposed edges of my brain.

'He rang Tessa, you know,' I said, still gripping his hand. I wasn't sure I could ever give it back to him. 'She told him she'd never heard of me, but he must be trying to track me down. He must be ringing all the hotels in the area.'

Richie looked unsurprised. 'Of course he is. He must be out of his mind by now, dealing with the kids and everything.'

'Please don't say that.'

He sighed. We were close enough for me to feel his breath. 'I'm sorry, but it's true. You've vanished, Olivia. You've been here for weeks, it must be a month already, and now you're missing your family summer holiday, as well. If that were me, I'd be off my head. I'd have had the police onto it a long time ago. I hope Tessa realised what she was doing when she covered for you.'

He was thinking about Lisa, not me. The mother of *his* child. He was thinking he wouldn't have let her go like this, like Russell was letting me go. I suddenly felt more profoundly than ever the sheer fluke of this summer, of today, this one free day. The only thing that had made it possible for us to be together here and now *was* Tessa's lie.

I tried to think reasonably. 'I don't think the police would get involved, would they? I'm not a missing person. I've made sure I've kept in touch so Russell knows I'm not in any danger or anything like that.'

'Maybe. But he'll still want to know the reason you're staying here so long.' Richie moved his body square to mine, causing the distance between us to shrink to a few inches. 'And I have to say, sweetheart, so do I.'

Sweetheart. The word stole my breath from me and I felt myself hesitate. But even as I did I knew it was the hesitation of a child at the top of a slide: I wasn't going to step back down again now. I was going to close my eyes and go. 'You know the reason,' I whispered.

'Do I?'

There was a sucking-in sensation between us as if we were each holding our breath and waiting to see who would exhale first. Neither of us spoke for what felt like a whole minute but was probably no longer than ten seconds. The sunlight was so intense I felt bleached, bleached to invisibility, which made it all the easier to do what I did next, which was to move my head the rest of the way to his. It was impossible to read his eyes as he squinted into the sun, but I thought I heard him swallow a groan just as our lips touched.

Once we'd started kissing we couldn't stop. The wind whipped my hair against his face, wrapping us together as we fumbled with our clothes. Bare skin, instantly goose-pimpled as it hit the air, was quickly warmed by the other's body heat and there was a faint, bony crunch of pebbles beneath our weight as we lay flat together on the rug. As he pushed himself inside me I opened my eyes wide, every millimetre of my vision filled with the blazing silver sky. For a moment I remembered this from before, not only the feel and smell and taste of him, but also the need for secrecy that had always seemed to strengthen the power our bodies held over us. Then we were both groaning and crying out and I abandoned all memory and clung to him harder than ever in the past. Moving apart, we were too dazed even to look at each other and I felt almost on the verge of blacking out. Coming to, I shaded my eyes from the sun and searched for his face. He was sitting up watching me, watching the hills behind me.

'You're there . . . I think I must have fainted for a second.'

'I have that effect on women. Swooning. You'd better come back here.' He reached out his hand and I crawled into his opened arms, gathering them tightly around me like a shawl. Now, with the sun behind us and his body shading me, I could see how gloriously blue the sky had become above the hills. The last cloud looked as if it had been pulled through with a fork, like patterned icing. We waited for our breathing to slow and then, at last, he spoke. 'You know, it's weird, but I've always found the scale of this place hard to get a hold of.'

'How d'you mean?'

'It just feels so much more epic than it is. You're lying there, eyes half-closed, and you see something moving in the distance and you think it's maybe a goat or a dog, and you open your eyes and it's a tiny bird. Everything here is always closer than you think it is.'

'Well, that sounds like the right way round to me. I hate it when you're walking forever towards something and you never actually get there.'

'Oh, I think you usually *do* get there,' he said, in a strange voice.

I turned my face to his and smiled. 'You seem a bit shell-shocked. And as you've pointed out before, I know how that feels.'

'Maybe I am.'

'Why?'

He chuckled. 'Why, she asks! Well, for starters, I'm not in the habit of sleeping with other men's wives.'

'It's only me.' My voice was a child's whisper.

'Yes. Exactly. Another man's wife.' *Or had you forgotten? We were just talking about him half an hour ago. (You'd really like him, Richie!) He's still out there, wearing your ring . . .*

'I don't feel like I'm anyone's anything,' I said, honestly. 'I know I *am*, of course, I know that's my name and my title and my position in the world, but that's not how I feel.'

Richie's face knotted. 'Well, that's kind of the problem, isn't it? *Why* don't you feel like you're supposed to? It's because you're . . .' – he searched painfully for the right word – 'you're vulnerable. I shouldn't take advantage of you. But what am I talking about? It's way too late for that. I knew this would happen.'

I gazed up at him. 'I'm not vulnerable. Not about this. I'm strong.' And in that cocooned moment I *did* feel strong, as if my only relationship in the world was the one I had with him. As if I belonged here and here alone. Again, neither of us spoke, but there was no longer any tension between us, only comfort. His face relaxed and his arms tightened: we were in this together now. 'You said for starters. What else?'

He raised his eyebrows. 'Well, there's the fact that I haven't had sex on a beach for about twenty years.'

'Well, I never have.'

'Really? Not even with me?'

I laughed. 'Don't make it quite so obvious you can't remember a single thing about what we did before.'

'Hey, I remember some things. The pill box, I remembered that, didn't I? And the first time, the little house where it rained all the time and I had to tiptoe along to your room at the back.'

'Very good,' I said approvingly. An echo, deep in my memory, of my mother talking to his father: *Well done, Warren!* I frowned, shook it clear.

'And in London, that big park we used to go to. You in your little pink bikini . . .'

'Clapham Common. And the bikini was red.' I knew all the locations, all the outfits, all the answers. I could have reconstructed that whole summer day by day, move by move. 'Did you really know this would happen?' I asked him.

He sighed. 'I had a feeling it might if you stuck around long enough.'

'So it's all down to my tenacity, is it? And there I was thinking I was being guided by the stars.'

'You're definitely being guided by *something* extra-terrestrial. I just haven't worked out what it is yet.' He stroked my hair, his blistered fingers grazing my face. 'Did *you* know it would happen?'

'Yes,' I said simply. 'I think it must be the reason I've stayed here so long. I couldn't take a step in any other direction until it did.'

There was a pause before he laughed. 'You mean you're gonna take off again now it has? You're a very funny girl. I wasn't joking about the extra-terrestrial, I seriously don't know what's going on inside your head. And I'm not sure you do, either.'

I burrowed my face into his neck, murmuring into the warm space under his chin. 'What I mean is I don't think it was ever going to be possible to spend time with you without wanting

236

this. I don't think these things die, do they? They get buried when you're not together, but they don't die.'

'Well, it's been well and truly resurrected now, hasn't it?'

I kissed him. 'I wonder if I knew right from that first day, when I walked up and you were painting the windows pink.'

I felt his throat stiffen beneath my lips. 'You mean you think seeing me again has *caused* what's going on with you?' And he shifted slightly away from me to get a clearer look at my face. 'Tell me that's not what you mean?'

'No, no, what I mean is . . . I couldn't be in my own life anymore. In London. Does that make any sense at all?'

There was a faint shake of the head. 'I think I see why you left, yes, but not why you haven't gone back.' He paused. 'Unless you're saying that if you hadn't found me you'd have turned around that first weekend and gone home like you were supposed to?'

'No,' I said, firmly, 'that's not what I'm saying. I would have stayed away wherever I went. A weekend . . . a weekend is nothing, it's not time to breathe. I really believe that.'

'Do you?'

'Yes, absolutely.' I swallowed a mouthful of air, scared suddenly of what I might say, what I might break. 'But it's not just that, Richie.'

'What? What else?'

'Us, the first time around. Because of the way it ended, I think I always needed you to want me again. It wasn't a natural ending back then, not for me. I haven't realised properly until now how it's . . . it's stayed with me all this time. Like I just said, the feelings never really went away.'

'Olivia, our relationship before was a lifetime ago.' I wondered if he sensed I was leaving out more than I was revealing. 'We're obviously both completely different people now,' he added.

You are, I thought, you've been changed by Wren and by Lisa, by your love for one and your loss of the other. They've made

237

you into the man I so wanted you to be when you were still years from becoming him. But was *I* so very different from before? Wasn't the past, for me, inseparable from this? Rather than having been transformed by life's subsequent events, hadn't I simply been held in suspension by the torment of what might have been?

The wind dropped and all at once I became aware of the sound of the sea, not a single collective sound, that roar you expected of the tide, but a thousand separate sounds from different parts of the water: the sweeping and spraying and rolling, the trickle somewhere of a single drop.

'Do you really think it's a good idea to go there again?' Richie murmured.

'No,' I said. 'Maybe we shouldn't. Not now.'

His breath was in my ear. 'Good. Because too much has happened in between. I can't think about how I was twenty-five years ago, I can't mess my head up like that.' He brushed his lips against my closed eyes, one after the other, and I could sense his exhaustion, a sad, war-torn exhaustion. 'And you shouldn't either, Dolly.'

We were kissing again, and it was then that I felt what I had not since our first summer together: hunger for another human being, compulsive hunger. Obsession. I was right: I hadn't changed. The way I was had never gone away, or at least it had always been going to return, from the moment I had taken up my mother's challenge and transported myself to Millington. I wanted to be with Richie. I wanted it more than life itself. I wanted to be close to him and be consumed by him, exactly as I had as a teenager. I'd tried to convince myself they were right, Mum and the other doubters, to convince myself that how I'd felt about him was adolescent and unreliable, that it had been in my imagination as much as my heart. But it had been real, after all.

All along, he had been in every cell of me.

Chapter 28

'Noah? *Noah?*'

Checking his watch, Russell tore himself from the early evening smoulder of the apartment terrace (never had a six-euro beer tasted so good!) and located his younger son in the boys' bedroom. After eight days of tenancy, it looked exactly as if an industrial skip of clothes and sports kit had been emptied onto the floor and left to rot. 'Didn't you hear me?'

Noah was still in his tennis kit, shins smeared with red dust from the court, dust that was now being transferred to the white bed covers as he lay watching TV. He didn't turn his head from the screen. 'No, what?'

'Your brother's half an hour late. Any idea where he is?'

'Dunno.'

'Didn't you come back from tennis together?'

Obviously not. Noah did that infuriating thing where he turned the volume of the TV up just as the other person was speaking.

'So he wasn't down at the courts with you, then?'

'Nope, I was with Finn and Rob.'

'Ah.'

Noah had made friends with a couple of other English kids in the resort, boys his own age, and it turned out Jamie was not a part of the gang. This happened every so often. Noah was more physical, he liked to mess about like boys did. In this type of environment, away from Herring's, he became more *typical* (they didn't use the word *normal* in their family; they no longer knew what normal *was*). He was quicker to conform. Russell's policy had always been to not interfere in friendships, to let the law of the jungle establish itself – if places as precisely landscaped as this lunar resort could be considered jungles.

'But he knows we're going to the grill restaurant tonight?' Russell asked, bemused. 'It was his choice.'

Noah nodded. 'Yeah, course he does.'

'OK. Well, you have your shower and start getting ready. He'll have to have his later when we get back from dinner.'

Dinner was generally an early affair here and at eight-fifteen, as the last of the families trooped beneath their balcony in the direction of the restaurants, Russell picked up the phone and dialled the manager's office. 'I think my son is missing,' he said.

The voice that came back was solicitous, but not so eager as to suggest this was the first announcement of its sort ever to have been made at the second-biggest family resort on the Algarve. 'Stay in your apartment and someone will be with you immediately.'

The man who came to the apartment was about Russell's age and instantly authoritative for being the only male he'd seen in the last ten days who was not dressed in pool shorts or golf gear. He introduced himself as the duty manager, Fabian, and he spoke English with a German accent. When he smiled it was as though his face had been forced open with some sort of tool, which was undoubtedly an all-weather physical peculiarity but in the current circumstances not at all reassuring.

'When did you last see him?' he asked Russell. He had elected not to sit when invited and so the two of them stood casually at the breakfast bar in what felt like a pastiche of a sitcom set.

'Um, at lunch. At the golf café.' It sounded so long ago, as though it were quite natural for him to abandon his children on holiday for half a day at a time.

'You did not spend the afternoon together?'

Russell shook his head. 'The boys usually do their own thing during the day, but we have a rule that we meet back here by six-thirty at the latest. They've never been more than fifteen minutes late. And now it's, what, almost nine o'clock. Something's got to be wrong.'

'Does he have a cell phone with him?' Fabian asked.

'No, his doesn't work outside the UK.'

'But he knew your dinner plans?'

'Yes. I phoned the restaurant, but he's not there. He wouldn't have gone on his own, especially not without changing out of his shorts.'

'Could he have gone down to the beach? He might have been swimming there earlier and fallen asleep?'

He might have *drowned*. 'Maybe,' Russell gulped, 'but he hasn't done that before.'

'Or might he have stopped to pick up a drink on the way back? Lost track of time?'

The time of sunset – around seven-thirty – was shown on clocks around the resort alongside large illustrations of cocktails, but for all his maturity Jamie had never shown any interest in alcohol; it was unfeasible that he would be sitting on his own in one of the bars, a sundowner on the table in front of him.

'And has he left the resort without you while you've been here?'

'No, not that I know of . . .' Suddenly all Russell could think of was the traffic. He'd seen it through the fences. Though all was calm and civilised within the resort – as well as the passing of an

241

occasional hire car or delivery van, a resort 'train' trundled along at slightly slower than walking pace – once beyond, the pace was frenetic, locals overtaking tourists in rental cars like bats out of hell. It was not hard to picture a British teenager forgetting that the traffic flowed in the opposite direction from home, that you needed to look left not right when you stepped out to cross . . .

Fabian's smile cracked open as a new solution struck him. 'Could he be having dinner with another English family and forgotten to tell you? Has he made new friends, perhaps?'

'Not that I know of. Let me ask Noah. Noah!"

Noah came sauntering in from the bedroom, bag of crisps in hand, maddeningly carefree. Russell wanted to shake him and yell, *Don't you know your brother's dead on the roadside!* He could sense his control of this situation slipping away fast.

'Has Jamie made any friends, do you know?' he asked.

Noah was blank. 'Don't think so.'

'What about the golf academy? Or the teen club thing, what's it called?'

'Young Explorers,' Fabian supplied.

Noah was obviously about to say something rude about this but miraculously remembered his manners and stopped himself, muttering only, 'He's not into stuff like that.'

That was right, Young Explorers was incredibly lame compared to the wicked stuff they'd done at Camp Able.

'He likes to read,' Russell told Fabian. 'If anything, he tends to come back early to read in the shade here.'

'OK,' Fabian said, coming to a decision. 'I am going to suggest a discreet search of the hotel grounds and the local area and then, if we do not find him, I will notify the police.'

'I'll try the beach,' Russell said, 'in case you're right and he's dropped off.' *Dropped off*; he didn't like the phrasing of that at all. 'You stay here, Noah, in case he comes back.'

Fabian reached for the phone. 'I will arrange for a babysitter to come here to your apartment.'

Noah looked ready to protest this indignity, but Russell gave him a silencing look. It was non-negotiable; the last thing he needed was both of them going missing.

The beach was virtually empty, with just the very last of the Portuguese packing up their belongings (they sensibly came to swim in the evening when it was cooler) and the children of diners at the beach bar who had broken loose to play in the sand below. Russell made straight for a promising silhouette of teenagers clustered against the cliffs, but Jamie's was not among the guilty faces that turned his way when he got close enough to see the bottles of Superbok in their hands. If he'd just slipped out for an underage beer, how happy the world would be!

He returned via the main entrance, unable to stop himself from walking out and patrolling the pavements for a few minutes, even though he knew Fabian had already sent out hotel cars in both directions. At every moment he expected to see the flashing lights and tell-tale ring of spectators that indicated an accident, a casualty. Seeing a low wall in front of him he sank onto it, his bodyweight at last too heavy for him to carry.

'Do *you* get this?' Olivia asked him once, 'this weird rushing through your head?'

He looked at her, worried. 'What, you mean like a pain?'

She gave her head a vigorous shake, as if something was stuck inside and if she could only loosen it she could show him physically what she meant. 'No, I mean thoughts, worries, kind of like worst-case scenarios?'

'Worst-case scenarios about what?'

'Everything. But mainly the boys.'

'Like what?'

Her brow puckered, the only expression that could make her look like her brother. 'Well, like I'll imagine they're crossing the road and a van's coming too quickly and it swerves to avoid Jamie and it kills Noah instead, and Jamie will never recover because of the guilt . . . so in effect both their lives are over. And in a split-second our whole family has been destroyed for ever. And the driver is probably a hit and run and won't ever be caught and even if we find him and punish him, *we*'ll be the ones to go to jail, not him. Then we'll lose our house as well as our family and prison will be so appalling we won't even recognise each other when we come out and we wouldn't be able to look at each other again anyway because of everything we remind each other of.'

It seemed to Russell that she said all of this in a single breath. 'Yeah, stuff like that,' she added.

He hesitated before replying. He wanted to say that the hit-and-run bit would never happen because Jamie would have memorised the number plate – he'd only need a quick glance for it to stick – but that was clearly an inappropriate response. She'd only turn it around so it was Jamie being run over and the less photographically accurate Noah standing watching. 'Um, sure, of course. All parents worry, don't they? It's only natural.'

He wasn't sure, though. His worries tended to be to do with specific physical problems, like what he was going to do about the crack in the kitchen wall, or, if it was about the boys at all, then something like how all their computer games might be damaging their eyesight. Not hypothetical stuff like this. What Olivia was describing sounded like a terrible waste of energy. It sounded exhausting.

Russell spoke urgently into the phone. 'Olivia, you need to phone me now! Call me back as soon as you possibly can!'

For good measure, and with some fumbling, he sent a text:

Olivia! Emergency
situation! Phone me
ASAP!

The bad news was she didn't phone. She didn't phone, even with *this*.

The good news was that Jamie was found. Just before midnight one of Fabian's security team picked him up on the road to Portimao. He had nothing with him, not even a bottle of water, which suggested a spur-of-the-moment bolt rather than a premeditated escape. All Russell could think once he was satisfied his son was safe and untouched was how much older he looked than he had at lunchtime. It was as if he'd departed a child and returned a young adult, someone who would soon leave his parents' charge altogether and go and do things of his own in the world.

'What were you trying to do?' Russell asked, when they were finally alone. 'Were you trying to hitch somewhere?'

Jamie's face didn't flicker. 'Nah, just walking.'

'But where to? Surely you weren't trying to get all the way to Portimao? That's almost twenty kilometres away!'

Silence.

'You could have been killed on that road, Jamie. It's easy to forget the cars are going the other way. Foreign kids get caught out all the time.'

'I'm not a kid.'

'It doesn't matter, the drivers don't care how old you are. Some of them are maniacs.'

Jamie shrugged. 'It's not that bad.'

'And where were you planning on sleeping, exactly?' He prepared himself for some smart-arse answer, like how Jamie had learned SAS survival skills at Camp Able and knew how to make a hammock from the skin of a grass snake and his own shoe laces, but he didn't get one.

'I don't know,' Jamie admitted, and that scared Russell much, much more.

He would say so little about his adventure that Russell accepted he was going to have to give up and try again in the morning. He'd insist both boys have a lie in and then he'd organise something special for them for breakfast. They would have a family talk.

Then, as Jamie was in the doorway headed for the bedroom, he suddenly turned back and asked Russell a question: 'Did you ring Mum?'

Russell paused, thinking as quickly as his exhausted brain would allow. Over four hours had passed since his call and Olivia had not been in touch. Surely it was better for Jamie to think she had not been alerted in the first place than to know that she had and yet had not been able to – had not *chosen* to – respond. 'No,' he lied.

'Why not?'

'Because I knew I'd find you. I didn't want to worry her. Now promise me you will go to bed and not disappear again.'

But Jamie just stood there, not reacting. 'It was her birthday today,' he said at last.

The news – for he had not remembered himself, *she* was the one who remembered birthdays – would have had a greater impact on Russell had he not been utterly flattened by the more life-threatening events of the evening. Olivia's birthday. Since they'd been married they'd never spent a birthday apart – another one of her golden family rules inspired by memories of Maggie's absenteeism. Twin bubbles of regret and anger burst in his brain before disappearing again without trace. There was simply no longer room. 'I don't suppose she's been celebrating herself,' he told Jamie, gently, 'but if you like we can try to phone her tomorrow and wish her happy birthday?'

Jamie neither nodded nor shook his head. He looked numb.

Russell placed a palm on his son's back, gave it a little rub. 'Hey, mate, you'll probably find she's phoned or texted you on your mobile today. When we get back to London you'll have a whole ton of messages waiting for you.'

He'd been careful until now not to make promises like that,

but tonight was different. He would say anything to reassure his son that his mum loved him.

'Come on, you're shattered. Into bed.'

He turned off the lights and positioned himself on the sofa between the locked terrace doors and the bolted front entrance; there was no way he was going to sleep tonight. He did nod off, eventually, of course. If there were resort clocks to record the time of sunrise too, then that was probably about the time that he succumbed. As he lost consciousness, Jamie's words repeated in his head: Did you ring Mum? Did you ring Mum? And then his own voice, not an answer, but only another question: Where are you, Olivia? Why didn't you phone back?

Why aren't you here?

Chapter 29

Not everyone knows about Richie and me, only the select few who we *want* to know. Being adult and illicit like this, it's so different from anything I've experienced before. I wonder if this is what it feels like to be an understudy when the lead actress falls ill. You know all the words, you just never thought you'd get the chance to speak them.

'So,' Dean says, 'you and Richie. Cool.'

We are in the garden at Dad's with Amy Jukes. She's been a permanent fixture since we came back from the coast and everyone likes her – even Mum. A ghettoblaster is playing a tape borrowed from Richie in his absence; he's been dragged off to the Tower of London – free tickets, apparently, through Mum's new boss, but since she's working for the local electricity board no one really believes that.

'Nice work,' Amy says, eyeing me with new respect. 'He's delish.'

'What's *delish*?' Dean asks, mockingly.

She gives him a womanly smirk. 'It means delicious. But don't worry, no one would ever use it to describe *you*.'

He winks. 'I'll remember you said that.'

'I just wish Mum wouldn't try to ruin it,' I say, nonchalantly. 'She's *obsessed* with keeping us apart. It's pathetic.'

Amy nods. 'It's not going to work, either. You'd have thought they'd know that by forbidding it they're only making it more attractive. I mean, it's *so* basic. Can't they remember what it's like to be young?'

'God, no, that's *way* too long ago,' Dean says, with contempt.

'Anyway,' I say, 'they haven't forbidden it, not officially.' I remember a phrase Mum used when I was little and struggling at school. She'd blamed the teachers. 'Don't let them nip you in the bud, Dolly. It's your life, not theirs.' 'They're just trying to nip it in the bud,' I tell Amy, squinting moodily into the distance, 'but it's my life, not hers.'

'Exactly,' she agrees. '*You* decide who you want to go out with.'

I marvel for a moment at the idea that I am 'going out' with Richie.

'She should just let you guys have your fun while you can,' Dean says. 'What's it to her? It's not like you're bonking *Warren*.'

'Eeww!' Amy and I squeal together.

'And he goes back at the end of the month, anyway, it's not like he's here forever and you're going to get *married*.' Dean's assumption is that our relationship will not last beyond Richie's return to California. He isn't being callous; he just doesn't know how I feel. He doesn't know that for me this is a life-changing love, a life-*starting* love.

Nor, apparently, does Dean notice the look Amy sends his way, an uncertain blend of amusement and hurt that I don't pick up on myself until I realise how hard she's trying to cover it up. Of course! She's relating all of this to them, to *their* holiday 'thing'. Like Richie, she is off to college next term, in her case to Durham University, to halls of residence and formal dinners and three-legged pub crawls. I watch as she pokes Dean in the ribs with her toes and begins to sing 'Summer Nights' from *Grease*. She has a really good voice and hits the notes sweetly.

'Oh, you and Richie,' she sighs afterwards, as if it's me she's been serenading and not my brother. 'You're just like Sandy and

Danny, aren't you? You'll have to follow him out there, Olivia, join the Pink Ladies, win him over with a raunchy new look. Do you have any black leather trousers?'

'I could always find some. Maybe in Maggie's wardrobe?' And we giggle and squeal again.

'Oh, give it a rest, you two,' Dean says, lazily. 'Can't we just listen to the tape and forget all that romantic shit.'

He turns up the volume on Richie's imported synth rock, but Amy gets her own back by launching into 'This Charming Man' right over the top of it.

It is not until the day before Richie leaves that we formally agree to keep in touch. We're in my room at Dad's, underwear off but clothes on in case of any surprise interruptions, and we're talking about the Christmas break. He's coming back to England again, he says, if Warren agrees to stump up the airfare.

'Richie, that's fantastic!'

'We should hook up again,' he says, fingers stroking my back, 'this has been *really* good.'

I am totally elated. It's like he's drawn a rainbow between us and no matter how far he goes from me the rainbow will stretch to reach him.

'I love you,' I whisper into his hair, the first time I've said it to him, to anyone.

He looks mildly amused. 'That's cool.' And then he bows his head again, lips reapplied to my breasts, and in a single moment the rainbow has snapped.

'You mean you don't love me?' I demand, squirming from his grip.

'Course I do.' He speaks so easily, fingers still stroking. He kisses my lips. 'Look at you. How could I not?'

And the colours are in the sky again, soaring upwards through the blue.

*

The next morning I walk through pale dawn streets to join the official line-up for family goodbyes. Warren is driving Richie to Gatwick alone – he has too much gear for anyone else to be able to fit in the car. Though I've allowed a whole half hour to walk the ten minutes' distance between the two houses, I'm horrified to find I'm only just in time. Warren is loading the luggage and Richie is out on the kerb with Mum and Dean.

Mum sees me first. 'Dolly!' she exclaims, brightly. 'We didn't know you'd be coming to see Richie off.'

I bet you didn't, I think. Since Richie is unbothered by such details as flight times, it was she who 'confirmed' his departure time to me when I asked earlier in the week.

I can't get Richie's attention straight away because Mum and Warren are instructing him on what he'll need to check in and what he might be able to cram in the overhead lockers (Mum talks so knowledgably on the subject you'd think she was moon-lighting as an air hostess). He's wearing jeans, tour T-shirt and a battered grey denim biker jacket, the wires of his Walkman already in place. I just stand there, memorising the sight of him, eager for a parting secret look, a last stolen kiss.

'Wow,' Richie says, when Mum hands him a gift-wrapped package. 'Thank you, Maggie.'

'It's nothing, sweetheart. We'll really miss you.' And she has tears spilling onto her cheeks as she hugs him. Anyone would think she was the one in love with him.

Dean says, 'All right, sucker? See you for Christmas – or whenever you're allowed back in the country. Never, probably.'

'Oh, we'll tempt him back,' Mum says. 'Don't you worry.' She produces her camera and starts taking pictures of him. I think of the farewells we have missed out on, Dean and I, the times we learned she had left only from the stricken look on Dad's face. Where were *our* final photos and special gifts? Where were *our* reassurances that it was not goodbye but *au revoir*?

I'm the last to get to him. For the sake of appearances, he

gives me brotherly squeeze and a chaste little peck on the cheek, but at the last moment, barely out of sight of the others, he presses his tongue against the corner of my mouth and whispers, 'I'm gonna miss you, baby.'

'I'll write tonight,' I whisper back. I'm already composing the sentences in my head.

Then all at once the last bag is pressed into the boot, the engine is running, Warren and Mum are discussing directions through the rolled-down window, and they are gone.

After a decent period of watching and waving, Mum hustles Dean and me indoors with the promise of bacon and eggs. I am welcome at the breakfast table again, it seems; presumably I can have my room back now, too. As I pass by I give her a long, steady look, a look that says, *I know you gave me the wrong time, I know you wanted me to miss him. But it didn't work, did it?*

She looks back at me, mother's smile intact but eyes empty. Then, reaching to pull the front door shut behind us, she spots a rain cloud coming in low overhead. 'Don't like the look of that sky,' she says.

Chapter 30

Even before we set off back to the cottage from Abbots Bay I had reconciled myself to the knowledge that I would never feel like this again. So removed from the rest of the world, so unmindful of it, and yet still so *full*. Today's joy had happened in a vacuum, on the water's edge of a parallel planet, and the fact that I knew I didn't deserve it made it all the more fragile. Maybe, in time, I would lose all memory of it.

But for now came something almost as special: the afterglow, the real rediscovery of each other. We couldn't stop touching; even in the tiny house on Angel's Lane, a room apart was still too far. When it came to night time I knew I would not be returning to my attic room at the top of the village. I left a message for Tessa, relieved she didn't pick up the phone and break the long stretch of Richie and me on our own, talking only to each other. If I thought about it, it was probably the longest we had ever been alone together.

That night we did what I had not done with Russell for years and years: lay in bed together and talked until dawn, one of those limitless, meandering conversations in which an account of a five-minute event can last three hours while whole years get dismissed in a single sentence, maybe altogether.

He was still careful about Russell and the children but asked me about the rest of my family, my father, the last time I'd seen them. Inevitably I was reminded of Mum's funeral, the eulogy Dad had given.

'It was sweet the way he remembered those stories. I mean, he didn't just do it for Mum, he did it for Dean and me, in case we'd forgotten that there *were* good times. Funny little moments that he must have known had become outnumbered by the bad times.'

A reading book of Wren's on the armchair by the bedroom window reminded me of one story in particular, the one about the bedroom ceiling falling in, but not the sky. 'When I was little and something went wrong, Mum used to say, "Come on, Chicken Licken, it's not as if the sky's fallen down."' Later she had dropped the Chicken Licken, but the sentiment remained the same. 'She was very matter-of-fact, you know: "Come on, get up, you'll get over it!" She was never the kind of mother who got all gushing and soothing and wanted to kiss things better.'

'Not like my mom,' said Richie, with amused distaste. 'Even now, she grabs me like I'm five years old.'

'I'm more like that, too,' I smiled. 'And it's ironic because I was the kind of daughter who needed the kissing better, while Jamie and Noah just need the "Get over it".'

'Maybe you're looking at it the wrong way,' Richie said. 'Maybe you only needed it because you didn't get it, whereas they don't need it because they trust completely that they'd get it.'

I smiled. 'I'd forgotten how much I like your way of thinking.'

He played slowly with the fingers of my left hand, minutely exploring the knuckles and the nails as if identifying unknown objects in a game of blindfold. 'So what were all these crimes of Maggie's, anyway? You've never really told me.'

'How long have you got?' I said, darkly.

He motioned to the shadowed skies through the uncovered window. 'Apparently all night.'

256

'OK. Well . . .' I exhaled a long puff of air before beginning. 'You know about her leaving us when we were kids, of course. There must have been six or eight times before she went to the States and met your dad. She got back together with Dad again later, but she changed her mind again around the time I left home myself. I hated her for doing that. Suddenly Dad went from it being the three of us, with just Dean gone, to being left on his own. It ruined that first term for me, knowing he was completely alone. And Dean was studying abroad at the time, so he wasn't around to go home for weekends. I was convinced the timing was deliberate on her part, so I could be made to share the blame.

'Then, when I finished college, she missed my graduation cer- emony – she'd managed to make it to Dean's, but then she missed his wedding. We used to joke that she should just have had one child, because she went to most things *once*. We were so used to it by then, though, it had stopped bothering us so much, but then she started doing the same thing with our children and it all flared up again. If we hadn't turned against her we would have turned on each other, because you couldn't help feeling a bit competitive about it. Whose christening, Jamie's or Isobel's? Whose first birthday party, Noah's or Connie's? Whose house for Christmas? And of course there were in-laws to compare her with, which didn't help. It was over three months before she came to see Jamie when he was born, when Russell's mother had been on our doorstep practically before we got back from the hospital. Over three months! Her first grandchild! I was so embarrassed and ashamed.'

'Maybe she was struggling with the idea of being a grandma?' Richie said.

'Maybe she was struggling with the idea of being a *mother*?' And I sounded so bitter, just like Dean. Such a honed and fluent chronicle of her wrongdoings – there could no mistaking how often I must have repeated it in the past.

257

'Come on,' Richie said, gently. 'Isn't it possible to forget all of that now?'

'With you, here, yes, it is.' I adjusted myself so that his head was resting on my chest bone and I could comfortably cradle it. 'Oh, Richie, you're so much better than me at forgetting the past. I wish I had that ability. It really is a gift, and only some of us are lucky enough to have it. But no matter how much time goes by, I keep things alive in my head. I can't stop myself!' But even as I spoke I saw how out of date that notion was, for hadn't I done exactly what I claimed to envy in him? Forgotten, forgotten my own family. It was a memory slip that eclipsed any that he himself had suffered. And if not a gift, then it was certainly rare.

But I wasn't forgetting, I told myself, I was . . . I didn't know what the word was . . . *protecting*, perhaps. I was protecting my family from me, from this unreliable, half-hearted version of myself. No, that was wrong now, as well, now I'd given myself whole-hearted to someone else. I'd never felt *so* whole-hearted. All at once I heard Russell's question, 'Are you alone?' And the remorse in his voice afterwards, because he hadn't planned to accuse me, he'd just got carried away with the moment. He'd never suspected me of betraying him, and yet here I was, in bed with another man, pouring out my hostilities about Maggie in just the same way I had when he and I had first been together. And I felt something then for him, something real and recognisable and long overdue: guilt. Not a violent stab as it was supposed to come, but more a picking at my seams with a sharp pair of scissors.

'You know, it's not such a bad thing to keep stuff alive,' Richie was saying, his breath damp on my skin. 'That's what I tell Wren all the time about her mom. Thinking about her every day keeps her alive.'

'But she's a child. That's the right thing for a child to do. It's her mother, she didn't have her in her life for very long and it's right that you help her keep the connection.'

He ran his fingers over the curve of my hip, his touch causing a response deep in my groin. 'And maybe it's right that you're thinking about *your* mother so much, even if it does mean processing the bad stuff.'

I sighed. 'A part of me wants to forget about her altogether, if only I could let myself. I think I hoped that's what would happen when she died. I'd finally be free of it, all the resentment, the grudges . . .' My mind sped ahead, making links, links that in this hyper-real place I existed with Richie felt like epiphanies. 'Richie, don't you think it's weird how I'm able to behave as if I have no responsibilities, no other family, and yet I can't stop talking about *her*? It must be because our relationship was based on something besides love. There must have been something wicked to it.'

'You don't mean that,' Richie said, fingertips still caressing.

'I do mean it! When I think all about the bad times in my life, she's always been there, always involved.' Flustered, I slid from his touch, propping myself onto my elbow.

He peered at me through the thickening dark. 'You don't mean involved in making the bad things happen? That doesn't make any sense at all!'

'Maybe it's more that she just *made* things go wrong without trying.'

'Or it just seemed that way. She was actually there at those times because she knew you needed her, she just didn't know how to help.'

I shook my head. This time his way of thinking was a long way wide of the mark. 'I wish that were true, but it's not what happened. Ever. You know, in a way it's a good thing that she missed so many celebrations – the birthdays and everything. If she'd turned up she might have turned them sour, stopped them from being such happy occasions.'

As ever with my mother – and one thing had *not* changed – my brain would reach a point of near combustion, the point at which I *had* to stop thinking about her before I screamed, however unresolved my thoughts. For years I'd tried to squeeze her into a smaller space, to reshuffle her lower and lower in the pack of life's worries, but I'd never achieved it. Only here in Millington, with Richie, had I come close to succeeding – until now, until I finally shared my deck with Richie, only to find that the first card I turned over had her face on it.

'Let's talk about something else,' I whispered. 'Tell me about Lisa. I don't know anything about her. What was she like? Was she a lot like Wren?'

I heard his smile in his voice. 'In some ways, yes. She was great. She was very . . . determined.'

'Determined about what?'

'Determined about what she wanted.'

'And she wanted you?'

'Among other things. And I wanted her too. At least I realised that eventually. I suppose that was when I finally grew up, the day I worked out that there wasn't that one moment where you suddenly love someone, like in the movies. It's like Wren growing. One day she's so high and the next she's this bit higher. No one saw it happen, but the point is that it did.'

I could no longer make out the features on his face as he told me what had happened. He had met Lisa in his mid-twenties when he was travelling around Australia. They were working in the same town in Queensland and had ended up joining forces to tour New Zealand. After the trip had finished and they'd both returned home she'd shown up on his doorstep where he was living in San Francisco and said, 'How about I hang out for a while and we see what happens?' But Richie had said no. He couldn't explain why he'd done it, other than he'd just thought it might get awkward and ruin the great memories they had of the trip. Then she'd gone away again and he'd realised he'd made the biggest mistake of his life, so he'd come to England to find her again. He'd tracked her down to an office in Southampton, waited outside the building at the end of the day. When she came out he walked up to her and said, 'How about I hang out *here* for a while instead and we see what happens?'

'If you said yes the first time around, you might still be in the States,' I said.

'Yep. And Wren would be a California girl.'

He told me that it had taken over ten years to conceive her. No child had been more wished for. She'd been determined into life. Silently I thought what he must have thought a thousand times over: if they hadn't had their struggles, if Wren had come sooner, then Lisa would have had more time with her daughter, a greater stake, a surer love. And even though I couldn't see his eyes in the dark my fingers touched the wet on his face.

Forty-eight hours after leaving Tessa's that blissful August Sunday, I finally returned home from Angel's Lane. As I slipped through the front door and up the stairs, she came out of the kitchen and stood in the hallway, calling up after me in unconscious but obvious mimicry of some earlier stand-off with the teenage Amanda.

'Your phone's been ringing up there . . .'

'Sorry,' I called back over my shoulder. 'I hope it didn't bother you. I'll go and check it now.'

'Is everything all right?'

'Yes, thank you. I hope you got my message that I was staying at Richie's house?'

'I did, yes . . .'

Whatever she said next I didn't hear because I was in my room with my phone in my hands, staring at the first words of a message from Russell:

Emergency situation!

Reading the full text, my body went liquid with terror. My first and only thought was the boys: something bad had happened. I dialled my voicemail, at the same time searching my brain for the

261

name of the hotel in the Algarve. Why couldn't I remember it? What the hell was wrong with me? Next thing, Russell's frantic voice was in my ear: 'Call me back as soon as you possibly can!'

Fumbling with the keys, I dialled his mobile number, but was diverted after a single ring to his message service. 'Russell, I've just got your messages! What's happened? Please call me. *Please*.'

For a wild, instinctive moment I reached for my handbag, thoughts of the train station, the airport, a dash to wherever they were, but my body buckled under me and I dropped the bag, clutching at the edge of the bed to break my fall. Breathing heavily, I forced myself to sit upright as I checked the details of the voicemail: nine o'clock, Sunday night. It was now Tuesday morning. There had been three further missed calls from Russell since he left his desperate message, all on that same evening, but no second voicemail and no follow-up texts. If anything serious had happened he would surely have phoned yesterday as well, again and again until I picked up.

But thirty-six hours I'd been out of contact! And even if I had thought to take my phone with me, there would have been no signal in the cottage in Angel's Lane, so I still wouldn't have noticed the calls. Would I have been dutiful enough to leave Richie's bed for the ten-minute pilgrimage to the village car park to pick up a signal? I knew the answer to that only too well.

All that time I'd spent complaining to Richie about Maggie, listing her crimes one after the other, but the terrifying truth was right here in the missed call details in front of me: I was no better.

Then, in little more than the time it could have taken him to listen to my message, Russell sent a new text:

False alarm, all fine,
on way home.

I didn't know which it was for – the confirmation that my family was safe or the removal of any need for me to leave Richie – but the relief was so forceful it knocked me flat onto my back. I lay on the bed, body depleted but mind alive, trying to understand what had just happened in my head. Had the news been bad – whether it involved one of the boys or Russell himself – *would* I have gone? Had the terror I had just felt really been for them, or had it been for myself? For Richie and me? Reaching once more for my bag, I pulled out the passport-sized school photos of Jamie and Noah I kept in my purse, staring hard at the faces that were dearer to me than my own life. But all I felt was mild curiosity, as though I were examining clues found on the corpse of someone I'd never met.

This was all wrong.

I tapped out a text to Russell:

Phone when you can.
I'm worried.

But when I read it back it sounded trite, much too little much too late, and I deleted it without sending. In any case, he beat me to it:

Please don't contact
us again unless you
are ready to tell us
where you are.

I looked at the words for a long time. I noted his use of 'us' rather than 'me'. And then, as the relentless mill of my thoughts brought them back around to my mother, I told myself again:

You are no better.

PART THREE

'Swans are normally very placid creatures, but they are very strong and can use their wings to good effect when defending themselves.'
    Royal Society for the Protection of Birds

Chapter 31

'Oh-li-vi-a!' Wren's voice rose excitedly from the kitchen doorway until it reached a full-blown squeal. 'Oh-li-vi-a! We've got a surprise for you!'

The cake was made of three higgledy-piggledy layers of chocolate and cream and sloped at a good twenty-degree angle. Mini eggs had been procured out of season and were arranged in a nest made of Shredded Wheat. In the middle of this was a candle, its flame swerving from side to side as Wren wobbled across the room towards the sofa where I sat. At the last minute, Richie swooped from behind, his arms appearing on either side of her to guide the plate safely onto the coffee table.

I leaned forward to take a closer look. 'Wow! This is amazing! What did I do to deserve this?'

'It's your birthday cake,' she announced, breathless from her exertions. 'Do you like it? I made it! Do you like my cake?'

I pulled her to me and planted a kiss on the top of her head. 'I *love* it, it's fantastic! I had no idea you were such a talented baker.'

'They're not real eggs, you know,' she said, lest I misunderstand. 'In the nest. They've actually got chocolate inside.'

'Ah, probably just as well,' I agreed, smiling up at Richie. I wanted to hug him, too, but we were careful not to touch in front of Wren.

Then the two of them sang 'Happy Birthday' to me, Wren's face as solemn as a chorister's, Richie's twitching with suppressed amusement.

'Thank you, this is very kind. Actually, my birthday was two weeks ago, but that doesn't matter. It makes this even more of a surprise.'

'Bugger,' Richie said under his breath, then, checking Wren hadn't heard, 'I couldn't remember the exact date. August, that's as far as I got.'

Since I had not mentioned the occasion to either of them, or anyone else in Millington, this could only mean he'd been thinking of the only birthday we had shared before: my sixteenth. For me, the details were as clear as his were hazy: a cake made by Maggie, my childhood favourite of vanilla sponge with cherry jam, and squirts of the fluffy fake cream we all loved (Dean used to put the nozzle into his mouth and blast it straight from the can). Sixteen red-and-white striped candles; I'd had to blow three times to put them out.

'I think your birthday must have been when I was in France with Grandma,' Wren said, with all the confidence of one who understands that every cake-eating occasion must take place in her presence.

'I think it was, yes.' In fact it had been the day Richie and I had gone to Abbotts Bay, a symmetry so perfect I hadn't breathed a word for fear of tainting it. Nor had I reported to him what had happened afterwards: the emergency messages from Russell, the news of a false alarm, the request for me not to phone again. No, with Wren away in France, Richie would only have done exactly what he'd previously threatened: taken me home himself. And if I knew anything at all in those first days of our being together again it was that leaving – leaving *him* – was unthinkable. Besides, once I'd recovered from the shock of it all I'd made a level-headed deduction of my own. Of course! Russell's call had been made on the Sunday, my birthday. *That* was why he had needed to get in touch with me so urgently. He'd wanted to wish me happy birthday, no more, no less. That hour of raw panic I'd felt at Tessa's looked to me now like a tornado witnessed from a great distance, already twisting out of view towards someone else.

But now Russell did not want to speak to me at all. I had lost his good will, I understood that, and his refusal to acknowledge my further attempts at contact was no more than I deserved. True to his word, he had blocked each of my calls and ignored every one of my texts. Even the Sterling Avenue line went unanswered. Once, when I phoned him at the office from Tessa's landline, he was tricked into taking my call, but the moment he knew it was me he said simply, 'Are you going to tell me where you are? Yes or no?' and when I admitted I was not, he ended the call without another word.

I had phoned the boys on their mobiles, leaving messages I wasn't confident they would pick up any time soon, knowing as I did that they used their phones almost solely for texting. 'I'm sorry I wasn't with you on holiday,' I said, 'I hope we can speak soon. I really miss you.' I had to fight to keep the despair from my voice and, terrified I had failed, hung up with the hope that they *wouldn't* ever hear it. I knew Russell would be discouraging them from contacting me, to safeguard them from me, just as my father had once safeguarded Dean and me from Maggie. In my heart, I knew I would probably have done the same.

'I *love* birthdays,' Wren was saying in her happy little singsong. 'When will it be *mine*? How many more days, Daddy?'

Richie considered. 'About another two hundred and eighty, but don't worry, angel, there are lots of exciting things happening between now and then. Like Halloween and Christmas and Easter.'

She pincered a chocolate egg from the top of the cake and slipped it into her cheek. 'And can we go and see Olivia in London soon? That would be an exciting thing.'

269

Richie and I exchanged a look. 'If she's back in London, yes,' he said, smoothly. 'If she invites us.'

'Brilliant. Oh! Can we all go and see *The Lion King*? Did you know *Chas* has seen it?' She spoke as though this were totally against the natural order of things and Richie and I laughed, relieved she'd not probed any further. Even a second question might have been enough to stump us.

'Now,' Richie said, 'are we going to cut this cake? D'you want to do the honours, Olivia?'

'Yes please.' I picked up the knife.

'Can we take a photo first?' Wren begged. 'For my special album?'

Thanks to a new printer – a present from Grandma Jane – the picture was printed out in colour and pinned to the wall above the desk before the first slices of cake had been finished. There we were, Wren and I, sitting arm in arm, the cake in front of us angled in such a way that it looked as if it might slide into the camera lens at any second.

It was odd to see a photograph of myself in Richie's house. Not odd because it looked out of place, but odd because it didn't.

It was soon after this belated birthday celebration that Tessa asked me outright about my past – or as outright as she was ever going to get. What she actually said was, 'I've been meaning to ask you, would you like to borrow some clothes?', but the look on her face made it clear she saw the subject as a gateway to larger truths.

'*Clothes*?' A couple of times I'd noticed her inspecting my tiny laundry pile with a bewildered air; it was a justifiable enough reaction. I had three changes of clothes in my possession and had been alternating them, changing only when something was obviously muddy and marked. I hadn't bought a single new item since coming here and the only time I'd dressed differently was

270

when I'd stayed at Angel's Lane and worn a shirt or a T-shirt of Richie's around the house. Otherwise it was the same jeans, the same tops, the same single green sweater every day.

'It's strange how few things you have. Not just clothes, *everything*.' But Tessa's eyes were less bold than her tone; they were, if anything, injured. She didn't want to have to pry like this: she wanted me to tell my story of my own accord.

'Thanks for the offer,' I said, 'but I'm fine. I really don't need much. And I've got my mac if the weather breaks.'

She looked me up and down in fresh appraisal, hardly necessary since the jeans, white vest top and sandals must have been as familiar to her as they were to me. 'It's just that everything looks a bit big for you. You must have lost weight since you've been here.'

'Maybe.'

Another disappointed pause. She tried again. 'Perhaps there's something of Amanda's you could wear? She's very slim. I could look in her wardrobe for you? I'm sure she wouldn't mind.'

The irony of my dressing in a teenager's clothes as I relived my teenage love affair was not lost on me and the chuckle came out before I could stop it. 'It's very kind of you,' I smiled, 'but, honestly, this is all I need.'

Now Tessa looked as though she thought I might be laughing at her and I felt ashamed, eager to give a little more. 'You know, it's an interesting exercise in a way, seeing how little you can manage with. None of us needs half the things we have.'

But this only appeared to confirm her worst suspicions. 'So where are the rest of your things, then? Can't you get to them?'

'They're back in London,' I said.

There was a silence as we looked at each other, and then she said, 'I can't imagine your life in London.'

I didn't know what to say. I certainly couldn't give the answer that came into my head: in London I was heavy, and it was nothing to do with how much I weighed or how many layers of clothes I wore. It was a heaviness so profound that I could only hope I'd never be dropped in deep water, because if I was I knew for sure I wouldn't be able to make it to dry land. What would Tessa say to *that*?

'I don't want you to imagine it,' I said, in the end.

'You don't ever talk about it,' she said, simply. 'It can be such a good thing to pour it all out, especially to someone who doesn't know any of the other people in your life. It might help you.'

I thought of the counsellor at my GP's practice in London who had used exactly those words when I'd gone to see her. She'd said I should see our time as 'talking therapy'. And so I had talked; I had described my feelings just as I felt them. But it made no difference, because my feelings were all questions and she didn't have any of the answers. There had seemed no point in returning for more.

'I do talk,' I said, 'I talk to Richie. He's been a really good friend.' Again, I wished I could say more; she was so obviously hurt and puzzled by my refusal to trust her, despite all the kindnesses she'd shown me. I didn't blame her; how could she possibly know how complicated this was, that as much as I feared her disapproval of my actions, I equally couldn't bear to burden her with the knowledge of them?

To my great relief she appeared to have given up. 'And I don't suppose you've got any idea yet how much longer you'll be wanting the room?'

'No. I still haven't made any decisions about my next move. But I know Amanda's back—'

'Second week in September,' she supplied, promptly. She was counting down the days, wishing them gone, which gave me a wretched, guilty feeling because I was doing the opposite. I wanted to prolong them, to preserve them for ever.

I turned to leave. I was expected at Angel's Lane and could feel the pleasure any prospect of seeing Richie and Wren stirred in me. 'Well, I promise you'll be the first to know when I've decided what I'm doing next.'

She followed me to the front door, watching as I pulled on my jumper. 'It'll be September soon. You'll need something warmer for autumn, a jacket.'

Was it my imagination or was there something in her voice that implied she didn't think we'd get that far?

'What do you tell them about me?' I asked Richie, when we alone that evening.

'What do I tell who?'

'The people in the village. Tessa and Sarah. Anyone who asks.'

He shrugged. 'I don't tell them anything. Sarah's been a bit nosy, you can't blame her for that, but I just say if they've got any questions they should ask you themselves.'

As if it's too horrible to be owned by anyone but me, I thought. 'So they do have questions then?' I persisted.

Richie sighed. 'Olivia, if you're getting people to lie for you, then sooner or later you're going to have to expect to give something back, don't you think?'

'Don't say that, you make it sound like . . .' I broke off, unwilling to spell it out. *A deliberate deception.* And wasn't it? If it hadn't been at first, then it surely was now. '. . . something it's not,' I finished, uncertainly.

'Well, maybe that's because I still don't know what it *is*, eh?' He kissed me, as adept as I was at changing the mood, if not at evading reality. I knew I was putting him in an impossible situation: torn between his sympathy for those I'd deserted and his enjoyment of having me here with him to share his evenings, share his bed.

There was another kiss then, this one almost painfully hard and I put my fingers to my lips. 'That hurt!'

'I know.'

'Why?'

'Because you're driving me crazy with this double life of yours! No wonder no one around here knows what to think, Olivia, you're making it so much weirder than it needs to be!'

I fell silent, more scolded by his words than by the kiss.

'Anyway,' he said, 'forget Sarah and Tessa. I'm more concerned about what I should be telling Wren. She's getting very attached.'

'So am I,' I said.

'This is what happens,' he said, his blue gaze unblinking. 'This is the danger.'

I nodded. 'What *have* you told her?'

'I've told her you're here for the summer.'

'OK. Well, that's true, isn't it?'

He kissed me again, this time sweetly, tenderly. 'Yes, it is. But at some point we're going to run out of time. You do realise that, don't you?'

'Yes.' But my answer was not a willing one.

Chapter 32

'All set for the party tomorrow?' Duncan asked Russell, as the two rode the lift together to their twelfth-floor office. Though the number of people squeezed in with them surely exceeded the maximum legal capacity, Duncan had still managed to find the elbow room to reach up and pat at his hair in the mirrored wall, while Russell, shoulders pressed painfully against a ninety-degree angle, was literally cornered.

'Er, sure. Looking forward to it.' He hoped Duncan hadn't noticed the missed beat there. It was paramount to conceal from him that he had in fact forgotten all about the office summer party, and this in spite of the perpetual low-level anticipation of it among the rest of the staff since – well, pretty much since the gossip died down after the Christmas do. Somehow he had imagined the event was still weeks away or at least that it wouldn't be happening until . . . until he knew what the hell was going on with his family.

'What's the venue like?' he asked in his best approximation of a normal person's voice.

'What?' Now Duncan was busy inspecting his shave. His jaw line, Russell noticed, was perfectly taut. Had he had some kind of cosmetic procedure? Flab removal, perhaps, or extra bone put in? Or was Russell just imagining these things out of sheer dismay at the contrast with his own physical (and marital) collapse? 'Um, yeah, it's quite cool actually. I went the other night to check it out. You know what those rooftop places are like.'

Russell did not, unless the roof of his own house counted. He'd been up there at the weekend in a bid to clear the guttering – and his head. He'd failed on both counts. 'Got a swimming pool, has it? Swim-up bar?'

'Thank the Lord not. We don't want the girls stripping off.' Duncan lowered his voice to a roguish whisper. 'Well, maybe a select few. But we're not allowed to say that kind of thing any more, are we?'

A fellow passenger – male – chuckled loudly at that and Russell couldn't help doing the same. At times like this he was reminded of how much he and Duncan had shared over the years; how *long* they'd known each other. Whatever separated them these days in the workplace, they were still the same age, the same basic model. They'd got married the same year, had had kids at roughly the same time, their wives got on fine; he wondered if Duncan might actually have something useful to say about Olivia's desertion. But the next moment the lift doors were sliding open and Duncan had exited with only a flick of the hand for goodbye. The moment was gone.

Russell made for his work station, the key strategic question of the day already clear in his mind: was it going to be possible to avoid the summer party and, if so, was it better to make his excuses now or to wait until after the event when people had, by definition, more exciting things to talk about? There was, of course, a third way: he could just go. He could pretend to himself that his life had not caved in on itself and he could let his thinning, greying, desiccating hair down. Just a few drinks with colleagues, *free* drinks (that was worth bearing in mind, if nothing else). Then he remembered that Jamie was scheduled to stay over at a friend's after school tomorrow night. Noah was not.

He would need supervision. Sod's law it wasn't the other way around.

He sighed, reached for his mobile and began to text:

Aniela, can you babysit
tomorrow evening? R

He'd found that texts were easily his most effective form of communication with his cleaner-cum-right-hand woman, though it was only a matter of time before Jamie would be able to take over in more traditional form, having picked up quite a bit of Polish from her over the summer holiday.

Her message came back, prompt as ever:

I am musical concert.
My friend Jana comes.
Time?

Great, Russell texted, 7pm please.

By the time he'd got home, briefed Jana in his own retarded dialect of sign language and apologetic grinning, changed his clothes, got back on the Tube and made it to the venue nowhere near the office but out in west London, it was already eight-thirty. Still, it was just in time to grab the last of the circulating champagne cocktails before it would be necessary to start queuing at the bar.

At once he was glad he had come. There was something about the rooftop location that loosened a valve in him: the (slightly) fresher air and the sense of removal from the world below, the way the planes ground excitingly low overhead as they descended into Heathrow and all about him the percussion of a hundred voices, not crashing into angles as they would have done indoors, but rising to the sky like a crowd of well-wishers at a royal parade.

Mercifully partners had not been invited, so there was no conspicuous absence to explain. Even so, it wasn't long before the first person, one of his own team in new business, Lizzie, revealed herself to be tipsy enough to make the kind of comment a plastic cupful from the water cooler had never quite inspired.

'Hey, listen, I've been meaning to say, Russ, I'm really sorry about your wife.'

'Why, what have you done with her?' Russell cracked. Then, when Lizzie looked discomfited, he added, more soberly, 'What about her? Seriously, what have you heard?'

'Just that she's, you know . . . taking time out. Not feeling herself.'

Even before several others made similar drunken approaches of condolence, Russell told himself that it was nothing to get dramatic about, it simply confirmed what he'd already known: people were treating Olivia's 'time out' as indefinite, maybe even permanent. He had a feeling some of them thought 'not feeling herself' might mean a full-on nervous breakdown.

Nervous breakdown: how old-fashioned the phrase sounded, like something that went with lunatic asylum and straitjacket. *One Flew over the Cuckoo's Nest*. There was that awkward link, too, with Noah's random question at the airport: *Like, has she been sectioned?* Was that what he was telling his friends? How long before people started speculating about electroshock treatment and lobotomies?

All, in all, Russell thought he preferred Beth's way of putting it (and she was, after all, the only one of them with any vaguely clinical experience): a loss of confidence. She'd popped over at the weekend, all suntanned and recharged from her holiday, laden with Spanish cakes for the boys and Rioja for him. She had the air of someone with an awful lot of urgent matters on her list – none more pressing than Russell and his situation – and exactly the transfusion of energy needed to tackle them. (Olivia had been like that as well, once.) Reluctant to share the scare of

278

Jamie's disappearance and Olivia's inglorious reaction to it, he'd offered instead the account of his meeting with Joanna Lilywhite and the revelation that Olivia had turned down her dream job. Next to all that had followed, its magnitude had diminished somewhat for Russell, but, as expected, the story was grist to Beth's mill.

'Hmm, yes, the work thing. I did wonder about that. It always seemed just a bit too hard for her to find what she wanted. I put it down to a loss of confidence. That's incredibly common with mothers, you know.'

Sometimes Russell wondered why no one ever spoke about things being incredibly common with fathers. What was it that was *so* different for mothers? Was their lot *really* so terribly unbearable? 'I just don't understand why she didn't discuss it with me,' he said. *That and everything else*, he thought, bitterly.

'Because she was in denial,' Beth explained. 'Someone with a loss of confidence doesn't necessarily recognise it as such. She would have blamed the job itself, told herself it was an insurmountable workload, impossible for her to manage. That makes no sense to us, but she would have really believed that.'

Russell struggled to understand. 'Maybe it wasn't too much to cope with, maybe she just found it boring?'

But Beth dismissed this at once. 'We all find our jobs boring, but we still do them. Believe me, when you're a working mum you take what you can get. For money and independence and, God, just the need to plug into the rest of society outside your own four walls! And even if the hours weren't perfect – which they were – the boys didn't need her at home the same way. They're at secondary school, they're growing up.'

Russell nodded. Again, he found it impossible to argue with the mum collective – even if he had any decent arguments against it, which he didn't. 'You're right. She hasn't needed to be at home for years, that can't be the reason.' The reinstatement of the present tense fortified him a little. 'I wonder if part of the reason for

279

her putting off work was because of the way Maggie kept disappearing when they were kids? She was overcompensating a bit?' This was more than mild suspicion, it was firm knowledge: right from the time of Jamie's birth, Olivia had told him almost as a pledge, 'I will *always* be there when they come home at the end of the day'. But there was now a ghastly flaw in the theory, because she *wasn't* there when they came home, not any more. However much she'd hated it as a child, she'd still gone and done it herself: she'd disappeared. And on the one occasion when he'd demanded that she get in touch, when it was a question of life and death, she'd responded with silence.

He still wasn't sure if he could forgive her for that, not when he remembered Jamie's face as he walked back into the apartment, the whole resort silent and asleep around them. He'd looked so *haunted*. It was as if he'd witnessed something dark and terrible out there that night. Sure, Russell knew in his heart that Olivia hadn't picked up the messages in time – he'd been able to tell from the panic in her voice when her message finally came – but even so, it had been the death blow as far as his patience was concerned. Whatever her state of mind, whatever her medical history, her neglect was wrong. He wouldn't let her treat them like this, not him, not the boys.

Then, like a little piece of whispered good news, an idea struck him. 'You know what I've just realised, Beth? That job offer must have been about the same sort of time that Maggie was diagnosed. Maybe Olivia saw she was going to be running backwards and forwards to Cheltenham and didn't want to take on the extra commitment? That would explain it, wouldn't it?'

It would explain the return of the depression, too. Perhaps what Olivia had discussed with her GP was not, as Russell feared, a general despair with her home life, her marriage, but the simple shock of discovering her mother was terminally ill. That was enough to send most people to their doctor, wasn't it?

Beth nodded. 'Possibly. But plenty of women combine a part-time job with looking after an ill parent. And Olivia was never Maggie's main carer, was she? She had Lindy living in, plus that whole agency rotation of nurses.'

'Yes, but Olivia wouldn't have known that at the time. She might have imagined Lindy was going to leave and the burden would fall automatically on her. And Dean,' Russell added in polite afterthought.

'Maggie would certainly have been a factor, one way or another,' Beth agreed. 'Like we said before, she always is.'

'You know, I thought it would all come to an end when she died,' Russell said, 'but I don't think it did. If I could just find Olivia to talk to her in person! It's so frustrating!'

'I've been thinking a lot about this while we were away,' Beth said, 'and, you know what? I think the reason she left was she didn't want the boys to see her like that. She recognised how she was feeling from the struggles she had when she was younger and she thought the best thing was to take herself off to get better. It may *look* selfish, but it's incredibly brave when you think about it.'

'Yes, that's true,' Russell said, doubtfully. It occurred to him for the first time that he and the boys were not the only ones who might be dealing with adjusted ideas of Olivia's position in the world. To Beth, for instance, she'd been a constant, one of her tribe, a fellow female in whom she'd confided more than Russell cared to imagine. She needed to rationalise this for herself, she needed to prevent Olivia from becoming the accepted villain of this – just as Russell had begun to convince himself she was. The realisation that he might now be out of synch with his only ally and confidante crushed him even lower.

Sensing his agony, Beth leaned forward and touched his arm. 'Russell, has something else happened? I mean, besides bumping into this old colleague?'

He shook his head miserably.

'It's just, you seem like you're giving up.'

He felt like a child with a grazed knee as he turned to his sister-in-law, hating the feel of tears in his eyes. 'Maybe I *should* give up. Maybe it's time I accepted she's not coming back?'

Beth's gaze was as strong and compassionate as he needed it to be. 'Oh, I'm sure she is, Russell. I'm sure she is.'

Aniela's friend Jana was considerably more alluring at one o'clock in the morning than she'd been six hours earlier – not that Russell had had time to scrutinise the woman he'd left to look after his younger son (or indeed to ask her for written references), he'd been in such a rush to get a free drink down his gullet. But now he saw she was wearing very short shorts and a vest top, a boyish get-up that only exaggerated the femaleness of her figure.

She had put music on; he recognised the songs but not the singers.

'*Mamma Mia*,' Jana said. 'I see this now eight time.'

'Oh, right, the stage show. Good. Would you like a glass of wine, Jana?' Having been drinking ceaselessly since eight-thirty, he found he didn't want to stop.

'Of course,' she said.

'That's what I like to hear!' Russell cried, losing his balance slightly as enthusiasm rocked his upper body. 'Let's sit in the garden, it's still warm out there and I want a cigarette.' Samantha in HR, from whom he'd cadged several cigarettes during the course of the evening, had sent him home with two spares and a lighter, and he now offered one to Jana, exclaiming with approval when she accepted. She seemed to find him hilarious, laughing a surprisingly husky, sexy laugh.

There was an open bottle of Sainsbury's Merlot on the kitchen counter and he poured the remains into two large glasses before joining his companion on the terrace. It was much sultrier here than it had been at the party venue, the day's heat trapped within three dense walls of untended ivy, and it felt fantastic to loll about on a pair of deckchairs as if it were early afternoon at the beach.

'So where is Aniela tonight?'

Jana dragged on her cigarette. 'She is skansert.'

'Skansert? Is that a town?'

'No!' Her laughter spilled towards him like music. 'The Queen. *We Rock You.*'

She was saying concert, he realised. *We Will Rock You.* He'd obviously infiltrated some Polish ladies' crap musical appreciation society. The thought made him laugh again.

'How's Noah been?' he remembered to ask. The notion of homework occurred, but then he recalled it was still the school holidays. Thank God for that. All things considered, he didn't think he could cope with the complications of termtime.

'OK,' Jana said. 'We play Wii.'

'Oh, what, the tennis one?'

'No, not tennis. Golfing.' After a moment of thinking, she added, 'Tiger Woods.'

'Ah, Tiger Woods, good.' Russell lifted the fingers of a nearby fern and tapped his cigarette ash into the flowerbed; the back of his throat felt exactly as it did when he was about to come down with a stinking cold. 'Do you play any sports, Jana?'

She just shrugged, almost in protest, which caused one of the narrow straps of her white vest top to fall to her elbow and uncover a small corner of lacy pink bra. She didn't seem to notice, or at least didn't bother to push the strap back up. 'I dance,' she said, finally, and fixed him with a gaze that seemed to sizzle like liquid on his hot skin.

Next thing he knew they were kissing, or she was kissing him, because she had left her deckchair to share his, which felt extremely good, and she seemed to think so too the way she deftly slipped out of her short shorts and straddled him, slotting her slim legs between the fabric and the frame. There was a clear

283

straining sound as the canvas took on their combined body weight, and then they were having sex in a weird, stationary but rolling sort of way, as if there were arrhythmic currents involved, like swinging in a hammock on an anchored boat. Russell felt drugged by her hot breath in his face, all the currents from his brain scorching south, even the impulses in his lips felt ripped out and re-routed.

When she had gone, he fell into bed with the vague notion that it was good that he'd paid her for the babysitting before they'd had sex and not after, but then, unable to close his eyes because of the spinning room, it occurred to him that prostitutes took the money up front anyhow. Not that he was in any way likening Jana to a prostitute, it was just that for some reason he felt like a bit of a punter. What did they call them in American TV shows? A John. He felt like a John, not a Russell. This struck him as a great witticism and he chuckled aloud to himself as he lay there. But after a while he started to think about Noah, mercifully sleeping farthest from the back garden in an attic room at the front of the house and, Russell prayed, oblivious to the intimacies that had taken place tonight. And Olivia – poor, emotionally broken Olivia – who Beth was now declaring a feminist hero for removing herself from her family rather than subjecting them to her distress! Who he had had the gall to accuse of infidelity! Unbelievable!

Still the room spun. Why was it that the guilt had to kick in before the sobriety? They might at least have the good grace to come together.

Chapter 33

Now that Richie has gone I am only too pleased to be living back with Dad. He allows me greater freedom to daydream. Mum reads me too closely for comfort. Not once since that first crowing accusation of a 'crush' has she made an explicit reference to my feelings for Richie, but not once do I think that she has stopped suspecting. Or discovering. 'We're so similar, Dolly,' she says, but it doesn't feel like a compliment, it feels like a warning.

I am in the sixth form now, officially a young adult and therefore encouraged to practise being a college student. We have our own common room with kitchen facilities and leaflets about teenage pregnancy and anorexia; we have shorter days and unmonitored study periods. The teachers say they respect our need for independence, and they won't supervise us unless we think we need it. I'm not sure what we think any more; already, in the first few weeks of term, I've started to separate myself from the 'we' – at least where it counts the most: boys. I might think about Richie every waking moment, but I don't want to share him with anyone else. Every day at breaktime new love affairs are dissected more thoroughly than any frog in the biology lab, but mine alone remains secret.

I become obsessed with my appearance, my 'image'. The fashion sketches I produce now are really just idealised versions of myself, how I wish I could look when I see him again at Christmas, like a movie star or a model. I remember him saying how different I looked from the girl in Mum's photo, how pleasantly surprised he was when he met me. I'll make him happier still next time. I experiment with make-up in front of the mirror like a bride rehearsing for her big day, trying hundreds of minute variations – a third slick of mascara, a lower lip glossier than the upper one – until I find the one I think will please him the best.

Gradually the weeks of my relationship with Richie contract and are outnumbered by those that have passed since he left. Gradually the extent to which my happiness hinges on the morning post grows. Soon I am able to judge the relative heaviness of the types of mail hitting the doormat from anywhere in the house; differentiating, for instance, between the sound of a single airmail envelope and that of a handful of circulars. The sight of the postman bypassing our door is so crushing it can even make me cry, though nothing hurts quite as much as the news that a letter has arrived from Richie for someone else. On those occasions, I prefer to hear snippets in passing from Warren, or third-hand from Dean. Mum is too casual, too cruel – 'I'll read it later, there's no rush' – when she knows I'm in earshot and ready to rip the page from her hand. It irritates me that she speaks of Richie as if he is her son ('Back on the party circuit – that's my boy!' Unbearable) but, more important than that, that she's getting letters from him in the first place. Doesn't she remember that it is only a matter of months since Dean and I had *no* address to write to her at? Richie gets the full beam, but her own children she chose to keep in the dark.

As for *my* letters from him, Mum is soon back in cahoots with Dad about those. I'm sure she's asking him to spy on me, to steam open the envelopes and find out what's going on. They are fighting a losing battle, however, for my new adult school timetable gives me plenty of extra hours at home. Nine times out of ten Dad is out when the post arrives. Nine times out of ten I have opened, memorised and hidden my precious missive before he puts his key in the door.

I sign each of my letters, 'I love you'; Richie his 'Love ya!'. It is, I tell myself, the same thing.

Dean and I are getting used to our dual-centre family now, comfortable with shuttling between the two houses and picking and choosing from the meals and entertainment on offer. Which of course makes it the perfect moment for our parents to call us together one evening and declare an all-change.

'We've got some news for you,' Mum trills. 'It may be a bit of a surprise.'

My brother and I don't even need to exchange a look. If there's one thing we're agreed on it is that *nothing* will surprise us when it comes to our mother. She is the limit.

In fact, it is Dad who does the honours. 'The tenancy on the Acacia Street house is up before Christmas and your mother will be moving back in with us.'

I frown, confused. 'You mean her and Warren? But there's not enough room. Where are they going to sleep?' And where will Richie sleep when he visits over the holidays? It barely worked out for us when we had the privacy of his basement room, but sneaking up and down the tiny creaky landings here is going to be impossible!

Beside me, Dean opens his mouth, incredulous. 'Don't tell us you're going to try and make us bunk up together? Er, no way, José!' As his thoughts move on, his face twists with contempt and I know *exactly* what he's thinking: Dad's going to give Mum and Warren the master bedroom and move himself onto the sofa bed downstairs! His humiliation is complete!

But Mum gets in first. 'Actually, I'll be coming on my own. Warren's going back to the States.'

'*What?*' I cry out. In a split second I've made the only connection

287

that matters: no Warren for Christmas, no Richie for Christmas. 'But *why*?'

She throws her hands up dramatically. 'Because he's homesick, Dolly, he misses Richie.' Is it my imagination or do those soft eyes of hers harden with satisfaction when she says my lover's name?

'Well, maybe Richie could transfer to a university here?' I say, wildly. 'Then they wouldn't have to be apart so much?' (And nor would we.)

Mum and Dad share a hurt look. 'We thought you'd be pleased about this,' Dad says, gently, 'us all being back together again.'

'I am,' I say, automatically. Too late I realise I should have been more careful. I've betrayed myself, I've betrayed *us*.

'Anyway,' Mum says, 'it's not just Warren's family. There's the weather, his friends, his business. It was crazy to think he was ready for retirement. He's always on the phone to Brad. He's been itching to get back to work from the moment he got here. He's made the right decision.'

As Dean and I just gape back at her, she tries to reach for our hands. I let her take mine for as long as I can bear before sliding it limply away. She's like a snare; one touch and you're captured.

'Look,' she says, adopting a saintly tone, 'I want you to know the truth. You're grown up now and you have a right to it. Warren doesn't want to break off our engagement. He wants me to go back with him and settle for good in California. He's even offered to pay for you guys to visit *us* at Christmas . . .'

My heart leaps at the idea, before squeezing painfully back into its hole.

'. . . But I've decided I want to stay. Guys, I realise I've made a mistake. I should be here with you, with my family.'

I'm aware of Dean's chest rising and rising as he listens to this, a diver about to plunge. So this is it, *finally*, the big apology! He waits to hear how sorry she is that she could ever have done it to us; he waits to hear how leaving us tore her apart as much as it did us. And that's when I know that I've separated myself even from my brother, my last ally. Because I don't want Mum's apology any more. I only want Richie.

But the apology doesn't come after all – or perhaps she thinks she's already given it. Dean has no choice but to expel the air from his lungs and it's Dad who breaks the silence. 'The divorce is on hold,' he says, and he and Mum exchange a coy smile. (And to think, a year ago this was what I *prayed* for. I *must* have grown up, she's right about that.)

'What about Rowena?' Deans asks, glumly. 'Is *she* being returned to sender as well?'

'She's not being "returned" anywhere,' Dad replies, sharply. 'We're very good friends, but nothing more than that.'

His tone is enough to let us know how disappointed he is with us, but Mum, of course, can't leave it at that. 'Whose side are you on?' she screams at Dean and me, as though *we*'re the ones who go around abandoning people, not her. 'Honestly, guys, I give up!' And she sweeps out of the room like Scarlett O'Hara, no doubt to phone Warren and complain how awful her children are being about her leaving him.

'Dad must be mental,' Dean says to me afterwards. 'What the hell's he doing having her back? It's humiliating!'

I nod miserably. Already I miss the days of Dad and Rowena and Mum and Warren; I miss them as much as I ever missed her. 'Yeah, I know.'

'"*I want you guys to know the truth . . .*"' He mimics her Hollywood movie voice. 'How come all Mum's truths are about how great *she* is? Have you noticed that? God, I'm so glad I'll be out of here by next summer. Roll on A-levels!'

'Thanks,' I say. 'Leave me to deal with the fallout.'

'You can handle it. Anyway, she'll be off again before you do yours, you can count on it. Dad's in a dreamworld, poor bastard.'

But for me there's something far worse about all of this than the possibility that Mum will mess Dad around yet again (after all, he must be as prepared for it by now as we are), something worse even than the fact that she really doesn't seem to care how any of us feel: I don't buy her story. I think she's faking.

I think she's split up with Warren because of Richie and me. She wants to cut ties between the two families and this is the cleanest, most effective way of doing it. Had it been a straight choice between Dad and Warren she would have gone back with Warren like a shot, but that would have meant she'd have to have Dean and me out for holidays – a detail she mentioned quite deliberately. Why do that if she weren't sending me a message? Taunting me with what *could* have been between Richie and me if only *she* had wanted it for us. No, whatever it is that bothers her so much about us, it is powerful enough to make her choose Dad and soggy English suburbia over Warren and Californian sunshine. Funny to think I could take the credit for getting my parents back together – if she hadn't already done so, of course. *I should be here with you*, my foot.

I decide against sharing my theory with Dean, not because I doubt he'd be open to a whole new dimension of criticism of her but because it would mean sharing my secret about Richie and me wanting to be together for ever. Not even my best friend Melanie knows the full extent of my dreams. (OK, not even Richie does.)

'I suppose this means Richie won't be coming for Christmas?' Dean remarks, dispiritedly, when boxes of Mum's belongings appear one morning in our hallway. 'He was going to play guitar at my eighteenth. *And* make kamikazes.'

Mum overhears him. 'Sorry, sweetie, but how could he now his dad's going back? He's not going to come on his own – the flight would be too expensive. And it wouldn't be appropriate now, would it? Warren might not like it.'

I feel her eyes on me as I perch halfway up the stairs, but I refuse to meet her gaze. I think to myself, *I hate her*.

'When's Warren actually going?' Dean asks her.

'Next week. But don't worry, everyone's being very grown up about it. He'll want to say goodbye properly, and I'm sure we'll all stay friends.'

Just as long as that doesn't include Richie and me, she means.

As it goes, Warren says something strange to me when we part. He says, 'I just want you to know that I don't agree with your mother about this. Let life go its own way, that's my view.' I'm so taken aback I don't dare ask whether the life he's talking about is theirs or ours.

Within hours of his departure the rental house on Acacia Street is emptied and locked up, their car sold. And not only has Mum left him, but she has left her new job as well. She wants to be a housewife, to 'go the whole hog', as she puts it. Now, when the post comes flying through the letterbox, she is the one waiting for it.

I waste no time in writing to Richie and asking him to address all further correspondence to Melanie's house.

Chapter 34

It seemed to me that being with Richie that August felt more like a honeymoon than my original one (my *real* one) ever had. It seemed to me that the shock of having almost been removed from him so soon after coming together again only made the time that followed more precious. Once, I even allowed myself to wonder if Russell had made up his 'emergency' to try and force me back, but I knew that was a bad thought, more than bad – hateful. The kind of thing my mother would do.

In any case, it was an illusion, this joy of ours; it was another in a succession of stays of execution. I may at times have felt like an angel (or at least guarded by one) – inviolable, protected, immune to *proper* guilt, *proper* pain – but it must have been clear to those around me that I was actually something far more prosaic: a pressure cooker, my lid starting to clatter.

One by one the senses I'd mislaid began to prickle back to life. And apparently in the wrong order, for the first was the least relevant, the least useful: jealousy. I couldn't stop thinking about Richie's memories of Lisa, of her having travelled to see him in California, putting all her hope and pride in his hands before returning home, resigned to a life without him – I was certain she must have considered it the bravest thing she'd ever done. And that phrase he'd used, *The biggest mistake of my life*, that's how he felt when he let her go. When he let *her* go.

It was too close to the bone. I could no longer carry the burden of the unfinished business of our past: I *had* to know how he had interpreted our ending, how he had lived those years, what he made of my certainty that Maggie had acted to keep us apart. It was time for him to know how devastated I'd been, how close I'd come to being extinguished completely, and not because I wanted to punish him but because I needed to show him the last part of me, the part I'd been keeping hidden: the broken bit in the middle. If we could somehow heal that, then perhaps the outer layers might start to heal themselves.

Well, it was an idea, at least. And with a husband who didn't know where I was, a lover who expected me to vanish as suddenly as I'd arrived and two sons who I seemed no longer to know how to love, I wasn't exactly overwhelmed with rival strategies.

As with most conversations here, the backdrop was idyllic. It was late afternoon, the sun slow to sink, and a mother swan and three cygnets had made their way downstream to Angel's Lane, paddling onto the lawn for a feast of clover. Wren was at Chas's house for a sleepover and Richie was just home from work, marshalling the birds gently, careful not to get too close to the cygnets and upset the mother. He caught sight of me watching him from up on the deck and called out, 'They like the clover because it's so sweet.' Then, seeing me laughing, 'What?'

'Nothing. I was just thinking how well you fit in here in paradise.'

He wandered up the lawn towards me, smiling in a way that made me want to lurch without warning into his arms. As he leaned against the gatepost, fingers wrapped lightly around the handrail, there was something of his father's old cowboy physicality in the stance. 'Paradise?'

294

'You know what I mean. The church bells, the meadows, the swans . . . and now I've met the swanherd, as well!'

He grinned. 'They are pretty cute. I told Wren I'd keep an eye out for them this evening. They swim down every so often. She'll be really disappointed to have missed them.'

He climbed the steps and joined me. I threaded my arms around his waist to pull him close. 'I didn't mean to tease. I'm still getting used to you as a country boy. You were such a city creature before.'

'I was a beach bum, more like.'

'Not in London. I remember you as a crazy party animal, always out with Dean, getting drunk. Playing your guitar, teaching us all how to smoke illegal substances.'

'You remember me in high school,' he said, and I became aware of a tensing of muscles through the length of his body. 'Everyone partied. But it's been a *long* time since I did anything crazy.' His body relaxed again as it pressed against mine. 'Well, except for the last few weeks, of course.'

He dipped his head to nuzzle his lips into the hollow above my breastbone and I spoke into his hair. 'Even so, sometimes I can't believe you're the same boy who broke my heart . . .'

Though his lips didn't stop moving, the defensiveness in his body returned – and with an extra charge. Suddenly I knew that this was my moment to decide, once and for all: should I let the past rest for ever or should I shake it awake? But I had made my decision already. I felt the same sense of compulsion I had at Abbots Bay that day, only this time I was aware of its power to destroy.

'The same boy who left me in despair,' I whispered, and it sounded wrong, like a taunt.

No wonder Richie's head came up and he drew away from me as though I'd pushed him. '*Despair*? *Broke your heart*? Come on, it was a mutual thing, wasn't it? If you can even remember that long ago?'

'How can you say that?' I cried, startling both of us. 'I loved you, and you *said* you loved me!'

Richie took a moment to consider how to deal with this sudden flare-up. He chose a manner I'd seen him use with Wren when she had one of her rebellions: dignified, deliberately unprovoked. 'When I left, sure, but we grew up fast enough, didn't we? I went to college, you went back to school, got yourself a new boyfriend. We both—'

'I did *not*!' I burst out, hotly. 'Not for years, not until after the end of college. My next boyfriend was Russell and I married him!'

'OK, take it easy.' Clearly he couldn't quite believe the transformation taking place in front of his eyes. I was finding it pretty hard to handle myself. Suddenly I was sixteen again, raw and untried and frighteningly quick to hurt. 'Maybe I'm not remembering right,' he added, still hoping to pacify me, to coax this little revolt back out of sight.

'I don't think you are.' I sounded shrill and insecure. 'What would make you think that? That I was going out with someone else?'

The strain of delving into forgotten history showed on his face and for the first time I understood that he *didn't* remember us, he really didn't; it needed physical effort for him to half-recall episodes that took only a hair-trigger for me to bring to life in complete detail. Then his eyes cleared. 'I guess that photo Maggie sent was the main thing, the one with you and some friend of Dean's.'

'What photo?' I demanded. 'What friend of Dean's?'

'I don't know. You had your arms around each other. Maggie called him – what was it? – your new beau or something like that. No, "suitor", that was it. I can't believe I even remember this! "See photo for Dolly's new suitor." That kind of thing.'

His words had an ominous ring of authenticity to them, they sounded like Mum's phrasing and, more to the point, Mum's deviousness. 'I don't know what you're talking about. There was never any "suitor". Do you still have this photo?'

'Yep, sure, upstairs, wrapped in silk.' He smiled mischievously at me, hoping to joke a way out of this unpleasantness, but I was much too stirred up for the humour to register.

'Where is it? Show me!'

'Of course I don't have it,' he said, groaning. 'Come on, why would I keep a letter from the ex-girlfriend of my father? From twenty-whatever years ago?'

For the same reason I kept yours, I thought, and any of Warren's I could get my hands on. My files had been regularly purged over the years, but never of Richie Briscoe.

'How could you believe her?' I asked. 'You knew she'd do anything to keep us apart!'

'We already *were* apart, weren't we? Anyway, what are you saying? That she doctored a photograph? That was the eighties, Olivia, they didn't have the software. You were with some guy in this photo and as far as I was concerned that was completely cool. No problem whatsoever.'

No problem whatsoever? I glared at him, my heart rate tearing ahead of my brain processes, my breathing too fast for the natural rhythm of my lungs. I tried to remind my body that this was not the fight or flight emergency it seemed to think it was, that it wasn't even a confrontation between right and wrong, but it was far too late for that. I'd unleashed something inside me that could not be controlled and the only chance I had of conquering it was to give it a life of its own, to find out how *big* a part of my problem it was. Maybe then, as I dearly hoped, it would shrink to its right size and give the other pieces the space they needed to fall into place.

'Just try and remember what the letter said, Richie,' I pleaded. 'I know it's a long time ago, but it's important.'

He frowned. 'But that's just it, I don't think it *is* important. How can it be?'

297

'It is to me. Please, just try to remember. You'd gone back to the States, but was it before or after your father went back?'

'I have no idea.' Again he had to drill deep for long-buried memories. 'I think Dad *was* back, yeah. Maybe it was your brother's birthday. No, hang on, were there Christmas decorations in the picture, maybe?'

I nodded. 'Let me work this out. Mum and Dad had a party to celebrate her coming back and it ended up being a joint thing with Dean's eighteenth. His birthday is December the twenty-ninth, so the decorations would still have been up.' To my intense frustration, Richie was right, it *was* impossible to remember. Having been oblivious to the event's significance I had not archived the images in their correct place; they had not been ordered and coded and subjected to years of microscopic analysis. He could be talking about any one of countless photographs taken that evening for almost everyone had had a camera and prints circulated until long after.

'She must have set up the picture,' I told him. 'It must have been a group shot or something and she cut the others out. Oh Richie, how could you believe I was with someone new when I'd told you I loved you?'

Still he didn't seem to understand. 'Maybe because you were fifteen years old and you didn't have a clue *what* you were feeling?'

I stared at him in dismay. 'I was *sixteen*! Don't you remember we spent my birthday by the sea? That was the first night we were together. Or have you forgotten that as well?'

'Come on, you know I haven't. Fifteen, sixteen, either way it was totally believable that you'd get together with someone else.' He dragged his fingertips over his closed eyes, before looking warily back at me. If I weren't in such a maelstrom I might have spared a moment's sympathy for him. Here we were, the first night alone together since Wren had been back from her holiday and I wanted to spend it reconstructing events from over twenty

years ago. He couldn't imagine how we had moved from cluck-
ing over cygnets to arguing about events that had taken place
almost a quarter of a century ago. Or where I might take this
next. 'We'd only been together a few weeks,' he said, with forced
calm. 'I didn't think for a second you'd be saving yourself for
me.'

'But my letters . . .'

'They were sweet, sure.'

'And so were yours.'

The air between us was flammable. 'Come on, there weren't
that many, Olivia, think about it. I was a terrible correspondent,
still am. Do you think maybe you made more of the whole thing
than—'

'Than what, Richie? Than you did? Are you saying I *imagined*
how we felt?'

As he stood floundering in front of me, unable to keep pace
with my wild leaps of argument, a new fear seized me by the
throat: 'What about how we feel now? Am I imagining this, as
well? I know everyone thinks I'm crazy, so tell me: is *this* in my
head, as well?'

His chest heaved in exasperation. 'Of course it isn't. That's the
point. Compared with what's going on now, the past is nothing,
is it? Raking over the details that neither of us can remember
properly, it doesn't solve what we're going to do about us here
and now!'

I watched as he retreated to the shaded bench and, not knowing what else to do, sank to my knees in front of him. I wished I
could accept what he was saying, his clear good sense, I knew it
was the sensible thing to do, but I could not. To the ears of the
teenage me, the girl to whom I believed I owed this confrontation, his logic was not sensible, it was insulting, poisonous. 'If
there was nothing special between us back then, then how would
you have recognised me when I came here?' I demanded. 'If I
hadn't meant anything to you before? If you hadn't thought

about me at some point over the years, I would have been a total stranger to you, wouldn't I?'

'I'm not saying it didn't mean anything,' he said, quietly, 'I *did* think about you. But it made no difference to what we both did with our lives afterwards. I mean, *obviously*, otherwise we would have seen each other before now, wouldn't we? But we didn't, we both went to college, we both grew up. You married Russell and I married Lisa. We had our children. *Those* were the lives we chose. It's nothing to get upset about, Olivia, it's just the facts.'

'The thing is,' I said, tearfully, 'I thought we *were* going to see each other again. I thought that was what we agreed. I remember when you stopped writing, I was out of my mind.' I paused, wiped my nose with my fingers. 'Things happened, Richie. That was when I started saving. I had to see you in the flesh. I even bought my plane ticket.'

He looked up sharply. '*What?*'

'That's right. Lisa wasn't the only woman to decide to fly across the world to come after you. I did it ten years earlier.'

He was aghast. 'You're saying you came to the States to find me?'

For a brief moment I was tempted to rewrite history – Lord knew I had lived the trip in my head a thousand times – but I couldn't do it. I got to my feet, took a step from him. 'No, I didn't, but I was planning to. I booked a flight to San Francisco, but I cancelled it.'

He reached for my wrist. 'Don't walk away now, I don't know anything about this! When was it, exactly?'

'The summer of eighty-five.'

His gaze narrowed as he calculated the dates. 'But you're talking about, what? A year after I went back?'

I nodded. 'That's right. I was working like a dog; I had two different jobs on top of school. I remember I didn't get my money back when I cancelled the flight and Mum and Dad couldn't understand what I'd spent all my earnings on. At least Dad couldn't. But Mum knew what was going on, that's for sure.'

'Hey, come here.' Richie pulled me to the seat beside him, took my shoulders in his hands in an attempt to get me to hold his gaze for more than a single angry second. 'Why *did* you cancel it? I don't understand.'

My brain had to remind my body to breathe before I could answer. 'Because the letter came. The one with your news.'

His brow knotted. 'What news?'

Finally I held his gaze. 'You know what news, Richie.'

He parted his lips, closed them again. This he really was not expecting. When he spoke again his voice was hardly audible. 'How did you hear about that?'

'Warren wrote to Maggie. I got it hot off the press.'

He absorbed my words slowly, one at a time, as if needing to deconstruct and build them again from scratch. 'OK. If you felt like you say you felt, then I guess that must have been pretty hard, hearing like that.'

'Yes.' And, absurdly, frustratingly, it was almost as hard now. For it was only here and now, in the set of his face in front of mine and in the words of agreement from his mouth, his and no one else's, that I truly accepted it had happened at all. All these years, a part of me had continued to will it into fabrication, to make it unreal again.

Holding my hands in his, Richie leaned forwards to kiss me on my eyelids, first the right one, then the left. It was what he did with Wren when he knew she was about to cry. Then he pressed his cheek against mine and murmured into my ear, 'OK, well it looks like I owe you an airfare. Can I pay you in kind?'

I shook my head, wanting, but not physically able, to pull myself from him. His grip on my wrists was too strong. 'I still remember her face, her voice. The way she read out the letter, like it was all a big joke. She didn't even look at me, just at Dad,

301

as if it was nothing whatsoever to do with me. It was so *cruel*. After everything I'd just been through, it felt like the end of the world.'

'Everything you'd just been through?' Richie repeated. He still had my hands, palms pressed between his as if in double-layered prayer. Only now did he say what I'd needed him to say from the outset. 'Tell me what happened,' he said, 'tell me the whole thing, right from the beginning.'

Chapter 35

I am not one of those naïve teenagers you hear about who doesn't realise she is pregnant until it's too late. One who goes into hospital with a stomach-ache and comes out with a baby. After two missed periods, I go with Melanie to the chemist on the high street and we buy a pregnancy test. It doesn't feel real yet; we even giggle in the queue.

'Fucking hell,' Mel says, an hour later, as we move from her bathroom to her bedroom. 'Are you going to tell Richie?'

'Oh, I'm sure he would want me to sort it out,' I say, dismissively. 'But I'll write and get his phone number at college. Then we'll have a big talk.' Already the cold shock of the positive result is being thawed by an odd pleasure in the unknown adultness of it all. I swear Mel to secrecy, though we quickly decide we must draw her older sister Susie into the plot. (That's how it feels, like a plot that someone else has come up with. I wonder if it's a natural thing: to make the decisions easier, to help me feel less responsible for them.) Susie knows of a clinic where you can speak to a doctor confidentially, where they won't tell your parents or your GP. Soon I have a hospital appointment for December.

Only occasionally does it feel like a crisis. When I wake up in the dead of night having dreamed of being laid out naked in one of those Victorian surgery performances we've been studying at school, cut open between the legs for all to see, a public disgrace. Then, I'm sweating and crying and grasping at the sliver of hope that it *is* only a nightmare, nothing that exists in the waking day.

Otherwise, it's a strangely content period of waiting. I'm used to waiting by now, after all: waiting for Richie to write back to me, waiting to find out when I might see him again, waiting to start living again. In better moments, the knowledge that the pregnancy will soon end makes me cherish the weeks of it I *am* allowed to have, the feeling of having something of his inside my body. It makes me feel close to him when he's so far way.

My main fear, of course, is that Mum will guess. My symptoms are not severe and so, other than the nocturnal terrors, it seems to me that I'm acting normally. The problem is that almost supernatural vigilance of hers. When I pick at my food and she says, 'What's got into you, Dolly?' I wonder if she's chosen those words especially. Several times, I think I see her gaze lower to my stomach. I imagine her searching my room while I'm at school, combing the surfaces for evidence of my crime. To cover myself on the day of the termination, with its 6.30 am hospital arrival time, I tell her there is an ice skating trip planned for the sixth form, a treat for our hard work, and we must all be at the school earlier than usual. (Ice skating! I haven't set foot on an ice rink since I was eight!)

At least I needn't fear her double-checking with another parent, because since her abandonment of us she's lost touch with most of them. The 'normal' mothers don't approve of her.

There is no ice skating. Three days before I'm due at the hospital, I'm in the toilets at school when I find blood in my knickers. Looking into the bowl I see that the water is bright, bright red and near the surface there are traces of something dark and clotted. At once I feel so light-headed I have to steady myself by pressing my palms against the cubicle door in front of me. I sit

for a minute, waiting for the spangles to fade, trying to understand, and then I cushion myself with loo roll, pull up my jeans
and walk out of the school grounds towards the bus stop. When
I take my ticket I notice I still have blood on my fingers, dried
tight on my skin like glue. There is no pain, but I feel weak and
disorientated; a fawn struggling to find its way without its
mother.

At the Casualty reception, I'm asked to describe what is
wrong with me.

'Blood is pouring out,' I say, simply, and it's true; I can feel it
seeping through the tissue and into my jeans. I imagine it on the
denim, a black saddle getting lower and lower.

I'm ushered through at once, scanned and examined by a
doctor. 'I'm afraid you've miscarried,' he says. 'Did you know
you were pregnant?'

'Yes, I did.' And the past tense feels very sad.

'I'm very sorry.'

I'm grateful for the way he speaks to me, like he assumes this
must be a disappointment because I wanted the baby and
expected to have it. I'm also grateful for the own-clothes policy
of our sixth form, which makes it possible for me to tell the
nurse I am eighteen and employed in an office nearby. When she
asks who she should phone to pick me up, I say no one. I will
make my own way home.

I don't tell Melanie until the next day.

'Do you think it was a boy or a girl?' she asks, as if this is
somehow significant.

I shrug. 'Maybe a girl.'

'A girl?'

'Yeah. Maybe.'

Richie never does send me his phone number. His next communication is a Christmas card to the whole family and when I
write back I don't mention what has happened. It's not that I'm

pretending it never took place; it's more that I've developed a way of not thinking about it. I see it as an illustration in a book, neatly squared off with a black border, and once I've checked its four corners I just turn the page and make it go blank. It's quite easy.

After a few weeks the last of the bleeding stops and soon my period arrives as expected. At my next hospital check up I'm told it's safe to have sex again. I tell the nurse that my boyfriend is away, that I won't be having sex with anyone until I see him again. She gives me condoms anyway. As I leave the room, I feel her fingers on my back, the gentlest of guiding touches, and when I turn to look at her she is smiling at me as if she actually cares. She is about my mother's age.

I take two jobs – one as a waitress and one in a card shop – and shoehorn the hours around my schoolwork. One Saturday, between shifts, I go to the library and find out how you work out the due date of a baby. Then, when the day in May comes around, I give myself a treat: a whole day of fantasy, a movie in my head of Richie and me with our newborn daughter, our happy sunny life together.

I calculate that at the University of California Santa Cruz he is just finishing his spring semester. He has not written to me for months now, but that's fine. I understand. Letters get lost in the post all the time, and I know he's busy with his studies. Mel says I must 'keep the faith' and wait to see him again before confessing. Our kind of conversation needs to take place face to face, we agree. I imagine telling him about the baby with tears tipping down my face, and him cradling me, murmuring into my hair, treating me as if I'm the lost infant in the story.

I buy my plane ticket the very day I've saved the full ticket price. Unable to wait a second longer than I have to, I leave my waitressing shift on the dot and walk straight into the travel agent's across the road. Every one of my weekly pay packets, every single shiny new pound coin I've been tipped, every fifty pence, it's all there in the line that reads *Depart LGW 11:25, Arrive SFO 14:15*.

Sitting at the agent's desk and watching her take down my details, I feel the happiest I've been since I was last in Richie's arms. There's dread, though, too, eating away at the edges, dread that the girl is going to produce a form and insist I get it signed by my parents, laugh at me for believing I could fly off to another continent without anyone's permission. (I've already decided that if it comes down to it I'll forge Dad's signature. Not Mum's. I don't want her name on this.)

The flight is booked for the day of my seventeenth birthday. I think of it as our anniversary, something auspicious that can only bring luck to the adventure. I imagine the perfect serendipity of Richie being home by himself when I walk up his path in the Californian sunshine and rap my knuckles on the door. He takes one look at me and pulls the door wider. He says, *Olivia! Wow!*

Once or twice I allow myself to include our baby, her soft head resting on my right shoulder so that it brushes against my cheek as we move. In this version Richie opens the door in time to watch our approach, his expression overjoyed. I start to make a pencil sketch of the scene but, hearing my mother move around in the room below, I tear it into pieces and put it in the bin.

Two weeks later, the letter comes.

It's a Saturday. Dean is staying with a friend for the weekend, allegedly cramming for his final A-level papers, and Mum and Dad and I are having breakfast together ('Are we breakfasting this morning?' she'll ask him, making a verb out of a meal, yet another of the affectations my brother and I still like to keep a tally of). She's brought the morning post to the table and sits it in a stack in front of her, sifting through the bills and circulars as she eats and saving the only two personal items till the end. One is white, with the unmistakable blue and red edging of airmail, and I hold my breath, praying it is for me. With Dad there, she'll have no choice but to pass it across the table without interference.

'Hey, it's from Warren,' she exclaims, examining the gold address sticker in the left-hand corner. Then, a tear and rustle later, 'Oh my gosh!'

Dad doesn't seem to have heard; I pretend not to have. Already I'm in my room, licking my wounds, telling myself I will hear from him on Monday. I add more honey to an already sticky slice of toast.

'Oh my gosh,' Mum repeats.

'What?' Dad asks.

'You're not going to believe this.'

'*What*, Maggie? Spit it out!'

'Remember Warren's boy, Richie?'

'Of course I remember Richie.' It's a ridiculous question: Dad got to know him pretty well last summer. But she's aware of that, of course; she's just warming up her audience. I do my best not to oblige, to look unbothered as I crunch into my toast, but every nerve in my body is alert to her voice and I don't taste a thing.

'Well, according to this, he's just got married!'

I put my toast down and for the next ten seconds its dry scrape as it touches the plate is the only sound in the world. I think I might have gone deaf. Then, across the road, a car engine flares to life and a woman calls out to her children.

I've misunderstood. That's it.

Dad's face is puckered with confusion. 'Who, Warren? He didn't hang about, did he?'

'No, not Warren!' Mum sends him a look that says, What, you think he's not still pining for *me*? 'I'm talking about *Richie*, of course.'

Inside my skin my organs hiss like raw meat hitting hot oil and then the whole lot goes into some form of arrest and I can no longer move. I don't know why I'm not falling from my chair; somehow my skeleton is keeping me seated without the aid of my muscles.

'Married?' Dad frowns. 'But he can't have, he's only . . . what? Eighteen?'

'Nineteen by now. His birthday was in April.'

'Is that even legal in the States? I thought you had to be twenty-one to do anything over there?'

'Depends on the state,' Mums says. 'And pretty much everything's legal in Nevada.'

'*Nevada*?'

'Las Vegas, Nevada.'

'Ah, Las Vegas. Say no more.'

'Exactly. It seems they took off there for a weekend and when they came back they were man and wife.'

'Warren wasn't invited to the ceremony, then?'

'Nope. I'm not sure it was much of a ceremony. He says here they wore swimming costumes.'

'*Swimming costumes*?' Dad looks stupefied. 'Why on earth would they do that?'

Mum smirks. 'Well, I assume there was some sort of Hawaiian theme.'

'Ah, yes. Elvis was involved as well, perhaps.'

For me, sitting at the end of the table between them, this question-and-answer set piece causes a scream inside me so violent, so savage, I can only be grateful that my vocal chords have shut down and the sound is killed before it is born. And then, at last, Dad asks the only question I *need* answering: 'Who's the girl?'

Mum turns back to the letter. 'She's called . . . where is it . . . Danielle. Another freshman at his college, apparently. Oh dear, Warren doesn't sound happy at all. I must write back this weekend and point out the positives.'

'What positives?' Dad chuckles. 'I'm not surprised he's up in arms. This is the last thing you expect when you wave them off to university.'

Mum smiles the virtuous, smug smile of someone who is (mistakenly) sure *she* has never done the last thing you'd expect. I want to stretch across the table and slap her. If my hands could move, I'd have to sit on them to stop myself doing it. 'Well,' she says, all playful now, 'let's hope Dean doesn't decide to spring something like that on us when he goes to university in September. York isn't *that* far from Gretna Green—'

Dad cuts in. 'It's far enough. Don't tempt fate, Maggie.'

During the whole exchange I haven't said a word; nor have I made eye contact with either of them. I feel as if I'm not there; I'm far away listening to a radio play, the words supplied by a professional scriptwriter, someone who knows what I will feel before I feel it.

Finally free from paralysis, I slip from the table. 'I'm going to my room.'

As I leave, I hear Mum say to Dad, 'He must have got the poor girl pregnant, d'you think? It's the only possible explanation.'

It's only a matter of hours before I get the idea that she must have faked the letter. She must have found out I've bought a plane ticket and worked out a way to stop me from going.

I wait until I'm on my own with Dad and I ask, 'Can I read the letter that came from Warren this morning?'

'I don't see why not,' he says. 'Is it on the desk in the living room with the other mail?'

'No.' That was the first place I looked.

'You'll have to ask your mum where she's put it then. She's always moving stuff around, I can't keep up with her rethinks.'

There was a time when Dean and I would have leapt on a comment like that, but now it scarcely registers.

'Did you see it?' I demand.

'What? The letter?' He frowns at me. 'Weren't you there when it came?'

'Yes, but did you read it yourself afterwards? Did you actually see the words?'

'Well, I didn't have to, did I? I'd already had most of it read out to me.'

'But it was Warren's handwriting?'

'I wouldn't know, but I assume so.' As he looks more closely at me his frown melts into something more tender. Maybe he's remembering *We're fine on our own*. 'What's this all about, love? You've been very up and down lately.'

I don't answer. I can't handle the kindness in his voice.

'Look, I know you were close to Richie when he was over here, but he's back in his world now, Dolly. He's a college student. It'll be exactly the same for Dean in the autumn, and then for you next year. Though I hope you'll both behave with a little less recklessness than our American friend . . .'

I stop listening then. I feel exhausted and alone. 'Please don't call me Dolly,' I whisper, finally.

'Sorry, Olivia. Hey, don't fret, Mum will be back in a while, she's just gone to the shops. I'm sure she'll find the letter for you.'

But I can't bear to give her the satisfaction of watching me grovel. Instead I wait till the following morning when they're both out somewhere together and I search for the letter then. But of course I can't find it. There are others from Warren, kept among correspondence in a desk drawer, and for a wild moment I hope they might give me the next best thing to the letter itself: something I might be able to blackmail her with, the information that she's still intending to join him, perhaps – just as soon as she's sure she's destroyed my dreams once and for all. I imagine saying to her, 'Tell me the truth about Richie, show me *proof*, and I'll keep your secret for you.' But Warren's letters are brief and bland, beginning with news of his safe landing after a turbulent flight and after that focusing on the fortunes of his

311

company. Congratulations on Dean's university offers; commiserations about the terrible weather. The *weather*? There is nothing remotely controversial in them.

Dean comes back that evening and we sit together on the sofa watching TV. 'Weird news about Richie, isn't it?' he says, cheerfully.

I swivel my eyes from the screen. Will I ever be able to hear that name again without my whole body firing instantaneously? 'Have you heard from him as well?' I ask, hopefully.

'God, no, he never writes to me, he's useless. Mum told me just now.'

'You read the letter?'

'No, but she told me what it said. Fucking hell, what's he on? That's *way* too young to get hitched, however much of a babe she is.'

I swallow a mouthful of saliva and bile. 'Mum seems to think the girl's pregnant?'

Dean doesn't notice how haunted my voice sounds. He just shrugs. 'Wouldn't have thought so, Richie's not a total idiot.' He gives me a wicked look. 'Anyway, you're the one who would know about that, aren't you? *Is* he a total idiot?'

I stare, horrified. It takes me a moment to realise he isn't accusing me of anything. He doesn't know. I change the subject. 'So you wouldn't consider asking Amy to marry you, then?'

Now it's his turn to stare. '*Amy*? Are you taking the piss? I haven't even left school yet! She'd think I was totally off my rocker!'

'No she wouldn't. She really liked you last summer.' I remember her face in the garden that day. She felt the same about him as I did about Richie.

'Last summer, yeah. A million years ago. Anyway, she's seeing someone up in Durham now, a Scottish bloke.'

'Is she? Oh.' I'm shocked. 'I'm really sorry, Dean, I didn't realise.'

He gives me a strange look. 'What are you sorry for? It doesn't bother *me*.' And seeing how easily he moves on to the next subject, how quick he is to laugh at the actor on TV, it seems he's telling the truth. On the subject of love and marriage he really doesn't care.

I write to Richie, just one sheet of paper, one line: *Is it true you got married? I really need to know.* But I don't hear from him, not then, not ever.

I cancel my seat on the birthday flight to San Francisco. And with it I cancel any trust in my mother that has lingered this last year. The little chemical traces of loyalty that the Lane blood washes through my heart every time it beats, I cancel those.

Chapter 36

Richie's eyes had taken on a daze. It was as if the rays no longer converged on the procession I'd conjured up before him of lost summer holidays, lost girls, lost freedoms. Then he said, very quietly, 'Wow, Olivia.'

I smiled sadly. 'I always thought you'd say that.'

About forty minutes earlier he'd opened a bottle of wine and already it was finished, both of us having drunk eagerly as though quenching thirst. He went to the kitchen to fetch another.

'I hate that you went through all that on your own. You never told anyone in your family?'

I shook my head. 'But I always thought Maggie suspected about the baby. She just seemed to know everything, but without ever admitting to it. It felt like she could read my mind or something.'

'You should have tracked down my number. I know I was useless at answering your letters, but Maggie would have had Dad's number, you could have called him and got to me that way.'

'I couldn't ask her. She would never have helped. And then when I decided I was going to come and see you, it didn't seem to matter that we hadn't spoken. I thought . . .' I paused to fight a rush of shame and regret, the last vestiges of the original pain, '. . . I suppose I hoped that once I'd gone to you I

315

would never come back. We'd have all the time in the word to talk.'

'Oh, Olivia, I had no idea. *No* idea.'

We stared at each other. 'Why did you do it, Rich? Marry this other girl? Was *she* pregnant?'

He gave a dry chuckle. 'No, she was high. The same as me.'

'And you got divorced, I suppose?'

'It was annulled, actually, if I remember. I'm surprised Dad told Maggie about it. I thought the general idea was to keep the whole thing quiet. My dad, her dad, they made us feel grateful we didn't get ourselves hauled into jail. This is freaking me out, Olivia! I haven't thought about any of this for years, maybe twenty years!'

'I'm sorry. I hadn't realised how much it had all festered. But I had to tell you. I've always known I would, eventually.' It had scared me how easily my feelings had come – and with what force. It was as if there'd been no break between then and now, nineteen eighty-five flowing into two thousand and eight without the smallest pause for question or announcement. 'I suppose because I never got to the bottom of what Maggie was up to, I imagined all kinds of stuff.'

Richie nodded. 'She should have been looking after you, comforting you. You did well to get through it at all.'

'It took a while. Years, if I'm honest. I was in a bad way pretty much until I met Russell.' But I didn't want to think about that now; my story was exhausted, and so were we. 'I should have just caught that plane and come and seen you anyway. At least I could have seen it all with my own eyes, told you what had been going on with me. I could have walked away.' I stared out to the fields beyond the brook. The swans were long gone.

'You need to forget about all this, sweetheart,' Richie said, gently. 'We were never going to have a baby, we were kids ourselves, we were way too young for anything serious.'

'Not too young to get married,' I pointed out.

316

'Yeah, for about two days,' he reminded me. 'Think about it: if things hadn't happened the way they had, would this be happening now? I don't think so. It would have been good riddance a long time ago – and I mean you to me. You would have seen I was a waste of space who couldn't deal with what you'd been through and you'd have wanted nothing more to do with me.'

'Don't say that,' I whispered. 'I would never have thought that.'

He looked hopefully at me, searching for a clue that a resolution might be in sight. 'Do you blame me for not supporting you, for not knowing?'

I bit at my lower lip. 'No, I don't blame you. The only person I blame is Mum. She made sure we never had a chance.'

His face fell. 'Maggie? But why? She might have disapproved of us, but she had nothing to do with me getting together with someone else. How could she?'

'I don't know. Maybe she willed it.'

'*Willed* it?'

'I don't know,' I repeated. I'd expected this conversation to bring clarity, but instead my brain was a knotted ball of wool, and the more I pulled at the ends the tighter the knots got. 'All I know is that she split up with Warren so you could never come back, so you would—'

Richie interrupted: 'Hey, that really is crazy. Those two were never going to work out, anyone could see that. They were a complete mismatch. Next you'll be saying they only brought me to England in the first place to torment you!'

'No,' I said, seriously, 'I've thought about that. She wouldn't have expected you to be attracted to me. Remember, she was surprised by how I'd changed, she wasn't expecting me to be so . . .'

'So beautiful?' He looked tenderly at my hot, blotched face. 'Because you were.'

'So much of a temptation,' I corrected him, bitterly. 'She remembered me as a child. Because she was such a great mother she hadn't seen me herself for almost a year.'

'Hey,' he said, again, 'I wasn't serious. Of course that's not why they brought me. I'm just trying to stop you wasting your energy on all this anger.'

My mouth trembled. 'I can't help it. I can't stop resenting her and I always thought I'd be able to, as soon as she was dead. I thought it would be over, but it's not. I can't escape her, Richie. I'm *never* going to escape her.'

'But you shouldn't be trying to; she's your mother. And there's no such thing as a perfect one.'

'I know that!' I cried. 'I only have to look at myself!' As fresh tears streamed down my face, he drew me towards him, mopping the flow with his shirt sleeve.

'Maybe you're right. Maybe our parents did stitch us up a little bit, but—'

'*She* did,' I cut in. '*She* stitched us up. She wouldn't have rested until you were out of range. If I had told her I was pregnant she would have *made* me have an abortion. And when she heard about you and Danielle . . . all that gloating was real! The reason I couldn't find the letter was because she was getting it framed in solid gold!'

Richie groaned. 'Come on, stop doing this to yourself. Maggie was a pain, yeah, but she wasn't the devil incarnate. And we were kids! We were only together for a couple of months. She might have helped us along, but we wouldn't have continued, period.' He tried to smile, but only one corner of his mouth registered the effort. 'Look, if everything you say is true, then think about *why* she did what she did. She obviously thought you were too young to be hanging out with someone like me, that I was a bad influence and not good enough for you. And she was right. I got you pregnant and didn't even bother to find out I'd done it. I was toxic.'

'No,' I said, 'you don't get it. That wasn't Mum's reason.'

'Then what was?'

I turned my face to his, eyes still damp. 'She saw me as her rival. She didn't want me to have the kind of boy she'd never had. She didn't want me to have the beautiful one, the special one, the free spirit.' And in that moment I knew it was true. There had been something about Richie that Maggie had wanted for herself: his attitude to life, his fearlessness in breaking the rules. 'She was jealous,' I said. 'It's as simple as that.'

Richie shook his head. 'She didn't want me in her precious daughter's life. It's as simple as *that*.'

'I was never her precious daughter,' I said.

'Oh, you were. She may not have shown it very well, but I promise you, you were.' He clasped me to him even more tightly now, as if smothering any further argument before I could make it. His voice was a command. 'Listen to me, Olivia, you will never know for sure what Maggie did or didn't do. And even if she was here in front of us and we had the opportunity to ask her outright, she still might not tell the truth, she might not even remember. You have to accept that she will never give you the answers you want. You have no choice but to forgive her.'

It was the one thing I'd thought impossible to accept, the one thing I'd thought impossible to forgive. And hard though it was to hear, I knew he was right.

Later, in bed, in the dark, Richie said, 'If you want me now, you know I'm yours.'

I didn't say anything, just responded with my body, curling closer into the warm crescent of him.

'I'm different now. You do know that, don't you?'

'Of course,' I murmured.

'I was only interested in having a good time back then, I didn't have the ability to care about anything for more than five minutes. I didn't think I needed to. But I do now and I want to take care of you. Properly.'

My body went still against his. 'What do you mean?'

319

'You know what I mean. Divorce Russell. Move in here with Wren and me. You're halfway there already.'

My breath caught in my throat. 'But . . . the boys.'

He was merciful enough not to spell out the heartbreaking obvious, that I'd already left my boys; we'd been apart for almost six weeks.

'Bring them to live down here. We'll get a bigger place. Or we'll work it out so that they stay in London and you split your time between them and us. I'd love the chance to get to know them. You already know Wren so well.' He paused. 'In fact, seeing you together is what makes me know this is right. It's like you've known each other before or something.'

I didn't know how to absorb this declaration. Though he sounded spontaneous, I knew he had to have been thinking about this properly; for Wren's sake, he wouldn't say it lightly. 'I don't know if Jamie and Noah would want anything to do with me after this,' I said, caught between hope and hopelessness.

'Of course they would. You've been together your whole lives. This break you're having is nothing compared to that. Kids are the most loyal creatures in the world – surely you've noticed that by now? And besides, you know my opinion about the boys.'

'What?'

'That as soon as you see them again you'll come to your senses.'

I felt myself tense. The evening's confessions were not yet complete, it seemed. 'I did see them,' I blurted out, 'well, I didn't. But I tried to. I went to the camp.'

'What are you talking about? What camp? When?' Richie snapped on the bedside lamp and I squinted up at him, adjusting my eyes to the dazzle.

'That week I was looking after Wren, I went to see them. They were in Hampshire.' I pulled myself up into sitting position and hugged my knees to my chest.

He stared at me. 'You went on a trip to Hampshire with Wren?'

'It's all right, she was completely safe. She was asleep the whole time, actually. We'd been at the swings all morning.'

He digested this. 'OK. So what happened? How come you didn't see them?'

My body felt impotent at the memory. 'I couldn't, I just couldn't, Richie. When it came to it I was too scared. I couldn't risk it. If it wasn't like you said, if I didn't come to my senses, then they would have *seen* me turning away from them, not wanting them. I couldn't risk that happening.'

'Oh, God, Olivia.'

All the hidden anguish of the last weeks finally poured from me: 'And then Russell rang me from Portugal and said there was some sort of emergency, but I didn't go, I was too late, and he said it was fine, nothing had happened after all and we haven't spoken since and it's because he thinks I'm evil and don't deserve to be their mother . . .'

As I spoke I could see that Richie was as much at a loss as I was, that he'd finally run out of answers to my troubles. But we were bound into this together now; one of us had to pick a way free, and he was the one with the strength.

'I wish you'd told me this before,' he said, 'or at the time – I'd have gone with you to the camp, to Portugal, wherever you needed to be. We could have sorted this out already, sweetheart. Look at you, you're not coping with this stuff! You need to understand that you don't have to feel all this on your own, not any more!'

'Thank you,' I whispered. 'Thank you.'

He held me close to him, waiting for my breathing to calm. 'Better?'

I nodded. 'I don't like this, Richie, I don't like not feeling what I should be feeling. I should be like you and Wren, or Sarah and Chas. I always *was*. What's happened to me? Why don't I want to be with my children?'

But there was no answer, of course. If there had been an answer, I would not be lying here asking the question.

321

'Maybe a better way to look at all of this is to concentrate on what you *do* know you want,' Richie said, slowly, 'what you *are* feeling rather than what you aren't. Are you feeling anything at all?'

'You know I am . . .'

As my voice faded to a whisper, his grew stronger, more insistent. 'Then what is it? What is it you feel?'

I couldn't see beyond Millington, beyond this room, beyond his face. 'I want you. I love you.'

'And I want you. I love you.' What felt like eternity stretched between us before he added the 'but'. 'But I'm not sure this is real, not for you.'

'It *feels* real,' I breathed.

'OK. But even if it is, you must see we can't make a plan that doesn't include your family. Sooner or later your feelings for them *will* come back, whether you believe that or not. We need to think about how it's going to work.'

'I know.'

'The summer's almost over. At the very least it's time to let everyone know where you are. And if you can, you should explain to Russell what's been going on. It doesn't have to be perfect; you're not on trial. Just tell him what's in your head right now.'

'I don't think I can . . .' It was inconceivable that I should say to Russell what was in my head at that moment, it was too shocking. For what I was thinking was that *Richie* was my family now – that *he* was all I knew for sure.

Losing the others I might one day be able to cope with. But I would not survive again without him.

Chapter 37

It was a pathetic psychological trick that wasn't fooling anyone, least of all himself, but Russell *still* had not saved and named Jana's phone number on his mobile phone, despite the dozen or so times she had texted him (and he her). He recognised her number, of course, he couldn't stop his mind from doing that. Nor could he stop the instant physical reaction in his trousers when her messages contained unwitting grammatical errors such as You want babysitting again? Was this the sex-texting he'd read about in the papers? If so, it was as sordidly compulsive as it was cracked up to be.

He found her last message and hit 'Reply': J. change of plan. don't come over. Rx

'Not interrupting anything, am I?' asked Dean, by his side, and Russell pressed 'Send' before slipping the phone back into his pocket.

'No, course not. How're you getting on with that beer?'

'Good, thanks. Sorry to barge in unannounced, I just thought you might like a bit of company.'

He'd popped around at Beth's suggestion, that was obvious from the fact that he had nothing new to report, only the usual sympathetic noises about Russell's domestic chaos and mildly hostile speculation about Maggie's will. It was nice, though, just what

Russell needed. They were on the terrace, slowly reddening under the paper-thin parasol that Russell had bought for a bargain price and discovered to provide little or no actual shade. Now he'd put Jana off, he found he was very much enjoying the illusion that he and Dean were just two blokes having a beer on a hot evening. Perhaps he could fool himself into thinking the wives were off somewhere together, a girls' night out or something.

'So the boys are at your mother's then?' Dean asked.

'Yep, they went this morning. I'd forgotten they usually go there for a week in August. It couldn't have come at a better time; work was getting a bit tricky.' He was sure Duncan was scheduling meetings later and later in the day, knowing Russell was trying to slope off early.

'I suppose you told her what's going on?'

'I had to.' Russell winced at the memory of his conversation with his mother, who had actually put the phone down on him in her haste to call the police and report Olivia missing – this despite the fact that her local constabulary was hundreds of miles away in Lincolnshire. And she would have gone ahead and done it as well had Russell not kept the line open himself for the next half-hour and prevented her (though she owned a mobile phone for emergencies, he was confident she did not know how to turn it on). When he'd phoned a second time, he'd had to be more emphatic than he would have liked: 'All I'm asking is that you take the boys for a week while I try and keep my job. Will you do that? Yes or no?'

Her 'yes' had been almost meek enough for him to regret his belligerence. (Had he ever spoken to Olivia like that? He hoped not.)

Lord only knew what scenes she was now filling their heads with, or they hers, or what the young geniuses could possibly find to occupy themselves with in rural Lincolnshire for a week. All he knew was he needed a break from it all, before he threw himself under a bus.

'What have you been up to?' he asked Dean. 'How's your work?' He wished his brother-in-law had not opted for the deckchair because it was impossible to look at him without experiencing split-second mental reconstructions of that erotic encounter with Jana. Jana. How easily he spoke her name, how readily he pictured her face. What had he intended for this evening had Dean not appeared and forced him to put her off? Naturally, he had not confronted the issue in any detail, even though he had been the one to propose the meeting. Having learned she worked most evenings in a bar and babysat only occasionally, he'd promptly 'booked' her for her next night off: tonight. Well, clearly any babysitting was to be purely metaphorical; there was obviously serious chemistry between them, however unlikely on her part (she, on the other hand, was indisputably gorgeous – he couldn't imagine any man disagreeing with that, Beth-worshipping Dean included).

What, then? A repeat performance of the deckchair straddling? Or would he have taken her out for dinner first, like on some sort of *date*? Well, it would have had to have been somewhere cheap. Finances had never been in such straits, it was touch and go as to whether he'd manage to avoid the bailiffs before the share of Maggie's estate was finally revealed (and how long after that before the money actually came through? He'd read of probate delays that ran into years, even when one of the main beneficiaries wasn't incommunicado).

'. . . the usual story,' Dean was saying. 'If I wasn't tied into this share option thing I'd seriously think about making a move.' He sucked his beer, tipping his head back with the focus of a newborn, before resurfacing. It was time to get to the point of his visit. 'So have you heard from her lately?'

He means Olivia, Russell reminded himself, guiltily. He grimaced. 'Yes, but I haven't spoken to her. Enough is enough. I've told her I don't want to talk again until she tells me where she is. And when she does, I'll go straight down there and get her.'

'Good for you.' Dean threw him a one-caveman-to-another look of solidarity and for a short, lovely moment Russell almost believed his own bravado. 'I mean, how long has it been now? What the fuck does she think she's doing? This is getting beyond a joke, don't you think?'

'I do,' Russell agreed. After Beth's professional soothing there was something refreshing about Dean's bombastic approach to the situation (it was no longer a crisis; crises couldn't go on indefinitely, sooner or later they had to be downgraded to situations). Officially he backed Beth, of course, but off the record he'd begun voicing the primitive instincts that Russell felt himself in darker moments but couldn't possibly vent in front of the boys. Yes, what the fuck *did* his wife think she was doing? When the hell *was* she planning on coming back? Anger, basically.

'She'll be back for the reading of the will,' Dean said, confidently. 'Next Friday.'

'What makes you say that?'

'Oh, it's far too big a deal for her not to turn up.'

Bigger than her own children? Russell thought. Bigger than one of them going missing in a foreign country? Of course she didn't exactly know about that but, still, wasn't there such a thing as maternal intuition? Back when he'd still been phoning her, catching her for those strange, dry exchanges that left him so unsettled, she'd seemed to assume that her sons had no more need of her. She'd seemed to think they were already grown up. 'Well done,' she'd said once, as if her work with them was over and she was trusting him to finish the job!

It was true, though, that for the rest of the family the reading of the will *had* formed a natural deadline, falling as it did towards the end of the school holidays. (That was another thing he needed to do: find out what new bits of uniform the boys needed, where he was supposed to buy them and what sizes they took. He hoped there were no badges to be sewn onto pockets or anything technical like that. And were there any forms to be filled in? Olivia had always been knee-deep in school forms. He resolved to make a master list of all these things once Dean had left; there was no way he could keep track of them otherwise.)

'Maybe,' he said, nodding at Dean. 'I hope the will *is* enough to get her back here. But to be honest I don't think it means that much to her. I wouldn't be surprised if she's forgotten all about it.'

Dean's reaction to this was explosive even for him: he cracked down his bottle on the nearby brick border and yelled, 'Well, bully for her that she thinks money grows on trees!'

'Hang on a minute—' Russell began, but he might have known that Dean was not going to, and sure enough his brother-in-law simply ranted over the top of him.

'Our mother was exactly the same, fucking everything up and leaving other people to worry about how to pay for it. You'd think they were royalty the way they behave! Feel a bit bored with your life? Well, just run off and pretend it doesn't exist! No thought to the kids you've left behind, how *they* might be feeling. Getting the piss ripped out of them for not having a mum. How can she not remember how that felt? Not to mention the sad bastard left behind to sort it all out. Can she not remember how crucified Dad was? Maggie turned him into a fucking eunuch!'

Unavoidable – not to mention soul-destroying – though the parallel was, there was no point in Russell trying to interrupt. He wondered where all this had come from: the lack of Beth's warning presence, for one, and from a bad day at work, as well, perhaps (unlike in his own 'career', Dean still had enough good days to make the bad ones stand out). In any case, it appeared he was through the worst of his outrage now, losing his puff and reaching for his beer again. 'All I'm saying is, maybe some of us don't buy this depression line. Maybe she's just doing what she saw her own mother do, putting herself first, simple as that.'

'That has occurred to me,' Russell said, mildly, 'of course it has. But I don't think it *is* as simple as that. After all, *you* haven't run off and left your family, have you?'

'I'm not a woman,' Dean shot back, as if this explained everything (which it possibly did). 'I'm telling you, Russ, what this is is history repeating itself. God, we probably won't see her for a whole year and when she comes back we won't even recognise her. She'll have a new name, a new face, a new voice!'

He was getting a little too refreshingly candid now and Russell had to work to keep his voice from quivering as he answered: 'You think she's with another man, don't you? Is that what Beth thinks, as well?'

Dean shrugged awkwardly. 'What do we know, mate? All I'm saying is that's what Maggie was up to. And why else would a mother leave her children? It's not natural, is it? It's *got* to be to do with sex.'

Remembering both the mounting evidence of serious depression and his own newly-marked slate in matters of sexual fidelity, Russell finally found his pride. 'Not if it's to do with what's in her head,' he snapped. 'For all we know she could really be in real trouble somewhere and we're just sitting on our arses doing nothing about it! Don't forget what happened to her when she was younger. You of all people must remember that?'

'What?' said Dean. 'Oh, you mean that thing with the American kid?'

'The American kid?' Russell was thrown by this. 'I'm talking about her breakdown. When she was at college.'

'Yes,' Dean agreed, 'after he left she was in a bad way. But that was a long time ago, mate. There's no reason to think this is anything like that.'

Russell sighed in despair. 'There's every reason! If you don't mind me saying, Dean, you don't seem to know your sister very well at all.'

The riposte was instant and inevitable. 'You don't seem to know your *wife* so well, either.'

Before he could argue further, Russell became aware of a rapping sound from inside the house. He looked through the open French doors and through the series of arches to the front window, where Jana stood peering in, one hand shading her eyes from the reflected sun. Catching sight of him, she smiled and waved.

'Who's the totty?' Dean asked, craning to get a better look.

'It's our babysitter. I'd better—'

'Babysitter? But the boys are in Lincoln, aren't they? Anyway, I thought you just left them home alone when you went out?'

Russell was getting tired of this. 'Not if Noah's on his own. Has everyone forgotten he's only twelve years old? You make it sound like I don't know how to look after my own son. Anyway, she must have got the wrong day – let me just go and see.'

To his relief Dean did not follow, but took the opportunity to pluck his mobile phone from his pocket, turn his shoulders to the house and make a call (to Beth, presumably, perhaps to phone in a real-time account of his visit. Russell wondered if he'd 'fess up about his rant; that had *definitely* strayed from the party line).

He hurried to open the downstairs door. 'Jana, hi. You obviously didn't get my text.'

'When you send?' She smiled at him, her blue eyes spectacular in the evening light, and gave one of her distracted one-shoulder shrugs. The sight of her all clean and shiny and flirty, the pale summer clothes cut in curves around those divinely smooth limbs, her top with its little ruffles at the shoulder and a low, low scoop over her breasts, well, it made him want to keep her here, not send her away.

She leaned closer, not quite touching him. 'I like you, Russell.'

He gulped. 'I like you, Jana.' And that was all it took for him to part ways with his sensible self and add, 'Forget the text, you're here now, so why don't I get you a drink and meet you upstairs in the living room in a sec? I'm just in the garden saying goodbye to a buddy.'

329

A buddy? Why had he said that and not brother-in-law? It was hardly the time to start pretending he wasn't married, even if his wife *had* left him, and anyway Aniela would have filled her in on all of that, surely? He didn't know what he was playing at, or how long he thought he was going to play it, but it was clear he wasn't going to be summoning up the moral fibre to end the game tonight. Luckily Dean was still absorbed in his phone call and Russell managed to open a beer, hand it to Jana and shepherd her up the stairs without being observed.

When he returned to the terrace in hopes of getting rid of his buddy, he found he was in luck. Dean appeared not only to be much chastened, but also preparing to leave of his own accord. 'I owe you an apology, mate. Forget what I said just now. I was talking crap. I know nothing about mental ill—' He halted, correcting himself in a belated attempt at tact, then added, 'That kind of emotional stuff.'

Definitely reporting to Beth, then; she'd brought him up sharp.

'Already forgotten,' Russell said. 'It's a weird time for all of us, not just me. I really appreciate you coming around.'

Dean slapped his back, gratefully. 'Thanks, mate. I should get going, Beth's doing dinner. Oh, she says do you want to join us?'

'I won't, thanks,' Russell said, smoothly. 'I've got a ton of mail to open, as you can see. Why don't you come out the bottom way? Much quicker.'

Closing the door behind his guest, he deliberately avoided looking at the kitchen table, piled high with the post he had failed to tackle over the last month and – despite claiming otherwise just now – intended to leave there indefinitely. About a week ago he'd started opening letters and had stopped after reading two from the mortgage company, the first (sent second, as it transpired) informing him that their rate had reverted automatically to the shockingly high variable, a difference from previously of over two hundred pounds a month, and the second (sent first)

330

reminding him to renegotiate his rate because only two weeks remained before his current deal elapsed and he'd no longer be eligible to switch to the soon-to-close once-in-a-lifetime discounted rate reserved for really special borrowers like him. Blah, blah, blah. No doubt the many unopened letters from the insurance and utilities companies told of similar ambushes and missed windfalls. It was extraordinary how many of these letters arrived every day, a full-time job's worth of admin. And to think he'd found Olivia's evening updates tedious. Tedious! When all along she'd been brilliantly condensing them and spoon-feeding him the highlights.

Grabbing himself another beer, he considered that it might be easier if they did lose the house, if they no longer needed insurance because there were no contents to be insured, if he just cut his losses and found some shoebox for himself and the boys, some place where the heating, water, everything came included in the rent. For the first time in the last month – in the last year – he felt the physical necessity to be free of it all. And upstairs, Jana awaited.

'Look, mate,' Duncan said into his right ear, and Russell's shrunken, dehydrated, guilt-infested brain sparked just enough to wonder why everyone was calling him mate all of a sudden. Pity, of course, always it came down to pity. 'Mate' was shorthand for *I feel really, really sorry for you and I'd do anything not to swap places with you.* 'We all know you're having a tough time at the minute, but that doesn't mean you can take the mickey.'

'Duncan, I'm not feeling well. I have a cold and so I'm taking one day off. People do it all the time.'

'Is this to do with the kids?'

No, it's to do with regressing to the me of twenty years ago, to three consecutive nights of alcohol and music and sex and smoking – what were those disgusting cigarettes Jana had had with her last night – *Sobranies*, for Christ's sake. And no doubt he'd let it continue tonight as well if Jana hadn't told him she had to work beyond her usual finishing time of eleven.

'Haven't you sorted out help yet?' Duncan said. 'When do they go back to school?'

Russell sighed. 'You can't ask me about that sort of thing, Dunk. HR'd have a field day.' Was that even true? They were perfectly reasonable questions, after all. 'At least you couldn't if I were a woman,' he added.

Duncan snorted. 'Seems to me women have it all their way. Is there anything left we *are* allowed to have a go about? Anyway, I shall leave you to your period pains, mate, I've got to go, my car for the airport's just arrived. Quick meeting in Frankfurt. I'll see you first thing tomorrow, OK?'

'OK.'

He'd be sacked soon, that would be the next thing. The boys would have to come out of Herring's and go into whichever failing secondary the council couldn't fill except with the worst local scum. Jamie would be bullied the second he opened his mouth; Noah would cross over to the dark side and *become* scum. Before he knew it he'd have a Cane and Abel scenario on his hands. Seated at the kitchen table, he cast about for a suitable penance, not needing to look far before he came to the pile of mail and, at its base, his list of Dorset accommodations. He saw he'd reached the letter 'U' before finally abandoning the project. That must have been just after coming back from Portugal, when he'd made the decision to ask Olivia not to phone, when his spirits had reached an all-time low.

What was the sense in phoning hotels? he'd thought. Even the humblest of these B&Bs would have charged weekly sums far larger that the withdrawals Olivia had been making from their joint account. Wherever she was living she was paying a pittance. It was suddenly incredibly depressing to note that she'd continued to use cash throughout her absence; there'd not been a single credit card purchase this whole time. And she never used the same ATM, either, but different ones in Weymouth and other towns in the county, just spread out enough to make a fool's errand of any local search. Despite being in the throes of whatever it was she was in the throes of, she was covering her tracks quite competently.

You don't seem to know your wife so well, Dean had said, and he'd been right.

Now Russell wished he'd just gone into the office, where at least he'd be able to torture himself against a backdrop that didn't include a hat stand loaded with his lost wife's coats, not to mention a little display of their wedding photos above the radiator, or, if that toaster and bread bin were as old as he thought they might be, their wedding *gifts*, too. What else had Dean said that night – it seemed so long ago already – oh yes, about being bored with your life. Well, he'd thought he was bored, too, chronically bored, and he'd give anything to get bored back. Anything.

He picked up the B&B list. Usborne Terrace in Abbotsbury was the first of the remaining untried places. He dialled the number and heard the voicemail click on, cut the line dead with frustration. The next was Valerie's, Millington: that was engaged. He hit the call-back option and moved to the next, Verwood Lodge in Verwood. Abbotsbury, Millington, Verwood: where were these places? He remembered he'd originally used a map of the Dorset coast for his investigations, dismissing any that looked too far for the cashpoint run to Weymouth to be feasible. That was before she'd made a withdrawal from a bank in Lyme Regis and his system had been thrown. He'd been too reactive in his approach, not to mention completely unscientific. Perhaps when term started he should ask Jamie and his classmates for help. He imagined himself going in to Herring's to address the class, as movers and shakers among the parent body sometimes did. *Hello everybody! Today I have a special task for you all. I need to harness your special gifts to help me hunt down Jamie's mother . . .*

A voice bubbled into his ear. 'Hello, Verwood Lodge?' *Finally*, a living breathing person.

'Oh, hi, I wonder if you can help me. I'm looking for a guest called Olivia Chapman, who may have been staying with you this summer.'

'Let me just check for you, sir.'

It was incredible how obliging they were, quite happily searching files and ledgers when he could be a mad axeman sitting in a car across the road. But then, if you really wanted to shake someone off you'd use a false name, wouldn't you? Yes, Dean's hysterical ravings about a new identity were looking less and less unlikely with every minute.

'I'm afraid we've got no one by that name on our records.'

'Would you mind trying Olivia Lane?' Her maiden name. Damn, why had it taken him this long to think of something so simple? And should he try Alice, as well, her favourite name, the one she'd wanted for her babies had the boys turned out to be girls? The thought caused a violent bolt of guilt and love to drill through the wall of his stomach. Did that mean he should go back to the As and start all over again? Perhaps this time he could do it properly, no omissions but every single place in the whole county of Dorset, maybe even across the borders into Hampshire and Devon and Somerset. If he started now and didn't take a break, could he get through them all in this one day off? Perhaps if he worked into the night . . .

'Hello?' The voice was back. 'Sorry, I've just checked the register and there's no Olivia Lane either.'

'OK. Thank you.'

No sooner had he hung up than the phone was ringing, and a voice said 'Valerie's, how can I help you?'

'Oh, yes.' He re-launched his spiel. 'This is a long shot but I'm looking for someone called Olivia Chapman. She may be a guest with you.'

'Olivia? Hang on.' The girl didn't cover the mouthpiece so he could hear the exchange that followed quite clearly. 'Mum? What's Olivia's surname?'

'Olivia? I can't remember offhand, love. Look under July, when she was still here.'

'Is it Chapman? I can't find it . . .'

'I don't think so, but Tessa would know.'

The girl returned to Russell. 'No Olivia Chapman, sorry.'

'Wait!' Russell cried, before she could hang up. Had the girl no sense of curiosity? 'This Olivia you know, is she not staying with you now, then?'

'No, she was here for a few days ages ago, but then she moved up to Tessa's.'

In the background he could hear the second voice saying, 'Who is it, Martha? Tell them to leave a name and number and she'll call back.'

'Who is it?' The girl repeated, obediently.

'I'm from Abbotsbury Deliveries,' Russell improvised. 'I'm just trying to sort out a delivery and this is the last address I have for her. But don't worry, I'll just change the details to Tessa's. Can you remind me which street that is?'

'Yes, it's Barn Lane, number 55.'

'Barn Lane, Millington?'

'That's right.'

On the page in front of him Russell saw he'd been circling the word Valerie's over and over, pressing so hard the nib of the pen had broken right through the paper to the wood of the table. 'Thank you,' he said. 'You're a real lifesaver.'

Chapter 38

Am I imagining her scorn for me, her rivalry? Am I inventing a position on my own mother's part that doesn't really exist? Am I thinking so differently from everyone else in this world that the truth I believe in is actually false?

Even at the time, I do wonder, I do doubt. When I listen in the common room to the stories of my classmates, whose love lives are so similar, so *typical*, that only the names of the boys vary (and even then not always); when Melanie's eyes no longer gleam at the whispered mention of Richie's name or spark in indignation at my report of another treacherous remark; when I feel completely alone – I do wonder, I do doubt.

Most of my friends have abandoned me – if anyone can smell when gloom is terminal it's a teenage girl – and judging by some of the comments that come my way, Mel has finally caved in and revealed the secret of last year's pregnancy. I suppose I should be grateful that she's at least waited until I don't care any more.

There is a limit to how many times a teacher will take someone aside and ask what is wrong, and it was reached a while ago, about the time Samantha Culler was made sports captain and I gave up on the idea of art college. In the end, they had to set my predicted A-level grades lower than they would have liked because my mock results were so poor. Now my future education is not to be in one of the top universities like Dean's, but in a humbler institution, one of the ones our school doesn't boast about much at prize giving.

I changed my mind about art school the minute I discovered it involved a one-year sandwich course at the local college, an extra year under my mother's roof. But I still draw. When I'm supposed to be revising I while away the hours in my bedroom sketching portraits of old movie stars, the ones with the heavy-lidded eyes and sad mouths. I use lots of heavy soft pencil or charcoal. Lots of black.

The only time I truly feel any energy is when Mum and I have our big fight. I've skipped a double history to come home and listen to music, to smoke out of my bedroom window and dream I am someone else. But either I've lost track of time or Mum has changed her shopping day, because suddenly she is in the house with me, storming up the stairs, shouting, 'Is that cigarette smoke I can smell?'

She sounds like the ogre who smells the blood of an Englishman. There is lust in her voice, she *wants* to find me guilty, to grind my bones.

I look up from the window ledge as she bursts in. 'What's the problem? It's only a Camel.' Richie's brand, not easy to find around here.

'Put it out right now!' She snatches up the pack from my desk and breaks the remaining cigarettes into pieces, releasing the scent of dry tobacco between us. 'The problem *is* we will *not* have these filthy things in this house!'

'You smoked yourself until a few years ago,' I remind her. 'You were happy to have us grow up with these "filthy things"' – I ape her habit of putting inverted commas around the words – 'so why not now?'

'We didn't know they were so bad for us then!' she splutters. 'Or that they smelled so vile!'

'Yeah, right,' I mock. 'You thought they were just like Chanel

338

No.5, didn't you?' I wonder if she's tempted to push me out the window – it's wide open and there are skull-cracking patio stones below. 'You know, your brother wasn't half as bad as this. At least he had a sense of humour about being a bloody annoying adolescent!'

I feel venom sliding up my throat and it's too late to stop myself. 'Yeah, he had to, otherwise you'd have seen how much he *hated* you.'

All at once her hands are flying at me; not fists, but fingers, nails, catching in my clothes and hair. I fend her off, falling to the bed under the window and dodging out of reach. For a few moments we just stare at each other, breathless. I'm less shocked by her attack than by the realisation that she has nothing better to offer. She is just the same as me, but older. She is what I have to look forward to.

'You're pathetic,' I say, speaking first.

'I *must* be to have come back to this house,' she mutters under her breath.

'Why did you?' I taunt her. 'And don't give me that crap about wanting to be with your dear darling children.'

'What on earth are you talking about?' she gasps. And she takes a step back as if to rid herself of the itch to grab me again.

'*I* know why you came back,' I say, coldly. 'And it was nothing to do with Dad, either. You don't love him at all.'

She sucks her teeth, furious. 'That's a despicable thing to say. You can't just say these things and not expect to upset people! What comes around goes around, you know.'

But she doesn't ask what I mean – that would be the natural thing, wouldn't it? – she doesn't demand, What do you mean, what is it you think you know?

'What about the letter?' I go on. 'Are you at least going to tell me if that was real?'

She throws up her hands. 'What letter? What is *wrong* with you, girl?'

'The letter from Warren. The one about Richie getting married.'

She frowns. 'Of course it was real. What, you're accusing me of holding a blank piece of paper in front of me and pretending to read from it? Why would I do that?'

She remembers the whole display of it then; her performance at the breakfast table. How could that stick in her mind if it hadn't been of unusual significance to her?

'Show me it, then,' I say.

She returns my challenging look with one of sheer disbelief. 'I can't show you something I've thrown away, don't be ridiculous!'

'I don't believe you threw it away. I think you would have kept it, like a trophy.'

She shakes her head. 'You're in some kind of fantasy world, Dolly. I think it must be the pressure of exams or something.'

I know then that I'm never going to find out the truth, she is never going to admit to it, which means there will be no end to this. Out of nowhere I think of the nurse I saw after the miscarriage, her hand on my back, the expression on her face, and the thought of her kindness makes me unutterably sad.

'Why do you want to ruin my life?' I ask, simply.

And Mum looks at me before she turns to go, a slow, disdainful look, as if to say, 'I think it's the other way round, dear.'

That night I'm trapped inside my dream. I'm struggling to breathe freely. It feels like I've been buried alive, the soil damp and heavy on my face, caking tighter into my mouth and nostrils the harder I flail.

'Just tell me! Just tell me!'

'Tell you what, Dolly?'

'I need to know, did you make it up? Did he really do it?'

'She's talking in her sleep, listen . . .' Someone is speaking to me through the warm earth. Is it Richie? No, it's my father, and he's turning in panic to a second figure. 'What's she saying?' he asks. 'What does she mean?'

'You stopped us from being together! I know you did!'

And Mum says. 'She was behaving very oddly earlier as well. I think she must be hallucinating or something, poor love. We'd better talk to the doctor in the morning.'

I tell the doctor nothing. He says exam stress is a big problem for my generation, a modern epidemic, and I should seriously consider deferring my A-levels for a year. With an August birthday, I'm one of the youngest in my class, so no one would think anything of it.

'No, definitely not!' The idea of that extra year at home is more unendurable than ever.

'All right,' he says. 'But I want to see you regularly, keep an eye on you. If you don't feel better soon, I'd like to arrange for you to see a psychiatrist.'

And so I do the studying, take the exams, do enough to get the new low grades I need to get out of here.

It's a blazing yellow day when the last exam finishes and everyone is tearing out of the common room doors and running down the bank to the playing fields. They're ripping up old timetables, hurling biros into the sky like javelins, screaming that they're free at last. You can see the faces of the younger kids at their classroom windows, ready to wish away the years ahead if they could be down here with us now.

And I run, too, really fast, almost tripping over my own legs, until I come to a halt somewhere in the middle of the hockey pitch and sink to the ground, spreading out my arms and legs like a starfish. There's a plane overhead, I can see it's a 747, and it's climbing steeply through the blue. I have no idea where it's going but the sight of it changes my mood completely, right then and there. For the rest of the day, all I feel is jealousy.

I'm jealous that when those people get to where they're going they'll be closer to him than I am.

Chapter 39

The leaflet about Weymouth's illustrious royal history was open on the café table in front of me, but I couldn't absorb a single word of it. I'd already forgotten which George it was who took to the waters here in his famous bathing machine – II or III? – even though I'd read it only two minutes ago. Nor could I apply myself to the excitements of the town's future, emblazoned on posters everywhere I looked. The Red Arrows would be here next weekend, hurrah! The countdown to the Olympics had begun, tick-tock! But I couldn't bring either of those events into focus.

No, all I could think was, *In ten minutes' time I will be face to face with Russell*. At exactly this moment he would be parking his car (*our* car – did he think of anything at Sterling Avenue as shared any more?) and strolling down to the harbour to find this café, to find me, his runaway wife. And when he opened the door and walked over to my table, when he said my name, how would I respond? Would I pass back through the looking glass and feel *myself* again?

His text had come last night, my first word from him in two weeks:

O. I know you're in
Millington. I'm coming

tomorrow. No
arguments. R.

I'd known, of course, that it was only a matter of time before it happened, and not just because of that phone call to Tessa ('I got the impression this wasn't the first place he'd tried'). If I was honest, I'd known from the moment the Weymouth train returned to London without me that first Sunday night in July. These six weeks may have felt like a gift from the gods, but they had really been a loan. Borrowed time. Whichever way you looked at it I was badly in debt, and a face-to-face meeting with my husband was the very least I owed him.

No, I had no arguments. The only detail I could hope to influence was the meeting place. I couldn't see him in the village, where I was Olivia Lane, where I was Richie's girl. It had to be somewhere else, somewhere busy and full of strangers.

I texted back:

Meet me in Weymouth
at Old Pump Café by
harbour, 12 o'clock?

His response was immediate: I'll be there.

I didn't know if he was bringing the boys – they would still be on school holidays, so it was quite possible – and a part of me responded to the prospect with a sweet, soaring feeling. I knew that it wasn't a quarter of what I'd watched Richie contain the night before Wren came back from France, or a half of the breathlessness that came over Tessa whenever a postcard arrived from Amanda, but it was still joy and to that I clung for dear life.

In the café, I chose a table for four, just in case, and tried to imagine the three of them filling the empty seats around me. 'The three of them': it was a familiar phrase to me, I must have said it and thought it thousands of times over the years, as I had 'the

344

three of you'. But why never *the four of us*? Why did *that* sound so foreign? Had I begun separating myself from them before I came here? Had I *always* been doing it?

I'd told Richie I was meeting Russell – lying to him now was the same as lying to myself and, in any case, this was exactly what he'd campaigned for himself. Though he'd offered to drive me into Weymouth and wait for me somewhere out of sight, we both knew there were pressing things for him to be getting on with in Bridport mid-week. His job there was finally almost over, only the finishing touches remaining, and the sooner he did them the sooner he could bank his cheque and move on.

Tessa ordered me a taxi. 'You look as if you're going to the gallows,' she said, sitting with me while I waited.

'Maybe I am,' I said, disconsolately.

'Who are you meeting in town?'

'My husband.'

Misunderstanding clouded her face. 'Your . . . oh, you mean your ex-husband?'

'No, my husband.'

She blinked, processing this. She hadn't put on any make-up this morning and her natural lashes were pale and powdery. She made me think suddenly of Lindy. I imagined her thoughts: Who *is* this woman? What is she hiding? Is she really in trouble?

'But you're in the process of divorcing, are you?' she asked, at last.

'I don't know,' I said, 'I think I'm about to find out.'

She considered this. 'Do *you* want to?'

'I wish I knew.'

'You'd know if you did,' she said. 'So if you don't know, then you probably don't want to.'

'But I'm happier here,' I said, 'here in Millington.'

'Are you happy?' she asked, gently. 'To me, you seem . . . not unhappy, but . . . adrift, I suppose.'

When the car pulled up, she told me the best place to pick up a taxi back to Millington, but it was obvious from the way she squeezed my wrist at the door that she was seriously considering the possibility that I might not come back.

The sound of gulls and rushing wind signalled the opening of the café door, but I couldn't bring myself to look over my shoulder as I had the last twenty times.

'Olivia, you're here.'

'Russell.'

He was right in front of me and I was out of my seat but we didn't hug, neither wanting to presume; he just pulled back the seat opposite mine and slipped quietly into it. He was on his own. He looked exhausted, almost glazed, like a security guard who has watched for so long he can no longer see.

'I wasn't sure if you'd be bringing the boys with you?' I said.

His eyebrows drew together. 'Jamie and Noah? Surely you agree it's more appropriate for us to meet on our own?'

'Yes, absolutely.' Too late I saw that my question was a catastrophic opening gambit. It must have sounded as though I'd been treating this meeting as some sort of official visitation, the kind of thing a divorced parent might be required to attend. It wasn't surprising that when he spoke again there was an edge of reproach to his tone, despite the words.

'You look very well. Completely different, actually, I almost didn't recognise you. Your hair's longer.'

I could do nothing but treat these as casual compliments. 'I haven't had it cut all summer.' I smiled. 'I can see you're in the same boat.'

'Yeah. I keep meaning to sort it out, but . . .' Russell pawed absentmindedly at the point where his hair met the collar of his charcoal-coloured shirt. The shirt was long-sleeved, his throat pale, he looked such a cold, wintry creature, tired and underslept.

'Anything for you, sir?' The waitress was at his side and he ordered a black coffee, looking first to me in case I needed something besides the tea I already had in front of me. I asked for a new pot, though I didn't really want it. But I didn't want him to think I was in any hurry to leave.

The waitress turned on her heel and our small talk resumed. 'Nice old town.' Russell gestured through the window to the harbour. Above the red, white and blue of the fishing boats, rain clouds gathered vertically, like smoke-stacks. 'Haven't been here before, I don't think.'

'No,' I agreed. 'I don't think we ever got further than Poole, did we?' The past tense sounded brutal, as if I meant something by it, and his face darkened.

'So why didn't you want to meet in Millington?' he asked. 'That's where you're staying, isn't it? And it's obviously not far from here.'

I had expected this question and decided that a lie was probably best. 'I thought you might be coming on the train; the station's just up the road from here. Millington isn't on the train line, you have to get a taxi.'

'Oh. Well, it wouldn't have mattered, I drove. But this is fine,' he added. 'I'm just glad to have finally found you.'

'I'm sorry I didn't tell you where I was,' I said. 'I know I should have.' The words were caught in a cough, making them even more absurdly inadequate than they already were.

'Got there in the end,' Russell said, shortly.

Despite the risk of displeasing him again, I was unable to hold off any longer. 'How *are* the boys? Are they OK?'

He nodded. 'They're good. They're up at my mum's – you know what her place is like, no Internet or cable TV or anything – but they seem to be coping with the deprivations. I told them to treat it like an exercise in how Cro-Magnon man lived. Maybe she could host school trips.'

I laughed unnecessarily hard, not so much for the joke itself

347

but for the fact that he was speaking exactly as he would have had I last seen Jamie and Noah just a day or two ago. I knew then what I'd most been dreading of this meeting: some definite sign that he considered himself solely responsible for them now, that he'd presumed me gone for good. I wasn't ready for that.

'They go back to school soon,' Russell continued. 'I'd like to say the summer's raced by but I can't, because it hasn't. It's been the longest in living memory.'

His tone had changed to something more openly castigating and pride made me stand my ground, in spite of my obvious guilt. 'Yes,' I said, 'the school holidays can seem very long.' I topped up my still-half-full cup with some of the new tea. The hotter liquid made patterns in the surface of the colder.

'So . . .' He waited for me to stop staring into my cup and resume eye contact with him. His right thumb played on a bump in the glaze of his mug handle, back and forth, as if working it smooth. He was going to graze his skin. 'Tell me, then. Why are you still here over six weeks after you went away for the weekend?' The strength of will required to condense everything he wanted to ask, everything he had the right to know, into that single question was evident in his face. He wanted the truth from me, even if it was going to tear him apart.

I took a long, slow breath. 'I've been seeing someone down here. I mean, not for long, just the last few weeks, but that's part of the reason I'm still here.'

The thumb stopped moving. Briefly, pain turned Russell's eyes childlike before the shutters closed. 'Who is he?'

I took a gulp of tea, hand trembling. 'He's an old friend. I knew him when I was at school. Before this summer I hadn't seen him since then. He was my first real boyfriend, I suppose.'

Russell's eyes were dead. 'What, the American kid? The one Maggie didn't want you to go out with?'

'I didn't know you remembered that story,' I said, uncertainly, 'but, yes, it's him. He lives down here now.'

348

'Evidently.' He didn't demand a name or any of the rest of the story, but asked only, 'Does that mean you want to stay down here permanently?' The contraction in his throat was visible, but I could only guess what it was he was swallowing: an insult, a demand, a scream? Finally, he shaped the words: 'Come on, Olivia, answer the question.'

'I don't know,' I said.

He sighed in mock amusement. 'Oh no, I don't want to hear "I don't know" any more. All this time you've let us believe you've been on the verge of some kind of nervous collapse, when the truth is you've been . . .' He broke off, hardly believing what he was finding himself saying. 'I really thought you've been down here getting your head together, getting over Maggie!'

'That's how it started, yes. And in a way I still am.'

'Well, you've obviously over it enough to start a new relationship,' Russell sneered. 'Or should I say pick up where you left off?'

'It wasn't a deliberate thing,' I protested. 'He's helped me resolve everything that happened with Mum.'

'Well, I'm very pleased for you both.' His voice was frighteningly emotionless as he asked, 'So, now you've finally spilled the beans, should I be talking to someone about a divorce? Is that the next step?'

I shook my head, not daring to say the words, but he leapt on them anyway.

'Don't say it again, OK? If you say you don't know one more time I'll walk out of here, I swear.' All at once his voice was flushed with disgust: 'You may not realise this, but none of us knows anything ever, we're no different from you. It's all pretty fucking confusing for everyone in this world, believe it or not. But we still manage to get on with our lives, to honour our commitments. Yes, even when terrible things happen, like someone in the family dying . . .' he paused, '. . . or a child going missing.'

I looked up, a cold, black feeling on my skin. 'What d'you mean, a child going missing?'

He drew back from me. 'Nothing. Forget it.'

'What, Russell?' Panic sucked at my breath exactly as it had that morning I'd heard his stricken plea on my voicemail. 'Is that what your message meant? Tell me, what's been going on? You never explained—'

His expression was thunderous. '*I* never explained! That's a joke!'

'Please,' I begged, feeling tears rise. 'Please, just tell me.'

He closed his eyes as if summoning strength he wasn't sure he possessed. 'When we were on holiday, our son vanished.'

I stared, appalled. 'Noah?'

'No, Jamie. We found him again, obviously.'

'Where was he?'

'He'd gone off on his own, made a break for the nearest town. Nothing a million teenagers haven't done before, huh?' Russell's mouth twisted in derision, he was trying to shrug this off, but I knew from the set of his shoulders that the memory shook him badly.

'You mean, he went off without telling you? He *ran away*?'

'Yep, that's the gist of it.'

'But why?'

He scoffed, incredulous. 'You tell me, Olivia. A cry for attention maybe? Could that be possible? It didn't work, though, did it? When I phoned you that night, you didn't even phone back.'

Shame washed over me. 'I did phone back,' I cried, 'I phoned the second I got your messages!'

'That was two days later. It was way too late by then.'

'But I didn't have my mobile with me before. I'd left it at Tessa's, that's the place where I'm staying—'

He cut in, coldly: 'While you were off shacked up with your childhood sweetheart, I suppose? How romantic. There's a nice story for your eulogy, eh? Don't tell me, you'll be expecting *me* to deliver it?'

I gasped. 'Russell!' His insult cut deeper than any other, as he'd known it would. 'I'm not like her,' I said, fighting to keep my voice steady.

'No?'

'*No*. And I'm sorry about Jamie, I'm really sorry. I had no idea something like that was going on. Poor, poor kid.'

'You do remember they're still kids then, do you?'

We stared at each other. The emotions in his face were changing so rapidly, they were scrambled; I couldn't track them.

'Kids need a mother, Olivia. I know they're a bit different – "exceptional" if you believe that ridiculous school of theirs. But kids need a mother and there are no exceptions to that.'

'I know,' I said.

'You know something, then? That's a relief.' Fear filled my lungs. He had the air of someone who had reached his final position far earlier than he'd hoped or planned. 'You have to make a decision,' he said at last. 'If I don't have it by the end of this week, then I'll be calling a solicitor first thing on Monday morning and getting the legal process started. You have to choose: him or me.' He didn't say 'him or us' and for that I was profoundly grateful. He gave me a tense, pained smile. 'I won't make it difficult for you, you needn't worry about that, but you *have* to choose. Do you understand?'

'Yes.'

His eyes narrowed again; something had occurred to him, something that conflicted with this ultimatum, and I felt a gush of hope inside me. 'You do realise it's the reading of Maggie's will on Friday morning? At her solicitor's office in Cheltenham. Do you plan on being there? According to Lindy, one of us needs to be.'

'The will?' A memory bubbled up as if from decades ago, predating all the relived teenage anguishes that had hijacked my thoughts these last weeks, and yet I didn't need Russell to tell me it was only a matter of weeks since it had happened: I was on the phone to Lindy, turning the pages of the pink calendar in the kitchen, chewing the end of a pen as I listened to her speak. 'We've agreed a time for the last week of August.' And I'd thought, *That's a lifetime away, hardly worth making a note of yet*. Well, evidently the lifetime had passed.

'I don't think I can handle it,' I said, truthfully.

'So you'd like me to go in your place?' Russell asked, sourly. 'To take more time off work?'

'No, you don't have to do that. We'll tell them not to expect either of us. I'm sure we'll find out soon enough if there's anything to find out.'

'*I* will, yes, but I don't suppose your teenage lover's address is known to the legal authorities.' He swallowed the last of his coffee and pushed his empty mug away from him in an angry gesture.

'Russell . . .' All my instincts urged me to do something to show him I was not the lost cause he thought I was. I might not be able to find the right words but that didn't mean I wanted the wrong ones put in my mouth for me. 'Please, Russell, try to understand . . .'

'Understand *what*?'

There was a sudden clamour in the café – customers' voices competing with the hiss and splutter of the coffee machine and the hard crack of crockery being stacked on the marble counter – and I had to raise my voice to be heard: 'Understand that something is wrong with me. I know I've hurt you, I know I've been a terrible mother, but I want to explain how completely *lost* I've been feeling.'

Not too lost to have found Richie or to have discovered I loved him all over again. Not too lost to have formed an unshakeable sense of belonging in the place he'd made his . . .

'Well, you have till Monday to find yourself again,' Russell said, as icily as if he'd read every last word of my thoughts.

We gazed at each other, utterly at odds. Irreconcilable, that was the word the courts used. Was that going to be the word that formally separated me from my family? The café sounds were all but extinguished as the thick white noise of terror filled my ears. 'What should I do, Russell? What do *you* want me to do?'

The question seemed to affect him physically. He was inhaling deeply, draining all available air between us and leaving me breathless. 'Do you really want to know?' he asked. 'Would it really make a difference if I told you?'

'Yes,' I whispered. 'It would. Of course it would.'

His eyes lost their hardness then; they were Noah's eyes, innocent and trusting. 'I want you to choose to come home, that's what I want. I want you to come back with me now, today, then go up to Cheltenham on Friday and bury this crap with Maggie once and for all. I want you to be who you really are, that's what I want!' His face was twitching with emotion. 'Listen, if you're feeling confused or overwhelmed, then let's get you some help. Beth will know the right person, a grief counsellor or something. Or maybe someone longer term, some kind of professional support that's always there for you. I don't care how much it costs.'

I felt completely disarmed by this. I responded instinctively, without thinking. 'But how could I come back after what I've told you? I mean, I couldn't even if I . . .'

I stopped myself. There was a ghastly silence.

'Even if you wanted to?' Russell said, voice flat, face crushed. 'That was what you were going to say, wasn't it?'

'No,' I stammered. 'I meant, how could I expect you to forgive me for what I've done?' How could my children not turn on me as Dean and I had Maggie? How could they not replicate our mutiny, a mutiny that had lasted a *lifetime*? And how could I explain to Russell that whatever my future, whatever 'help' I received, my original treachery could only get bigger and bigger in my head because of that one terrible parallel I could never escape?

There was another painful silence. 'I don't think you're yourself, Olivia,' Russell said, as if finally understanding what this conversation had been about. 'Of course it would be possible to forgive you, because it's not you who's doing it. Whoever it is who's moved down here, started up with this old boyfriend, it's not you. I can see it now, you're someone completely different.'

The sense of revelation in his voice was powerful. I suppressed a shiver. 'What do you mean?'

'God, I don't know how to describe it. I suppose it's like seeing a film of you or something, how you might have been if things hadn't turned out the way they did . . . you know, if we'd never met and got married, done the stuff we've done. A kind of alternative history.'

'That's how I feel myself!' I cried. 'That's how I've felt since I got here. It's not me, or at least it's the me I'd forgotten I ever was. It feels like, oh, like the body snatchers or something. And I don't know if I can ever get myself back!'

Russell blinked. 'Well, forgive me if I don't find that terribly reassuring.' His fingertips began to massage his temples, his tongue licked dry lips. It occurred to me that he must have been driving for three or four hours to make this twelve o'clock meeting time, maybe longer in morning traffic. And he faced the same journey back – alone and with only stalemate and ultimatum to replay for company. Finally, I understood what I had done to him: I had almost destroyed him.

'I'm sorry,' I said, simply. 'I wish I could make things better, like they were.'

For the first time Russell touched me, reaching forwards and gripping my hand in his. 'Listen to me, Olivia, they *can* be like they were. I think we can get over what's happened these last few months, this last year, two years, however long you've been feeling like this. Everyone's entitled to a bit of time out, a few crazy mistakes . . .' Something private and unreadable crossed his face before he added, 'It's nothing in the long run, is it?' His eyes were

354

intense, all fear and anger set aside, and I felt the urgency of his love inside me as well as in the pressure on my fingers in his hand. 'I want you to know that if you do come back I wouldn't hold any of this against you. The opposite! I would make it my business to make sure you never felt unhappy enough to want to do this again . . .' The words broke apart then, just as tears began to fall down my cheeks, and it was almost as if they'd sprung from the crack in his voice.

'Don't cry,' he said, sadly.

'I can't help it. I don't deserve what you're offering.'

'Of course you deserve it. You're my wife, Olivia. You're my *life*.' He returned my hand to the flat of the table, gently, carefully, as though lowering something breakable from a great height. 'If you don't deserve it, then nobody does.'

He had never said anything like this to me before. And as he stood and turned to leave, his posture still that of a burdened man but his eyes strangely free, I understood that he would not come back and say it a second time.

Chapter 40

Broken both by emotion and heat, I decided that the only way to process my meeting with Russell was to sleep. Arriving back in Millington, I avoided Tessa's querying presence by dialling Richie's number as I walked through door and retreating upstairs with the phone clutched to my ear. I got his answerphone, which was partly a relief, and after leaving a brief message of reassurance I pulled down the blinds and sank low into my teenager's bed under the eaves.

Lord knew what connections took place in my mind, but I came to early the next morning thinking about my mother's funeral. I had a perfect bird's-eye view of the gathering, far removed from my actual experience of it – and more disturbing. That uneasy black oval we made around the freshly dug grave: from above it resembled nothing more than a ring of beetles advancing upon an open mouth, not uneasy at all but intent and pitiless.

As I washed my face and cleaned my teeth, the words of the committal played on my lips like a song I couldn't shake off: '*We therefore commit her body to the ground; earth to earth, ashes to ashes, dust to dust; in the sure and certain hope of the Resurrection to eternal life.*'

The phrasing was familiar from a thousand television dramas and yet somehow, on the day, to me it had been quite foreign, the meaning impossible to grasp. To hear those words, to step forward and scatter earth on your own mother's coffin (the sound of it was much more solid than you might have expected, like a proper blow) and to not feel anything deep inside . . . To think instead of – what had it been? – superficial things like how cold my feet were, how fidgety the couple behind me. I should have noticed then that something wasn't right.

Lindy had noticed. She'd said to me, 'Give it time,' and I had given it time, I'd given myself so much of the stuff I'd been able to create a second life from it, a second family. And now Russell had taken events to their logical conclusion and named the day – Monday – when my time would finally be up. I couldn't blame him for that; I couldn't blame him for anything. Having begun our meeting hardly recognising him, I'd left it haunted by memories of how he had appeared to me when we'd met twenty years ago, when I'd still borne the bruises of Richie's casual betrayal and was struggling to understand my new independence from Maggie. I hadn't yet connected to adult life, to life outside my own head. Russell had rescued me from myself, he had shown me what normal meant. A life with fewer dramas but greater safety. A home with children in it. A rhythm to the years that had comforted before it had suffocated. He'd rescued me then and now he was willing to do it again.

I wondered if he'd told the boys about our meeting yesterday. He must surely be preparing himself to break the news, the news that I had not come through for them, that I was a coward and a deserter. My phone had remained silent for the rest of the day, in fact since Russell's last text late on Tuesday night: *I'll be there.* No family, no friends, no cold callers. It was as if the world had finally given up on me.

Today was Thursday. I had until Monday morning to decide if I was ready to give up on the world.

Fuelled by fourteen hours' sleep and two mugs of strong instant coffee, I left the house before Tessa was up and walked downhill into the centre of Millington. After a moment's hesitation, I passed through the kissing gate into the churchyard. As with most corners of the village, this was a beauty spot in its own right, with its moss-cloaked golden stone and deep borders of late summer flowers; it didn't feel like a sad place at all, more a private garden meant for pleasure. I moved carefully among the headstones, trying to decipher the inscriptions, many of the letters lost long ago to the elements and only traces left now of those spare, heartfelt phrases: 'entered into rest', 'devoted wife', 'in sacred memory', 'beloved mother'.

'Beloved mother' came up a lot. I wondered if it was the adjective mothers most desired for themselves; having devoted their adult lives to loving others, they wanted to be remembered as having been loved in return.

That made me think of something one of Mum's nurses had said – Joyce, she was called, a woman not much younger than Mum herself but as overflowing with vim and vigour as Mum was depleted of it. We had gathered in the kitchen around a pot of tea, she and Lindy having finished their bustling. All that replenishing of supplies, renewing equipment, cleaning and airing – it always reminded me of a new baby's nap, when the day's chores had to be fitted into that golden hour of silence. Unfamiliar with the medical practicalities of dosage calculations and plastic under-sheets, I would busy myself with the flowers, refreshing the water, cutting another centimetre off the stems to give them a last suck at life.

'It's important for Maggie to have you here,' Joyce told me. 'What we find at this stage is it's the emotional needs not the physical ones that need the most attention. All they want at the end is to feel it's been worth it because they've been loved. That's their proof of life, if you like.'

Maybe it was my own guilt working on me, but it had felt as if she were not so much telling me this as *tasking* me with it. Her life's almost over, you're her only daughter – so get on with the devoted act, whether you feel it or not!

Now, in the churchyard, sitting in the sunshine my mother no longer shared, I couldn't bear to evaluate whether or not I had succeeded.

Too restless to sit for long, I left the churchyard and climbed to the ruin on the hill, a pilgrimage I had not made since my first week here. At the top, a couple with a terrier argued hotly about which path to take and just as I thought they would never stop they made their decision and were gone. I sat on the grass with my back against the thick stone of the outer wall, the ocean to one side of me, the village to the other. From here Millington's unique and precious position in its cradle of hills was fully revealed – you could almost stretch out your finger and trace the streets below. But for the occasional gust of wind or bleating sheep, it was quite silent. I should have come up here more often, I realised, because this was where you could really dig deep inside yourself.

And that was when it happened, just as Richie had been confident it would and Russell feared it might never; just as I had despaired of being locked out of myself for the rest of my days, it happened: I had my answer. Richie, Russell: they had been at the centre of everything for me – not just this summer, but ever since I'd been old enough to love for myself – and yet all along I had been paying attention to the wrong man.

Pulling myself upright against the cold stone, I dialled Lindy's number, quite clear about what I had to do. I would see him tomorrow.

She answered on the second ring, her voice bright with delight. 'Olivia, how wonderful! Oh, we've all been so worried about you! Are we going to see you at Mr Bellamy's office tomorrow?'

'Yes,' I said, 'that's why I'm calling. I don't have the address with me.'

'I've got it right in front of me.' She gave me a street name in Cheltenham, straightforward enough for me to commit it to

360

memory. She knew better than to press me with questions, but said she hoped we would have time to catch up the next morning. Though I doubted that, I thanked her, as grateful as ever for her sensitivity, and said I was looking forward to it.

Next I texted Russell to tell him I would be attending the meeting after all and he need not take the day off work. He texted back three words: Thanks, that helps. There would be no final speculation about tomorrow's revelations, nor even a simple 'Good luck'. When the time came, he would get his news of the outcome from another source – Dean, perhaps, or Lindy. But he and I, we were no longer in this together.

I put my phone away, looked about me once more. Below, still bathed in cloudless sunshine, the perfect imprint of Millington streets was beginning to lose its clarity.

Chapter 41

This time, Richie insisted on driving me to the station himself. We were both grateful for Wren's presence in the backseat, for her quick-fire, comically misspelled 'I Spy' games that stopped us from talking about what was ahead.

Before we parted a kind of chill passed between us, an unspoken fear that this might be the last time we saw each other. In the streets by the station, normal people were going about their business, making short work of their goodbyes. I felt sure ours was the only farewell like this one, just as my greetings later in the morning would be the only ones like them. I was the common denominator in all this doubt and unease, and the burden of it threatened to overpower me all over again. Get through today, I told myself, and then the way will be clearer.

'I feel weird about saying goodbye,' Richie said, in a low voice.

'I *am* coming back to Millington later,' I told him. 'I'll come straight to the house, like we said.'

Satisfied that Wren was distracted by the gulls on the pavement below her window, he leaned across to kiss me: 'I hope so.'

I knew what he feared without him needing to tell me: that I would abandon him as I believed he had once abandoned me, that this would complete the symmetry between us. Then something made me remember a detail from the Acacia Street days. 'Hey, do you remember, in the old days, you never used to say goodbye?'

'What?'

'You used to say "sayonara" instead.'

'I did?'

'Yes. You said you got it from your friend Troy. "Sayonara, sucker!"'

He began grinning. 'Troy . . . that's right. What was his last name again? Wow, I'd forgotten about him. Did we really say that? What a pair of clowns.'

I reached for the door handle. 'You got us all saying it. I remember we thought it was so cool.'

He looked fondly at me. 'You wouldn't say it now, though, would you?'

I smiled, brushed my fingers over his. 'Maybe you can teach it to Wren instead.'

I knew exactly what I wanted to say to my brother. If I hadn't been quite word-perfect before I negotiated the join-the-dots rail route from Weymouth to Cheltenham, then I certainly was by the time I got there.

And I was lucky, too, because he was as early as I was, arriving a good half-hour ahead of the scheduled time. I caught him as he parked his car across the road from the solicitor's office, his quick, critical eyes taking in the gracious Regency address near Imperial Square. From my seat on the grass bank nearby, I'd had an opportunity to study it myself. It might have been a grand family home, with its fashionable pale green woodwork, baskets of flowers, well-scrubbed stone. Only the small brass plaque gave a clue to the business within.

I scrambled to my feet and called out: 'Dean!'

He turned at the sound of his name, key fob still outstretched, not seeing me yet.

I waved. 'Over here!'

A break in the traffic, a dozen long strides, and he was next to me. He didn't come quite up to me, though, as if fearing I might have turned feral. 'Olivia! Thank Christ you're here! Russell seemed to think you'd be giving it a miss. So where did you—'

'I'll explain that later,' I cut in, my throat too full of my own prepared speech to allow me to hear out his questions. 'Listen, Dean, can we talk before we go in? We've got a few minutes and I really need to speak to you, just you and me.'

He snorted. 'Two months of complete silence and that's what she says! Speak away, darling!'

'Can we sit down? What about here on the grass?'

'If we must.' He lowered himself into a schoolboy pose, knees up in front of his face, awkward to manage in his tailored suit. It occurred to me that he was far more smartly dressed than he had been at the funeral.

'Well, well, well,' he said, raising his eyebrows. 'I *told* Russ this would bring you out of hiding.'

Hiding? But I was much too fired up to argue the implications of *that*. 'We need to forgive her, Dean,' I said, leaning eagerly towards him. 'No, more than that, we *have* to forgive her if we want to have any chance of enjoying the rest of our lives.'

His mouth twisted to one side. 'I assume by "her" you mean our dear departed mother?'

'Dear departed', not once had I seen that well-worn phrase on a headstone in Millington graveyard. It sounded sarcastic, unloving, and not just because it was Dean who was saying it.

'Maybe we'll have a better idea of whether we can forgive her in about half an hour's time, eh?' he suggested.

'I'm not talking about that,' I said. 'It doesn't matter what her stupid will says.'

His face was a picture of scandalised horror, but nothing could derail me now. I *had* to get him to understand, it was crucial that we both did this, not just me. His influence on me was too powerful, it always had been. I couldn't break from Mum *and* him, not both at once. 'Seriously, we've got to stop letting her ruin our lives, once and for all. We've got to sort it out between us – you and me. I mean, I know we've said it before, but we've never actually let it go, have we?'

'What are you talking about?' He had begun fidgeting with his mobile phone and without thinking I snatched it from his hands and tossed it away from us. Unnerved, he made no move to reach for it and I continued speaking as if nothing had happened.

'Yes, it was awful when we were kids and we didn't know where she was or if she was ever coming back, but after we grew up and she moved down here with Alec, we should have changed the way we behaved with her. That was our opportunity, I see that now. But we wanted to continue the bad feeling. We still do!' I paused for breath, willing his agreement as if my life depended on it – or at least life as I now knew I wanted to live it. 'Every time something happens it's like we can't wait for her to slip up again so we can make her feel guilty and tell ourselves we were right all along not to trust her. And because she knows what we're expecting, she goes ahead and does it . . .' In the rush of emotion I'd switched, unwittingly, to the present tense – and at exactly the point where I'd finally understood the need for the past one! – but that didn't matter. What mattered was that Dean wasn't interrupting me, he was listening properly, his eyes were fixed on me, not searching for opportunities for escape. 'But now we have to end it, we have to break the pattern. *We* have to be the ones in charge of *her*. *Surely* that must be possible now?'

It occurred to me that this might be the longest speech I had ever made to my brother without his breaking in (or vice versa).

He cleared his throat. A flicked glance at his watch was barely discernible. 'Olivia, this is all very . . . *passionate*. And I know what you're saying. It's pretty much what Beth has said all along. You mean we need to get closure, right?'

I heaved with frustration. Beth was an ally, a well-meaning

one, but this wasn't to do with her any more than it was to do with Russell: it wasn't to do with anyone but Dean and me. 'It's more than that. We need to take some of the blame. Did I tell you she tried to apologise to me at the end? To us?'

That surprised him. 'What are you talking about?'

'The night she died, she wanted to say she was sorry. But I didn't let her.'

He looked completely askance. 'Why the fuck not?'

'Because I thought we'd made her suffer enough. I thought we were as much to blame as she was. We made a feud out of it, Dean, however we like to pretend it was just us reacting to her faults. It's been self-perpetuating, and if we're not careful we'll keep on with it even now she's gone, reliving the old stuff, just out of habit. What a waste of our lives! We've got to end this now, no loose ends, nothing. I know you felt she didn't love you, love us, but we can make up for it ourselves. We've still got Dad, *he* loves us. And *I* love you. That needs to be enough for us now!'

As I pressed fervently towards him, he shuffled out of range, his discomfort tangible. I pulled myself back; outpourings of love were perhaps best left for another time.

'So what exactly are you proposing?' he asked, warily.

I clutched my hands together in my lap. 'First of all, that we stop talking about her, maybe even ban her name from being spoken when we're together, at least for a while. We have to set the agenda now.'

He checked his watch again, this time with a significant flourish. 'If you don't mind me saying, your timing couldn't be more ridiculous – we're just about to hear the details of her will. How can we not mention her name? How can we "set the agenda", as you put it?'

I breathed in. 'We can if we decide not to take her money.'

There was a slow moment when the words hung in the air, swaying to and fro between us, before he grimaced. He grimaced so deeply it twisted his body, crumpling his posture as well as his face. 'What? Have you gone mad? Did Russell not tell you the house has just been valued at a million?'

'No, he didn't.'

'That's half a million each, Liv! Think about it!'

'You think about it,' I said. 'If we give it up, we'll be quits. We'll be free.'

'You've *got* to be kidding me.' His tone and his body language were a restless mix of threatening and threatened, as if he were dealing with a conman at his front door. 'This is our compensation, Olivia! There's no way I'm going to turn down her pay-back.'

'But that's my point, Dean, we shouldn't feel like we *need* pay-back. If we really forgive her then we can enjoy the rest of our lives for what they are.'

'I think I'd like to enjoy the rest of my life with the help of half a million pounds. Call me shallow.' He pushed himself to his feet and stooped to retrieve his phone. 'Come on, let's at least go and see how much exactly it is you've decided to turn down. Maybe your half will automatically come to me, eh?'

And I could do nothing but follow him up the steps and into the solicitor's office.

We didn't speak while we waited for Lindy to arrive. Dean huffed his way through a property magazine while I looked absently about the waiting room. Despite the smart exterior of the building, the offices inside were scruffy, the familiar scruffy of Sterling Avenue, with discoloured cornicing and scuffed woodwork, rugs and sofas that had seen better days, better decades. It was comforting to see a space so well worn.

Lindy slipped into the room with a few minutes to spare. Having last seen her in head-to-toe black, I was instantly warmed by the prettiness of her soft auburn features against the smoky pink of her dress and jacket. She looked younger, unshackled. Earlier thoughts of how I hoped Maggie would remember her generously returned to me.

'Olivia! Dean! I hope you haven't been waiting too long for me?'

But we were hardly able to exchange greetings before Adrian Bellamy was in the doorway, ushering us through.

'Everyone here? Let's get you all some coffee and we'll get started.'

As we trailed him to his rooms on the first floor, Dean cast me a look that told me I'd taken the joy out of this for him. But I refused to be downhearted; he was my brother, and I would try again when the right time presented itself.

In his office at the rear that overlooked simple bordered lawns, Bellamy continued with the pleasantries, asking about our summer holidays. I'd met him once before; he was a business acquaintance of Alec's, not quite a contemporary of Mum's but senior enough to bring an air of seasoned perspective to these proceedings. I liked his unkempt silver hair and hastily rolled-up sleeves.

'Well, thank you all for coming. It's been an unusually long wait, I know.'

Despite the melodrama of the delay, the 'all' he addressed comprised just Dean, Lindy and me.

'Where's Beth?' I asked Dean.

'Mum only asked for us,' he said, shortly. And his demeanour, if not his words, made it clear he considered Lindy one too many.

Bellamy looked up from his papers. 'That's not quite true. Mrs Harrison did request the presence of one other party, but I haven't been able to make contact with him.'

I wondered if he meant Dad, staying for the summer with his wife's sister in her house in Menorca. Now *that* would be pay-back.

Bellamy began with the smaller gifts: trinkets for three of

369

Maggie's favourite nurses, including Joyce; jewellery for Beth, the girls and me; an antique desk for Dean; a painting for Alec's sister; a few other items of sentimental value for friends and neighbours. There was also a cash legacy for Lindy (that drew nothing from Dean beyond a brief acknowledgement that he was deigning to listen).

'And so,' Bellamy continued, his tone announcing that we'd reached the main event, 'subject to the payment of debts and other expenses . . .'

I allowed myself to fantasise that my brother would leap up and relinquish all claims on both our behalves.

'. . . Mrs Harrison leaves her estate in equal shares to five beneficiaries—'

'*Five*?' queried Dean at once. 'Who are the other three, then?' His suspicious glance in Lindy's direction told me he was ready to treat the gift already announced for her as some sort of deviously placed red herring.

'Five,' Bellamy repeated after him, as if agreeing that this was indeed surprising and exciting news. I tried to recall details of our early speculation. Alec had had no children of his own, but had been close to his only sister's two children, and though they had received settlements in his will, it was sensible to assume he might have agreed with Mum that she should make additional provision. That was probably it.

'And they are as follows: Mr James Chapman, Mr Noah Chapman, Miss Isobel Lane, Miss Constance Lane, and Miss Wren Briscoe. None of the beneficiaries inherit until he or she reaches the age of twenty-five . . .'

Though he continued with details of the formal arrangements, trusts and executors and substitutes and so on, I barely heard a syllable of it. Had he said *Wren Briscoe* or had I just imagined that? Put the name in myself in a slip of concentration? I looked to Dean for guidance, but he was busy agitating for his own – more obvious – reasons. '*What*? Hang on a minute, Adrian! Let me get this straight: she's left Olivia and me *nothing*? She's left *her own children* nothing?'

'That's correct,' Bellamy said, pleasantly, 'the estate passes to her grandchildren. It's not as uncommon as you might think.'

'But you said *five*? This other kid, who the hell is *that*? *That*'s not a grandchild!'

'You mean Miss Wren Briscoe?'

My pulse drummed in my chest and skull. So I hadn't imagined it, then. I didn't know what on earth was going on here. I opened my mouth to protest, but nothing came out.

'She is listed simply as a friend,' Bellamy clarified.

'Do *you* know who it is?' Dean demanded of Lindy. Given that Wren's gender had been made quite clear from Bellamy's phrasing, I resented his contemptuous use of the pronoun, making a beautiful girl sound like some lower animal.

Lindy shook her head, as at a loss as the rest of us.

Dean was turning puce. 'So you're saying that some kid who none of us has met in our lives gets a fifth of the money! That's going to be two hundred thousand pounds! Talk about a kick in the teeth. Wren, what like the bird? Fucking stupid name!'

As his fury rose, I was aware of both Lindy and Bellamy looking to me for some kind of leadership in calming him, but I could only stare in confusion. How fitting, how terrifying, that I should lose the power of speech just as I had discovered what it was that I needed to say. In desperation I looked over Lindy's shoulder to the gardens outside. All was completely still, giving the illusion of a photograph, until, almost startlingly, a figure emerged onto a balcony and began motioning with his arms to someone indoors.

My focus returned to the room. Dean was making extravagant leaps in imagination, his thoughts coming in gushes. 'Right, let's think about this. Briscoe, Briscoe . . . She might be related to Warren, do you remember, Liv? That American guy Mum brought over when she came back from California? Richie's dad – well, I know you'll remember him. He's the only Briscoe I can think of though, knowing Mum, there could have been dozens more. But say it *is* him, then I'm guessing Warren must have had another child later in life, a second family, something like that.' There was an odd pause and then a ghastly dip in his voice, like a break to a bone. He turned to me. 'You don't think, you don't think Mum might have had another kid herself, you know, *secretly*?'

Bellamy and Lindy exchanged appalled looks. I flushed, managed to croak my first intelligible syllable for some time: 'Dean!'

'No, seriously. That year she was gone, she might still have been young enough . . . But that can't be possible, can it? She couldn't have hidden a child all these years, could she?'

'No,' I said, finally finding a solid vocal. Though it was a preposterous theory and one that deeply embarrassed the other two people in the room, I knew Dean needed a sincere denial from me. 'Of course not. Even she wouldn't have done something like that. No, forget that, that's not what this is.'

'Then maybe this is Warren's grandchild, d'you think?'

'Yes,' I said, levelly, 'I think that's exactly who she is.'

'But *why*? Someone from Alec's family, I get, but Warren's? It was years ago, they weren't even married!'

Reading my hesitation as some sort of betrayal, he turned back to Bellamy, demanding, 'What's the kid's address?'

Bellamy placed a protective palm over his papers. 'I'm afraid I can't disclose that. I can only say that it is her father, Mr Brian Briscoe, who was invited to attend this morning and who failed to respond to my letters.'

'*Brian*?' Dean echoed, mystified. 'Who's that?'

'Richie,' I told him. 'His first name is Brian, but he doesn't use it.'

Dean ignored me. '*You* must have it,' he said to Lindy, 'in one of Mum's files or something. Go back to the house and see what you can dig out.'

As she recoiled from his rough tone, I spoke up. 'This is nothing to do with Lindy, Dean, so please stop bullying her.' I caught Bellamy's eye. 'Is it Millington? Is it Angel's Lane, Millington?' My voice sounded no stronger than a disembodied echo spliced in from a crossed line, but it drew immediate attention from the others.

Bellamy nodded. 'It is. Do I take it you know the place? Somewhere down on the Dorset coast, I believe?'

I nodded. Somewhere on the Dorset coast where the colours shone like jewels and the sea spoke in a thousand voices and in wintertime the mists hid it from the rest of the world. Millington, a name that Russell would have recognised the moment he heard it. He couldn't yet have told Dean about finding me, or about my confessing I was seeing someone I'd known when I was young, otherwise Dean would have made the connection already. There was no question that he would. The next time Dean and Russell met my past and present would finally collide.

Dean looked at me with growing disgust. 'What, you mean *you* know this bird girl? You know where she lives? How?'

'She's Richie's daughter,' I said, quietly. 'And I know where she lives because that's where I've been this summer. In Millington, with the two of them.'

'You mean you knew about this all along?' He was remembering my petition on the grass before the meeting. 'Bloody hell, don't tell me this was your idea? Part of your closure scheme? Talk about the enemy within!'

'No,' I said, curtly, 'it was *not* my idea. Mum never spoke to me about her will. But I have to say that now I've heard it, it makes sense.'

He laughed scornfully. 'Well, how nice for you!'

'What do you mean, Olivia?' Lindy asked, softly. 'How does it make sense?' But I shook my head. How could I tell them the truth, that Maggie had simply wanted Richie here today? She'd wanted him here whatever it took.

Dean was looking in disbelief from Lindy to me. 'Fine, well, if you know where she is, lead the way! Did you drive here?'

'No.'

'Then I'll take us down there in my car—'

At this suggestion, Bellamy and Lindy both spoke at once:

'Now, Mr Lane . . .'

'Dean, what can you achieve . . .?'

'Mrs Chapman, can you ask your brother—?'

'Olivia, please don't let him—'

I got to my feet. 'Please, everyone, leave this with me. Give me a day or two to sort it out. Can I phone you all on Monday morning?'

'That sounds reasonable,' Lindy said, hopefully. This, and Bellamy's nod of agreement, drew a fresh scowl from Dean.

'I want to appeal this, no matter what,' he said, but the comment had the air of a parting shot, which was a relief to us all.

'Fine. Then let's review the situation on Monday,' Bellamy said. 'Now, before anyone dashes off, we haven't *quite* finished here. Mr Lane, Mrs Chapman, I also have a letter for each of you from the deceased.'

He passed us one each of a pair of small white envelopes. Dean ripped his open at once, but I didn't have the stomach for mine right now and slipped it into my bag. I had no need to open it, in any case. No explanation was necessary. I understood it all.

Anxious to be gone, I said my goodbyes to the others.

'Please phone me,' Lindy said, no longer the transformed figure we'd greeted in reception. 'I know you have to do things your own way, but I'd like to help if I can.'

'Oh, Lindy!' I exclaimed. How I wish you were my mother, I thought. If Maggie had just once spoken to me like that!

As I stood on the pavement outside, filling my lungs with the hot midday air, I felt Dean's bony fingers on my shoulder. In his other hand a single page of handwritten text flapped in the breeze. Maggie's handwriting. 'You were right about something,' he said, screwing the paper into a ball and tossing it into a nearby bin. 'She did want to apologise. And now we know what for.'

374

Chapter 42

I was back in Millington by four o'clock, which meant I must have been sitting on the veranda steps at Angel's Lane for two hours waiting for Richie to come home from work. I'd lost track of the church bells, by which I usually kept time, but the sun was low enough in the sky for me to shuffle a step forward out of the shade and into its amber glow.

'Hey,' he said. 'I tried to call you. How did it go at the solicitor's?'

I nodded. 'It was fine. Maggie left Dean and me out of her will.'

He looked shocked. '*What*?'

'No, it's really not a problem. It's exactly what I wanted.'

'Oh-kaay . . .' His eyes searched my face, judging my mood. I was so used to people doing that now I scarcely noticed it. 'Will you be all right for another ten minutes while I go pick up Wren?'

I got to my feet. 'Can you leave her with Sarah for a little while longer? I need to talk to you.'

'Can it wait till after she's gone to bed? It's Friday, Nick'll be home by now. I need to take her off their hands.'

'I'd rather we were on our own,' I said, quietly, 'just for a few minutes. I don't want her to be upset.'

He stared at me. 'Why would she be upset?'

'Please. Just a few minutes.'

Frowning, he forked his fingers through his hair and dust rained down. 'Fine. But let me just call Sarah and tell her I'm delayed.'

I followed him inside, watched him make the phone call and then gestured to the sofa. 'Sit with me.'

He put his arm around me and squeezed. He smelled of plaster and sweat and impatience. By the end of the week he grew jittery from so much separation from Wren.

'So you're OK about everything, then? How did Dean take the news?'

I didn't answer. 'You were in touch with her, weren't you?'

'Who?'

'Maggie. My mother,' I added, unnecessarily.

'I know who Maggie is,' he said, but he didn't answer my question.

'Please, Richie. Can we just be straight? It will be quicker.'

After a long pause, he met my eye and nodded.

'She met Wren, didn't she?'

'Depends what you mean by "met", but yes, we did see her once. She looked me up a few years ago.'

'She came here?' I looked about the room. It didn't seem right that she should have been here in our private space.

'No,' Richie said, 'it was before we moved to Millington. We were still living in Southampton.'

'How did she find you?'

He removed his arm from me and scratched at his forehead, leaving a faint trace of red across the skin. 'When Lisa died, she saw the obituaries in *The Times* and recognised my name. She made a few phone calls, found out where I was working – it's not hard to find someone these days, as you know.'

I felt a sudden spasm of understanding of how it must have been for Richie this summer, to fall in love with a fugitive – and not only a fugitive from present troubles, but from past ones, as well. Someone who couldn't tell the two apart. With me, he'd been edging further and further from the shelter he'd built for himself and his daughter, and all because I had been sent a slip of paper with his address and made the decision to present myself to him.

'I know you're tired of talking about her,' I said. 'I'm getting pretty tired of it myself, but I promise this will be the last time. What did she want?'

He shrugged. 'Nothing much, to be honest. We met for lunch. She said how sorry she was about Lisa, how fond of me she'd been when she and Dad were together. I got the feeling she just wanted to see how I'd turned out.'

'Really? That was all?' Despite myself, my tone sharpened and he turned wearily to me.

'Sure. It was just a flying visit, a quick chat. I didn't think much of it. You've said yourself, she did things on a whim, didn't she?'

'And she particularly wanted to meet Wren, did she?'

He was taken aback by the question. 'No, not at all. Wren was with me, yeah, but she was obviously much younger then. She might even have been asleep, I honestly don't remember.'

It was a glum thought, the three of them together: Richie, newly widowed, still in his thirties, too young to be on his own; Wren, toddler-sized and adjusting to life without her mummy – did she wake up from that lunchtime nap and reach for Lisa? (How old did a child need to get before the instinct vanished?); and Maggie, ageing and alone, still grieving for Alec. 'She would have been recently bereaved herself,' I said, thinking aloud. 'I wonder if she saw you as kindred spirits or something.'

'Probably,' Richie said. 'Listen, babe, I know it must have been tough for you today, but shall we talk about this when Wren's in bed?'

As he made to rise, I pulled a breath from deep in my chest.

'Richie, you obviously don't know, but Maggie included Wren in her will.'

He slumped back into place and turned dumbfounded eyes on me. '*Wren?* How come?' Face creased, his eyes began scanning the room as if for a clue to this latest madness. And then, to my surprise, he seemed to find one: his gaze came to rest on a pile of mail on the desk by the door and at once his brow cleared. 'You know what? No, I'm pretty sure I've thrown it away now, but there *was* a letter from a solicitor. I didn't recognise the names, though, I thought it must be some kind of administrative mistake.'

I nodded. 'That will have been from Maggie's solicitor, Adrian Bellamy, giving you notice of the meeting this morning. And he probably used her married name, Harrison – she hadn't been known as Maggie Lane for twenty years.'

'As I say, I assumed it was a mistake.' He smiled a small, regretful smile. 'I've been distracted.' He was a fraction quicker than I had been, however, to follow the thought through. 'Hang on a bit, you were there . . . how weird if that had been how we'd met again!'

Not weird, I thought, planned. Plotted. Just in case I'd thrown her letter in the bin and never seen his address. Or I'd seen it and *still* discarded it. This was Maggie's contingency, albeit a more expensive one than she'd imagined (I was sure she hadn't been aware of the surge in property prices; even Dean had been surprised by that). What she also hadn't counted on was Richie throwing *his* letter in the bin; she'd expected the promise of money to be enough to turn anyone's head – the exact sum gifted was almost irrelevant.

'She's left Wren a fifth of her estate. It will probably end up being close to two hundred thousand pounds.'

'I can't imagine why she would have done that,' he said, disbelievingly. 'I was right: there's obviously been a mix-up.'

'Has there? Isn't it clear to you what she was up to?'

He looked at me, mystification now joined by a trace of irritation. 'No. *What?*'

'She wanted to bring us together again. She knew it was the real thing first time around – for me, anyway – and she wanted to give us a second chance. She knew that if she hadn't interfered the way she did, life would have been different for me, with or without you.'

'Why? Why would it have been different?' And he shook his head, thinking, but not saying, Not this again. Not another scene. But there was a difference this time, a difference in me. This again, yes, but I was no longer the hot-cheeked and hysterical antagonist of our previous confrontation. I was cool, dry-eyed and quite clear about what was to be said and done. Finally, I had got there.

'Because there wouldn't have been the "what if?"s. I mean, imagine if you *hadn't* followed Lisa back here to England? That's what I'm talking about. You said it yourself, you have to make the leaps for yourself, there's no one golden moment when you know what to do. But if you *don't* take the leap . . . 'What if?'s are what drive people mad in the end. That's what's driven me mad.'

He heard me out, before exhaling wearily. 'But I don't see what any of that has got to do with her leaving all this money to Wren. She could have got me into a room with you without going to those sorts of lengths.'

'Ah, but you don't know how she thought. Everything to Maggie was worthy of "those sorts of lengths".' Painful though this conversation was, there was a pleasure in having access to the answers, to having all those strands untangled and laid out in parallel lines in front of me. 'She made crazy sentimental links, especially in the last few years. I wouldn't be surprised if she saw Wren as the daughter we never had.'

For the first time true anger sparked in Richie's eyes. 'What? That *is* crazy. There's no way she saw Wren as *our* child, no way. How could she?'

But his indignation dissolved as he remembered my bombshell

379

of a few days' ago, and I touched his hand to show that I understood both his frustration and his remorse. 'Not literally ours, I don't mean that. But I always thought she knew about the pregnancy. She may not have known exactly how it ended, but I'm fairly certain she knew there was a "What if?" in there somewhere.' Suddenly I remembered Russell's comment in the café about my looking like someone else, someone who'd been living an alternative history. He'd sensed it instinctively, without even knowing about Wren, about the natural binding she had made between Richie and me.

'Finding you widowed, just like she was herself, well, she would have seen that as a sign that you needed her help. She was romantic and melodramatic, Richie, that was just the way she was. She was on a mission to make amends. The problem was that because it was her, her idea of amends always involved trampling on someone else.'

She'd known it was dangerous to bring us together again, that it would hurt too many others; that was why she'd done it secretly. All her other eleventh-hour wrong-righting had been in the open, involving Lindy, phone calls and bedside reunions, but not this one. This righted wrong had been hers alone.

The only person she didn't try to appease was Dean, because he was the one person she knew she had no chance of winning back. I thought of the letter, then, his face as he dropped it into the bin; whatever she'd written to him, it had not been good enough. There'd been too little thought for him at the end of her life and too much, *far* too much, for Richie and me. She'd been intent on reuniting us; she'd been going to do it if it was the last thing she did.

'The only thing I don't understand,' I said, 'is why you didn't tell me she'd been in touch? We've talked about her so much these last few weeks.'

He nodded, as if to say at least I had a point on *this*. 'I was going to tell you. When you first came here it obviously made me think of it, but I could see straight away you still had a lot . . . a lot of stuff to resolve. It didn't seem worth introducing another complication.'

'Fuel my fire, you mean?'

'Basically, yes.' He fixed me with the candid, unblinking Briscoe gaze that Wren had inherited. 'And it obviously has, hasn't it?'

'It's helped me with the missing pieces of the picture, yes.'

We fell silent. There was an unfamiliar flatness between us; the sound, I supposed, of a stalemate. The truth was I was never going to be able to persuade him – or anyone else – of Maggie's machinations, good or bad. I had not the tools to explain caprice, enigma. An unexpected thought presented itself, but I did not speak it aloud: Russell understood about Maggie. He always had.

'The thing is,' I said slowly, 'I needed you to be untouched by her.'

'I *am* untouched.' His present tense was emphatic.

'But you're not,' I said. 'All along she's had a stake in you, and in Wren.'

Richie shook his head, his face in profile to me as he answered. 'She had no stake, I assure you. This is all in your mind.'

'No, not in my mind. Sitting in black and white in her file in the solicitor's office, just waiting to be opened.'

He threw up his hands. 'Forget the will, Olivia, forget the money. We don't want it any more than you do. I'll just refuse it, or gift it back to whoever you want me to, however it works. I honestly don't know what else I can say. I certainly haven't meant to mess things up by somehow getting involved in her will.'

I caught his hands, enclosing them in mine. I could feel the shake in them. 'No, you've done nothing wrong. As you say, you didn't think anything of it, and why would you? You didn't even

381

think it was worth turning up to the meeting. You haven't jumped in the way she thought you would because you're better than all of this. Everything you've done just proves how strong you are. But *I* have, Richie, *I*'ve jumped. And what I've been concealing from you is far worse than anything you haven't told me.'

Alarm seized every feature of his face. 'Jesus. I can't take much more of this. What have you been concealing?'

I felt in my pocket. 'She was the one who sent me here, Richie.'

'What do you mean?'

'She sent me your address, a few days after she died. Look.'

As I showed him the frayed piece of paper he looked relieved, as if he'd expected far worse. 'She must have got this from Warren after you moved.'

'No. This isn't Dad's writing,' Richie said, examining it. 'I wrote this. That's right, Maggie asked me to let her know of any change of address and I sent her a note. This must be it.'

There was a rising note to his voice, the triumph of being able to explain *one* thing, at least, but as his spirits rose mine only sank. Richie's own writing! The man I'd thought I'd loved my whole adult life I'd actually known so little I hadn't even been able to recognise his handwriting.

'Am I missing something here?' he asked, seeing my face. 'I knew you must have got my address from somewhere – why not from her? So maybe she wanted us to meet again, fair enough. But she didn't ask you to leave your husband for me, did she? All along you've told me you were leaving Russell anyway. I would never have let anything start between us if I thought that wasn't the case.'

My voice implored him to understand: 'I *was* leaving, that was absolutely the truth, yes. But don't you see, she chose to send me to the only person in the world who could make me feel like this? In my whole life you've been the only one, and she knew that.

382

She knew that everything I did after you left, after you married that girl, everyone I was with – it all felt like it didn't quite match up to my dreams, because it was *instead of you*.'

I waited as Richie buried his face in his palms in sheer exasperation. Resurfacing, he looked on the brink of explosion. 'I don't get this, I really don't get it. What are you saying, Olivia? That she wanted you to see me again so you could finally be happy? Or she wanted you to see me again so she could destroy your family? Which is it?'

There was undisguised sarcasm in his question, but I answered it quite seriously. 'Both, Richie. She believed it was worth risking one to have the other. That was how *she* lived, after all.'

We were both breathing audibly as we gazed at each other. Fresh clouds passed across his eyes and I had a feeling they might never clear.

'It's already eaten away at half my life, Richie. I'm not going to give it the second half. The rest of my life is going to be my own.'

'Good,' he said, standing. 'Then we agree. Let me call the solicitor, this Bellamy guy, and we'll work out how we can refuse the inheritance. Then things will be as they should be. Now, I *have* to get Wren.' His eyes strayed past me towards the front door but he didn't move, catching on the edge of his vision my slow shake of the head.

'The money isn't important. Actually, I would love Wren to have her share. There's a kind of justice in it. But either way things won't be as they should be, Richie. We both know that. You've known longer than I have.'

'What does that mean?' He went very still, then, the only fragility detectable in his eyes, and at that moment I knew I loved him even more deeply than I'd believed I did, I loved him more deeply than the first time. And that, I was somehow going to have to accept, *that* was the very last irony of all.

'I have to go back, darling,' I whispered. 'I have to live my life the way it should be lived, how it would have been lived if I'd never been given your address. I have to rewind to the day after the funeral.'

He paled. 'But how can you know what you would have done? How do you know that if you did rewind you wouldn't go and do the same thing again? You might meet some other guy, start again somewhere else, stay away forever?' As he rallied, the colour returned to his face. 'We talked about this – I remember your exact words! You said a weekend wasn't long enough to breathe. That's what you said. *Not long enough to breathe.*'

I stepped forwards to take back his hands, threading our fingers together, breathing his breath. 'You're right, I did say that, and I meant it. I still do. But I'm fairly sure that if I hadn't come here and found you again, I would have just taken the time I needed to rest and to think and to remember, and then I would have gone back home. Yes, maybe I'd have met someone while I was away. I might have been unfaithful to Russell. But there's no one else in the whole world I could have fallen in love with except you.'

He crushed his lips into my cheek, murmuring over and over against my skin, 'Please don't go, I don't want you to go.'

Having managed to stay dry-eyed throughout the conversation, I was now sobbing hard. 'I know. I know. But that's what I'm going to do.'

Chapter 43

Jana's flat was in the kind of Brixton street that, even to Russell's untrained eye, had the look of one with little likelihood of being gentrified any time soon. The house next door was derelict, a rectangle of stained board in place of the front door, and where his own neighbours had artful tangles of jasmine and rose, Jana's had only bins, rows of them choked full, their mouths agape like piranha. He had second thoughts about approaching her door even before he saw the bare legs of a sullen-looking black guy draped out of an open ground-floor window, his companion on the ledge a cartoon-snarling bull terrier. The man's outfit of vest and shorts, along with the sight of a rumpled mattress just inside the window, gave the impression the pair might not in fact yet be formally up. It was Saturday, two o'clock in the afternoon.

'Afternoon,' Russell said, amiably. He inspected the two doorbells, faintly labelled 'Ground' and 'First', before pressing 'First' with confidence – there was no way someone as freshly scrubbed as Jana could be sharing with this hobo.

'Who you want?' the guy called out.

Russell was sufficiently reassured by the sight of his hand on the dog's neck to attempt a reply. 'Er, I was hoping to find Jana.'

'Jana's not in.'

'Oh, really?'

'You not believe me? You saying I'm lying?'

The dog, sensing discord, growled. Russell felt frightened.

'No, yes, of course I believe you. I'll just . . .'

His stammering was interrupted by the thud of heavy footsteps on the stairs inside and a faint shake to the ground before the door was opened. Having expected a Gruffalo, or at the very least a large man in hob-nailed boots, Russell was surprised to find a lightly built young woman before him. On the filthy brush doormat her feet were bare, the toenails painted shell-pink, incongruously clean and pretty in such squalid surroundings.

'Yes please?'

The accent sounded similar to Jana's. That was right, she'd mentioned a flatmate from her home town but he couldn't remember the name.

'I'm sorry to disturb you. I'm looking for Jana. You must be . . .?'

'She is not here.' Clearly she didn't care to elaborate. Nor did she smile or make eye contact. Jana alone had graduated charm school, then.

'I told him that!' exclaimed the character at the window and, hearing him, the girl stepped forward from the doorway, moving as if Russell were not standing there and forcing him to shuffle out of the way to avoid a painful collision.

She put up a hand. 'Hey, Douglas!'

Since man and dog perked up equally at the greeting Russell couldn't be sure which of them she'd meant it for. 'Do you happen to know where Jana is this afternoon?' he asked, growing tired of the general rudeness around here.

She merely petted the dog, tickling its neck and stroking its ears between forefinger and thumb.

'Jana's already at the club,' Douglas/his owner replied in her place.

'The club?'

'Yeah, where she works.'

'Who are you?' the flatmate asked, suddenly turning back to him with a suspicious frown. 'Are you a police?'

'Police? Er, no, I'm Russell,' he said.

She looked blankly back at him, but once again the neighbour proved to be better informed, nodding in recognition. 'Me wonder when us meet the new boyfriend!' he called out, sounding quite jolly. He was even roused to swing a leg over the ledge and place his slippered foot on the concreted ground. The adjustment revealed a glimpse of the largest ashtray Russell had ever seen, as well as an amplifier that would do Wembley proud.

'I'm not . . .' Russell trailed off, some ancient sense of chivalry (or was it the opposite, self-protection?) stopping him from completing the denial. 'OK.' He addressed the neighbour. 'Could you tell me where the club is? Is it near here?'

'On the High Road. Next to Hot Chilli's. You know Hot Chilli's?'

'I'm guessing it's a restaurant? I'll find it. Thank you.' He sought the girl's eye, feeling the need to make amends before he left. 'So you must be from Poland, as well?'

'I am Slovakian. Like Jana too. I think you should know this if you are *boyfriend*.' She lingered just long enough for her contempt to penetrate fully, before slipping back inside and closing the door in his face. This time there was no sound whatsoever of her footsteps on the stairs, which caused him to suspect she might simply be crouched under the letterbox, hiding (he was getting paranoid).

'Nice to meet you too!' he called out, petulantly.

When he backed out of the doorway he found that the man and his dog had withdrawn from the window and a grubby net drape had been rolled across. A second later music pounded out. He'd been well and truly dismissed.

Shame washed through Russell as he made his way back to the high street. Was it really possible that he hadn't grasped

Jana's correct nationality? Because Aniela was Polish he'd simply assumed she must be as well. He'd asked her which town she was from and the name she'd given him had been unfamiliar. It had *sounded* Polish enough.

He hoped this 'break-up' wasn't going to be trickier than he'd imagined. It had crossed his mind that he might get away with texting, but he'd seen Jana enough times – four, five? He pretended he didn't know exactly how many – to warrant an in-person explanation. Which was this: since he'd seen his wife again, irrespective of whether or not she was going to divorce him for another man, the insanity of his association with Jana was clear. Call it a holiday fling, a cry for help, or a plain old-fashioned mid-life crisis, but it was not a tenable long-term relationship. It was not love.

He would need to paraphrase this for Jana, obviously.

OK, Hot Chilli's. In his mind, he was picturing the club as that trendy new members-only drinking place that had opened with great fanfare a year or so ago and now attracted models and musicians from the West End. He knew that Jana's main job was in a bar, but he had not imagined anything quite so glamorous. Now he felt an absurd flush of jealousy as he imagined some twenty-year-old rock star casting an eye over her thighs as she poured his champagne. But reaching the high street, thronged with the aimless Saturday shoppers and assorted idlers only Brixton could produce in such swarms, he saw that the place he'd been thinking of was in fact a couple of blocks beyond Hot Chilli's, the brash red and green frontage of which was instantly identifiable to his left. From where he stood there was no sign of any bar or club next door, only a shoe store on one side and a discount plumbers' merchants on the other. Great. The bastard with the dog had sent him on some kind of wild goose chase.

It was only when he was standing directly in front of the restaurant that he saw an open doorway between the Hot Chilli's take-out kiosk and the shoe shop. It was painted matt black, with the word 'Curves' in pink over the entrance. Inside, with his back pressed to the wall as if he hoped to bring it down with sheer brute force, was a very large man in black who appeared to be muttering crossly to himself – until Russell worked out there was actually a hands-free mobile involved and this was in fact a bouncer. Beyond, steps led up to what must be the club itself, presumably housed in the rooms above the restaurant with the pink blinds at the windows. Without breaking his hostile stream into the mouthpiece, the doorman spied Russell and at once indicated a sign on the wall half-obscured by the door: '£25 minimum charge.' He held out a hand for the cash, but Russell shook his head, craning forward to get a better look at the montage of photographs on display to the right of the sign. Protected behind glass like prized stills from the Olympics were pictures of girls in thongs twisting around a shiny steel pole; others, in floor-length dresses of turquoise or orange, held aloft trays of cocktails that didn't look real, like props in a Bond movie. Jana was not featured, but he didn't need an identity parade to know that someone of her allure would not be employed in a place like this to mix the banana daiquiris.

The bouncer raised a querying eyebrow and Russell averted his eyes. He was an idiot for a thousand reasons, he knew that, but he was at least sensible enough to know that this was not the venue to break up with one's lover; especially not now the term 'boyfriend' had been bandied about. Jana could be pals with this twenty-stone bruiser, there could be teams of them inside; Douglas the pit bull might be part of the operation (perhaps that was why the window was kept wide open – so he could tear out and savage Jana's lovers at a single whistle). One teardrop from those pretty blue eyes and Russell would be tenderised and devoured in turn. Or shot by the bouncer or whoever the sleazy despot was who ran this place. *Local Dad Gunned Down for a Lapdance!* The boys would be orphans, mocked for the sordid circumstances of their father's demise and adopted only with great reluctance by Dean and Beth – or, far worse, by Russell's mother.

Breathing heavily, he ducked out of the doorman's range and made for the department store across the road. He needed pen, paper and envelope, and a space to sit and think. The store had an old-fashioned layout and an unthreatening atmosphere, and once he had his stationery and was in the café – a familiar high street concession – he was feeling considerably calmer. He ordered a large black coffee and began to compose his letter:

> Dear Jana,
>   I had hoped to see you in person, but you were at work. Sorry to write this in a letter but I'm afraid I can't see you again. There have been some family changes and we no longer need a babysitter.

Reading back to himself this ridiculous euphemism, he realised he was going to have to ring the cleaning agency and tell them he no longer needed Aniela, either. He would have to sever all links with these women (perhaps even move house? The fantasy of the shoebox resurfaced briefly). He'd have to do the cleaning himself until he found someone new, or perhaps he could pay the boys to do it; they'd been campaigning for extra allowance lately.

> It has been lovely getting to know you. Thank you.
>   Best wishes, Russell

Once he'd read in one of Olivia's magazines a feature entitled: 'I've Never Been More Humiliated', in which women from all corners of the UK contributed anecdotes about bastards they had dated. One that had stuck in Russell's mind was a Valentine's card sent to someone called Fliss, signed 'Best wishes, Dave'. Nothing wrong with that, Russell had thought, it was hardly the work of an evil genius, but Fliss had had a quite different reaction. 'So much for true love!!' she wrote. 'How lily-livered is that?!!' A caption added the good news that she had found her One soon after the Valentine's devastation and was lucky enough never to have laid eyes on the pathetic jerk again.

As Russell slipped the note through Jana's letterbox, careful not to cause a clanging that might alert the house's occupants, he felt a pang of solidarity with Dave.

By the time he got home he was feeling quite upbeat – albeit in a down-beat sort of way. Jana or no Jana, he was resigned now to losing Olivia. The continuous tense looped around his mind like silk ribbon around a wound, his last comfort, for he knew in his heart that it had already happened: he had lost her. *How could I come back,* she'd said, *even if I wanted to* . . . And why *should* she? He had not appreciated her and he had not recognised the despair building in her. In a funny, gallows-humour sort of a way, he now admired her for her vanishing. She'd broken the mould, even if he and the boys were the mould she'd broken.

He, meanwhile, had been prepared to drift from year to year, decade to decade, letting her – correction: forcing her by default – to make every last decision about the children, the household, their jobs, their futures, all the while waiting for her mother to die and save his skin financially. Well, that hadn't come off, either, had it? Lindy had phoned yesterday to explain the terms of the will. The boys wouldn't get their inheritance until they were twenty-five – not in time to help with university fees, let alone school ones. So what was his plan now? To wait for his own parents to pop their clogs? Either that or start buying scratch cards.

Upstairs Jamie and Noah circled; they were in their holding pattern between arrival home from independent adventures and touching down to demand food. How familiar he was now with their daily rhythms, rhythms he had never noticed in the past. He waited for the call: 'Da-ad? Is there anything to eat? When's dinner?' He could set his watch by it.

391

And thank God he could. Otherwise he might never set it again, he might never move a muscle for the rest of his days. The boys were the reason to sort himself out and renew his efforts; the reason, when he thought about it honestly, for disentangling himself from Jana, and even for issuing Olivia with an ultimatum. If it had just been about him, with only a marriage in jeopardy rather than two childhoods, he'd probably have waited for ever.

And there was at least *some* good news. Lindy had offered to come and help him when term began, to act as a housekeeper during the week, returning to her new flat in Cheltenham at weekends. She didn't want to charge him, she said; it was what Maggie would have wanted (Russell couldn't help doubting *that*). Just until Olivia came back, of course, she'd added.

Of course.

The landline rang and Russell looked limply at it before picking it up. There weren't many people left in his world who phoned him on his home line, not his colleagues nor his children nor Jana, but only cold callers and his own mother (the ultimate cold caller). He supposed it might be for one of the boys.

'Hello?'

'Russell?'

'Yes.'

'It's me, Olivia.'

'*Olivia?*' She'd taken his ultimatum seriously, then, and this was it, her formal withdrawal. *This was it.*

'Yes. I wanted to tell you I'm getting the ten-thirty train home tomorrow. It arrives at Waterloo just before two. I wondered if you would come and meet me?'

He gulped. 'You mean you want to have another talk?'

'No, I mean I'm coming home. If you meant what you said and you'll still have me.'

He closed his eyes. 'Are you sure that's what *you* want?'

'Yes, it's what I want, more than anything.' She sounded calm and happy and sane. Not the old Olivia, but not the new one either. 'But I thought we should chat before I see Jamie and Noah, decide what we should say to them. What *I* should say. I don't want them to think for a second that they've done anything wrong, that they're the reason I've been away. Well, I know you've already been amazing about everything, but if you could update me, help me work out what to tell them . . .'

'OK,' Russell said, 'that sounds sensible. But Olivia?'

'Yes?'

'I have something of my own . . .' He paused, knowing that if he chose to he could still hide this if I wanted to. 'When we meet, I have something to tell you. I haven't been as amazing as you think.'

As she considered this, he listened carefully for any cooling of atmosphere, but there was none. The temperature did not flicker.

'I imagine it's all relative,' she said, at last. 'So two o'clock at Waterloo?'

'Two o'clock at Waterloo,' he repeated.

There was a whole minute after he'd put the phone down when he wondered if he might have imagined the conversation. It was only when he began crying and couldn't stop that he knew it must have been real.

Chapter 44

It was early on Sunday morning when Richie phoned, still silent in Millington, the sunlight fresh and soft. I was at my attic window at Tessa's, taking a last turn at my lookout point over the village. You couldn't see Angel's Lane from here, it was hidden from view by the church, but my picture of his house was in bold relief. I suspected it always would be.

There was little trace of me now in Amanda's room. The bed was stripped, towels returned to the airing cupboard, my few possessions gathered into a bundle no bigger than Dick Whittington's. My own keys to the city I'd remembered to retrieve from the pot on the dressing table and they were now tucked safely into my jeans pocket.

'I need to ask you a favour,' Richie said.

I held my breath. 'Anything.'

'Please don't go without saying goodbye to Wren. She won't understand.'

'I would never do that,' I said, in a small, cracked voice. I had not said goodbye to Jamie and Noah, I had not said goodbye to Dean or Beth or Lindy or Dad. And I had not said goodbye to Mum, not properly. All in all, I had woefully under-valued goodbyes. But when I thought about Richie's lost farewells, and Wren's, theirs to Lisa and hers to them, I knew I had not done too badly. They would never get the second chance I had now.

'I could come around in a little while?' I suggested. 'Are you up?'

'We're up. I'll put some coffee on.'

'Richie?' I said, nervously. 'I wanted to ask *you* something, too, before I see her.'

'Yep?'

'I wondered if you might let me keep in touch with her? I mean, only if you think that would be a good idea. But if you do, I'd really love to.'

He didn't hesitate. 'Of course you can. Though I should warn you she's an extremely ardent correspondent. Her last email to her grandma featured at least two hundred kisses and smiley faces.'

I could hear the smile in his voice and felt my own on my face, the easy smile that Wren drew from me, and everyone else, so naturally. 'Maybe I could tell her I'd like to be a new auntie, something like that?'

'Let's just stick with friends for now, shall we? See what pans out. But, yeah, it would be great if you don't disappear for ever.'

'I'm not going to disappear,' I said. 'I'll just be in London.'

There was a pause. I could hear no sounds of Wren in the background; I imagined her outdoors already, down by the brook in her nightie, craning upstream for a glimpse of the swans.

'You're sure, then?' Richie said. 'You're really sure this is your decision? You're not going to change your mind?'

'No,' I said. 'It's the right decision. And I . . .' Again I faltered. After weeks of searching every corner of our souls together, I didn't know how to hold back from him. I didn't think I could do it, not yet. 'I know how this sounds and I hope you'll understand what I mean, but I couldn't have found the strength without you. You've saved me.'

As my words faded, there was only the ache of silence between us. My face flamed; *you've saved me!* I'd gone too far, carried away to the end: my mother's daughter. But I had on my side the fact that Richie was Richie, he was one of the good guys. He had no interest in making me feel low, however low he felt himself. He had *never* wanted me to feel low.

'Thank you,' he said, finally. 'I guess I know what you mean. But I maybe wouldn't put it quite like that to your husband.'

I smiled, relieved. 'I'll take your advice on that.'

'So, are you looking forward to seeing Jamie and Noah again?'

'Yes, I can't wait. They'll both be home when I get there. There's another week before they go back to school, so we can have some time together.'

'That's good. That's really good.'

There was another silence, this one a little less sore. Down below me, the weathervane on the church spire moved a whisker to the west and connected with the sun, suddenly shining a golden light of its own.

'OK,' he said. 'Well, we'll see you in a little while, then.'

'Richie?'

'Yes?'

'I love you.'

'Love you too, Dolly. Always have.'

Before I set off for the cottage, I went to settle up with Tessa. I found her in the conservatory with notepad and pen, making a list of all the things Amanda might need to take to her student hall of residence with her. 'Is it too much to pack some groceries, do you think? Just pasta and rice, some chocolate, that kind of thing? Is that what you did, Olivia, when yours went to university?'

'You mean a care package,' I said, even now evading her direct question, though I felt certain she knew I had not yet been

397

through this particular parenting rite myself. 'I think that's a lovely idea. Some staples and a few treats. Maybe a bottle of wine, as well, to have a drink with her new neighbours.'

The parting meant more to me than it did to Tessa for she'd shared with me so much more of herself than I had her. In a way, our children had been our barometer: I knew her daughter's exam results, the reason her first boyfriend had dumped her, her favourite flavour of ice cream – and now the contents of her first college care package; Tessa didn't even know my sons' names. I wished I had handled things differently with her, but I hadn't, and now I had no one to blame but myself.

'Can I write to you?' I asked, spontaneously. 'When I'm back in London? I know I owe you some proper answers, but I think I'd do it better on paper.'

She looked up from her pad, pen immobilised and mouth half-open with surprise. 'That would be very nice,' she said. And she offered to take me to the train station, when I was back from Richie's, when the time came for me to go home.

Richie let me into the house and made himself scarce. There was little for us to say to each other, not while the heat from our summer together still hung in the air, not after what we'd just said on the phone. Small talk would have been wrong.

Wren had been told I was going away. She was watchful of me, nervous, old enough now to be sensitive to adults' moods. I gripped her in a cuddle, making her giggle and protest. I could smell the warm, rumpled cotton smell of sleep on her.

'I've got something for you, look.' I showed her the first page of the purple silk-covered journal I'd chosen for her and in which I'd inscribed our names. 'This is my address in London. This is my email address. These are my phone numbers. I really hope we can speak to each other a lot. Daddy says he wouldn't mind and I know you love sending emails.'

'I'm writing Chas one later,' she said. 'I could write you one as

398

well? Daddy has to tell me the spellings. I can only spell "Wren" and "swan" on my own.'

'I see. Well, I'm sure you'll build up more words when you go back to school next week.'

She groaned. 'Mrs Matthews says we have to do *spelling* tests in year one.' And she took the book from me, stroking its soft cover with pleasure. 'I've decided I'm going to keep it *here*.' She placed it on the desk in between the phone and the 'I Love My Daddy' mug she and Richie used to store pens. Pinned on the wall just a few inches above was the photograph of the two of us from my birthday celebration: my eyes on the camera, Wren's on the cake.

The picture reminded me of something. 'It's my son Noah's birthday soon, you know. September the twenty-seventh. He'll be thirteen.'

'It's good you're not going to miss his birthday,' Wren said, gravely. 'Even *teenagers* want their mum to come to their birthday.' Were these Richie's words or her own? Who knew? In her mind, a birthday was as good a reason as any to pack up and go and live somewhere else.

'Perhaps I can come back for *your* birthday in April? That's if you have a party and want to invite grown-ups to it?'

She addressed the suggestion immediately and seriously. 'I'll definitely have a party. I don't know if there'll be grown-ups allowed. There's still Christmas to go, *and* Easter *and* Bonfire Night. But I don't like fireworks and nor does Chas. They're too loud.'

'I know,' I agreed. 'I'm the same as you. But my boys love fireworks, so we always have to go to lots of different displays. One year, we went to a tall office building where you could see all these different shows going on at the same time.'

She looked as if she'd never heard anything so silly in her life.

'Anyway, you'll have to think about your birthday nearer the time and let me know what you've decided.'

399

I hugged her little body to me again, kissed her cheek, memorising the feel of its softness on my lips. 'You're my favourite girl in the whole word, Wren. Thank you for making my holiday here so special.'

'That was a *really* long holiday. Was it your all-time best ever holiday?'

'Yes, it was. Especially the bits with you, like going to the park and the swannery.'

'When you come back there might be another in-ter-loper to see,' she said, pronouncing the word carefully. Her eyes looked hopeful.

I grinned at her. 'Maybe *I*'ll be the interloper? Maybe you'll find me sitting in one of the pens with a swan family! Wouldn't that be funny?'

'That's not allowed,' she said, frowning. 'The daddy wouldn't like having a human in the family.'

I straightened my face. 'You're right. Then I won't do it. When I come back I'll come straight to your door.'

'It's the pink one,' she reminded me. 'The only pink one on the street.'

'Yes, the pink one. I remember the day it was painted.'

When Richie reappeared her mind was already on the next thing and as they followed me out to wave goodbye from the veranda, she demanded, 'Can we finish the magic mouse story now, Daddy? *Please*, there's only a few more pages to go. I'll play the maracas for you afterwards.'

'Hmm, a tempting offer,' Richie said, smirking. Then he picked her up and, one hand cupping the back of her head, winked at me over her shoulder. For a moment I thought he was going to say it, *sayonara*, but he didn't. He didn't even say goodbye. He just took Wren inside and closed the door.

Chapter 45

On the train, with three and a half hours of nerves and excitement ahead of me, I decided it would do no harm to open Mum's letter. Her official apology, or rather – if I'd understood Dean correctly as we parted outside Bellamy's office – her official reasoning for having left us out of her will. She couldn't possibly have known how *that* would please me.

No, having had a close-up view of my brother's disgust as he'd tossed his copy into the bin, I had no great expectations.

But it turned out Maggie Lane had the ability to confound to the last:

Dear Olivia,

I am sorry for so much. I am sorry for what I did to you and Richie. I should not have forced you apart, and after I did I should have realised that your distress was something different from the normal teenage heartbreak. I should have cared for you better – not only then, but before and after, as well.

I can only pray that you will now understand why I sent you his address. It is my hope that you will already have gone to him and made your peace with the past. If not, then you will know by now that I have

401

> created a second opportunity for you to say
> goodbye . . .

I stopped short. I looked away and then back again. I re-read that last sentence, sure that I must have misunderstood, but there it was:

> If not, then you will know by now that I have created a
> second opportunity for you to say goodbye . . .

I felt a shiver on my thighs and upper arms. *Say goodbye? Make my peace with the past?* I read on, hardly daring to move my eyes from one word to the next:

> Either way, I hope that seeing him again has brought you
> new perspective. You have your husband and children and
> it is important you know that they are not, and never
> have been, second best. Thinking there is something better
> out there in the world, something worth more than you
> already have – of all my mistakes, that was my biggest
> and I cannot bear to think of you repeating it.
>
> Olivia, I don't deserve your forgiveness, I know that,
> but I beg you to consider my words. I am at last in a
> position to say that only certain things count in life –
> and this counts.
>
> All my love,
> Mum

That was when I finally cried for her. Not for the formal confirmation that she had been guilty of all I'd suspected her of, and, worse, that she'd willingly made me doubt my own mind – what crueller misdeed for a parent to do to a child? – but for that one final act that I'd been wrong about. In the end, she hadn't meant to destroy my family at all: she had meant to save it. She had

402

seen I was allowing it to disintegrate and she had understood why. Then she had devised a way for me to put it back together.

She couldn't have realised the risk she was taking, she couldn't have predicted how close I would come to calling her bluff and getting it wrong.

But, in the end, I had done what she had wanted me to do without even knowing I was doing it.

And, when I finally stopped crying, I had to smile at that.

When the train arrived at Waterloo station, I stayed in my seat for a short while as the other passengers competed with one another to get off first – anyone would think they were handing out medals at the end of the platform. The train was late getting in and so coming in the opposite direction in equal numbers were those who'd been delayed in leaving the city. After a little awkward weaving, each group adjusted itself and began surging through its own invisible corridor, electric with purpose. It was fascinating to watch, as though the current were being passed from person to person. I remembered myself here before, at weekends and rush hours and peak seasons, with Russell or the boys, hating the crowds and walking in their slipstream for protection. I'd forgotten that there'd been times, lots of times, when the slipstream had suited me just fine.

The last time I'd been at Waterloo, of course, I'd been alone. I couldn't recall what I'd worn the day I left, which of my three changes of clothes it had been. The way I remembered it, I'd been a weak, pale figure, the colour all washed out of me. Perhaps I had vanished altogether. Perhaps, when I sat on the train, eyes cast down for fear of catching sight of my own reflection in the window, the ticket collector had not paused at my seat, thinking it empty. Had I not thrown the original ticket away I might have been tempted to dig it out and check for his stamp.

But now I was back. As the carriage filled once more around

me, I finally collected my bag and stepped firmly down onto the grey stone platform. In my hand, the ticket was thick and substantial; in the train window, my reflection was satisfyingly sharp.

And at the barriers, on the other side, Russell waved hello.

I'LL BE THERE
FOR YOU

Louise Candlish

When life goes wrong do sisters
make the best friends?

*Hannah hugged her sister tightly. 'I know you don't trust life any more. But
you've still got to live it – and so do I.'*

Hannah and Juliet Goodwin have been best friends since childhood,
but when Juliet's boyfriend Luke is killed, just as Hannah marries the
affluent Michael, the divide between the two sisters is suddenly too
painful to bear. While Hannah prepares for the birth of her first child,
Juliet begins to neglect her job, her health and all those who love her
the most. Hannah is the last person she'd appeal to for help.

Until Juliet finds herself drawn into a secret betrayal that threatens to
destroy Hannah's happiness before she even has a chance to enjoy it.

Praise for Louise Candlish:

'A wonderful novel about friendship and heartache'
Elle

'Utterly compelling. We love, love, love Louise Candlish's writing'
Heat

General fiction
978 0 7515 4123 6

THE SECOND HUSBAND

Louise Candlish

She had always put her daughter first – until
one man changed everything

*His voice was sweet, intimate, demanding: 'There is a way out of this, you
know. You could agree to marry me.'*

When Davis Calder moves in next door to Kate Easton and her
seventeen-year-old daughter Roxy, neither has any idea of the
devastation about to be unleashed. With Kate struggling to accept her
daughter's independence and Roxy getting more secretive by the day,
there's enough family tension to go around already.

Before they know it, glamorous, charismatic Davis is the only one who
seems able to keep the peace. Until, one wedding day later, Kate makes
a discovery that blows the whole family apart . . .

Praise for Louise Candlish:

'Not afraid to tackle darker issues . . . moving
and thought-provoking'
Daily Mail

'Heart-breaking and heart-warming – we couldn't
read it fast enough'
Cosmopolitan

General fiction
978 0 7515 3988 2

Other bestselling titles available by mail

☐	The Double Life of Anna Day	Louise Candlish	£6.99
☐	Since I Don't Have You	Louise Candlish	£6.99
☐	The Second Husband	Louise Candlish	£6.99
☐	I'll Be There for You	Louise Candlish	£6.99

The prices shown above are correct at time of going to press. However, the publishers reserve the right to increase prices on covers from those previously advertised without prior notice.

――――――――――――― sphere ―――――――――――――

Please allow for postage and packing: **Free UK delivery.**
Europe: add 25% of retail price; Rest of World: 45% of retail price.

To order any of the above or any other Sphere titles, please call our credit card orderline or fill in this coupon and send/fax it to:

Sphere, PO Box 121, Kettering, Northants NN14 4ZQ
Fax: 01832 733076   Tel: 01832 737526
Email: aspenhouse@FSBDial.co.uk

☐ I enclose a UK bank cheque made payable to Sphere for £ . . . .
☐ Please charge £ . . . . . . to my Visa/Delta/Maestro

Expiry Date ☐☐☐☐   Maestro Issue No. ☐☐

NAME (BLOCK LETTERS please) . . . .

ADDRESS . . . .

. . . .

. . . .

Postcode . . . . Telephone . . . .

Signature . . . .

Please allow 28 days for delivery within the UK. Offer subject to price and availability.